WWW.BEWAREOFMONSTERS.COM

PRAISE FOR JEREMY ROBINSON

"[*Hunger* is] a wicked step-child of King and Del Toro. Lock your windows and bolt your doors. [Robinson, writing as] Jeremiah Knight, imagines the post-apocalypse like no one else."

—The Novel Blog

"Robinson writes compelling thrillers, made all the more entertaining by the way he incorporates aspects of pop culture into the action."

—Booklist

"*Project 731* is a must. Jeremy Robinson just keeps getting better with every new adventure and monster he creates."

—Suspense Magazine

"Robinson is known for his great thrillers, and [with *XOM-B*] he has written a novel that will be in contention for various science fiction awards at the end of the year. Robinson continues to amaze with his active imagination."

—Booklist

"Robinson puts his distinctive mark on Michael Crichton territory with [*Island 731*], a terrifying present-day riff on *The Island of Dr. Moreau*. Action and scientific explanation are appropriately proportioned, making this one of the best *Jurassic Park* successors."

—Publisher's Weekly - Starred Review

"[*SecondWorld* is] a brisk thriller with neatly timed action sequences, snappy dialogue and the ultimate sympathetic figure in a badly burned little girl with a fighting spirit... The Nazis are determined to have the last gruesome laugh in this efficient doomsday thriller."

—Kirkus Reviews

"*Threshold* elevates Robinson to the highest tier of over-the-top action authors and it delivers beyond the expectations even of his fans. The next Chess Team adventure cannot come fast enough."

—Booklist - Starred Review

"Jeremy Robinson is the next James Rollins."

—Chris Kuzneski, NY Times bestselling author of *The Einstein Pursuit*

"[*Pulse* is] rocket-boosted action, brilliant speculation, and the recreation of a horror out of the mythologic past, all seamlessly blending into a rollercoaster ride of suspense and adventure."

—James Rollins, NY Times bestselling author of *The 6th Extinction*

PRAISE FOR SEAN ELLIS

"What follows in *Savage* is much more than a political thriller. Robinson and Ellis have combined technology, archeology, and even a little microbiology with the question they ask better than any other authors today: what if?"

—Suspense Magazine

"Sean Ellis is an author to watch closely."

—David L. Golemon, NY Times bestselling author of *The Mountain*

"Sean Ellis has mixed a perfect cocktail of adventure and intrigue, and [*Into the Black*] is definitely shaken and not stirred."

—Graham Brown, NY Times bestselling author of *Ghost Ship*

"Some books are just plain unbridled fun; others are edge of the seat gripping entertainment. Some make you think; a few open your eyes. Sean Ellis is a magician, doing it all with a deftness that pulls you in and draws you along from page one breathlessly to the end of the book, offering mysteries galore, bad guys with the blackest hearts and a good old fashioned hero to kick their evil arses. I had a blast."

—Steven Savile, international bestselling author of *Silver*

"Sean Ellis writes action scenes that rival those of Clive Cussler and James Rollins."

—James Reasoner, NY Times bestselling author of *Texas Rangers*

"Sean Ellis delivers another high-octane romp [with *Magic Mirror*], exploring mythical lost civilizations and alternative histories, with the unrelenting pace of your favorite summer blockbuster."

—Stel Pavlou, bestselling author of *Gene*

"I'll admit it. I am totally exhausted after finishing *Oracle*, the latest Jade Ihara page-turner by David Wood and Sean Ellis. What an adventure! I kept asking myself how the co-authors came up with all this fantastic stuff. This is a great read that provides lots of action, and thoughtful insight as well, into strange realms that are sometimes best left unexplored."

—Paul Kemprecos, NY Times bestselling author of *Medusa*

"[*Dodge Dalton* is] high flying adventure at its best. Cleverly conceived, original, and multi-layered, the action literally jumps off the page and takes the reader through unexpected twists and turns."

—Rob MacGregor, NY Times bestselling author of *Indiana Jones and the Last Crusade*

ALSO BY JEREMY ROBINSON

The Jack Sigler Novels
Prime
Pulse
Instinct
Threshold
Ragnarok
Omega
Savage
Cannibal
Empire

Chess Team Universe Guidebook
Endgame

The Chesspocalypse Novellas
Callsign: King
Callsign: Queen
Callsign: Rook
Callsign: King – Underworld
Callsign: Bishop
Callsign: Knight
Callsign: Deep Blue
Callsign: King – Blackout

Standalone Novels
The Didymus Contingency
Raising The Past
Beneath
Antarktos Rising
Kronos
Xom-B
Flood Rising
MirrorWorld
Apocalypse Machine

The Jack Sigler Continuum Series
Guardian
Patriot
Centurion (2016)

Cerberus Group Novels
Herculean

Secondworld Novels
SecondWorld
Nazi Hunter: Atlantis

The Antarktos Saga
The Last Hunter – Descent
The Last Hunter – Pursuit
The Last Hunter – Ascent
The Last Hunter – Lament
The Last Hunter – Onslaught
The Last Hunter – Collected Edition

Nemesis Novels
Island 731
Project Nemesis
Project Maigo
Project 731
Project Hyperion

Horror
(Writing as Jeremy Bishop)
Torment
The Sentinel
The Raven
Refuge

Post-Apocalyptic
(Writing as Jeremiah Knight)
Hunger
Feast (2016)
Viking Tomorrow (2016)

ALSO BY SEAN ELLIS

Jack Sigler/Chess Team
Callsign: King
Callsign: King – Underworld
Callsign: King – Blackout
Prime
Savage
Cannibal
Empire

Mira Raiden Novels
Ascendant
Descendent

The Nick Kismet Adventures
The Shroud of Heaven
Into the Black
The Devil You Know
Fortune Favors

The Adventures of Dodge Dalton
In the Shadow of Falcon's Wings
At the Outpost of Fate
On the High Road to Oblivion
Against the Fall of Endless Night
(with Kerry Frey)

Cerberus Group Novels
Herculean

Novels
Magic Mirror
Wargod
(with Steven Savile)
Hell Ship
(with David Wood)
Oracle
(with David Wood)
Changeling
(with David Wood)
Destiny
(with David Wood)
Flood Rising
(with Jeremy Robinson)
Camp Zero
(with Sharon Ahern & Bob Anderson)

Secret Agent X
The Sea Wraiths
The Scar
Masterpiece of Vengeance

EMPIRE

A Jack Sigler Thriller

JEREMY ROBINSON
AND SEAN ELLIS

Sean Ellis dedicates this novel to Dan and Elayne Mason...
Thanks for being there.

EMPIRE

"If I had a chance to ask God just one question, it would be, 'What really happened to my friends that night?'"

~Yuri Yefimovich Yudin,
Sole Survivor of the 1959 Dyatlov Expedition

"If you want to talk about a nation that could pose an existential threat to the United States, I'd have to point to Russia. And if you look at their behavior, it's nothing short of alarming."

~General Joseph Dunford USMC,
Chairman Joint Chiefs of Staff, in testimony to Congress

"My family is my strength and my weakness."

~Aishwarya Rai Bachchan

PROLOGUE

The Ural Mountains (Sverdlovsk Oblast), U.S.S.R.
February 1959

Bent over her skis, head down and focused on ascending the slope, Zinaida Kolmogorova almost collided with her teammate, Rustem Slobodin. If they had been on flat ground or descending, she probably would not have had time to stop at all. Because they were climbing, and had been for hours now, she was just able to stop short when she glimpsed the back ends of his skis.

She planted her ski poles in the snow and craned her head around to make sure that the rest of the party behind her was aware of the halt. Through the veil of falling snow, she could just make out Alexander Kolevatov. He was twenty feet behind her, methodically stepping with his skis in the herringbone pattern she and Slobodin had left.

"Stopping!" she called out. Kolevatov raised his head in acknowledgment. She returned her attention forward and called out to Slobodin. "Why are we stopped?"

"We are lost, I think," Slobodin replied, his voice muffled by the heavy scarf covering his face. "Igor says that we are on the wrong mountain."

"This is not Otorten?"

Slobodin shook his head. "He thinks we are on Kholat Syakhl."

Kolmogorova groaned in dismay. Given the restricted visibility, it was understandable that they might have wandered a few degrees off course, but to lose track of an entire mountain was unforgivable. She expected better from their leader, Igor.

Beneath her face covering, Kolmogorova cracked a smile as she thought about what Dubinina would say. Lyudmila Dubinina, the only other female member of the team, would not let Igor off lightly. Her tongue was as sharp as a Cossack rider's sword, and twice as quick. Kolmogorova almost felt sorry for the man.

Kholat Syakhl.

She recalled seeing the name on the map. It was not a Russian name, but Mansi—the language spoken by the native tribesmen who inhabited the region. They grazed their herds on the steppe below, when the days were longer and warmer. They avoided the mountains because nothing grew here, even in the favorable season. That was how this mountain had earned its name.

Kholat Syakhl translated to 'Dead Mountain.'

It was an ominous name, but the Mansi, like most Russians, were prone to pessimism. Otorten, the name of the mountain the team had intended to traverse, was taken from a Mansi phrase that literally meant: 'Don't go there.'

The Urals apparently had a sense of humor. Since the team had rejected that sage advice, the mountain had tricked them, sending them more than five miles off course.

Don't go there? she thought. More like 'can't get there.'

Kolevatov caught up to her a moment later, by which time Igor and the others ahead of Slobodin backtracked to explain the mistake.

Dubinina was surprisingly subdued in her reaction. "We are lost?"

"No," Igor explained. "We just aren't where we are supposed to be."

"Wonderful. We'll be trekking half the night."

Igor shook his head. "It will be dark soon. We'll make camp here."

"We passed some trees a ways back." This came from Alexander Zolotaryov. The man, an instructor at the polytechnical college where the rest of them had met as students, was a voice of reason if not necessarily experience—he was older than any of them by more than a decade. "It is more sheltered there."

Igor rejected the suggestion. "I don't want to have to make this climb twice. We'll pitch the tent here. It's good practice for camping in winter conditions."

"You call it 'practice'?" Dubinina said with a snort. "How will this be different from what we've been doing every night for the last week?"

Igor did not reply but instead began delegating responsibilities. While Kolmogorova and several others began stamping out a flat ledge where they could erect the tent, he and the others began unpacking. The tent went up quickly, the moment preserved forever on film by Yuri Krivonischenko, who had dutifully kept a photographic record of the expedition with his beloved Zorki camera. Soon they were all ensconced within, stripping off their damp winter clothes to avoid becoming chilled. Despite the navigational error, the mood stayed light. Zolotaryov began brewing a pot of tea from melted snow, though only a few of the group expressed any interest in the warm beverage.

It was too early to retire for the night. The sun, though obscured by scudding clouds, was just beginning to set, plunging them into a darker shade of twilight. At this latitude in February, sunset came at five o'clock in the evening. Nevertheless, Kolmogorova had learned from experience not to drink tea or anything more than a few sips of water before getting into her bedroll. Nothing ruined a good night's sleep more than waking up with a full bladder in the dead of night. Easing the call of nature meant slipping past eight other sleepers and then venturing out into the frigid night to squat bare-assed in the snow. She was content to simply lie back on her sleeping mat and relax.

She was not exhausted by any means. A full week of trekking and skiing had left her well-seasoned. Her muscles, which had been sore for the first two days, despite the fact that she was in excellent physical condition, were now supple and toned. At the beginning, she had dreaded going to bed. She had known that waking up would mean another day of endless misery, trudging hour after hour through the snow. Now she looked forward not only to sleeping but also to rising in the morning for another day's activity. Even this minor misadventure was not enough to dampen her spirits. It would make for an amusing anecdote to tell at parties.

After what felt like only a few minutes, she heard a strange humming sound and felt a blast of bitterly cold air on her face.

She sat up and was surprised to see her teammates gathered around the open flap of the tent, staring out into the night.

"What time is it?" she mumbled.

"Almost nine," Slobodin said without looking back.

I must have dozed off, she thought.

The incongruity of the persistent humming sound finally penetrated the fog of drowsiness. It sounded like an electrical transformer, but they were miles away from anything powered by electricity. In a leap of intuition, she grasped that the others must have been similarly curious about the noise, prompting them to open the tent to the frigid night. She rose and moved to join the group.

"What's going on?"

Even as the words left her mouth, she saw the light. It hung in the sky above the distant treetops, brighter than any star. It was almost as bright as a full moon, though she knew that was more than three weeks away. "What is that?"

"I don't know," Slobodin admitted. "It just appeared."

"It is a flare," another voice supplied.

This comment came from Nicolai Thibeaux-Brignolles, the engineer. "The army must be conducting an exercise nearby."

"It's too bright," Igor countered. "And a flare would not last so long. It is a searchlight from an aircraft."

That explanation was only slightly more plausible to Kolmogorova. The noise did not sound like a helicopter, but perhaps the snowfield was playing tricks on her ears. She shivered, but not because of the cold.

"Searchlight or flare," Thibeaux-Brignolles said, "it is of no consequence to us. Close the tent. You're going to freeze us all."

"Let me get a photograph first," Krivonischenko said, positioning his camera on its makeshift tripod. "Just a moment." There was a click as the shutter snapped open and closed. "Got it."

Someone drew the flap, blocking out the light, but the noise immediately grew louder, more intense. The canvas structure acted like the body of a drum. Kolmogorova could feel the deep bass vibrating in her bones. She felt faintly ill.

"What is that?" Dubinina complained. "Make it stop."

Kolmogorova opened her mouth to commiserate, but then the other woman clutched her head. Dubinina writhed in agony. Kolmogorova knew that what she was feeling was nothing compared to what Dubinina was experiencing.

Thibeaux-Brignolles clapped his hands to his head and let out a harsh oath, which devolved into a tortured howl. Slobodin reached out to him, resting a concerned hand on the engineer's shoulder, but Thibeaux-Brignolles rounded on Slobodin and gave him a shove that knocked the man off his feet. Slobodin's head struck one of the backpacks piled near the center of the tent, rebounding off something solid inside with a crack like a shot from a starter's pistol.

Kolmogorova gaped in astonishment, but instead of signaling a climax, the sudden act of violence was like the opening of a floodgate. A shriek rose, not one voice, but three—Dubinina, Thibeaux-Brignolles and now Zolotaryov. All of them were writhing as if their very bones were on fire.

"They're mad," someone shouted. "Get out before they kill us all."

The cry, even more than the screams, unleashed total pandemonium. Someone crashed into Kolmogorova, knocking her into the stunned Slobodin. She raised her head cautiously and saw Doroshenko tearing at the side of the tent. The heavy fabric yielded to his bare-handed attack, opening a gaping wound in the shelter. Icy air poured in. But the strange hum relented by a few degrees. Doroshenko plunged through the hole, tearing it even further, and then he was gone. His panic was infectious. Two others—barefoot and wearing nothing more than long undergarments—scrambled through the gash.

Idiots, Kolmogorova thought. It's twenty degrees below freezing. They'll die out there.

But then in the corner of her eye, she caught a glimpse of the others. Hypothermia was the least of her worries.

Something was happening to them. All three convulsed, as if their skeletons were about to explode. Dubinina's head shook back and forth, her face a blur. The woman's skull was changing shape, ballooning outward as if her brain was expanding.

The shaking stopped as abruptly as it had begun. Dubinina's face and head appeared normal again, but her eyes were ablaze with rabid fury and she was staring right at Kolmogorova. With hands curled into feral claws, the woman charged.

Suddenly, Igor was there, intercepting Dubinina, deflecting her into the side of the tent. He whirled around to face Kolmogorova. "Get out!"

When she remained rooted in place, he reached out, took her arm and propelled her through the hole. She caught her foot and went sprawling, face down in the snow. A moment later, Igor, supporting the dazed Slobodin with one hand, emerged from the tent and lifted her to her feet with his other.

The strange light was still blazing in the sky above, and while the riddle of what caused it was now the last thing on Kolmogorova's mind, it provided enough illumination for her to clearly see. The footprints of the others led away, down the slope toward the edge of the forest.

Out in the open, the hum was much harder to hear, but she could still feel it shaking her bones. Dubinina and the others' shrieking was still audible, but now a new noise joined the cacophony—the sound of tearing fabric.

They're shredding the tent!

Kolmogorova could see the others who had fled—Doroshenko and someone else, Krivonischenko perhaps—far ahead, still running as if chased by ravenous wolves. The forest was almost a mile from their campsite, and each step away from the terror they had just escaped took them deeper into the throat of the storm.

She took a few tentative steps after Igor, who was still helping Slobodin stay on his feet. The snow was infiltrating her socks, melting and refreezing around her toes. "Igor," she shouted. "We cannot survive out here. We must..." She trailed off as her gaze was drawn once more to the light in the sky.

Is someone up there, watching us? She thought about Dubinina and the others, driven mad by pain that seemed to have no apparent cause. But something did cause it, she thought. Poisonous gas? Or some kind of strange mind-control weapon? Is that why they are up there? Watching to see what will happen? Watching us die?

Will we also go mad?

Behind her, the tent came apart like a banana peel, revealing the four figures that had remained inside.

Dubinina's head was tilted back, like a wolf howling at the light blazing in the sky. Thibeaux-Brignolles and Zolotaryov were still tearing at fabric like insects caught in a spider's web. The fourth person was Kolevatov, but unlike the others, he did not appear to have been possessed by the madness that had come over the others. Instead, he simply knelt in the midst of the ruined tent, weeping like a frightened child.

Dubinina's eyes found Kolmogorova again. The woman's shoulders rose up, like a cat about to pounce. Then the broad cone of light in the sky tightened into a searing, bright circle no more than twenty feet across. It focused on the tent and the three afflicted skiers.

All three flinched, hissing in pain. Then, as if driven by a single mind, they erupted out of the tent's shredded remains and bolted out into the snow.

The circle of light chased after them.

The narrow beam, defined by snow flurries, led back to its source in the sky. Kolmogorva was certain now that it was a helicopter with a searchlight, but why it was there and whether its presence boded good or ill, were questions to which she feared she would never know the answer. The bright circle was now just a pinpoint of light, at least a hundred yards away. The three fleeing figures were just indistinct silhouettes dancing in and out of its glare. She did not see Kolevatov. She wondered if he, too, was out there, chasing after the others or perhaps chasing the light.

"Zina," Igor said, shouting to be heard over the wind. "Hurry. We must get to the woods. We'll be safe there."

She turned to face him, wishing she could share his certainty. Perhaps he did not truly believe it himself, but the possibility of being affected—or infected—by the madness that had come over the others was a greater threat than the elements. He started down the hill, in the direction Doroshenko and Krivonischenko had gone, urging Slobodin to keep up.

Kolmogorova followed, but with each step forward, she could feel the energy—her very life force—seeping away. Her body heat melted the snow clinging to her thermal undergarments, and just as quickly, the frigid night turned the dampness to ice. Physical exertion was no longer enough to ward off the chill. Her teeth began to chatter. In some remote corner of her mind, she realized that she could no longer feel the strange vibration in her bones. Whether that was because it had stopped or because she was losing feeling in her extremities, she could not say.

She quickened her pace and caught up. "Igor. We must go back."

Before he could disagree with her, Slobodin stumbled and went down, nearly taking Igor with him. The expedition leader tried to lift him up, but the injured man pushed Igor's hand away. "Zina is right," he said through chattering teeth. "We will die out here. I am going back to the tent."

"The tent is wrecked," Igor said.

"We can still salvage blankets," Kolmogorova said. "Our packs. Warm clothes."

Igor shook his head. "We will make a fire. Build a shelter. We can survive."

Slobodin paid no heed. He struggled to his feet and turned, heading back the way they'd come, but after only a few steps, he staggered and pitched forward again. Kolmogorova went to him and knelt to lift him up, but her fingers refused to work. Her hands were like two dead things at the ends of her arms.

"Igor, help me!" She raised her head and saw Igor, still trudging down the slope toward the forest. The woods were at least half a mile away. "Igor!"

He did not look back.

She turned back to Slobodin, but her efforts to raise him up were futile. "Rustem! You have to get up."

When there was no response, she rose and started after Igor. The cold had settled into her joints, and it was all she could do to keep shambling forward. "Igor! Help me or Rustem will die!"

The reality of what she had just said hit her like a slap. It was already too late for Slobodin. She could not compel him to move, and she doubted Igor could either.

I have to save myself, she thought, but doing that seemed almost as impossible as saving her teammate.

She staggered after Igor Dyatlov, recognizing that with each step she took, she was committing to a course of action doomed to failure. The woods offered no salvation. Even if they could get a fire burning, it would not be enough to keep hypothermia at bay, not in their underwear and stocking feet.

"Igor. We must go back." She tried to shout, but all she could manage was a hoarse whisper, swept away by the wind.

No, she thought. I must go back.

She turned and gazed back up the slope. The wreckage of the camp was hidden beneath a shroud of blowing snow, but she could still distinguish the footprints in the snow. If the storm did not cover them over, she might be able to find her way back.

And if she did, what then? The camp was in ruins. She would never survive the night, much less the long trek back to civilization. It could be days before anyone even thought to look for them.

But somebody already knows we're here.

She raised her head and scanned the sky, searching for the helicopter with its searchlight. The army, she thought. The army did this to us. To Dubinina and Thibeaux-Brignolles and Zolotaryov.

They had done something to cause the madness, the transformation, and then they had watched from a distance to see the results.

But surely they won't let all of us die.

She knew that was wrong, but in the absence of real hope, the lie kept her going until she could go no further.

The Ural Mountains (Sverdlovsk Oblast), Russia
The Present

"**This is King.** Radio check, over."

"Queen. Five by, over."

"This is Bishop. I hear you."

"Knight, loud and clear."

"Rook, here. Loud and proud, over."

King allowed himself a faint smile. The last reply, brash and irreverent, with little regard for protocols and standard operating procedure, was typical of the man who went by the callsign: Rook. "Good news. Our radios work. King, out."

He switched off the throat mic and rolled over to look at the four people to whom he had just been speaking. They were arranged in a circle, facing out to provide three hundred and sixty degrees of security for their position. No more than ten feet separated the individual team members. Even though they were facing away from him, he could have easily heard their voices without using the short-range comm unit. But the radio check was standard operating procedure. The best time to identify a malfunction was before going into the sandbox, though technically they were already hip deep—and it wasn't sand but snow.

Russia.

He shook his head. Five hundred miles from anything faintly resembling friendly territory. They had no safety net and no one standing by to pull their asses out of the fire if things went south.

And if that happened, if they screwed up, it would mean war between nuclear-armed superpowers. Hell, even if they succeeded, it might still mean war. The Russkies were pushing hard, testing the limits of American resolve, intent on exposing NATO as nothing more than a paper tiger. If the unit—his unit, US Special Forces, Operational Detachment D/Chess Team—could bring back proof of the Russian president's true intentions, it might just be enough to unite the fractious European partners comprising the North Atlantic Treaty Organization (NATO). That might—just might—be enough to make Crazy Vlad take a step back from the brink.

The sky overhead was now a deep shade of purple, growing darker by the minute. It was go time. "Knight, head out. Set up an overwatch position. Where, is up to you."

The figures were all wearing white winter camouflage shells, making it virtually impossible to distinguish one operator from another. One of them rose from his position and hefted his SVDS, the shortened variant of the venerable Russian 'Dragunov' sniper rifle.

The 7.62-millimeter long-range weapon wasn't Knight's tool of choice for the killing trade, but beggars didn't get to be choosers. It was much easier to procure equipment on the local black market than it was to transport it across international borders. That was especially the case in Russia, where corruption was endemic and military-grade hardware, stockpiled since the Cold War, was easier to come by than reliable transportation.

The old pickup truck they'd driven from Yekaterinburg had given up the ghost halfway to the objective, forcing them to hump in the rest of the way on foot. It was a long slog through the snow to reach the place, which Rook had described, eloquently but accurately, as the ass-end of nowhere.

After moving only a few steps away from their release point, Knight seemed to vanish into the benighted landscape. King suspected that, even with sixth-generation night-optical devices (NODs), which were currently still in testing at DARPA, he would have been unable to locate the trained sniper. The man had an uncanny ability to disappear in almost any condition, but the snow and darkness greatly simplified that task. Unfortunately, they didn't have sixth-gen NODs or much else in the way of the kind of equipment that usually went in their tool box for a mission like this. Some things were easier to acquire on the black market than others. The closest thing they had to night-eyes were light-amplification scopes mounted to their weapons. The old, Soviet-era technology was about as useful as the 'night vision' app on King's iPhone, but it was better than nothing.

That was what he kept telling himself, anyway.

He turned his attention back to the objective, or more precisely, to a spot about a mile from their present location, which had been marked as the target site. He continued scanning the snowfield with his binoculars, looking for some hint of activity, anything to confirm their initial intel. But except for the darkness that now blanketed the landscape, the view had not changed appreciably since their arrival three hours before.

"Is anyone seeing what I'm not seeing?" he asked at length.

"I see jack and shit," Rook offered. "But if that's what you see, then...negative, over."

Queen shrugged. "A secret military research city wouldn't be much of a secret if it was out in the open for everyone to see."

"Nothing is that secret." King gestured in the direction of the emptiness they were surveilling. "No buildings, no roads, no LZ for helicopter resupply."

"Could be underground," Bishop said. "Self-contained. Or re-supplied by underground train. We've seen that before."

"If the place is dug in that deep," Rook opined, "not a hellava lot for us to do here."

"They have to breathe," Queen said.

"Air vents." King rose to his feet. "Let's get started. We don't have all night."

"Yes we do," Rook muttered. "Gonna take that long to find anything, too."

King did not argue. Rook was probably being optimistic. But Queen was right, too. Even if the secret research city was buried deep underground, accessible only by tunnels located miles away, there would have to be a ventilation system. The bigger the facility, the bigger the air intake would have to be. It would be camouflaged, of course, invisible to satellite reconnaissance, but much harder to conceal at ground level, especially in winter.

"We'll focus on that wooded area at my ten o'clock." He keyed his mic. "Knight, we're going to start our sweep. Keep an eye on us, over."

"Both eyes," came the reply. "Knight, out."

"Like there's anything else to look at out here," Rook grumbled.

"Rook," Queen barked. "Zip it."

Rook, surprisingly, did.

They moved out, traveling in single file, with King in the lead. The others followed, placing their snowshoes in his tracks. It was an unnecessary precaution. There was not a shred of evidence to suggest that the site was patrolled or monitored. King was beginning to share Rook's belief that the mission was a snipe hunt, but until they were safely back in the team room at Fort Bragg, he was going to continue operating as if every shadow concealed a Russian soldier with orders to shoot on sight.

Despite the utter stillness, he kept his recently acquired weapon—an AK-104 carbine, powder-coated white to blend in with both his camouflage and the environment—at the high ready. His index finger rested alongside the trigger guard, but it was poised to curl around the trigger at the first hint of trouble. He knew the others, even Rook, who was packing the squad automatic weapon—a durable PKM light machine gun—would remain equally vigilant until the operation was completed.

The stand of trees—cedars, judging by the smell and less than a square mile altogether—was a conspicuous green island in a sea of white. The trees were real, no doubt about that, but King got the sense that they had been placed, or more likely left behind when the surrounding area was logged. To hide something.

Something like the air intake for an underground research facility.

They were almost to the wood line when Knight broke radio silence. "Hold."

King froze in place, saying nothing, waiting for Knight to elaborate. Several seconds passed before the sniper spoke again. "It's gone. I think you're clear."

"I don't know which worries me more," Rook said before King could respond. "The word 'it' or the 'I think' part."

"Knight, explain," King said.

"Something big and furry came out the woods about a hundred yards left of your position, then it went back in. I don't think it was human."

"This is Russia," Bishop remarked. "The bear is the national symbol."

"Was it a bear, Knight?"

"Of course," Bishop continued without missing a beat, "bears should be hibernating right now."

"Maybe it's the other kind of bear. You know, a big hairy guy named Boris who likes—"

"Rook!" Although barely louder than a whisper, Queen's sharp exclamation ended Rook's commentary.

"One or the other," Knight said. "But my money's on the former. It didn't move like a man."

King scanned the trees but saw no sign of movement beyond the veil of darkness. "Tangling with either one is not how I want this to go," he said. "But what we're after is probably in those woods. Close on me. We'll go in tight. Maybe Boris will see that he's outnumbered and give us some space."

Before he could take another step however, Knight spoke in his ear again, and this time his voice was tinged with panic. "Stop!"

"Talk to me," King said. This time, he did not remain motionless, but swept a 180 degree arc with the barrel of his weapon. "Is he back?"

"If so, he's moving like the wind. Movement to your right, fifty—"

Knight's transmission ended with a scritch of static, as if Knight had let off the transmit button a moment too soon. King swung his carbine in the indicated direction. He thought he saw something moving in the green display of his light-amplifying scope, but before he could be sure, the shape shrank back into the darkness.

"What the fuck?" Rook growled. "Knight, are you sure that's the same guy? Bear? Whatever the hell it is?"

When Knight did not answer immediately, King started worrying. "Knight, talk to me."

"Shit," Bishop shouted. "Hostile, left. Twenty—"

The harsh report of gunfire drowned out the rest. King brought his carbine around and triggered two rounds into the woods, firing in the same direction as Bishop, even though he didn't have a target.

"Abort. Fall back to the—"

Rook opened up with the PKM. Some of the 7.62-millimeter rounds found their targets, tearing through fur and flesh, spraying the snow with blood, but the wounds seemed only to enrage the creatures further. In the strobe-light of muzzle flashes, King saw not one or two shapes, but dozens of shaggy forms, swarming toward Rook, moving up from their rear.

They were not bears. Bears he could have wrapped his head around, but these things? The creatures had gotten behind them, flanked them, as if to drive them into the woods.

What the hell are they?

Rook poured a sustained burst into one of the creatures. The bullets drilled through the beast's torso, tearing away huge chunks of ragged flesh, but even as the thing went down, three more rushed Rook's position. The machine-gunner disappeared under an avalanche of dark fur and the gun abruptly went silent, permitting King to hear Rook's screams.

Then those stopped, too.

"Close ranks! Back to back." King's voice cracked with desperation, as he shouted the order. He could not see Queen and Bishop behind him, but he could feel them, pressing against his back. He could hear the near constant report of gunfire. He added his own weapon to the symphony, peering through the scope at bestial forms that were moving so fast he couldn't get a clear look at them. There was barely time to fire, then reacquire and fire again. After a few seconds, there was no longer any need to aim or even look through the scope.

The creatures were everywhere.

He heard the other weapons firing on full automatic, and he switched his own weapon over as well. Then he emptied the rest of the magazine into the roiling wave of flesh and fur in a single trigger pull.

There was no time to switch out the magazine. He drew his secondary weapon, a sturdy semi-automatic pistol. But before he could raise it to trigger a shot, something struck his forearm, knocking the gun from his instantly numbed fingers. Then suddenly he was buried under a writhing avalanche of hair and muscle. The smell of body odor—rank and musky—filled his nostrils, stronger even than the sulfurous stink of burnt gunpowder. He started to gag uncontrollably. He fought back, trying to pull free of the creatures' grip, not because he was a Special Forces soldier, proficient in close-quarters combat and sworn to resist capture with his last breath, but because he was terrified.

Nothing in his training had prepared him to battle something like this.

His struggles were futile, and as the blows rained down on him, driving him to the edge of consciousness, the last coherent thought in the mind of U.S. Army Master Sergeant Joseph Hager—operational callsign: King—was that his mother and father had lied to him all those years ago.

Monsters were real.

SHELL GAME

Between him and blue eternity, there is only a window.

More precisely, a thin bubble of transparent polymers, deceptively thin, he knows, for the cockpit canopy has been designed not only to withstand the heat and shearing forces of supersonic travel but also the impact of anti-aircraft shrapnel and cannon fire. It is not a perfect defense against either by any means, but given the extreme environments in which the fighter jet was designed to operate, perfect is a relative concept. Humans weren't meant to travel at two-and-a-half times the speed of sound, twenty thousand feet above the Earth's surface. That he is doing it now would have been considered a divine miracle in centuries past.

His stomach drops as the nose of the aircraft rises abruptly, the G forces pushing him down and back.

"Hang on, Siggy!"

The voice, her voice…her clear, joyous, strong voice…resonates in his ears, reminding him that he is not alone. Or in control. She is.

Julie!

He feels an almost overwhelming need to speak to her. There is something she needs to know, something critically important, but what it is, he cannot remember. Something prevents him from remembering. From warning her.

The pressure yields as the jet brakes, shedding speed with such abruptness that it feels like they have come to a dead stop in mid-air. This is an illusion; the plane is still rocketing across the sky, but now it is merely traveling only about as fast as a commercial airliner. To either side of the cockpit, the wings swivel outward until they are perpendicular to the airframe. The teardrop shape of the airfoils supply lift when the aircraft is traveling at subsonic velocities. As the plane approaches the Mach barrier, traditional aerodynamic concepts will no longer apply, and the wings will fold back against the fuselage so the increased drag does not rip the aircraft apart.

Julie likes going fast. She always has. She is where she is, right here, right now, because of a line from an old movie about—what else?—fighter jet pilots. He can still hear her chanting that line:

"I feel the need...the need for speed!"

If she is slowing down, it can only mean...

He grips the base of his seat a heartbeat before the F-14 rolls over and remains inverted as it races forward. The acceleration holds him in his chair—that and the five-point restraint system. But aside from the stomach-churning suddenness of the maneuver, he has no sense of being upside-down. The only real difference is that, instead of blue eternity, he now sees where the sky ends and a different kind of infinity begins. The endless blue-green of the ocean stretches out in every direction, as far as the eye can see. Somewhere behind them, there is solid ground, but back is the one direction he cannot look.

The aircraft rolls again, but instead of returning to an upright position, the plane begins corkscrewing through the air. All he can see is the light blue sky, the dark blue ocean...sky...ocean...light...dark... Blue eternity flashes so fast that he has to close his eyes or be driven mad.

"Don't lose your lunch on me, Sig!" Julie shouts, playfully. "You know how hard it is to get the smell of puke out of these things?"

The twisting stops, and he feels acceleration again. His stomach is no longer lurching. It feels like it has been completely ripped out of him. He can see both sky and ocean now, the dividing line directly below, and he knows what this means, too.

A vertical dive.

He tries to shout, but no sound comes out. He pounds on her seat, his brain about to burst with the intensity of the words his mouth cannot form.

Pull up! Please, Julie. For God's sake, pull up!

But she is not there.

The front seat is empty.

His sister is gone. Evaporated.

The canopy is still intact. She didn't punch out. She's just not there anymore.

It's as if Julie Sigler never existed.

The endless sparkling blue resolves into cresting waves, rising and falling. Close. So close.

A loud hiss fills the cockpit. Alarms sound, warning of imminent impact. He tries to reach out for the ejection handle, but his arms won't work. All around him the sounds grow louder, deafeningly loud, as the blue ocean reaches up and...

ONE

Ashburn, Virginia

Jack Sigler started awake, clutching for the handle that would, when pulled, trigger a series of explosive bolts to first blow the canopy and then propel him, chair and all, away from the doomed fighter jet.

Except there was no handle, just as there was no jet.

The vehicle in which he sat was not a Grumman F-14 Tomcat fighter jet, but a rented 2015 Toyota 4Runner. Instead of plummeting toward the ocean at nearly five hundred miles an hour, the vehicle was stationary. It was parked on the roadside in the industrial zone of a Virginia town, surrounded by non-descript warehouses.

There were similarities though. He was in the passenger seat, and the person sitting behind the steering wheel was his sister. Not Julie, but Asya Machtchenko, a younger sibling that he had not even known existed when Julie Sigler's plane had drilled into the Atlantic Ocean two decades earlier.

Asya's orange-brown eyes, so much like his own, seemed to be peering into his very soul. "You are having dream again?"

Raised in Russia, Asya had lived in the United States for only about three years. It was not nearly long enough to lose her thick Slavic accent or to perfect the nuances of English grammar.

The dream, he thought. *Not* a *dream, but* The Dream.

He shook his head, a dismissal rather than a denial, though perhaps the distinction was lost on Asya.

"It doesn't matter." He rolled back the cuff of his black knit turtleneck to expose the black and silver face of his vintage Omega Speedmaster wristwatch. 2028 hours. Eight-twenty-eight p.m.

Close enough. "Go time. Let's do this."

After making sure the interior light was switched off, he opened the door and got out. The area, sparsely occupied during normal working hours, seemed deserted now with the fall of night.

Asya appeared beside him, hefting a backpack—black to match her attire—onto one shoulder. Sigler carried a similar pack, which combined with hers contained all the equipment they would require to infiltrate the target, and a lot more he hoped they would not need.

The target was not a hardened military installation or an ultra-secure government facility, but a sprawling 150,000 square foot, concrete warehouse. Presumably it contained endless rows of computer servers for off-site data storage. There might be some form of security—cameras, alarms, maybe even a rent-a-cop or two, armed with a flashlight and walking a patrol route—but nothing that would require the fullest expression of his skill set.

Or maybe they would not even find that. The building was new, and it was possible that the new tenants, a mysterious entity called TSAR Data Solutions, had not even moved in yet. The only way to know for sure, the only way to know if the answers he was looking for were there at all, was to get inside.

He and Asya were there for the same reason that he had started having The Dream again: Julie Sigler.

Julie's accident had happened when Jack Sigler was just a teenager, but for many years afterward, he had dreamed about the last moments of her life. He had relived the crash as if he had been right there with her. At first, he had wondered if there might be a supernatural explanation for The Dream, a psychic bond between himself and his beloved older sibling, similar to what identical twins reportedly shared. The dreams, or flashbacks or whatever they were, often came when he was experiencing a high degree of stress. Given his subsequent life choices, high stress was pretty much part of the daily routine.

Following Julie's death but inspired by her life, Jack Sigler had made the decision to enlist in the United States Army, a decision that culminated with him leading Chess Team. The five-person team had been assigned unique operational identifiers—callsigns—taken from the pieces of a chessboard. He was King. Asya had recently taken up the mantel of Bishop. While the rest of the armed forces had spent more than a decade fighting terrorists and insurgents, they had fought monsters.

Literal, actual monsters.

Somewhere along the way, the dreams—*no, The Dream*—had stopped. Maybe the old adage about time healing all wounds was true. But the mystery of why he had stopped having The Dream did not concern him. What did concern him was the mystery that had brought The Dream back.

Seven months earlier, a different kind of monster—this one a very human political beast—had slammed its fist down on the table, knocking over all the pieces and utterly changing the game forever. Senator Lance Marrs, an ambitious lawmaker with aspirations for the Oval Office and absolutely no scruples, had exposed Chess Team as a rogue paramilitary operation. While that was not entirely untrue, he had accused their handler, former President Tom Duncan, Marrs's longtime political rival, of treason, which *was* a lie. Duncan had allowed himself to be arrested in exchange for amnesty for the team. But letting their leader languish in prison was not Sigler's idea of an acceptable outcome. Chess Team had vowed to win Duncan's freedom by any means necessary, no matter the cost, but before they could embark on that new mission, something extraordinary had happened. King had discovered that his older sister Julie was still alive.

Or so it appeared.

All he really knew for sure was that a woman, who looked exactly like his deceased sister, had appeared on the podium behind the current President of the United States on national television. The woman might simply have been Julie's doppelganger. Everyone had a lookalike, and given the amount of time that had passed since he had last seen Julie, his memories were suspect. Yet all his efforts to identify the woman had yielded no information. No person or database could identify her.

She was a ghost.

But was she Julie's ghost?

Sigler had turned his attention to the matter of Julie's deadly accident. There had never been cause to question the official findings, but when he scratched the surface, he discovered unusual discrepancies. Julie, an Air Force pilot, had been flying a Grumman F-14 Tomcat, at the time, the primary air superiority fighter of the US Navy—not an Air Force F-15 Strike Eagle. She had been alone in the cockpit, and alone in the sky. There was no Radar Intercept Officer in the back seat, and no wingman. King's request to have Julie's remains disinterred had yielded another unpleasant surprise: there was an empty coffin in Julie's grave.

There was a plausible explanation for any one of these irregu-larities, but all at once? It seemed unlikely. And explanations were not answers.

Somewhere along the way, King had started having The Dream again. Only now, Julie was no longer in the plane when it arrowed into the Atlantic.

As the weeks turned into months, the team continued to search for leads, both to the identity of the mystery woman and to the location of the secret prison where Tom Duncan was being held. There were dozens of secret—and not exactly legal—detention facilities scattered around the globe. They were nicknamed 'black sites.' The odds were good that Duncan was being kept at one of them. But because of their secretive nature, the only way to determine whether Duncan was present at any of them was to put boots on the ground.

They had infiltrated eight sites so far without success.

Lady Luck was a fickle mistress however, and after seven months of spurning them, she had done an abrupt about-face and supplied them with actionable leads to both objectives.

Zelda Baker, callsign: Queen, had taken the rest of the team, Stan Tremblay and Shin Dae-jung—Rook and Knight—north to check out a possible black site location above the Arctic Circle. King and Asya had come here.

Solving the mystery was not just a personal indulgence for King. The woman had been standing next to the leader of the free world. The fact that she had evidently gone to great lengths to hide her identity was cause for concern—regardless of whether she was Sigler's sister. If she actually was Julie Sigler, back from the dead, then it was imperative that he learn the truth.

The team's technology guru, Lewis Aleman, had undertaken the tedious task of piecing together all the video and CCTV footage he could get his hands on for the twenty-four hour period surrounding Julie's appearance. Then he had subsequently tracked her movements across Washington, to Dulles International Airport. She had both arrived and departed aboard a Global 8000 private jet aircraft. That was where he lost her. Several false flight plans had been submitted for the aircraft, leading him down one dead end after another. The names on the passenger manifest turned out to be aliases. The aircraft itself was owned and operated by a private corporation—TSAR Data Solutions, Inc.—headquartered in Wilmington, Delaware, America's shell company capital. It had seemed at first like another dead end.

TSAR Data Solutions, Inc. appeared, at first glance, to be just one more phony shell company, but that did not stop Sigler or Aleman from trying to crack the shell. After weeks of relentless digging, they had caught a break when TSAR purchased a warehouse property in Virginia, ostensibly to establish a computer server farm. The purchase had been handled by someone named Genrikh Ludvig—another alias, and a curious one at that, since Ludvig was the name of an obscure Russian scientist from the days of Josef Stalin. Whatever its true purpose, the warehouse was their only lead. It was a loose thread that King hoped would lead him back to Julie...or the woman who looked exactly like his dead sister.

They stayed in shadows, skirting the edge of the empty parking lot until they reached the southwest corner. Their intended point of entry was a fire exit one hundred yards away on the south wall. To reach it, they would have to traverse open ground under the glare of parking lot lights.

King donned a Bluetooth earpiece, linked to the smartphone in his pocket. "Deep Blue, this is King. How copy, over?"

Deep Blue was the operational callsign for the Chess Team's remote intel and data analyst, and general all around handler. Up until seven months ago, Tom Duncan had been Deep Blue, but just before his arrest, he had handed the reins over to Lewis Aleman.

It still felt odd calling Aleman 'Deep Blue.' His old handle—more of a nickname than a callsign—had been 'R2D2,' a reference to his technical prowess, not his stature. There was nothing stubby or truncated about the lanky, six-foot-two, former track athlete, and there was no one better suited to managing Chess Team from the op center. Aleman himself had suggested they temporarily shelve the Deep Blue callsign, but the team had voted down the suggestion. Continuity was essential for optimal operational efficiency. When they were in the field, they used callsigns, and those callsigns did not change, no matter who filled the role.

He was King. Asya was Bishop. Aleman was Deep Blue.

Period.

"Read you, Lima Charlie," Deep Blue replied in his ear. "Wish I could tell you the coast is clear, but that warehouse is a tough nut to crack. I'll keep monitoring local emergency channels. That way, if you trip a silent alarm, I'll be able to give you a head start."

"Roger. I'll keep the channel open." He turned to Bishop. "Move out."

With King watching her back, Bishop started forward, moving at a determined but leisurely pace. A casual observer—someone driving by or even a bored security guard watching a CCTV monitor through half-lidded eyes—would be more likely to take note of someone hunched over and sneaking like the villain in an old Bullwinkle cartoon, than they would someone walking normally and purposefully. In fact, the latter might not even register in an onlooker's conscious mind.

Whether or not the approach went unnoticed, Bishop reached the fire door a few seconds later and immediately went to work. She took a small device about the size and shape of an electronic stud finder from her pack, and moved it along the door frame. The device—they called it the 'skeleton key'—could pick up electromagnetic fields, such as those generated by the current passing through an alarm system. It then generated an induction field to bypass the alarm, so the door might be opened safely.

As useful as the skeleton key was, it was rudimentary compared to some of the equipment that had been at their disposal when they had operated out of a secret underground facility in New Hampshire, before things went completely to shit. Now, instead of a sophisticated quantum computer network, integrating comms, video, night-vision, weapons targeting and a host of other functions, they had to make do with smartphones and other devices. While some of those were ingenious, they were far from state-of-the-art. Such were the limitations of the fugitive life. Aleman was working on a new version of the quantum computer, but their operating budget and resources, while not inconsiderable, weren't what they once had been. Acquiring the necessary materials discreetly was proving a challenge.

The tools however were not as important as the soldier skills that each team member brought to the table. Those were as sharp as ever. In addition to the ongoing searches for Duncan and Julie, the team had taken on a few special jobs, including a recent jaunt to Mongolia, where they had tangled with some run-of-the-mill terrorists, and some decidedly not-run-of-the-mill Mongolian death worms. The burrowing creatures had been the size of subway trains and sprayed corrosive acid. Even without quantum computers and fancy apps, they had neutralized the threat, because that was what they did. When they ran into an obstacle, they didn't let it stop them. They just blew through and kept going.

Bishop's voice broke through King's reverie. "We have problem. This door is...well, it is *not* a door. We can't go through."

TWO

Ellesmere Island, Nunavut Territory, Canada

"**Okay, I have** three questions. One. What the hell kind of name is 'Alert'? Two. Who even names an empty swath of ice?" Stan Tremblay—callsign: Rook, the Chess Team's heavy weapons and demolitions expert—waved at the featureless expanse of ice that stretched out in every direction. "And Three. Don't you think, 'Holy Shit-Balls, It's Cold as Fuck Here,' would be a more accurate name?"

"They named it for the HMS Alert." Zelda Baker—callsign: Queen—did not look up. She lay prone on the snow, peering through the lens of the night vision monocular strapped around her head. Beside her, and also lying flat on the ground, Shin Dae-jung—callsign: Knight—did the same. Though instead of a handheld lens, he had his night vision scope mounted to his M-21 rifle.

Rook also wore NODs, albeit without the addition of magnifying lenses, but he suspected that his teammates were seeing the same thing he was. Everything was the same sickly pale shade of green, or so it appeared in his night vision display. In reality, everything was white. The binoculars, the rifle, the custom-made environmental suits the three of them wore and everything in every direction, as far as the eye could see. White whiteness, everywhere. Somewhere underneath the blanket of ice and snow, the barren land transitioned into water—the Lincoln Sea, part of the Arctic Ocean—but this far north and at this time of year, it was impossible to tell the difference.

"HMS Alert," Rook echoed with a laugh. Though only a few feet away, he was facing the opposite direction, watching their six o'clock. Although given the lack of terrain features, there was little chance of anyone sneaking up on them. "That's a ship, right? British? Let me guess. They got stranded here trying to reach the North Pole. Froze their asses off and had to eat each other when the food ran out."

"Are you asking me?" Queen replied, with just a trace of irritation. "If you want to know, look it up on Wikipedia, like I did."

"Look it up on Wikipedia," Rook said, doing a sarcastic impression of Queen. "I think I'll do that, and then update the name to 'The Land of Perpetual Boredom and Endless Ice that Can Freeze a Deuce Solid in the Time it Takes to Leave Your Sphincter and Hit the Ground.'"

"That's a mouthful," Knight remarked.

"Ha. That's what she said."

"To be fair, I have a small mouth," Queen said quietly.

"Well, that's just rude," Rook said, grinning behind the mask that covered his mouth and nose, protecting his face from the frigid air.

"That's the place, right?" Queen said, turning her head a few degrees to look at Knight.

"That looks like the old weather station, but..." Knight shrugged without raising his head. "It looks completely deserted."

Rook twisted around again and squinted in the direction the other two were facing. "Wait, there's a building out there?"

Despite his earlier quips, he had actually read up on their objective, a decommissioned weather and radio monitoring station built by the Canadian government in the 1950s. Officially, the station—CFS Alert—was once staffed year-round by a roster of scientists and technicians. At just five hundred miles from the North Pole, it had been the northernmost permanently inhabited settlement in the world. But in 2013, the site had been leased to the US government and all the tech had been removed. It was an empty shell. A black site. Permanently occupied, yes, but by a small coterie of security contractors—mercenaries with a background in black ops and a Top Secret security clearance—and one very special prisoner.

Queen handed him the magnifying lens. "Several actually."

Rook scanned the foreground with the high-powered optics. There was nothing recognizable in his display, and certainly nothing that appeared man-made. "Those lumps covered with snow?"

"Could be camouflage," Knight suggested.

"What's the point of that?" Rook said. "This is literally the last place on Earth."

"As much as it pains me to say it," Queen said, "he's right. I think this is another dead end."

Rook tried to think of an appropriately off-color reply, but the realization that they had come so far for nothing took the wind out of his sails. It had taken the better part of three days to get to the location, which was so far north that satellite communications and GPS location systems were unreliable at best. The last leg of the journey, a nine-hour snowmobile ride from Grise Fiord—an Inuit village 500 miles away, whose name meant 'Place that Never Thaws'—had sounded a lot more fun than it actually was. Getting back would be no less tedious, but the return trip would take place in the shadow cast by a cloud of failure. "We should probably...you know, check it out."

"Yeah." Queen rose to her full, if modest, five feet, five inches—five-seven including the two-inch thick soles of her mountaineering boots. She clicked into the quick-release bindings on her snowshoes, and gripped the FN-SCAR-L assault rifle that had been slung across her back. "Let's go take a look."

Knight tilted his head back, revealing the eye-patch that covered the place where his left eye had once been—he'd lost it on a mission in the Congo—and he looked up at her with his one good eye. "Want me to do what I usually do?"

Queen stared back at him as if weighing the options, but Rook was not surprised at all when she nodded. "Yeah."

As the team's designated marksman, it was Knight's job to provide overwatch. Given the circumstances, it seemed like an unnecessary precaution, but standard operating procedures were called that for a reason.

Rook rose as well. He glanced down at Knight, who had already lowered his eye to the scope. "Don't eat the yellow snow."

Knight shook his head. "Is that the best you can do? It's like you're not even trying anymore."

"Ouch," Rook said, with a dramatic wince. He turned to Queen. "Do you think he's right? Am I losing my touch?"

Queen's face, mostly hidden behind a thermal mask, was unreadable. "I'll tell you if it gets to be a problem. Let's go."

Rook held his SCAR at the low ready and started forward, taking point. Normally, he would be packing the squad automatic weapon—an M240B or something with equivalent firepower—but this mission demanded a higher degree of mobility. A machine gun was useless without several hundred rounds of ammunition, and there was only so much the three of them could carry. With King and Bishop chasing after their dead sister, or whoever the mystery woman was, some adjustments had to be made.

There were other considerations, too. If Alert was the black site they sought and they had to fight their way to Duncan, their foes wouldn't be terrorists or enemy combatants. Trained killers, yes, but Americans, working under the auspices—albeit with questionable legality—of the United States government. While Rook and the others would not hesitate to defend themselves, the best outcome for the mission was one where they would not have to fire a single shot. Carnage was off the table, and that was probably for the best. Inasmuch as Alert appeared to be another dry hole, leaving the big gun behind was definitely the right call.

At least there was a silver lining to this dark cloud. He looked over his shoulder at Queen. "Now that we're alone—"

"Don't."

He grinned again. "Just looking forward to warming up when this is all over."

Despite her protestations, Rook knew Queen enjoyed his irrepressible wit. It was what had ultimately won her over. They had been an item for almost four years, and while their relationship was not exactly conventional—it was hard to imagine either of them settling into a house in the suburbs, with a couple of rugrats and a soccermobile—the bond between them had only grown stronger with the passage of time.

He let his eyes linger on her a moment longer. The custom-made combat-suit—an ingenious combination of high-tech liquid body armor and synthetic fur—left her virtually unrecognizable. Still, he had no difficulty visualizing the lithe, athletic body underneath. He was, after all, intimately familiar with it.

Maybe a couple rugrats wouldn't be so bad after all, he thought. *She would make beautiful babies.*

He pushed the idle thought away and returned his attention to the blank snowfield ahead. Truth be told, he sometimes entertained the fantasy of a normal, ordinary life with her. He would never say it to her face, though. Long before she became Queen—the strongest woman he had ever known—Zelda Baker had borne the unimaginable pain of losing a child. He was not about to do or say anything that might tear open that old wound.

The snow-covered lumps he had glimpsed through the lens gradually became more defined as they approached, though it was still a stretch of the imagination to believe that they were man-made structures. Even when he was standing close enough to touch the outermost drift, Rook got no sense of what lay underneath. He reached out with one gloved hand and began scooping away the snow. The action triggered a small avalanche from above that bowled him over and subsequently piled up around him.

"Damn it," he rasped, kicking his snowshoes in the air for a moment.

"You look like an albino turtle flipped onto its shell" Queen said with a chuckle. "You grew up in snow country. How did you not see that coming?"

"Stay in your lane," he retorted. "I do the jokes."

"I think the joke is on us. Take a look."

Rook rolled over onto hands and knees and wiped the powdery snow away from his face. The collapsed drift now revealed a squat, weather-beaten, pre-fabricated modular building. Sheets of plywood had been nailed into place over the windows and what he could only assume was a door.

"Well, at least we won't have any trouble getting a room."

"Nice," she replied, and turned away, heading for the corner of the structure.

Rook got to his feet again, which was no simple task in the deep snow. "Oh, come on. I'll build a fire. It will be ro—"

"Rook!" Queen's voice was unexpectedly sharp. "Get over here."

He was on his feet in an instant and reached her side less than two seconds later, his SCAR raised and poised to fire. Queen was pointing at a dark spot fifty feet away, halfway between the first building and the next.

"What is that, oil?"

"Switch off your NODs," she said. "I'm going to use white light."

He did as instructed, squeezing both eyes shut so that the brightness of Queen's tactical LED flashlight reflecting off the snow would not blind him. Even with that precaution, he still winced a little as the light stung his pupils. It took him a few moments to adjust. When he finally opened his eyes, he saw that the spot in the snow was actually a deep shade of red.

"That's blood."

"Yeah," Queen said.

"A lot of it."

"Yeah."

The blood had melted the snow a little before cooling and freezing, but it was still starkly visible. No snow had fallen to cover the stains, and the buildings had evidently blocked the wind that might have otherwise erased them from existence. The dark stain looked like a Rorschach ink blot from a distance. Up close, Rook could see that there were actually several splotches of red in the snow. "Someone got killed here."

"Or something." Queen pointed to something beyond the splotches. "We're in polar bear country, don't forget."

There was a long, mostly straight furrow, heading north through the snowed-over compound, toward the water. Drag marks. As if to confirm Queen's suggestion, there were several larger depressions in the snow, too big to be footprints but too small to be snowshoe tracks. A closer inspection showed the distinctive shape of a paw, with bloody needle-points at the end pointing away from the larger bloodstain.

Claws.

"Papa Bear walked out of here, dragging a kill." Rook shook his head. "Or at least that's how it's supposed to look."

"You don't think that's what happened?"

"This is a splatter pattern, caused by a high-velocity impact. Like from a bullet. I don't think Papa Bear would be able to pull a trigger."

Queen registered her agreement with a nod.

"This couldn't have happened more than a day or two ago," Rook went on. "Someone or something got shot, right here. Executed, maybe." He winced as soon as he said it. "I'm sure it wasn't..." He didn't finish. Meaningless platitudes and wishful thinking wouldn't change reality. Somebody had died on this spot, and it might very well have been Tom Duncan.

"Somebody fired that shot," Rook went on. "A person not a bear. Maybe the bear showed up later and dragged the body away."

"The shooter might still be here," Queen said. "I think this place just lived up to its name." She keyed her radio mic. "Knight, we need you down here. ASAP. Head on a swivel. Something's not right here."

Rook heard the sniper's reply in his earpiece. "Oscar Mike." Radio-speak for 'on the move.'

"We're gonna clear this place." Queen said, speaking over the radio net. "Every corner and crevice. We need to figure out what happened here."

Rook just nodded. They pulled back to the outer perimeter and waited for Knight to join them. Not surprisingly, the Korean-American made a stealthy approach, getting within ten yards of them unnoticed before clearing his throat to announce his presence.

"Show off," Rook muttered, but his heart wasn't in it.

Queen brought Knight up to speed and then outlined her plan of action. They would walk the perimeter, making sure that no one was lurking on the far side of the settlement, and then begin systematically clearing the buildings, even if they had to use breaching charges to get inside. They started out, moving tactically in short bursts, from one place of cover or concealment to the next.

Three minutes later, they found more blood.

As before, the snow told a tale of high velocity impact, a body dragged toward the water and bears. As before, the circumstances were suspicious. Knight noticed a detail that had escaped Rook's notice.

"These tracks weren't made by a bear."

Rook gave the bloody paw prints a second look. The foot pad and five evenly spaced toes certainly looked like every bear track he had ever seen.

"Hate to break it to you," Rook said, "but I grew up in black bear country. I know bear tracks when I see them. These are bigger, but they're definitely bearish."

"They are bear tracks," Knight countered. "But look at the spacing. Whatever did this was walking on two legs."

"Bears do that."

Queen put one booted foot, then the other, into the paw prints, and then started forward, stepping in the tracks without difficulty. "Knight's right. These tracks were made by a human."

"Wearing fake bear-paw boots." Rook shook his head. "That's some ninja shit right there."

"Ninjas wouldn't have been so careless. This was rushed," Knight said.

"Careless or not," Queen said, "somebody hit this place and then vanished. Where did they come from, and where did they go? There's no sign of snowmobile tracks, no helicopter LZ." She gestured in the direction of the pack ice. "They couldn't have left by boat."

"Submarine." Rook and Knight said it at almost the same moment, in harmony, then Rook continued. "Ninjas with polar bear feet and a submarine. Well that just clears it right up."

"I think this was the place," Queen said. "This is where they were keeping Duncan. But somebody got here before we did."

When neither man responded, she went on. "He's alive. That's why they tried to make it look like bears dragged the bodies away. To cover the fact that Duncan is still alive."

"So this was a rescue?" Rook was skeptical.

Queen shook her head. "It was an abduction."

"A sub that can break through pack ice," Knight said, as if thinking aloud. "Who has access to that?"

Rook knew that Aleman—Deep Blue, now—would be able to provide the answer, but this far north, satellite communications were practically non-existent and certainly not reliable enough for an encrypted transmission. The answer to the question of who might have orchestrated the raid on the Alert black site would have to wait.

"Let's finish our sweep," Queen said. "Maybe we'll get lucky and find a clue."

Knight abruptly made a hushing sound. Both Rook and Queen knew better than to respond with anything but total silence. Rook pulled his hood back a little and cupped a hand over his ear, trying to hear what it was that had caught Knight's attention. At first, all he could make out was the constant low hiss of the wind moving across the snow. Then he could make out the harsh roar of jet engines in the distance and the faint rhythm of helicopter rotors beating the air, growing louder by the second.

THREE

Ashburn, Virginia

"What do you mean it's not a door?"

Bishop searched her English vocabulary for the appropriate words to describe what she was looking at. "Is fake. Just there for looks."

King jogged forward to join her. As he reached her side, Deep Blue's voice sounded in her ear. "I've checked the blueprints on file. There's definitely supposed to be a fire exit there."

King took out a red LED flashlight and shone it at the edge of the steel door. There was no gap between the door and the doorposts. The builders had affixed a sheet of metal to the concrete wall, held in place with a frame of molding. From a distance it looked like a one-way exit, but it was merely a façade.

"Well, we've got them on a code violation," King said, "but that doesn't get us inside. I suppose all the other fire doors are bogus as well."

"Can't help you with that," Deep Blue said. "All I've got are the blueprints, and those are clearly wrong."

"We don't have time to play Monty Hall," King said. "Let's go to Plan B." He surveyed the breadth of the building, looking for the place that afforded the most concealment, but the wall was uniformly flat and exposed. "I guess here's as good a place as any."

Bishop unslung her backpack and knelt over it, rooting in its depths to retrieve a coil of black rope. Attached to one end was a collapsible grappling hook. She took a step away from the building, mentally gauging its height, and then she measured out several arm lengths of rope. While she did that, King doffed his pack and took out a black plastic object that looked a little like an over-sized workman's lunch box, with a strange pulley mechanism sprouting from the handle.

Bishop played out the rope and then began whipping the grappling hook around in an overhand motion. The hook made a faint whooshing sound as it orbited, gathering momentum until, after only a few revolutions, she extended her arm up and heaved both rope and hook skyward. The hook shot up more than forty feet on a slight parabolic trajectory, before peaking and arcing back down. A moment later, it disappeared beyond the edge of the roof. A faint clanking sound signaled contact. The rope slapped against the side of the building and remained there, while the excess slack clattered to the ground in front of Bishop.

"First try," King said, handing over the lunchbox-like contraption. "Not bad, little sis."

"I always get it on the first try," Bishop said, without a trace of humility. She had mastered the art of setting a grapnel long before joining her older brother's paramilitary team. She clipped the rope into the pulley handle and then used a carabiner to secure the device—an Atlas APA-5 battery-powered mechanical ascender—to the black nylon rigger's belt she wore around her waist. "Tell me. What is Monty Hall?"

Before King could answer, Deep Blue chimed in. "Monty is a 'who' not a 'what'. He was the host of 'Let's Make A Deal.'"

"I don't understand."

"It's a game show. You see, there are these doors—"

"She can Google it," King said, sounding a little annoyed. "We're on the clock."

Bishop shrugged then thumbed a button on the handle of the Atlas device. There was a whirring noise as the small but powerful electric motor engaged, and then a moment later, it lifted her into the air. She leaned back and planted her feet against the wall so that she was for all practical purposes, walking up the vertical surface. It took just a few seconds for her to make the ascent, after which she hauled herself over the roof's edge. She drew up several yards of rope and clipped the now quiet ascender to the end. Then she manually lowered it down to King. After one last check to make sure nobody was around to see, he clipped in and started up the wall to join her.

"That was fun," she said, when he was once more at her side. "Should have been A Plan."

"Plan A," he corrected. He unhooked the ascender and stuffed it back in his pack, while Bishop gathered up the rope into a coil, which she slung over her shoulder. "This was Plan B, because climbing up the side of a building like Batman may be fun, but it's also very conspicuous."

Bishop fought the urge to roll her eyes. King was right, of course. Although sometimes he was too cautious for her liking. Her brother was an exceptional leader, though. What was really bothering her was the fact that they were here at all. As far as she was concerned, rescuing Tom Duncan was their first priority. Their *only* priority. Julie Sigler was nothing to her but a name. Finding who the woman King had identified—questionably—as their long-dead sister was something that, in Bishop's opinion at least, could wait.

Deep Blue's voice sounded in her ear again. "There should be a maintenance door fifty yards from your location."

"I see it," King said.

"What if is another fake?" Bishop asked.

"Then we'll have to go to Plan C. Cut our way into the ventilation system."

"Nothing conspicuous about that. Maybe we should just go in front door." She made a gun-shape with her finger. "You know, ask politely."

"I doubt the rent-a-cop at the security desk will have the answers we want," King replied. "But we can make that Plan D."

Plans C and D proved unnecessary, however. The roof access door was not only unsecured, without any alarms or cameras, but it was propped open with a cinderblock. A pile of cigarette butts and a faint whiff of stale tobacco smoke at the doorway explained the evident lapse in security.

"Nice of them to leave door open," Bishop remarked.

"Someone has a serious habit. Odds are good we might run into them on their way up for another nicotine break." He drew his sound-suppressed sidearm, and said, "Stay frosty."

Despite the display of firepower, Bishop knew the optimal outcome would be one where they did not need to fire a single shot. Their objective was to gather intel, not go on a killing spree. Nevertheless, Bishop drew her own sound-suppressed pistol. "Always."

King approached the door and eased it open a few more inches until there was room enough for him to slip through. Bishop followed immediately and found herself on a metal staircase that descended about ten feet to an open catwalk suspended high above the warehouse floor. To either side, she could see the enormous conical reflectors of hanging, industrial-strength metal-halide lights. Only a few of them were turned on. They cast small islands of illumination in the sea of shadows that was the warehouse floor. Yet, despite the sparse light, one thing was immediately apparent.

"This is not server farm," Bishop observed.

"Nope. Looks more like a Costco."

King was not wrong. Directly below them were row after row of multi-tiered pallet racks, filled with stacked cardboard boxes wrapped in cellophane. They were too far away to make out the words stenciled on the containers, but the boxes, at least all those Bishop could see from where they were perched, were all nearly identical. "So is just warehouse?"

"Maybe." King sounded unconvinced. "Cover me."

He holstered his pistol and dropped flat on the catwalk, then lowered himself over the edge, down onto the closest pallet. Crouching there, he drew his KA-BAR knife, sliced open one of the boxes and inspected the contents. Bishop looked around, then leaned over to see what he had discovered.

"Recognize this?" King held up a small parcel, wrapped in a green camouflage pattern, which Bishop did indeed recognize immediately.

"That is..." She faltered for a moment as the English words to describe the familiar item escaped her. "*Individualnovo Ratsiona Pitanee*. How do you say? Food ration."

"MREs," King muttered.

"I ate this in Russian Army. Much superior to your MRE. The biscuits are..." She trailed off again, casting her gaze in either direction. There were hundreds of pallets, each one stacked with full cases of military food rations. She did a quick calculation. "This is enough to feed someone for a thousand years."

"Or a thousand people for a year." King stuffed the package back into the case. "Maybe even ten thousand."

Bishop tried to wrap her head around this discovery. They had been prepared for the possibility that TSAR Data Solutions was not what it presented itself as, but she could not fathom why the shell company would put thousands of Russian military food rations in their warehouse. "Are they going to sell these?"

"I don't think so. This is a supply depot."

"Supply? For what?"

King didn't answer the question. "We need to find out what else they've got here. Come on."

He crawled to edge of the rack and then began climbing down the upright metal frame. Bishop hastened to catch up.

Down on the floor, the warehouse felt more like a claustrophobic maze. The towering racks were like castle walls, looming above her and blocking out most of the available light. King, his pistol once more drawn and held at the ready, gestured for her to follow. Then they headed down the long narrow space between the racks. He paused at the end, pivoting around the corner slowly, employing a technique known as 'slicing the pie,' where he scanned each new degree of visibility.

They continued in this fashion for several minutes, slicing every blind corner as they made their way down the transverse aisle. After passing several more racks like the first, the floor arrangement changed. Now, instead of pallets loaded with cardboard boxes, there were several more rows of enormous plastic tanks marked with Cyrillic letters that Bishop had no difficulty reading.

"Water."

The vertical tanks, a dozen of them, were arranged in two back-to-back rows parallel to the last pallet rack. Each was large enough to contain a swimming pool worth of water, at least twenty thousand gallons. A quarter of a million gallons in all. Maybe more.

"Food and water," King said, nodding in comprehension. "Enough to supply an army."

"A Russian army." The implications of the discovery made her dizzy. "But why?"

She thought she knew the answer, but it seemed too improbable, too crazy.

"An army may travel on its stomach, but they don't fight that way. Let's keep looking. If we find some ordnance—"

Before he could finish the sentence, the overhead lights abruptly flashed on. It took a moment for the metal-halide lamps to warm up to their optimal output, but even the faint change in illumination as the lamps came on was enough to put both of them on high alert.

"Time to go," King said.

He darted back to the end of the aisle and edged around the tank, peering down the cross aisle into the unexplored depths of the warehouse. This time he took only a couple of slices of the pie before pulling back. He turned to Bishop and held up his hand, four fingers extended.

Four tangoes.

He then pointed down the aisle, the meaning of the gesture clear. *Check the other end.*

Bishop sprinted down the row, careful to roll from heel to toe with each step, minimizing the sound of her footfalls. She drew up short of the corner and then carefully sliced around the blind spot.

Four more men were moving up the transverse aisle. They wore casual attire—blue jeans and T-shirts—but there was nothing casual about their manner. All were tall and broad, hair cropped close or completely shaved, like soldiers. They walked in a tight tactical knot, clearing each row, just as a team of soldiers would do.

And they were armed. Like soldiers.

The four men carried compact submachine pistols with extended vertical magazines. Bishop couldn't distinguish the exact make of their weapons with her quick glance, but there was something eerily familiar about the disciplined way the men carried themselves.

She backed away and then turned to King, shaking her head and holding up four fingers just as he had done. King's silent reply was immediate. He pointed to the rack behind them and then pointed up.

Climb.

Bishop holstered her pistol and leaped onto the pallet racks, scrambling up the metal frame like it was a piece of playground equipment. At the other end of the row, King did the same.

She was twenty feet above the floor, and about the same distance from the top of the rack, when the shooting started.

FOUR

Alert, Nunavut Territory, Canada

Knight peered through the scope of his sniper rifle, searching the star-filled sky to the south of their position for any sign of the approaching aircraft. There was none. The helicopters—he was pretty sure that there were at least two—were running dark. There was no question that the birds were headed for CFS Alert. Where else was there to go?

The more important question was: why?

"Ghost time," Queen said.

He did not have to ask what that meant, but vanishing like wraiths was a tall order under the circumstances. Their camouflage would afford some concealment and their temperature-controlled winter combat gear would make them virtually invisible to thermal scopes. But there was no hiding the almost two-mile long trail of footprints leading from their parked snow-machines, straight to the black site. And while their tracks might not be visible from the air, it wouldn't take long for the men aboard those helicopters to spot them, once they were on the ground and searching the compound.

Queen said nothing more but started out at a run. Her snowshoes kicked up little puffs of frozen powder with each step, but she was careful to place her feet in the tracks they had left earlier. Doing so would not erase all signs of their presence, but it might serve to confuse the message left by their trail. Rook set out next, doing the same, though matching Queen's shorter stride gave him an almost comical gait. Knight went last.

Since any radio transmission might betray their presence that much sooner, they did not speak, not that any of them would have been inclined to waste time or breath on idle conversation. While they were all in excellent physical condition, running in snowshoes was as much a test of skill as it was of athletic ability. Nevertheless, as Knight fell into a steady running rhythm, the many unanswered questions began to intrude on his thoughts.

Had they really missed Duncan by mere days, or even just a few hours? And if so, who had beat them to the black site? The leaked intel that had brought them to Alert might have been picked up by someone else as well. Who? Foreign spies? A rival domestic intelligence agency? A private sector organization with a grudge against Duncan or an interest in picking the brain of a former United States president? Any of the above might possess the resources to send a fully crewed submarine to break through the Arctic ice and put a team of commandos ashore to raid the black site.

But who was on the helicopters? Someone coming to find out why CFS Alert had gone dark? Or someone who knew the Chess Team was there? Someone who was hunting them?

Was it possible that this entire scenario was an elaborate trap designed to catch the team?

Seven months earlier, following Tom Duncan's decision to surrender to federal authorities in a deal designed to protect the rest of them from prosecution, the commanding officer of the Joint Special Operations Command—the cross-branch military agency that had been the genesis of the Chess Team—had offered them all a chance to return to active duty, submitting once more to the chain of command. By unanimous accord, the five of them had refused, which effectively nullified the offer of amnesty. The JSOC commander, Admiral Ward, had elected not to pursue his legal options against them, though. It was tacit permission for them to continue battling enemies who were beyond the reach, to say nothing of the comprehension, of legitimate military units. But tolerating them was not the same thing as support.

Has something changed?

The roar of the jet turbines and the beat of rotor blades abruptly grew louder, as if the aircraft were about to pass directly overhead. Knight scanned the sky again and thought he saw a pair of black shapes moving in front of the star field. It could have just been his imagination, but the immediate change in the pitch and rhythm of the rotor noise, a Doppler-shifting as the source of the sound began moving away instead of toward him, strongly suggested it was not. The helicopters were headed for Alert, and they would be landing in a matter of seconds. It might take a while for the men in the helos to walk the site and realize that someone had come and gone, but they would eventually find the tracks leading out across the snowfield. And they would follow.

Knight judged they had covered less than a quarter of the distance to the spot where they had left the snowmobiles. With a little luck, they might be able to reach their rides before the hunt began in earnest, but what then?

One problem at a time, he told himself.

FIVE

Ashburn, Virginia

The smell of burnt paper and gunpowder filled King's nostrils as he reached the top of the rack. He rolled onto the six-foot-tall stack of boxes on the uppermost pallet, removing himself, temporarily at least, from the shooters' direct line of sight. He could feel the cartons shuddering with each impact and all around him, bits of debris were exploding into the air, as some of the bullets grazed the corner edges. The packed Russian army rations would provide next-to-no cover whatsoever. The only way he and Bishop were going to survive this was to keep moving. Unfortunately, there was nowhere to go. The aisles separating the pallet racks were at least fifteen feet apart. It was a distance that he might be able to leap across with a running start, but under the circumstances, that wasn't possible.

"King!" Bishop's urgent voice sounded over the comms, but the open transmission also amplified the near constant crack of machine-pistol reports. "Coming your way. Cover me."

He glanced down the length of the rack and saw her fast-crawling in his direction, surrounded by a cloud of smoke and debris.

Right, he thought. *Cover you.*

Trusting that Bishop knew what she was doing, he drew his pistol, extended the suppressor end a few inches out into the open, and started pulling the trigger. The .45 bucked in his awkward one-handed grip, sending the ACP rounds in a random spray, but accuracy wasn't his primary goal. He was just trying to draw fire long enough for Bishop to do whatever it was she was trying to do. With the silencer masking both the noise and flash of each shot, it took the shooters below a few seconds to shift their fire toward him. But when the incoming storm of lead intensified, he knew he'd gotten their attention.

"King! Come to me!"

Bishop was close enough that she did not need to bother with the comms, just twenty feet away, but reaching her was easier said than done. He looked around frantically, searching for some way to draw the heat off him.

There was a small gap between the stack on which he lay and the back of the metal rack. Not enough room for him to slip down behind the cartons, and doing so would have been a bad idea under any circumstances, but it gave him an idea. He did a quick combat roll toward the narrow space and jammed his elbow down into it. The top layer of boxes shifted a little, widening the gap and allowing King to worm his way deeper, but the shrink wrap around the stack kept them more or less in place. He kept shoving and burrowing deeper, even as the storm of incoming fire continued without letup. None of the rounds made it all the way through, but King could still feel each impact, as if someone was relentlessly striking the side of the stack with a sledgehammer. He shoved and shifted, shoved and shifted again, and then he felt the entire stack begin to move.

He twisted around, braced his back against the boxes and pushed hard against the metal rack. His intention was to shove the entire load off the pallet and onto the floor, but at that moment, the cellophane wrap, which was perforated by innumerable bullets, tore loose, spilling just the upper three layers. The boxes tumbled off one-by-one, instead of falling as a single unit, but it was enough to momentarily disrupt the fusillade from below.

King scrambled up onto the next pallet and saw Bishop, still a good fifteen feet away, crouching low and holding her pistol—

No, it's not a pistol. It's the grappling hook.

She played out a few feet of rope and then began whirling it overhand, lining up with one of the hanging lights. If she managed to snare it, she might be able to swing across Tarzan-style to the next row of pallet racks, but it was a big 'if' and an even bigger 'might be.'

Her eyes met his for just a second, then her gaze shifted past him and locked on something just beyond him. He ducked before she could shout a warning, and then he threw himself to the side. He was a fraction of a second ahead of the shots that were coming, not from the floor but from the end of the rack.

The shooters knew what they were doing. While the bulk of the element had maintained suppressive fire to keep them pinned down, someone had climbed up the end of the rack in a classic flanking maneuver.

King flipped onto his back, and even though he knew it was probably already too late, he raised his pistol to return fire. Before he could get a shot off, and before his would-be killer—a hulking man with a bullet-shaped head and wearing a T-shirt that could barely contain his biceps—could adjust his aim, something flashed through the air above King. The shooter ducked reflexively as the projectile arced toward his head, but he evidently did not see the rope attached to it. That rope landed on his shoulder a fraction of a second later, and then snapped taut as Bishop hauled in the slack with a sharp jerk.

The man was yanked off his feet, the hook set deep into his trapezius muscle between his shoulder blades. He flew through the air to slam into a pallet, right where King had been a moment before.

With the suppressor affixed to his pistol, more than doubling its barrel length, King was too close to aim the gun, so he did the next best thing. He swiped it across the side of the man's head. The blow was hard enough that King felt the impact vibrate up his forearm. The killer just shook his head, pushed away from the pallet and twisted around to face King.

King still didn't have a shot. Judging by the guy's size and ferocity, it would take more than a couple of bullets—even from a .45—to slow him down. So King used the only weapon he had left.

Himself.

"Bish! Belay on!"

He launched himself at the big man, wrapping him in a bear hug and driving him backward, off the edge of the rack. King knew he would be going over as well. There was no avoiding it, but if Bishop understood his last desperate command...

For a fleeting instant, both King and the shooter were in freefall, but then the downward motion ceased, as the rope attached to the grappling hook buried in the man's back went taut again. The man's weight and momentum tore the hook free, permitting King to resume his downward plummet. The pause gave him a chance to throw his arms around the rope.

The line jerked taut again as the hook snagged his arms, the talon-like claws digging painfully into his flesh. He swung like a pendulum back into the rack, slamming into a loaded pallet on the fourth level, a dozen feet down from where he had been a moment before.

Below him, the dazed attacker crashed down atop the litter of cartons that King had loosed a few seconds before. The other gunmen were in disarray, for the moment, but King knew it would not last. He tore his right arm loose from the hook, aimed the pistol in their general direction and emptied the magazine.

The gunmen scattered. King couldn't tell if he had scored any hits. He couldn't win the battle from his precarious position, but he *had* bought himself a few more seconds in which to find a better strategy.

He jammed the pistol into his belt—no time to futz around with the holster—and then knotted his fingers in the shrink wrap. Fueled by the urgency of need, he clawed his way up the pallet and then scrambled back up to the top rack, where he found Bishop. The rope was wrapped around her arms and her feet were jammed against an upright metal post.

"A little warning next time," she growled through clenched teeth.

"I did warn you," King said, as he heaved himself back up onto the half-emptied pallet.

"A little more, then."

King shrugged out of his backpack and delved inside. As he did, he nodded toward the enormous water tanks on the opposite side of the aisle. "Think you can hook those?"

"Of course I—" She stopped, her eyebrows furrowing in consternation. She bit back the unasked question and began furiously drawing the rope in. She whirled the grappling hook around several times and then heaved it out across open space. The hook sailed past one of the tanks and clattered down into the gap behind it. The throw had left Bishop with only a few remaining yards of rope, but she immediately began pulling in the slack until there was no more give. The hook had caught on something.

"Now what?"

By way of an answer, King clipped the Atlas ascender to the rope and then hooked the carabiner to the upright post. "Hang on to something," he said, and then he pushed the button to activate the device.

Almost immediately, the whir of the motor became a strained growl. The tension in the line increased until the rope was humming like a plucked guitar string. For a moment, King feared he had misjudged the capacity of the ascender or the load rating of the rope. Neither were meant to do what he was now attempting.

But then a new sound joined the din: the groaning of metal beginning to flex.

Then the entire section of pallet racking began to move. For a few seconds, it was barely noticeable, but as the degree of tilt increased, the equally distributed weight of the cargo loaded on the racks amplified the effect. Several loud reports sounded in quick succession—not gunshots but anchor bolts exploding out of the concrete floor, as the pallet rack leaned over like a toppling domino.

King and Bishop scrambled up the ever-increasing slope and heaved themselves onto the backside of the falling rack. King managed to wrap his arms around one of the uprights, but then the rack crashed into the row of water tanks with such violence that he was ripped free and hurled into the chaos below.

The water tanks split open like overripe watermelons. They instantly disgorged two hundred thousand gallons of water onto the warehouse floor. King had not even begun to recover from being body-slammed into a jumble of boxed food rations and metal posts when the tsunami hit.

SIX

Ellesmere Island, Nunavut Territory, Canada

Queen leaned forward, staying low over the handlebars of the Ski-Doo Expedition Xtreme, as she pushed the throttle to its stop. The spinning track underneath the vehicle threw out a horsetail of snow behind her, like an enormous exclamation point on the blank landscape.

"Open it up," she shouted into her radio mic, breaking radio silence for the first time since leaving Alert. There was no longer any reason to be slow or sneaky. The roar of jet turbines in the sky overhead was proof enough of that.

They had barely reached the snowmobiles when the helicopters idling at the deserted black site rose once more into the sky. At first, the three of them had kept the tracked-machines to a stealthy twenty-miles an hour, barely faster than their running pace—or at least it felt that way. But as the helicopter engine noise grew louder, louder even than the two-stroke 800 cubic centimeter 163-horsepower engine atop which she was sitting, there could be no doubt that the helicopters were headed their way.

Their situation was desperate, no question about that. Still, escape was not beyond the realm of possibility. An aircraft's strengths could easily be turned into weaknesses during a pursuit. The pilots would have no trouble catching up to them or matching their speed, but actually stopping them was another matter. It wasn't like they could run the snowmobiles off the road. There was also the question of how long the helicopters could sustain the pursuit. The Ski-doos could go for a couple hours, and at least a hundred and fifty miles, on a single tank of gas. The team had brought along more than enough fuel for a round trip back to

Grise Fiord. While the helicopters probably had a much longer range than that, they almost certainly had used up quite a bit of fuel just to reach Alert. The pilots would have to reserve enough fuel to get back to their base.

Of course, none of that would matter if the men on the helicopter opened fire on them. Trying to shoot the aircraft out of the sky with the weapons the three of them had brought along was a tall order. Not impossible, just very tall. Probably suicidal. Queen wasn't going to give the order to start shooting unless their pursuers gave them no alternative.

"Let's make 'em work for it," she said into her mic. "Rook, break left. I'll go right. Knight, go wherever the hell you want, as long as it's away from us."

Without waiting for a reply, she twisted the handlebars to the right, leaving the trail they had blazed on their approach to Alert. She plowed headlong across the pristine snowfield. Without reliable GPS navigation, the chances of getting lost were astronomically high, particularly if the weather changed. The batteries powering the heaters in their winter-survival suits would not hold out forever, nor would the fuel in the snowmobiles. But getting lost was a long-range problem. Eluding the helicopters was the immediate concern.

The roar of a jet engine overhead continued without letup. Queen tried zig-zagging randomly, but nothing changed. It sounded like the helicopter was right above her.

"It's working," Rook called out. "I think I lost them."

"Not me," Knight said, shouting to be heard over the helicopter noise in the background. "They're right on—"

The transmission abruptly cut out.

"Knight, what's happening?"

No answer.

Queen cocked her head to the side, straining to catch some change in the ambient noise that might provide a hint to Knight's fate.

Nothing.

Shit, Queen thought. "Rook, if you can, double back and find a place to dig in. Hide out."

"What about you?"

"What about me?" she snapped. "Just do it."

A sudden gale force wind ripped at her clothes, as the pale green landscape in front of her disappeared in a white haze of blowing snow. Her mask and NODs partially shielded her face, but she had to squeeze her unaided left eye closed to avoid being blinded by the icy blast. As the whiteout intensified, she realized what was happening. The pursuing helicopter was using its rotor wash to stir up a blizzard.

Clever, she thought, lowering her head. *But now you can't see me either.*

She let off the throttle, allowing the snowmobile to coast for a moment. Next she cut a turn so tight that she had to lean in the opposite direction to avoid flipping over. She dipped so low that she could feel the snow scraping against her shoulder. After a couple seconds, she straightened the handlebars and eased forward on the throttle, crawling the snowmobile forward through the whirling snow.

There was another blast of sound in her ear as someone broke squelch. She heard Knight's voice, a labored stage whisper, barely audible over the din. "Knocked me off...ride. Digging in."

When the transmission ended, Rook's voice replaced it. "They'll have to set down to take us. We can ambush them."

Queen nodded. An ambush was about the only chance they had. Unless the helicopters were big passenger ships—Chinooks or the like, which was doubtful—they would be dealing with no more than a squad or two. Ten to twelve shooters max, but probably not even that many. Their camouflage would give them a temporary edge. Her decision to have Rook and Knight disperse cut both ways though, since Rook might be too far away to make much of a difference. Still, Knight's prowess with the sniper rifle would more than make up for that.

The static haze cleared as Queen emerged from the snow vortex. The first thing she saw, a hundred yards away, was another huge column of blowing snow, marking the spot where Knight had been forcibly dismounted. Above it, barely visible, was the black outline of a helicopter. There was not even a glimmer of light visible from the aircraft. A glance over her shoulder revealed a similar shape hovering above and behind her.

Close. Almost too close. But do they see me?

She realized she might not get another chance to strike a blow against the hunters.

Releasing the throttle, she stood up in the stirrups and launched herself off the snowmobile. She twisted in mid-air, hands finding the FN SCAR a split-second before landing on her back in the deep snow. The strident whine of the snowmobile engine ceased as the throttle kill-switch—a safety measure to prevent a runaway sled—cut in. Queen barely heard the change over the roar of the helicopter's turbines and the rush of blood in her own ears.

"Take them out!" she shouted, and she aimed the assault weapon at the nearest hovering shape.

Before her finger could tighten on the trigger however, a loud voice—louder even than the deep bone-shaking beat of the rotors—boomed down from above.

"This is the United States Army. Stand down, and you will not be harmed."

Queen's finger came off the trigger, as if she had received an electric shock. The identity of their pursuers did not come as a surprise. In fact, she had assumed that the helicopters were military. Who else had the resources to mount an Arctic expedition and operate in total blackout conditions? Even the fact that they were Americans, conducting operations on Canadian turf, was not altogether unexpected. Somebody in the Canadian government had sanctioned the black site, so it only made sense that the same entity would have given the U.S. military authority to act in its defense.

What stopped her was the warning itself.

The soldiers aboard the helicopters could have opened fire at any time but they had not. If the disembodied voice was to be believed, they would continue to refrain from taking lethal action.

"Queen, what's the play?" Knight's voice was taut with urgency.

That he had not already taken a shot placed the burden of the snap decision entirely on her. She almost regretted that he had not fired when she had given the initial order. Now she was faced with an entirely different set of variables.

They could start this fight, and they might even be able to win it. Military gunships were up-armored against small arms fire, but they weren't invulnerable. A burst from the SCAR might strike a vital, exposed component and take the aircraft out of the sky, or the rounds might find their way into the passenger compartment.

But it would be a fight against American soldiers. There was no longer any uncertainty about that.

"Stand down," the voice repeated. "We know who you are. We mean you no harm."

"Queen," Knight said again. "Call it."

"Standby, Knight."

Queen shuffled through her options, but it was like rearranging a losing poker hand and hoping the cards would magically get better. Fight, and either lose and die, or win and cement their fate as fugitives. There would be no going back if they declared war on the Army.

Surrender was the wild card, but she couldn't see it making a bad situation any worse.

Unless they're going to cross us off anyway.

She realized that she had chosen the wrong metaphor. This wasn't a poker game where the bluff made all the difference. It was a chess game, and they had been outmaneuvered.

"Queen sacrifice," she muttered. "Knight, Rook, hold your position. I'm going to see what these guys want."

Rook's objection was immediate. "Queen, no. You can't trust them."

"I don't. That's why you're going to do what I said. Hold your position and be ready to light their asses up."

There was a pause, then Knight said, "Roger."

"I didn't hear you, Rook."

"This is a bad idea, babe."

"That's what they said about you and me." She took a breath. "Okay, I'm doing this."

She lowered her carbine, allowing it to hang by its sling across her chest. She stood up, raising her hands. She didn't know if the men in the helo could see her, white against a white background, so she swiveled the PVS-14 unit away from her face, and twisted the mode selection knob to activate the built in infrared light. Invisible to the naked eye, the IR light could offer additional illumination in conditions where there was not enough natural light for the NODs to function at their best. The light served a more important role as a sort of friend-or-foe identification system. In most combat scenarios, only the good guys had night-vision, so anyone with an infrared light shining from their face was probably someone you weren't supposed to shoot.

She hoped the men on the helicopters would understand that as well. Evidently they did, because instead of drilling her full of holes, the nearest bird shifted position slightly. The voice from heaven spoke again.

"I see you. Stay where you are and keep your hands away from your weapon, or we will act accordingly."

Queen was relieved that he had not said something like, 'We will open fire.' In a tense standoff, men with itchy trigger fingers tended to hear only the last two words.

"We're going to land now. Stay where you are."

"That's right," Rook muttered in her ear. "Come out of your nice safe helicopter and stand where I can kill you."

"Rook!"

"If they scratch their asses wrong," Rook said, undeterred, "*I will act accordingly.*"

"We got your back, Queen," Knight added. "If you even catch a whiff of this going south, hit the ground."

Lights began appearing on the exterior of the hovering black shape, bright enough for her to make out the familiar outline of a UH-60 Black Hawk helicopter. The aircraft's nose came up, and then the vehicle settled toward the ground fifty yards away, like a hawk coming to roost. A wild flurry of snow hid the final touchdown, but Queen could hear a change in the pitch of the turbines as the pilot reduced power to an idle and adjusted the collective so that the rotor-blades were no longer pushing air.

She remained where she was, arms raised high, and waited for the storm to clear. As it did, she saw two figures emerging from the flurry. Both wore white camouflage shells, their faces hidden behind matching masks and ski goggles. Both were armed with FN SCAR-L rifles, exactly like those she and Rook were carrying. The man on Queen's right held his weapon diagonally across his chest with the barrel pointing up, while his companion had allowed his weapon to dangle from its sling at his side. In his hand, he held a flashlight, aimed in Queen's direction, though he was careful not to point it directly at her face. They walked with some difficulty through the loose snow, finally stopping about twenty yards away. They stood there for almost a minute, staring at her and seemingly daring her to say the first word. She decided to oblige them.

"You guys lost? Or is this the start of Operation Canadian Freedom?"

There was a snort of laughter over the comm line—Rook—but the two newcomers just exchanged a glance. The man with the flashlight pushed his ski goggles up onto his forehead and drew down his face-covering to reveal clean shaven, handsome African-American features. That was about all she could tell about him from a distance. "You must be Zelda Baker."

It was the same voice she had heard over the public address. Queen was not surprised to hear the man use her given name. He had after all, claimed to know who they were.

"Callsign: Queen," he added. "Am I right? Who's with you?"

"That's not an answer. What the hell are you doing here?"

"Well, among other things, we're looking for you. We heard a rumor that you might be on your way to the station in Alert." He paused. "It's like a slaughterhouse in there. Your doing?"

"Didn't even go inside."

The second man emitted a harsh disbelieving laugh, but a sharp look from his companion squashed any further displays of skepticism. He turned back to Queen. "That's something we'll have to look into. For now, I'd appreciate it if you would instruct the rest of your team to stand down and join us. We've got a long ride back to civilization, and I'd just as soon not stand around here any longer than we have to."

"Thanks, but we've got transportation covered."

The man smiled but there was no humor in it. "It wasn't an offer. It was an order. Admiral Ward's orders."

"I don't take orders from Admiral Ward," Queen retorted. "Or you. And you don't have the legal authority to arrest me—not here on Canadian soil. Now, I don't want this to get any uglier, so why don't you get back on your whirlybird and tell Admiral Ward where he can shove it."

The man seemed genuinely surprised by her reaction. "Uh, I'm sorry. I think maybe we need to take a step back. I know all about your status. In fact, I might know more about it than you do."

"What the hell is that supposed to mean?"

"The Admiral could have rolled you up any time he wanted, but he didn't because you were far more valuable as a rogue element. Hell, he even called you our secret weapon."

Queen shook her head. "So...what? You're drafting us?"

The second man gave another snort of laughter. "That's funny. You know, 'cause this is Canada, and you're like draft dodgers."

"Don't mind him," the first man said, quickly. "His filter doesn't work."

"Yeah, we've got one of those."

"Love you too, babe," Rook said in her ear.

"But you're right," the man with the flashlight continued. "You're being drafted. Recalled to active duty. Call it what you want. Your country needs you." He gave her a long hard look. "The impression I got from the Admiral was that you would be down with this."

"Sorry you came all this way for nothing. I don't accept rides from strangers."

The man was taken aback for a moment. "Is that the problem? Why didn't you just say so?"

He raised his hands in a fair imitation of her own subservient pose and slowly began walking toward her. Queen tensed, ready to drop her arms and go for her rifle, but the man made no threatening moves. As he got closer, she was able to get a better sense of his size—he stood about five-ten, but was broadly built. She guessed that under his camouflage shell, he had the physique of a body builder. He stopped about three paces away and extended his hand.

"Master Chief Petty Officer Stefan Yehle."

"Master Chief?" She raised an eyebrow. "I thought you said you were Army?"

"TAD'd to Delta. You know how it works at JSOC. Your branch ain't as important as your skills."

"You're an operator? A SEAL?"

"That's right. Recruited into a special unit that Admiral Ward created. My handle is 'King.'" He jerked a thumb over his shoulder to his companion. "That's my boy 'Bishop.' We're the Chess Team." Then Yehle grinned. "Just like you."

Queen stared back, dumbfounded for a moment. "The fuck you are."

SEVEN

Ashburn, Virginia

The wave slammed the already dazed King into something hard and held him there. He was pinned momentarily by the crushing weight of so much water. Then, just as quickly, the weight was gone, and King crashed down into a mass of soggy cardboard. He raised his head and found Bishop, a few feet away, still stunned by the crash and its watery aftermath. All around them, the frame of the pallet rack rose like the bars of a protective cage. It had prevented the rushing flood waters from sweeping them away. If they didn't get moving though, it would become a different kind of cage—a snare trap to keep them immobilized until the shooters recovered from the deluge.

"Bish!" he shouted. "Still with me?"

She raised her head, shook it and then flashed him a thumb's up gesture.

His mind turned to the threat. There was little doubt in his mind that their attackers were Russians, and they almost certainly possessed military training.

There might have been an innocent explanation for the contents of the warehouse. Maybe Genrikh Ludvig, the mysterious CEO of the shell company had a soft spot for international military memorabilia and had gotten an insane wholesale bulk deal on Russian Army field rations. Maybe he was so paranoid about protecting his stash that he not only lied about the purpose of the building but also hired mercenaries armed with submachine guns to protect it. It was possible. Anything was possible, but King knew from experience that the simplest interpretation was usually the correct one.

The simple solution to the puzzle was that the Russians had established a military supply depot thirty miles from America's capital city.

The men guarding the cache were almost certainly Spetsnaz—Russian special forces. Russian rations, Russian soldiers. Hell, even the names, TSAR and Genrikh Ludvig, reinforced the Russian connection. Russia, or some faction within its military or political leadership, was setting the stage for an invasion of the United States.

And Julie?

That was the part that defied a simple explanation. It was the piece of the puzzle that did not quite seem to fit, and yet it was the very piece that had led them here.

He shook his head. The answer wasn't going to magically appear in the air. He gripped the frame of the rack and hauled himself up high enough to peek over the top.

The surrounding area looked like the aftermath of a hurricane. Although the rows of pallet racks behind them were untouched, a foot of standing water covered the floor in all directions. The vertical water tanks had been scattered like bowling pins. And toppling them had triggered a domino effect across the rest of the warehouse, almost completely obliterating whatever had occupied the rest of the floor space.

He put a hand to his ear, checking to make sure that his Bluetooth was still there. Miraculously, it was. "Blue, you still with us?"

Deep Blue's relieved voice came back. "I'm here, King."

"We need an exit."

"The front entrance is in the middle of the north wall. I can only assume it's not fake like the fire doors, but there's no way to tell from here. I wish I could be more helpful, but the blueprints on file are crap. You might be better off heading back to the roof and rappelling down."

King gave the immediate area a quick once over. "That ship has sailed. We lost our rope."

"And my grappling hook," Bishop added. "My big brother thought it would be good idea to use it to demolish everything."

"You destroyed an entire warehouse with a grappling hook?" Deep Blue's tone was a mix of incredulity and awe. "What do you think this is, a Matthew Reilly novel?"

"Whether we make it out of here or not, wrecking this place was a good idea. Someone was planning to use it as a staging area for an invasion." He drew the pistol from his belt and replaced the empty magazine, then turned to Bishop. "You ready?"

She ejected the magazine from her pistol, inspected it and then slotted it back into the grip. "Ready."

King clambered over the twisted wreckage of the pallet rack and dropped down into the water, the pistol extended in a two-handed grip ahead of him. There had been no sign of life in the flooded ruins of the warehouse, but he wasn't naïve enough to believe that the shooters had all been incapacitated by the destruction of the water tanks. They were still out there, and if they were Spetsnaz soldiers, as he believed, they would never give up.

He oriented himself toward the north wall and began advancing, leading with the suppressed pistol but checking every direction, slicing the pie at every blind corner. Fifty yards out, he spied what appeared to be an alcove, blocked off by a section of chain-link fence. It was presumably erected as an internal security barrier.

"There's our way out." He splashed forward with equal measures of urgency and caution. There was a reason the warehouse exits had all been blocked off. The entrance was a chokepoint. If the shooters were going to hit them, it would happen there.

They covered the intervening distance in several short bursts, one person moving while the other provided cover. When he reached the chain-link, King took out his Gerber Diesel multi-plier and used the wire-cutter to clip away several links, opening a hole big enough to crawl through. Beyond the fence lay a narrow corridor. The far end of it was cloaked in shadows. King took a step back, positioning himself so he could watch both the corridor and most of the warehouse. "Bishop, go."

She broke from cover and darted forward, barely pausing to duck through the hole he had cut. At that instant, gun fire erupted from the dark corridor. A few of the bullets rattled the chain-link above Bishop, but most passed through without making contact. King stabbed his pistol through the net-like wire mesh and squeezed the trigger, pumping several rounds in the direction of the unseen attackers. He changed his aimpoint with each shot, concentrating his fire along the walls a foot or two above the standing water—right where he would have positioned himself. Bishop squirmed the rest of the way through, then took a breath and plunged under the water, disappearing from sight. King fired a few more shots, higher this time, then pulled back, removing himself from the line of fire. Whatever Bishop was up to, she would be able to do it a lot more effectively without him firing blindly down the hallway.

Even as he turned away, he glimpsed movement from out of the flooded depths of the warehouse. Three men emerged from behind the wreckage of the water tanks, their guns already homing in on his position. He ducked low and returned fire without aiming. The men sought cover but kept up the barrage of lead. Their machine-pistols emitted a harsh buzz-saw sound with each burst. Given the distance separating them, there wasn't much chance of anyone hitting their intended target. King's intention was to make sure that the gap between them remained unchanged.

A few seconds later, Bishop's voice sounded in his ear. "All clear."

It was the signal he'd been waiting for. He ducked through the fence and splashed down the hallway at a full run. Bishop was waiting at a turn in the corridor. She had traded her suppressed SIG for a PP-2000 machine-pistol. The Russian-made sub-gun, with its distinctive angular trigger-guard/forward grip combination, was a favorite of the Spetsnaz. That was what he assumed the man floating face down in the water a few feet away had been, up until his first and only close encounter with Bishop.

"Nice work," King said. "Any more?"

"I do not think so."

"Three behind me. Time to go." King rounded the corner leading with his pistol. The bare concrete walls to either side were purely utilitarian. He had been in sewer tunnels with more aesthetic appeal. The corridor continued along for about fifty feet then made another turn, ending at a closed metal door. The hinges indicated that it swung out, but the pressure of so much water had jammed the latch bolt against the strike plate so tightly that it refused to budge. Recognizing that trying to force it open would be futile, King took aim with his pistol.

"Brace yourself," he told Bishop, and then fired.

The .45 caliber round split the latch mechanism apart, and the door burst open, propelled by a thousand tons of water. The outrushing water swept both King and Bishop off their feet and carried them through the opening like so much flotsam in the current. The outpouring lasted only a few seconds, as the water dispersed throughout a large deserted room that was probably intended to serve as a reception lobby. Large panes of tinted privacy glass comprised the exterior wall, and right in the middle of it was a glass door, likewise tinted to prevent anyone outside from looking in. King fired into one of the lowest panes, shattering the glass and triggering yet another outpouring. As the current caught hold of him, he curled up in a fetal ball and let himself be carried through the opening and outside the fortified warehouse.

Even before the water dispersed into a thin sheen on the asphalt parking lot, King and Bishop were on their feet and sprinting out ahead of the diminishing flood. They were a good seventy-five yards away before they heard the report of a machine-pistol behind them.

King didn't return fire and didn't look back, but he did alter his course by a few degrees, zig-zagging to make himself that much harder to track. There was the possibility that he would blindly veer into the path of a bullet, but that risk was no greater than if he simply kept running in a straight line.

Ahead of him, Bishop reached the perimeter and bounded over the landscaped border, out into the street. King realized the shooting had stopped, but he made a few more random course changes before lowering his head and pouring on a burst of speed to catch up with his sister.

Bishop reached the SUV first and went immediately to the driver's door. Before getting in on the other side, King looked back and saw a single man running down the street toward them, gun held out in front of him but not firing. King considered taking a shot at the guy, but at that moment, the engine turned over and the vehicle gave a slight lurch, as Bishop shifted into drive. Dismissing the gunman, King slid into the passenger seat. It was only as they pulled away and he glimpsed the man in the rearview mirror, speaking into a walkie-talkie, that he realized why the man had been alone.

"Damn it. We're gonna have company."

EIGHT

Bishop navigated out of the industrial park and followed the signs to State Route 28, heading south, following the primary exit route they had chosen when planning the op. King had not directed otherwise, and until he did, she was going to continue as if nothing had changed.

Except everything had changed.

She had gone into the TSAR Data Solutions warehouse with low expectations. Maybe King would have found some clue to the identity of the woman he claimed looked exactly like their sister. Maybe he wouldn't have. Neither outcome would have made much of a difference, as far as she was concerned. But finding a

Russian military supply depot on the cusp of the D.C. metro area was on a different order of magnitude from her expectations.

Strangely, she couldn't help but feel a twinge of admiration for her former comrades-in-arms. Russia would always be her mother, and while she felt no loyalty to its current political leader and his empire-building ambitions, establishing a forward supply depot on American soil was a bold move. Impressive. But it was also enemy action, and she could not ignore that. America was her home now.

Part of her wanted to believe that the supply depot was merely some kind of holdover from the Cold War, a precautionary measure, just like the nuclear arms race. A preparation made in hopes of preventing a war rather than triggering one. But the warehouse was a new structure, the rations no more than two years old, and the men guarding it... No, it wasn't some leftover from a different time, and it wasn't intended as a last resort. Russia was preparing for war with the United States. The warehouse was a powder keg, and the mere discovery of it might be enough to light the fuse.

In her brief time with the Chess Team, she had fought many strange creatures, but total war was a very different kind of beast. If it was unleashed, not even Jack Sigler would be able to stop it.

"King, this is Blue. What's your status?"

The transmission pulled Bishop's focus back to the moment. They were heading south on Route 28. Unless King called an audible, in about five minutes they would arrive at Dulles International Airport, where they would drop off the rental and board a flight to Atlanta.

That had been the plan. Was it still?

She glanced over at King, who had not yet replied to Deep Blue. He was looking into the mirror, watching the road behind them.

"King?" Deep Blue said. "Bishop? You guys still with me?"

Bishop waited a moment to see if her brother would speak, before replying. "We're clear."

"We're not clear," King said abruptly. "We made it out, but not clean."

Bishop checked her mirrors but all she could see were innumerable headlights. On the busy highway, it was impossible to tell if anyone was following them. "You think we have shadow?" she asked King.

"I'm sure of it. What we saw tonight? They absolutely cannot let us just walk away." He tapped his fingers on the dashboard. "Screw the airport. Take 267 east."

Bishop kept her gaze on the road ahead. She didn't know the Virginia roads as well as King, who had grown up in the state, but she knew that 267, was a major artery connecting Washington, D.C with points west, including the airport. "Just let me know where to turn."

"You're going to Washington?" Deep Blue asked.

"If those guys follow us into the airport, things will get ugly. They won't hesitate to shoot the place up, just to get us. A lot of innocent people might get hurt." He paused a beat, then said. "The exit's about a mile from here. Blue, if you can, access the traffic cams. See who else makes the exit with us. Maybe we can figure out who our shadow is."

"And you'll have plenty of road to shake them off."

"I don't want to shake them off. I've got a better idea."

"You're the King," Deep Blue said. "Okay, I've got the camera feeds up... You just passed one. I'm tagging all the vehicles that pass in the next minute. When you've got a second, I need to update you on what's happened up north."

Bishop's breath caught in her throat. With no reliable satellite coverage in the Arctic Circle, she had anticipated that it would be another day or two before they heard what, if anything, had happened at the Alert black site. She couldn't contain herself. "Did they find Thomas? What's wrong?"

To everyone else in the team, Tom Duncan was still Deep Blue or even Mr. President, but her relationship with him was different. She had met him after his resignation from office, and she had become his friend long before joining the Chess Team. She secretly hoped that someday they might be more than friends, which was why wasting time chasing after Julie Sigler's ghost rankled her.

She was grateful when King said, "Now's as good a time as any. Let's have it. Bad news first."

"The bad news is that Blue... Duncan, was already gone when they got there. It looks like a third party hit the site within the last few days."

"Gone?" Bishop said, before King could respond. "Where is he now?"

King pointed ahead. "That's the exit."

Bishop grimaced in frustration, but steered right, onto the clover-leaf interchange. A toll gate loomed ahead and she steered through the EZ Pass lane. They didn't have an EZ Pass, which meant that, as they passed through, a camera would photograph them and a fine would be issued, but a traffic violation was the least of their concerns right now.

King spoke again, this time to Deep Blue. "Who did it?"

"No way to know for sure, but it had to be someone with a sub and the resources to conduct Arctic ops."

"So we were close. Damn. We should have flown in." They had discussed, and ultimately rejected a plan to fly directly to Alert, not only because it would have been nearly impossible from a logistical stand-point, but also because a subsequent covert investigation of the site would have been impossible, and they had no real proof that Duncan was even there. "How was Queen able to make contact?"

"That's the other development, and I don't know if this is good news or bad. Admiral Ward picked them up."

Bishop let out another gasp.

"They were captured?" King asked.

"Not exactly," Deep Blue said. "He says he wants to meet with you. Time and place of your choosing, but ASAP. Queen seems to think the offer of a truce is genuine."

"I'll get back to you on that." He turned to Bishop and said just two words. "Go. Fast."

Bishop glanced at the speedometer. She was already doing seventy-five, matching the flow of traffic for whom the posted speed limit was merely a suggestion. She pressed the gas pedal to the floor and started looking for gaps in the traffic that would allow her to keep accelerating. Eighty-five mph didn't feel that fast, but as the speedometer crept toward the century mark, it required more focus. One of the tires, evidently not balanced properly, began to shimmy ever so slightly. If they had a blowout or if, God forbid, her timing was off by a fraction of a second, they would end up rolling down the expressway. The trees lining the roadside were an indistinct blur, and the cars in the four lanes all around them were like fixed slalom gates. She tightened her grip on the wheel and tried to shut out everything but the road ahead.

She barely even heard Deep Blue's voice in her ear. "A pickup just blew through the toll gate. That could be our guy."

"Roger," King said. "Anyone else suspicious?"

"I tagged twenty vehicles that went through the gate right after you. Let me check the next camera." A pause. "Okay, that pickup is definitely trying to catch up to you. Everyone else is falling behind. Except for the motorcycles. Four of them."

King craned his head around. "I see them. Bish, keep it on the floor. Just a couple more miles."

She wanted to ask what would happen in a couple of miles, but at their current speed, she would barely have time to pose the question. Sure enough, after only about a minute, King told her to get ready to exit the highway. An overhead sign advised that Interstate 495, the Capital Beltway, was approaching. Bishop let up on the accelerator.

"Not that one. Keep going."

Bishop had to swerve into the far left lane to avoid the congestion of vehicles taking the beltway exit. There was a sudden blast of air as King rolled down his window. From the corner of her eye, she saw him twist around and stick his head and arm outside.

"Next exit," he shouted. "You'll have to slow down. That's when they'll make their move."

She whipped the SUV back into the right lane, and when she saw the sign for the exit—State Route 123 North—she let off the accelerator. As she veered toward the off-ramp, she saw a second sign, warning that the maximum safe speed for the exit was just thirty miles per hour.

She applied steady pressure to the brakes but they were still going almost fifty when the turn began. She allowed the vehicle to drift to the far left edge of the road, shedding another ten mph in the process. Then she cut the wheel hard. As the SUV started to skid in the wrong direction, she let off the brake and punched the gas pedal again. The vehicle shuddered and whipped back and forth for an instant, but then the wheels caught and she regained control.

There was a flash of light in the side mirror and then the source shot past her. A black racing motorcycle—what Rook would have called a 'crotch-rocket'—slid past, hugging the left shoulder. Another bike passed on the right, and as it did, King opened fire.

Bishop didn't hear the report from King's suppressed pistol, but she saw the results. The rider on the right side jerked with the impact, pitching over the handlebars. Then suddenly both he and the motorcycle were cartwheeling across the road, right in front of them. Bishop had to jerk the wheel to avoid a collision. As bike and rider vanished off the side of the road, the motorcyclist who had passed on Bishop's side shot out ahead of them, completing the loop and merging onto the northbound highway. Bishop kept accelerating out of the loop and was doing seventy again when she reached the highway. There was no sign of the motorcyclist.

She ducked reflexively in her seat as a hailstorm of bullets tore into the SUV from behind. The rear window was obliterated in an instant. Some of the rounds passed through the interior, striking the windshield, sending long cracks like lightning bolts across the glass. Something struck her in the back, just below her right shoulder blade. It felt like someone had jabbed her with a sharp stick, but she knew it wasn't a serious injury. The bullet had probably been slowed down by all the things it had hit before reaching her, but with the window shot out, the next bullet might not be so forgiving.

"You going to do something about that?" she shouted.

King's answer was to take up the machine-pistol she had captured at the warehouse and let loose an earsplittingly loud barrage through the SUV's interior and out the hole where the rear window had been. Spent shell casings went everywhere, an added distraction she didn't need.

With the noise, the rain of hot brass in her lap and the fact that she was hunched over to avoid getting shot, she didn't see the motorcyclist that had passed them earlier until it was almost too late.

The rider had pulled off to the side of the road and was aiming his PP-2000 at them. He was a hundred yards away when Bishop saw a tongue of flame erupt from the muzzle off his weapon.

There was no time to warn King. She cut the wheel to the right, transfixing the gunman in her headlights. A few rounds sparked off the hood and gouged quarter-sized divots in the already damaged windshield. As soon as the shooter saw her change course, he let go of the trigger and leapt over his parked motorcycle, trying desperately to get out of the way. Bishop did not relent, though the gunman was not her primary target. At the last possible instant, she hauled the steering wheel to the left. The abrupt maneuver caused the rear of the SUV to whip around, striking the motorcycle like a horsetail swatting a fly. A sickening crunch of metal and fiberglass sounded as the motorcycle was punted into the concrete guardrail. Bishop couldn't tell if the shooter had gotten clear in time, but either way, he wouldn't be coming after them again.

King turned back around to look forward, his face a grim mask. He stared through the cracked windshield for a moment before speaking. "You hit?"

"No," she said. It was mostly true. "You?"

He shook his head. "Stay on this road."

Bishop kept the gas pedal pressed to the floor. She glanced in the side mirror to check on the pursuit, but a stray bullet had smashed it. The center rearview was gone as well, so she risked a quick look over her shoulder. A vehicle with only one headlight, presumably the pickup Deep Blue had identified, was matching their breakneck pace. "I don't think we can outrun them."

"We don't need to. Just stay ahead of them for a few more minutes."

She knew he was up to something, but staying ahead of their pursuers was going to require all her focus. The number of lanes available to her had been reduced to two, making the job of maneuvering around cars that might as well have been parked and abandoned in their path, that much more difficult.

The next three minutes were a blur as she wove back and forth across the road. She cut through suburban neighborhoods, and blew through intersections and red lights, using the horn to warn of her approach but never once touching the brakes.

"Get ready!"

King's warning snapped her out her trance. "Ready for what?"

"That!" he pointed to an official looking green highway sign. She tried to read the words printed upon it, but they were going too fast. All she caught were the words: GEORGE, CENTER and NEXT LEFT.

"Left!" King shouted.

Bishop saw the intersection looming ahead. The traffic light was green and cars were passing through in the opposing lanes on the far side of the grassy median. Beyond that, a road with bright yellow gates—open, fortunately—led into the woods.

Instead of easing off the gas and gradually slowing, she waited until she was just a few car lengths from the junction, then slammed on the brakes. The anti-lock-brake system kept the vehicle from going into an uncontrollable skid, but the SUV nevertheless left trails of rubber on the pavement. The brakes fought against inertia, the vehicle sliding halfway through the intersection.

Before the SUV could come to a complete halt, Bishop floored it again. She was afraid it might stall out, but after a slight lurch, the automatic clutch let go and the vehicle shot forward again. She punched the horn with the heel of one hand to warn oncoming traffic and shot toward the entrance. The headlights of unsuspecting drivers formed a crazy lightshow as they swerved to avoid hitting her, but a moment later she was through, racing down the seemingly deserted forest road.

She risked another glance back and saw the pickup and a pair of motorcycles, lit up by streetlamps and headlights, surging through the intersection after them. A quarter of a mile down the road, a well-lit structure, came into view. It looked like an oversized fast food restaurant drive-through over the roadway, but with one notable difference. Stretching across the lane was a two-foot high metal barrier.

"Keep going!" King urged. "Ram it!"

Bishop didn't question the order. She kept her foot on the accelerator, steering straight for the security gate. As it was eclipsed from sight by the SUV's hood, she let her hands drop from the steering wheel so the impact wouldn't break her arms. Then she closed her eyes.

The collision hurled her forward at the same instant the airbag deployed, punching her in the face and knocking her senseless for a moment. A haze of smoke—burning oil, scorched wiring and other strange smells she couldn't identify—filled the interior of the now motionless SUV. The engine, nearly overheated from the high-speed escape, was ticking like a metronome. Through it all she heard King, calling out to her.

"Stay down."

She struggled to make sense of the command, and then she fought against the seat belt across her chest and the pieces of the dashboard that had crumpled around her like a protective cocoon. Then the sound of gunfire drowned out everything else, and she somehow found a way to do as King had said.

Bullets raked the SUV, each impact shaking the entire vehicle. She could feel the heat of rounds passing above her, distorting the air with the distinctive cracks of miniature sonic booms. Then almost as quickly as it had begun, the shooting stopped. She waited for something else to happen.

She gradually became aware of Deep Blue, shouting frantically in her ear, asking for a status report. She didn't answer him. She had no idea what their status actually was. Another voice, louder and more immediate, sounded from somewhere outside the vehicle.

"You in the car. Show me your hands."

Bishop almost laughed at the suggestion. She could barely move her hands. Still, the command had been given in unaccented English, which meant that the speaker was not a Russian Spetsnaz killer.

"Don't shoot," King called out, much closer. "We surrender."

She allowed herself a small sigh of relief. Surrender was not good, but it was better than dead. She pushed up a few inches, raising her head just high enough to peek over the crumpled door panel. A squad of men wearing black battle dress uniforms, replete with body armor and Kevlar helmets, and brandishing M-4 assault rifles, had them surrounded. She raised up another inch and saw the body of one of the men from the warehouse lying on the ground nearby.

"King," she said in a loud whisper. "Where are we? What just happened?"

"Didn't you see the signs? We just tried to crash the George Bush Center for Intelligence, better known as the headquarters of the Central Intelligence Agency."

"CIA?" Bishop said, incredulous.

"It might be a good idea to let me do the talking," King said. "Blue, let Admiral Ward know that I'd be happy to meet with him. You can tell him where to find me. I don't think we'll be going anywhere for a little while."

NINE

Dubai, United Arab Emirates

By any metric, the Burj Khalifa in Dubai was the tallest structure ever built. Topping out at just over 2,700 feet, it was nearly double the height of the Empire State Building in New York City. It was over a thousand feet taller than Taipei 101, the previous building to hold the record. If the ability to look down upon others—to be the lord of all that one surveyed—could be considered an appropriate symbol of power, the 155th floor of the Burj Khalifa would be the likeliest spot from which to rule the entire world.

As it happened, Catherine Alexander, the nominal occupant of the highest occupied floor of the Burj, was very close to doing exactly that.

Catherine Alexander was not her real name, of course, but it suited her well, invoking not one but two world domineers who had earned the epithet 'the Great.' To her mentor, the man who had given her that public name, and whom she thought of almost as a father, she was also 'the Ice Queen.' That name suited her as well. Perhaps even better, for it emphasized her cool intractable demeanor as much as it did her authority. She was not a queen in any formal legal sense, though her mentor had assured her that she was descended from royal blood many times over. Instead, she was a different kind of monarch—an empress ruling over an empire that transcended national borders. She was the Chief Executive Officer of the Consortium.

Like the location of its headquarters, the Consortium did not officially exist. It was at once, too big, too complex and yet also so very simple in its structure, to be quantified as an organization. Like the concentric tiers and spires of the Burj, the Consortium comprised several large multinational conglomerates across a variety of sectors— banking and finance, media, energy and consumables—which were in turn made up of thousands of smaller corporations. They formed a veritable pyramid of free enterprise. And Catherine Alexander was the capstone.

Many of the men assembled in the room were household names, from families whose influence and wealth extended back many centuries. Those who had not inherited wealth or title were nevertheless well known and highly regarded in their respective spheres of influence. All were immensely powerful, dictating international policy, raising national leaders or bringing them down as it pleased them. It had been no simple feat to unite them all, to bend them to a common purpose. With guidance from her mentor, not to mention the considerable resources made available to her by him, she had done exactly that. She had spied, manipulated, threatened and when necessary, killed to forge a broad cartel that insured success for all involved. The men who had come here today feared her, perhaps even hated her, but they also loved her, or at least loved being so close to the top.

She listened patiently as each man gave a detailed report on the state of their respective enterprises, carefully parsing their words and sentences for any hint of duplicity. It was human nature to try to conceal one's shortcomings, and these rich and powerful men were not immune to it. Indeed, they were perhaps more susceptible to self-delusion. Whenever she detected a bit of evasive language, she would give them one chance to recant and speak plainly. Bad news did not trouble her, but deception could not be tolerated. In the five years she had presided over the Consortium, only once had it been necessary to take things a step further.

She paid particular attention to the report from the CEO of Consolidated Energy who, in a Texas accent and a halting manner, revealed the bleak horizon for oil production.

"We're hemorrhagin' money 'cause the Saudis are overproducin' and undersellin'. They think the writin's on the wall for petroleum, and they don't want to wind up with a fortune still in the ground, when the bubble finally pops."

Catherine leaned forward. Oil policy was of particular interest to her. "Cheap gasoline increases consumer confidence in a petroleum-based future. That's good for all of us. When prices at the pump are low, people are more likely to ignore fuel efficiency ratings and choose a luxury, gasoline-fueled vehicle, which means they're locked into purchasing gasoline, no matter the price. It's a feedback loop that works in our favor."

"Be that as it may," the oil man said, "most of our provable reserves are either in deep water, or in shale and tar sands. Those are mighty expensive. We can't even break even, unless we get the price back up to at least eighty dollars per barrel. The Arabs—" He said it with the emphasis on the first vowel, *Ay-rabs*. "—know it. They're doing this on purpose to keep us from exploiting those reserves."

"The Saudis can't sustain this gambit indefinitely."

"They don't need to. They just need to keep it up until folks wake up and smell the coffee about global warmin'. We can't pull the wool over their eyes forever. If we don't exploit those reserves and soon, then we all bought ourselves a pig in a poke."

Catherine smiled patiently. "Our friend from Texas paints with cliché like a true artiste," she said, addressing the room. "I can tell you only what I have told you so many times before. We are playing the long game. Though they don't realize it, the Saudis are doing us a favor by keeping oil prices low. I promise you all that soon..."

Something began vibrating in her pocket, causing her to falter for a moment. It was her mobile phone. A very special phone, one that she dared not ignore.

"Soon, we will all benefit from their..."

Another buzz from the phone.

"From the short-sightedness of our friends in the Gulf States." She took out the phone and stared at it as it shuddered a third time. "Pardon me. I have to take this."

She rose from her chair and moved to the edge of the room, where a plate glass window looked down on the city two thousand feet below. A low murmur rippled through the room. An interruption like this was unprecedented, and she was acutely aware of how this would look to the assembled group. Catherine Alexander the Great, CEO of the Consortium, the woman who had fused them together into an engine of unparalleled prosperity, was at no man's beck and call.

No man except this one, her mentor.

She pressed the button to accept the call. "Yes?"

He spoke directly, as he always did, without any familiarity or affection, and in Russian, a language that she had yet to fully master. "I need you. Immediately."

Catherine's gaze flitted about the room. Now, more than ever, it was imperative that she display complete control over the executive board, yet the Consortium existed for the sole purpose of advancing her mentor's agenda. To let the board dictate her schedule would be tantamount to the sword telling the warrior when he ought to fight.

"Of course," she replied in careful Russian.

She did not ask for more information. It was not her place to do so. She felt certain that he would tell her what she needed to know, and she was not wrong in that assumption.

"They are getting too close."

"I heard what happened—"

"This is something else," he said quickly, as if trying to prevent her from saying something indiscreet. Even though the line was encrypted, it was not beyond the realm of possibility that someone was eavesdropping on them. Her mentor's anxiety regarding electronic espionage bordered on mania. He almost never used mobile phones or the Internet, conducting most of his business on hard-lines, using an old fashioned private bank exchange telephone system. They recorded everything with manual typewriters instead of computers. "We must accelerate the timetable."

She considered her reply with great care.

In her opinion, the timetable for Operation Perun, the capstone of his grand plan, was already overly optimistic. Although she had delivered her part of the plan well ahead of schedule, there were certain realities that could not be ignored. It was winter, and the first phase of the plan would be severely hampered by adverse weather conditions. And then there was the matter of the Firebird. If the researchers at Volosgrad could not deliver what they had promised, it would all be for nothing. She was not as confident in the abilities of the lead scientist there as her mentor was.

Nevertheless, this was what he required of her, and she would not refuse.

"I will leave within the hour."

He rang off without another word.

She returned to the table. There was a palpable anxiety in the air. She put on her most confident smile. "I have good news, gentleman. I thank you all for coming and submitting your reports, but none of that matters any longer. Be assured that the game is about to change in our favor. Very soon, we will reap the bountiful harvest we have sown. This meeting is adjourned."

TEN

Limbo, Fort Bragg, North Carolina

As the government-issue van in which he rode pulled into the non-descript hangar—a gigantic Quonset hut not far from the flight line at Pope Field—King felt a strange sense of nostalgia. "Who says you can't go home again?" he murmured.

Bishop gave him a sidelong glance and then shrugged. She had never been to the Decon facility. Rook had nicknamed it 'Limbo,' the void between heaven and hell. It was where Delta teams staged their operations, and were debriefed upon returning. Along with the nearby team room, Limbo had been the home station for Chess Team while they had been part of Delta. When that relationship had ended, with the Team severing all ties to the military and moving to the Alpha facility in New Hampshire, they had scrubbed all trace of their existence. But memories were harder to erase.

Snapshots of the good old days flashed in his head like a slide show—throwing horseshoes in the pit out behind the hangar, drinking Sam Adams beer, eating barbecue and playing Go Fish to unwind after their missions. The dour face of Erik Somers—the former Bishop—bristling at one of Rook's incessant barbs. King had met his wife, Sara, here. As a disease detective for the Centers for Disease Control and Prevention, she had been temporarily assigned to the team to thwart an outbreak of the deadly Brugada virus.

It had been only a few years since they closed up shop, but for King, it had been many lifetimes.

Although he was not fully briefed on King's personal history, Admiral Ward seemed to sense what King was feeling. "Just like being back on the block, isn't it?"

"Yeah." He shifted to face the Admiral. "But if you think a trip down memory lane is going to convince me to re-up, you're sorely mistaken."

Ward laughed. "That ship has sailed, my friend," he said, cryptically. "Honestly, I don't want you back."

Pointedly ignoring King's questioning look, Ward opened his door and got out. "I'll explain everything inside. I don't like having to say things more than once. Your people are waiting in debrief. Before we go in, though, would you mind telling me what happened last night?

I called in a lot of favors to get you out of hock with the Company, and I'd like to know exactly what I paid for."

"A recon op turned out to be more than we expected," King replied, evasively. "I really don't know any more than that yet. I'll tell you what I told the CIA last night. Check out that warehouse. The answers are there."

"No, they aren't. Somebody torched the place. Used rocket fuel as an accelerant. The fire's still burning. It's so hot that it breaks down water molecules into oxygen and hydrogen and makes it burn even hotter. It's a total loss. We also came up with zilch on the guys who chased you into Langley."

King spread his hands. He wasn't ready to reveal his suspicions about what he and Bishop had discovered to Ward or anyone else. He needed to figure out what Julie's involvement in it was, and figuring that out meant having a conversation that he had put off too long already. Besides, until he had something more concrete in the way of evidence, it was all supposition anyway. "Well, keep me in the loop."

Ward's answer was a non-committal grunt.

They followed the Admiral into the conference room. Most of the seats at the table were already occupied, but King ignored the unfamiliar faces and locked eyes with Queen, his stare a form of nearly-psychic communication.

Is this cool?

She blinked once and gave an almost imperceptible nod.

It's cool.

He hoped that was what she meant anyway. Ward had succeeded in putting the entire team—even Lew Aleman—together in one place. If he intended to arrest them all and ship them off to the disciplinary barracks at Fort Leavenworth or worse, to some obscure black site, they would be SOL. Or very nearly, at least. Ward hadn't rolled up everyone. Knight's girlfriend Anna Beck—who sometimes worked with the team as Pawn—was conspicuously absent, laying low as directed by

King. And although his influence was no longer what it had once been, retired CIA director Domenick Boucher was also a friendly resource on the outside.

King's instincts, however, were telling him that Ward wasn't planning anything like that. King had a gift for reading people, and his read on the JSOC commander had always been that the man was a straight-shooter. Which made his comments about not wanting the team back under military control all the more confusing.

Bishop, looking both bewildered and a little bit intimidated, took one of the empty chairs. King remained standing, taking in the faces of the five men he did not recognize, who were seated at the table. One was African-American. Another had short dark hair and an olive-complexion—Hispanic or possibly Native American. The other three were Caucasian. All wore casual attire that could not hide the hard, muscled features of Special Forces operators.

Rook pre-empted the official introductions. "Hey, King. Meet our replacements. This is the new Chess Team. Note that I did not say 'new and improved.'" He leaned forward, cupping one hand to his mouth as if trying to hide a conspiratorial whisper. "Their Queen is a dude. I don't judge, but that's a little weird."

King rounded on Ward. "You formed a new Chess Team?"

Ward frowned. "Mr. Tremblay has it wrong. You haven't been replaced." He gestured to the chair. "Sit. I'll explain. And please, hold your questions.

"I'll skip the preliminaries and get to the point. After the incident in the Congo, President Chambers began looking at ways to expand the Chess Team program. Teams that could take on assignments that were either too sensitive from a national security point of view, or otherwise beyond the scope of normal special operations. A unit that answered directly to the President."

"Chambers wanted his own private black ops detail," King said.

Ward frowned at the interruption. "I believe that's what President Duncan intended when the original Chess Team was formed. You all were already off the books, and your..." He sighed. "Your loyalty was somewhat questionable, as you amply demonstrated last year, when you refused to come back into the fold. But that's beside the point. The Chess Team template was perfect for our needs, so we started recruiting operators to fill the ranks."

"You could have at least changed the name," Rook grumbled. "Retired our callsigns like the All-Stars we are."

"Wrong again," Ward snapped, with a little more heat. "The name is the most important thing. It's like football. The players come and go, but the Steelers are always the Steelers. And everybody wants to play for the Steelers."

"Steelers." Rook snorted. "Well that explains a lot."

"What the hell is that supposed to mean?"

King waved at the five men seated across from him. "So what's this, a change of command ceremony?"

Ward surprised him by grinning, though it wasn't a friendly smile. King thought he looked a little like the Big Bad Wolf about to pounce on Little Red Riding Hood. "Not at all. We created two new teams, White and Red, each with a specific area of operations. White's AO is international operations. Red team..." He nodded to the men at the table. "Is tasked primarily with domestic counterterrorism. Blue team is our wild card."

"You said two teams."

"I said 'two *new* teams.'"

"We're Blue team," Queen said, beating King by a fraction of a second.

"Red, white and blue," Rook said. "Cute. Very patriotic."

"When you went off the reservation last year," Ward continued, "our plan was to shut you down, but we realized pretty quickly that there were advantages to having a rogue element in play. You proved that in Mongolia, taking out a threat that no one else could touch. You've amply demonstrated that you're not going to work against the interests of the United States either. So while we can't officially sanction your activities, we think you're more useful out there as paramilitary vigilantes, than you would be in the stockade. In short, we want you to keep doing what you're doing."

Rook gave a dramatic whistle. "Wow. So it's like you're Commissioner Gordon and we're Batman."

King shook his head. "What's the catch?"

"Just that, from time to time, when we need a job done—a mission that only the Blue Team can handle—you do it."

"See what I mean?" Rook said. "Batman. Ward...can I call you Ward? We're all usually on a first name basis, but I don't know yours. How's this sound? Whenever you need us, just shine a big chessboard spotlight into the sky and we'll come running."

Ward gave Rook the stink-eye. "I just thought of one other *catch*. Keep your people on a shorter leash. Maybe teach them some respect." He pointed a finger at Rook. "As far as you're concerned, my first name is 'Admiral.' But you can call me 'Sir.'"

"Is that spelled C-U-R?"

Queen, ignoring the exchange, jumped in. "You could have told us all this in a backchannel e-mail. You sure as hell didn't need to go all the way to the Arctic Circle to roll us up."

Ward gave Rook one last withering glare, then turned to King. "As it happens, we presently have one of those situations. You may have noticed that White Team isn't here with us. They're MIA, deep in Indian country—" He stopped, frowned and turned to one of the men on Red Team. "My apologies, Hawk. Old habits."

The dark-skinned operator offered an indifferent shrug.

"They're missing," Ward continued. "Five men. Master Sergeant Joseph Hager—King. Sergeant First Class Marc McKeon—Queen. Chief Petty Officer Trace Williams—Bishop. Sergeant First Class Christian Baughman—Knight. Staff Sergeant Chris Baker—Rook. I don't know if they're alive or dead, but I do know that they are American soldiers, and they deserve to be brought home. If any of them are still alive, it's absolutely imperative that we rescue them."

Knight spoke up for the first time. "Why not send them?" He nodded at the members of Red Team.

"For starters, it's not their AO. Don't get me wrong. They've already offered, but there are other considerations. Political considerations."

"You need deniability," King said.

"We don't know how badly compromised we are, but an officially sanctioned rescue mission is out of the question. I won't leave those men hanging in the wind, but I can't send more troops across enemy lines."

"And which enemy is that?"

Ward didn't sugarcoat his answer. "Russia."

ELEVEN

"We've all got that stamp in our passport," Queen murmured, but King heard the apprehension in her voice. They had conducted anti-terrorism operations on Russian soil, and had tangled with Russian agents abroad, but they had never gone up against the full might of the Russian Bear in its own den. Queen's concern was justifiable.

And she doesn't even know what we found in Virginia.

King wondered if Ward knew his parents, and Asya's, were former Soviet agents. Bishop had been raised in Russia. What would Ward make of those relationships if he learned the whole truth?

King made a determined effort not to look at Bishop. "Why were they there? Russia's not exactly an ally, but when did they become the enemy?"

"You know better than that, Sigler. They've always been the enemy. It won't come as news to you that the current president of Russia is an ambitious son of a bitch. In the last few years he's become increasingly belligerent. Invading the Ukraine. Supporting

Assad in Syria and accusing us of collusion with the Islamic State. He's daring us to do something more than talk, and every time he gets away with it, he gets bolder. But he's also desperate. Russia's only real source of wealth is oil, and with oil prices bottoming out, their economy, not to mention his influence on the world stage, is sinking fast. He needs a game-changer."

"And picking a fight with us does that how exactly?" Rook asked.

"There are a lot of people out there who would like to see him win that fight. But the short answer is that war, or even the possibility of it, drives up oil prices. And if it actually comes to a shooting war, an oil surplus is a huge strategic advantage."

Queen shook her head. "We've still got a lot of nukes pointed at Moscow."

"Yes, we do," Ward admitted. "But would we use them? More to the point, would we be willing to go to war over some piece of Eastern European real estate that most Americans can't even find on a map?

"I'm going to assume that you're all familiar with NATO. Since the end of the Cold War, a lot of former Warsaw Pact nations, and even a few former Soviet states, have joined NATO. At the time, it was a big strategic victory for us. Better to have them on our team than allied with the Russians. Now, it's become a huge liability.

"Article Five of the treaty stipulates that if a member nation is attacked, all NATO countries must come to their assistance. Ukraine was on the path to joining NATO when Russia annexed the Crimea and began supporting rebel factions there. If they had actually been a NATO member nation, we would already be at war with Russia.

"And by 'we' I mean just that. There are twenty-eight member nations, most in Western Europe, but we're the big dog. Everyone knows it. Not everyone likes it. A lot of those folks think they're just—forgive me for saying it—pawns in the same tired old chess game that's been going on since the end of World War II. Russia versus

America. Russia thinks NATO is just a puppet for U.S. foreign policy, and that if put to the test, the alliance would crumble.

"As we speak, the Russian army is conducting winter exercises on the border with Estonia, a NATO member. If the exercise turns into an invasion, the treaty that all twenty-eight member nations signed will require an immediate military response. But several Western European countries have already gone on record as stating that they will not mobilize their forces in defense of Estonia. If that happens and those countries pull out of NATO, then the Russians will pretty much be free to do as they please in Eastern Europe."

King thought about what he had seen in the warehouse. The supply depot was most certainly *not* part of a plan to invade Estonia, but he did not doubt that there was a connection. Estonia would be the opening move in a game with much higher stakes.

"Would we?" he asked. "Even if a few countries pull out, we'd still honor our obligations, right?"

Ward raised his hands in a show of uncertainty. "That's up to the politicians. Frankly, if it comes to it, I don't think we will. Right now, the only thing holding him back is the fact that he's not one hundred percent sure what our response will be. It's a gamble, and if he's wrong, things could escalate all the way to DEFCON 1."

"Okay, I get all of that," King said. "It doesn't explain why you sent a team over there. What were they doing?"

"As I said, Russia knows that testing NATO's resolve is a gamble. All this saber-rattling could very well do the opposite, unify NATO instead of destroying them. If it comes to total war, they won't back down. They have to win it."

"They need to go back and watch War Games," Rook said. He affected a robotic voice. "'The only way to win is not to play.'"

"Well, the Russian president doesn't think that way. Remember, these are the folks that gave us that unique version of roulette. But to answer your question, we picked up some intel indicating that the Russians have re-opened an old Soviet research facility in the

Ural Mountains, north of Yekaterinburg. During the Cold War, Yekaterinburg—or Sverdlovsk as the Soviets called it—was a closed city dedicated to the production of WMDs. Nukes and bioweapons. We still don't know everything that went on there, but we *do* know that they were developing anthrax strains based on research conducted by the Japanese Unit 731 during World War II. In 1979, there was an anthrax leak that resulted in at least a hundred deaths, probably a lot more. The city was demilitarized in 1992, but there have long been rumors that the research continued underground, figuratively and literally, at a complex in the Urals near a place called *Kholat Syakhl.*"

Bishop looked up suddenly. "I know this place. It means Dead Mountain."

Ward's eyes went wide, and he stared at Bishop for several seconds.

Rook finally broke the uncomfortable silence. "Of course it does. Where else would a Bond villain like Crazy Vlad build his secret death lab? You know, I think we could solve all the world's problems if we just gave these places cheerful names. No one would even think about cooking up anthrax on Fluffy Bunny Hill."

King seized on the distraction to shift attention away from his sister. "So you sent White Team to investigate, and now they're missing. You want us to go find out what happened, get the goods on what the Russians are really up to and rescue or recover your boys if we can. Have I got that right?"

Ward slowly looked away from Bishop. "Pretty much. White Team has been disavowed. We can't admit that they're missing. We can't even acknowledge that they are American citizens, much less soldiers. We sure as hell can't send anyone after them. But you're outside our control. If, God forbid, things go south, your record as rogue operators will immunize the President from blowback."

Rook shook his head. "Dude, you need to work on your sales pitch."

King cracked a smile. "He's right, Admiral. You've pretty much made it clear why you want us to do this, but I haven't heard a word about why we should. What's in it for us?"

Ward appeared unfazed by the question. "It's pretty clear to me that you intend to keep operating as the Chess Team, regardless of whether you have official sanction or not. I can make that a lot easier. First and foremost, you would have an assurance of amnesty against any prosecution for any activities past, present and future, within reason of course. President Chambers has already signed off on that."

"Promises like that are hard to keep," King said. "Administrations change. Admirals get promoted...or fired...and people can become very forgetful."

Ward spread his hands. "I won't lie. You're right. But a presidential pardon still carries a lot of weight. Second, I know that you're trying to find Tom Duncan." He glanced at Queen. "That's how we knew where to find you. We got the same tip you did about that black site near the Arctic Circle. We knew you'd end up there eventually."

"Yeah, about that..."

"We're still trying to put the pieces together and figure out what happened, but I can assure you that the U.S. military was not involved in the operation of that site, nor in the death or disappearance of anyone there. I'd like to know what happened to Duncan as much as you. When you've finished up in Russia, you will have my blessing to continue looking for him, along with whatever help I can give you. Unofficially, of course."

"Is it possible the Russians are behind that as well?" Knight asked.

"Very possible. You may be killing two birds with one stone."

Or three, King thought. There was a connection between the woman that looked like Julie and Russia—that much was obvious. He didn't know if all these threads would connect, but he had already decided that they would accept this mission. Now it was just a question of seeing how much Ward would be willing to give them. "Okay, what else?"

Ward stifled a chuckle. "Playing hard to get, eh? I'll bite. What else would it take?"

"A tech upgrade would be a nice start." King looked over at Deep Blue. "Lew, can you put together a wish list?"

A mischievous gleam appeared in Deep Blue's eyes. "Absolutely."

Ward frowned. "That could be a sticking point. Even a black budget can get audited. The one thing I can't be seen doing is funding you."

"Money isn't a problem," Deep Blue said. "But a lot of the components I need are restricted for civilian purchase."

"This mission is time critical. We can't hold things up waiting for a FedEx shipment."

"Two days is all I need," Deep Blue promised.

"It will take us at least that long to prep," King added.

"But you will do it?" Ward pressed.

King looked to the others to see if they were with him. It was a formality. He did not doubt that they were on board, if for no other reason than to rescue, if possible, the missing operators. It was a part of the Soldier's Creed: *I will never leave a fallen comrade.* Their nods signaled that he had judged them correctly. "Lew, can you run the op from here?"

Deep Blue considered the question. "I can rig up quantum ansible audio comms—"

"Ansible?" Ward asked.

"A device for faster-than-light communications."

"Faster than light? Sounds like science fiction."

"It was. A science fiction writer, Ursula LeGuin, coined the word in 1966. It's a mainstay of science fiction stories. But quantum entanglement makes it actually possible to have instantaneous, undetectable and completely secure communication over any distance. Audio is no problem, but anything more than that would take time we don't have."

"So you won't be able to upload real-time satellite recon," King said.

"Unfortunately, no. And I'm not sure how reliable the satellite coverage is for that region. A better option would be to put a couple micro-drones in the air..." He trailed off as if lost in thought.

"Is there a 'but?'"

"I can't pilot the drones from here. We'll need to establish a mobile command center near the AO."

"If you're up for it, make it happen."

King had no doubt that Aleman was fit for field operations. "The rest of you head to Yekaterinburg. Travel separately and regroup when you get there. Start picking up whatever you think we'll need. Bishop, if you have any old black market contacts, see what you can get us, but be discreet. The Russians are probably expecting another team. Keep a low profile."

"I take it you're not joining us?" Queen said.

"I'll catch up to you, but there's something I need to take care of first." He turned back to Ward. "There is one other thing, and this is non-negotiable." He waved to the members of Red Team. "You need to come up with a new name for them. There's only one Chess Team."

BLOOD TIES

TWELVE

Bremerton, Washington

Gray drizzle dampened the observation deck of the commuter ferry as it plowed across Puget Sound. It was heading toward Washington state's Olympic Peninsula, but rather than diminishing the craggy Olympic Mountains, the weather seemed to accentuate their abrupt majesty.

The Olympics were nowhere near as imposing as the snow-capped triple-crested peak of fourteen-thousand-foot Mount Rainier, just visible to the southwest. But the contrast of dark rock, lush green forest and turbulent water was hauntingly beautiful.

King had the deck mostly to himself for the duration of the journey, which gave him plenty of time to appreciate the scenery. Unfortunately, it also gave him plenty of time to contemplate the upcoming reunion. As the vessel neared port, the view of the mountains was lost behind the no less imposing silhouettes of warships docked at the Puget Sound Naval Shipyard in Bremerton. Then those, too, were hidden from view, as the ferry pulled into the terminal.

He had made the trip alone, telling no one where he was going or why, but he had assured the team that he would be no more than a day behind them. He had debated bringing Bishop along, but had decided against it, not despite, but because of their familial bond. There was no telling how she would react when he accused their mother and father of conspiring to fake Julie's death and turn her into a Russian spy.

King had not seen his parents in well over a year, and while that last meeting had ended on a positive note—surprising given the corrosive nature of their family history—his feelings about seeing them again fell somewhere between ambivalence and dread. Seeing Julie again, whether it was really her or not, had ripped off a Band-Aid covering a wound that he had completely forgotten about.

When he thought back to his youth, he saw everything through the context of subsequent revelations. After Julie's accident, his father—their father—had left the family, disappearing off the face of the Earth. Yet the pain of abandonment that young Jack Sigler had felt had been somewhat eased by the knowledge that Peter Sigler had not simply walked out on his loved ones because of an inability to deal with the tragedy.

King's parents, Peter and Lynn Machtchenko, were former Russian spies, poised to carry out a campaign of sabotage, if and when the activation orders were given.

Those orders had never come.

The Soviet Union had fallen, and the Siglers, as they had called themselves, taking Lynn's maiden name as their surname, had fully embraced their new lives. Yet, despite their best efforts to keep the secret buried, the truth had eventually bubbled to the surface, and Peter Sigler had been forced to go into exile to protect his family.

King had lived nearly two decades believing that his father was a deadbeat. But the man had been living in Russia with Asya, a sister that King had not even been aware of. King had also learned that the secret that had wrenched the family apart had almost nothing to do with Peter and Lynn being spies, and everything to do with their bloodline. They were both the descendants of a man named Alexander Diotrephes—the man who had inspired the legend of Hercules.

Diotrephes—Hercules—was King's great-grandfather many times removed. The man might not have been a mythological demi-god, but he was an extraordinary man: an explorer from a parallel universe whose knowledge of science had given him almost god-like abilities. He had conquered death, remaining alive for thousands of years.

Following the sighting, King had avoided contact with his parents. The last thing he wanted to do was make them relive the pain of losing their firstborn daughter, especially if it turned out to be nothing more than a case of mistaken identity. But regardless of whether the woman was Julie or not, she was inextricably connected to a plot hatched in Peter and Lynn's homeland. He could postpone this meeting no longer.

His parents were waiting for him outside the ferry terminal, standing together under the protective canopy of an umbrella, holding hands like an old married couple in their retirement. They were that, but they were something more, too. Spies, trained in the art of deception. He wondered if he would get a straight answer from them.

"Jack!" Lynn stepped out from under the umbrella and moved quickly to embrace him. He returned the hug with all the enthusiasm he could muster. There was nothing insincere about his love for her. She had stayed, after all, raising him, guiding him through the dark years after Julie's death and Peter's disappearance. He had not always been an appreciative son, and he knew it, but all of that seemed so long ago.

"You look well," she said, though there was a hint of concern in her eyes. "Married life agrees with you."

There was a subtle dig in the comment. Circumstances had prevented Sara and King from having a public wedding ceremony.

Before he could respond, Peter came to his rescue. "Leave the boy alone, Lynn. We both know how tough it can be to live a secret life."

King managed a tight-lipped smile. "I was about to say that retirement seems to agree with both of you. I'm surprised you decided to come someplace so wet and gray."

"Are you kidding?" Peter said. "The rain is what brought us here. It's very soothing."

"I suppose it is," King said, evasively. "And no one will think to look for you here."

Following the events of what had been semi-officially labeled 'the Omega crisis,' Peter and Lynn had been forced to yet again rebuild their lives. They had taken new identities and relocated far away from anything familiar, covering their tracks, so that old enemies, or worse, old masters, would never again disrupt their lives. That was, in fact, a reason—though not the only one—why King had not invited his parents to the wedding.

Lynn spoke up. "Just because we love the rain doesn't mean we need to stand here and get soaked. Come on. Let's get you back to the house. I'll make us some hot cocoa and we can catch up."

"If it's all the same," King said. "Maybe we could just grab a cup of coffee somewhere. I've got to be on the three o'clock ferry back to Seattle, if I'm going to make my flight."

Lynn raised an eyebrow. "You came all this way just for a cup of coffee?"

Peter stepped forward, holding the umbrella high to partially shield all of them. "Your mother's right, Jack. We're glad to see you, of course, but if you couldn't stay at least a couple of days, why bother coming at all?"

"I'll explain, but I think we should all be sitting down."

Peter and Lynn exchanged a glance, and then Peter shrugged. "The wheel turns," he said, cryptically. "There's a place a couple blocks from here."

King just nodded. "Lead the way."

As they walked along, Lynn staved off the awkward silence by telling King about their house, a cabin overlooking Discovery Bay, midway between the touristy bedroom communities of Port Townsend and Sequim. The latter, she explained, rhymed with 'swim', even though it looked like it ought to sound more like 'sequin.'

King nodded perfunctorily, acutely aware of the fact that what he was about to tell them might destroy the idyllic existence they had carved out for themselves. He knew they sensed it, too, even if they didn't know exactly what shape the trouble he had brought would take. Finally, seated in a corner of a little café a few blocks from the ferry terminal, King dropped the bomb.

"Something has happened," he said, choosing his words carefully, "that has raised some questions about Julie's death."

Just putting it into words felt like shedding a tremendous burden. It was out there now, for better or worse.

Peter's eyebrows came together in an expression of dismay. "What kind of questions?"

King leaned forward. "I need you to be completely honest with me. Is there anything about your original assignment that you haven't told me?"

He paused, searching for the right way to ask the next question. He didn't want to come right out and ask if they had somehow contrived to fake Julie's death, just as they had, years later, faked Lynn's death.

"Something that might have involved Julie?" he said at length.

Peter shook his head slowly, a look of confusion on his face that was too sincere to be a put on. "We got our assignment long before your sister was born. Everything we did after you kids came along was to get us out of that life."

King took a deep breath. "I'm going to ask you a hard question, and I need you to be completely honest with me. A lot of lives might depend on it."

His parents returned solemn nods. "We owe you complete honesty," Lynn added. "Don't be afraid to ask."

"Were you grooming Julie to take over your mission?"

Peter let out a snort of harsh laughter. "That's your question?"

Lynn laid a hand on her husband's arm. "He has a right to ask, Peter." She looked King in the eye. "I can't imagine why you would wonder that, but the answer is an unequivocal 'no.' We didn't want anything to do with that life, and we certainly didn't want our children following in our footsteps."

In a quieter voice, Peter added, "You know that's why I opposed Julie's decision to join the Air Force."

King continued to scrutinize them. They seemed so very sincere, and yet if they were play-acting, would he know the difference?

Peter held him with a stare like a laser beam. "You said this had to do with Julie's death. What's this really about? Do you think someone killed her? That it wasn't an accident?"

"There's a possibility that..." He faltered. Took a breath then another. "Are you sure that Julie really died that day?"

The stunned silence that followed was sufficient to alleviate any concerns that his parents were keeping something from him.

After almost a full minute, Peter found his voice. "What are you saying, Jack? Is our daughter still alive?"

"I honestly don't know." And then he told them everything, starting with the one and only time he had seen the woman with Julie's face, and ending with the discovery in the Virginia warehouse.

"The dots connect," he finished. "I don't know if that woman was Julie, but she's involved with this somehow. That's why I had to ask."

He glanced at his watch. The next ferry back to Seattle would not leave for another hour, but he felt an overwhelming need to get moving, to escape. He stood up. "I'm sorry. I know what you must be feeling right now. I'm feeling it, too. I won't rest until I know what's really going on. I promise you that."

Peter stared up at him with that same intense gaze. "You're going to Russia, aren't you?"

"I'll go wherever I have to," King said, trying to dodge the question. "Can you get us to Moscow?"

King looked back at his father, momentarily dumbfounded. He resisted the immediate impulse to flatly deny the request. "Why? Do you know something, after all?"

Peter shook his head. "No. I mean, I don't know anything about this, but I do know where to look. If they did this—"

"They?"

"The SVR. Foreign Intelligence Service. Successors to the KGB's First Directorate. If someone in Russia abducted your sister and covered it up by faking her death, that is the agency that would have carried it out. If you can get me to Moscow, I can learn the truth of it."

Before King could answer, Lynn spoke up. "Jack, you need to trust us. But you should also know that, with or without your help, we're going to go. You can't stop us."

King saw the determination in her eyes, Peter's too, and knew that she was dead serious.

He had anticipated stirring up pain and grief. He had even tried to prepare himself for the gut-wrenching possibility that Julie's accident was yet another part of their unending spy saga. This was something he had not expected, and yet he should have. Julie was their first-born, and even though more than a score of years had passed since she was torn from their lives, they had a connection to her that time and death could not erase. They were Julie's parents. If she was still alive, there was nothing they wouldn't do to find her. Moreover, they had the skills and connections to actually make a difference. And having a pair of Russian-born, Soviet-trained agents on the team might just give them the edge they needed in carrying out the primary mission.

"If you're going to do this," he said, "it has to be right now."

Lynn glanced at Peter who returned a reassuring nod. King felt a twinge of guilt for even contemplating allowing them to put themselves in harm's way, but it passed quickly. Life was full of hard choices. Peter and Lynn Machtchenko knew that better than anyone.

THIRTEEN

Yekaterinburg, Russia

"Better or worse?"

Knight felt a lump the size of a cue-ball rise into his throat. "Oh my God," he whispered.

"Sorry. Eye doctor joke. I guess that was in pretty poor taste."

Knight felt moisture welling up in his eyes. Both of them. Intermittent and uncontrollable lachrymal discharges from his left eye socket had been an ongoing side-effect of wearing a prosthetic eye, but this was not that. He turned to face Aleman. "Lew. I can see."

To call what was happening in his left eye 'seeing' was perhaps an overstatement. But compared to what he had 'seen' a moment before the activation of the new optical device, it was like comparing night and day. He had immediately been able to distinguish light, and shortly thereafter, shadow. The longer he looked forward, the more he was able to differentiate shades of gray, textures and depth. The lines and shapes gradually resolved into a hotel room, strewn with equipment and components. He had no trouble at all distinguishing the face of the man who had just restored his sight. Deep Blue, though in this context, he was just plain old Lew. "This is incredible. I'm actually seeing with my left eye again."

Aleman grinned, and the best part was that Knight could see him do it with both eyes. "Glad to hear it. I didn't want to tell you about this until I had all the kinks worked out. When Admiral Ward cleared up my supply issues, I was able to get the last few components I needed to get it working. I know it will never fully replace what you lost, but it's something."

Aleman was speaking from experience. The tech expert's own career as a sniper had been cut short by a battlefield injury. After several surgical procedures, he had made a complete recovery. But by that time, he had demonstrated that he was far more valuable to the Chess Team and by extension, to the nation, as a gadget guru than as a field operator. He was also considerably happier in his new role.

"I've learned a lot from my mistakes with the Knight-Eye Mark 1," he went on. "There have been some awesome technological and medical developments since then. But before you go all googly-eyed—pun most definitely intended—there are some drawbacks, too. To begin with, you're probably only seeing black and white right now, and a little fuzzy, too."

"I'll take a little fuzzy any day over zilch," Knight said.

"The device works by translating light into electrical impulses, just like what your real eye does. Because of the damage to your optical nerve though, those electrical impulses are just sort of randomly shooting into your brain."

"Uh, okay. When you say it like that, it doesn't sound so good." Knight could still vividly recall the searing migraines he'd gotten from the previous optical device Aleman had designed to help him overcome the disfiguring eye injury he'd suffered in the Congo.

"No, that part is fine. You won't feel a thing. The problem is that your brain has to learn to interpret those impulses. The good news is, it can do just that. The brain is much more plastic and adaptable than we ever thought possible. And your good eye is facilitating the process by helping your brain make sense of the fuzzy black and white blur. Try closing your right eye for a second, and you'll see what I mean."

Knight did as instructed and suddenly everything he thought he was seeing vanished, replaced by a murky blob of light and dark. He opened his good eye again and the image quickly resolved. "You said it will continue to improve?"

"I did, but in the near term, you'll probably feel some mild eye strain. Maybe some headaches, but I promise you, nothing like before. You'll need to keep both eyes open. And you may have difficulty tracking fast-moving objects. That's a hardware problem I hope we'll be able to overcome, if I can build us a new quantum computer."

Knight thought he heard a hint of grief in Aleman's voice at the mention of the quantum computer. When they had been operating out of the former Manifold Alpha facility in New Hampshire, Aleman had built a beyond-state-of-the-art supercomputer. It had utilized the phenomenon known as quantum superposition, in which a subatomic particle could literally be in more than one place simultaneously. Unlike digital binary processors, quantum superposition allowed for instantaneous computation and data transfer. Aleman's quantum computer had enabled him to create gadgets that would have made James Bond's Q-section green with envy. Glasses with a retinal projection system, networked to the sights on their weapons had allowed for multiple target tracking, and adaptive camouflage had made them very nearly invisible on the battlefield.

That computer and everything it had made possible, including the first version of a replacement eye for Knight, was gone now. It was all a casualty of the full-on assault that had very nearly destroyed the Chess Team. But the technical know-how to build the computer anew had not been lost. Aleman was already working on a new and improved design, but as he had told Admiral Ward, many of the components he needed to make it a reality were not available for civilian use. It would be several weeks, perhaps even months, before it was up and running, which meant they would have to go 'old school' for the current mission to Russia.

But at least Knight would be able to go in with both eyes open.

"I did manage to add a couple of special features to this one," Aleman said. "Focus on something. Anything. Doesn't matter what."

Knight glanced around the room. He finally settled on a notice sign posted on the door. The optical device did not have sufficient resolution for him to differentiate the letters, but he could see that they were there, black ink on white paper. He squinted and was surprised when the sign, and the surrounding door, suddenly got bigger. Now, he actually read the fine print on the hotel fire evacuation map. "Magnification. Nice."

"Ha. You spoiled my first surprise. But yes, squinting will automatically increase magnification. It's an intuitive system, kind of like autofocus on a camera. Now, relax your eye to go back to normal perspective, then very quickly, blink twice."

Knight did as instructed. When he opened his eyes the second time, he saw a tracery of red around the door. Floating in front of it, also in red, was the display. '4.3 m.'

"A rangefinder," Knight said with a grin. "In metric, even."

"Of course. I can change that to standard measurements if you prefer. Now, the rangefinder doesn't work very well with the magnification optics or with an external device like a scope or binoculars. So if you can't see the target with the naked eye, it won't be of much use. Hopefully, that's something else I can address in the next update."

"Cool." As Knight looked away from the chair, the display faded and returned to normal vision. "Anything else?"

Aleman leaned close and spoke in a low whisper. "Okay, you should probably keep this next feature a secret. It could cause... friction."

Knight was intrigued. "I'm almost afraid to ask."

"Blink three times slowly."

On the third blink, his sight abruptly dimmed to a slate gray hue. After a few seconds, images began to resolve, but they were nothing like what he had been seeing before. He looked at Aleman, but the question on his lips died when he realized that he was looking *through* the man. In his right eye, he saw Lewis Aleman's lean, smiling face and tousled blond hair, but in his left, he saw what looked like a skeleton made of black mist.

"X-ray vision," Knight said, incredulous. "Un-fucking-believable."

The skeletal form shook with laughter. "Just like those glasses they used to advertise in the back of comic books, only this really works."

"This thing isn't going to cook my brain or give me cancer, right?"

The skull bobbed from side to side. "It's a passive backscatter receiver. Uses background radiation. Cosmic rays. Radio waves. Stuff that's all around us all the time. Stuff that can pass through solid objects. The device is able to render an approximate image based on the diffusion rate, which basically means that bone shows up because it blocks more radiation than flesh or clothing.

"Like with regular vision, your brain will learn to distinguish exactly what it is you're seeing the longer you use it. The range depends on the density of the objects you're looking at...er, through."

"Could I see through walls?"

"Depends on what the wall is made of. You would probably be able to see shapes. You'd be able to see the outline of a person standing behind a closed door, but you wouldn't be able to tell who it was. And, of course, as you can tell, it's not much good for ogling."

"So why did you advise me to keep it on the down low?"

"If people think you can see through their clothes, they might get a little nervous around you."

"Our little secret then." Knight grinned, but he knew it wasn't a secret he would be able to keep for very long. Chess Team was effective because each member—each piece—knew the capabilities, strengths and weaknesses of the others. Keeping an ability like this from the others might have fatal consequences.

"Backscatter mode can also function as a sort of night vision, though not quite as well as NODs. Just blink again to return to normal mode." He paused a beat, and then added. "Seriously. Turn it off. You're creepin' me out."

Knight laughed and blinked, restoring the eye to normal function. "I can't thank you enough, Lew." Even that somehow felt insufficient, but a knock at the door spared him the need to reach deeper. He swiveled his head toward it and activated the backscatter function, to reveal two spectral figures—one at least a full seven inches taller than the other. "Rook and Queen," he said.

The pair of very solid-looking pistol shapes resting on either side of the taller person's rib cage confirmed that identification. Knight didn't know how Rook had contrived to smuggle in his Desert Eagle XIX semi-automatic hand cannons—which he had lovingly nicknamed, 'the girls'—but if past experience was any indication, everyone would probably be glad he had.

Aleman stepped in front of him. "Ixnay on the X-ray," he said, then he turned to admit the pair.

Queen stepped inside. Without preamble, she said, "FRAGO."

The term was military shorthand for 'fragmentary order'—an adjustment to an ongoing mission that did not necessitate a change to the overall objective. Or as most soldiers put it, 'a change to the mission, but the mission doesn't change.'

"King just called," she went on. "He's making a detour to Moscow. He wants Bishop to meet him there. The rest of us will head out and start preliminary recon."

Knight frowned. "King and Bishop running their own op? What a surprise."

"I know, right?" Rook said. He crossed over to the bed, and sat down heavily on the corner. "It's getting to be a bad habit with those two."

"Stow that talk," Queen said. "King knows what he's doing, and we've got work to do. We've got a long drive ahead of us, and an even longer hump into the wilderness. Hope you packed your long-johns. I want to roll out by eighteen-hundred hours."

Eighteen hundred. Knight shot a look at his wristwatch. It was almost fifteen-hundred now—three p.m.

The sudden change of focus momentarily confused his new optical implant, making everything fuzzy for a few seconds. It was a none-too-subtle reminder that he was far from one hundred percent battle-ready.

But who really ever is? he thought.

FOURTEEN

Moscow, Russia

Moscow in winter looked like something out of a fairy tale. The ornate and colorful buildings in Red Square—most notably St. Basil's Cathedral and the Kremlin Palace—looked like confectionery sculptures, liberally dusted with powdered sugar.

Appearances were deceiving. What the postcards sold in airport gift shops and street corner kiosks could not adequately depict was the bitter cold.

It had been a moderately chilly sixty-five degrees Fahrenheit in Dubai. In Moscow, it was minus six degrees—almost forty degrees below freezing. Catherine Alexander felt certain she would never get used to the frigid winters. The nickname her mentor had given her was a private joke about her ability to be coldly logical, even ruthless, when they played chess together. It was most certainly not an indication of her love for the long dark winters of her adopted homeland.

No wonder this place makes such hard people, she thought, though in fact, she was really thinking only of him.

The car he had sent to meet her at the airport kept most of the cold at bay, as did the sheltered portico where she transitioned from the limousine to the magnificently domed Kremlin Senate Building. Once inside, she doffed the heavy sable coat and matching Zhivago-style pillbox hat, handing them to a waiting aide.

"Take me to him," she said in an imperious tone, just as her mentor had instructed her. *The subservient class will not respect your kindness*, he had told her. *They will mistake it for weakness and begin looking for ways to destroy you*. She knew he was right, but learning such disdain for other people had not come naturally to her.

The aide, knowing her reputation for long quick strides, fairly ran ahead of her. They bypassed the security station—no one would dare accost her—and negotiated the corridors of the Senate building to the modest office of Catherine's mentor, the President of the Russian Federation.

The President looked up from behind the simple wooden desk, met her gaze with his own piercing eyes, and then turned to the aide. "No interruptions," he said simply.

The man nodded and left the room, closing the door firmly behind him. The Russian President returned his stare to her but said nothing.

"I am surprised to find you here," she said, trying to fill the uncomfortable silence. "I thought you would be at Novo-Ogaryovo."

While the Kremlin complex was still the seat of power for the Russian Federation, the President had in recent years transferred his official presence to his primary residence, an elegant 19th century estate situated to the west of Moscow. Ostensibly, it spared him the ordeal of daily commutes through heavy city traffic, but Catherine knew there was a more compelling reason for his decision. Here in the Kremlin, he was exposed. Exposed to the ministers of Parliament, who understood that access to the President gave them political power. Exposed to his critics, who sought ever to trick him into admitting that he was not a constitutionally legitimate ruler, but a dictator, intent on establishing himself as the head of a perpetual autarchy. Exposed to the scrutiny of the world. As Operation Perun gained momentum, building to its world-altering climax, that level of exposure was increasingly dangerous.

He ignored the casual inquiry. "I need you in Volosgrad. The Firebird must be ready within the week."

"Within the week? Is that even possible?"

"You will make it possible."

"Me?" The order stunned her. She had spent years creating the Consortium, almost single-handedly bending the leaders of nations and corporations to their will. And now, instead of rewarding her, he was demanding more. Demanding the impossible. She could not snap her fingers and produce the Firebird out of thin air, nor was it simply a matter of working the scientists harder. Threatening and cajoling them would not change the laws of physics, any more than it would magically increase the limited supply of organic material necessary for the research to continue. "Forgive me, but I must ask. Why? What has changed?"

"One of the supply stations was hit yesterday."

Catherine's eyes went wide. The supply stations were among her greatest accomplishments. With the wealth and influence of the Consortium behind her, she had personally overseen every aspect of the creation of the supply stations. There were eight of them in all, ringing the American capital city. From establishing the shell corporations that owned the properties, to hand selecting the Spetsnaz soldiers who would provide security for the sites, she had done it all. "That cannot be. How did they learn of it?"

He shrugged. "Perhaps one of the American agents got a message out of Volosgrad before their capture. It is irrelevant."

"The chess pieces?" Catherine shook her head. "No. That's doesn't make any sense. There was nothing at Volosgrad to connect—"

"It does not matter. It is done. If the Americans do not already know about Operation Perun, they soon will. They must already suspect what we are planning. We must act while the element of surprise is on our side. The operation will commence in one week, whether the Firebird is ready or not." His lips curled in a faint smile. "I would prefer if it was, of course, but a pyrrhic victory is better than no victory at all."

Catherine heard the note of finality in his voice. She knew there would be no dissuading him from this path.

It was a pity, really. She had already given him so much. With the Consortium, his dream of an empire to rule the world had already become a reality, but she knew that he would never consent to ruling from the shadows. "Very well. If it is what you wish, I will push Alexei harder."

"That is not why I am sending you there."

"I don't understand. If not that, then why?"

He held her gaze. "None of the captured Americans were viable candidates."

Catherine's eyebrows drew together. "Are you certain? All the evidence indicated that the team leader would be a match."

"Perhaps he is, but the Americans did not send *him*."

This revelation, while discouraging, was not entirely a surprise. Using her influence as the head of the Consortium, Catherine had been given extraordinary access to key figures in the American government, including President Chambers himself. Subsequently she had learned everything there was to know about a special operations unit that did the jobs no one else could do. The information confirmed what SVR operatives had been reporting for years regarding the role of this team—the Chess Team—as the tip of the spear for American forces. She had also learned their identities—most notably the team leader King, who it was believed possessed unique genetic attributes necessary to the success of the Firebird project.

Acting on the information she had supplied, the SVR had set a trap, leaking information about increased activity at the Volosgrad facility in the Ural Mountains. They had hoped to draw the Chess Team to them. The chess pieces were the logical first choice for such a mission, but evidently the Americans had sent another group of agents in their stead. That had always been the flaw in the plan, as far as Catherine was concerned.

"Then I do not understand. Firebird cannot proceed without King. He is the only source of genetic material we've identified."

"No. Not the only one." Her mentor was as impassive as a statue.

The declaration hit her like a gut punch. "Me? You would sacrifice me?"

"I would sacrifice everything and everyone." His voice was flat and dispassionate, but then he put on a patronizing smile. "Do not worry, my Ice Queen. The procedure is painful, but the damage is not permanent. You will make a full recovery, I promise. You know this is true."

Anger—an emotion that she rarely felt—flashed through her, melting the ice in her veins. "This was always your plan. To use me this way."

"You know that is not true. You are as a daughter to me."

She spat out a laugh. Publicly, the Russian President was known to have two daughters, but that, like everything else in his public life, was a carefully constructed fiction designed to create an illusion of normalcy. The rarely seen young women were actresses hired to play the part of daughters, as was the woman who posed as his ex-wife and made occasional benign yet critical statements about him and their life together.

"How long have you been with me? Twenty years? We did not even know this was possible until just a few years ago."

He was not wrong about that.

Although the Firebird project had its genesis in research begun nearly seventy years earlier, at the dawn of the Atomic Age, the breakthrough had come just five years ago. A man named Richard Ridley, the head of a leading bio-gen firm, had offered to share research with the Russian government in exchange for their help in tracking down a unique genetic population that Ridley had called 'the Children of Adoon.' The subsequent search had produced a very short list of candidates who met an additional criterion, a list that included King—a.k.a. Jack Sigler. However, Catherine's mentor had revealed that she was also a child of Adoon.

Had he known about her true genetic potential all along? It had never occurred to her to ask. She doubted he would tell her the truth unless doing so somehow served his purpose.

He was right about one other thing, too. The procedure he was ordering her to undergo would not kill her. And if it worked as the scientists promised it would, she would rule the world at his side. The pain—not just that of the invasive procedure that awaited her at Volosgrad, but also from his callous betrayal—was a small price to pay.

She took a breath to regain her frosty composure. "Very well. Will you see to my travel arrangements, or am I to also gather the firewood for the altar?"

She knew he would grasp the significance of the reference. In the Bible, God had commanded Abraham to make a human sacrifice of his son Isaac. In what seemed like a particularly cruel twist, the elderly patriarch had directed Isaac to gather wood and build the altar upon which he would be slaughtered.

Before the President could answer, an electronic trilling noise signaled an incoming telephone call. A look of irritation flitted across his face—he had explicitly instructed his aide that there should be no interruptions. He broke eye contact with her and looked at the blinking light. His frown deepened as he lifted the receiver to his ear and pressed the button to accept the call.

"Da?" He listened intently for nearly a minute, then said, "Call me again in one hour. Use a different phone."

He returned the receiver to its cradle and turned back to Catherine. "You chose an apt metaphor, my child. Like Abraham, my faith had been rewarded."

FIFTEEN

Moscow, Russia

She had been a child when the Soviet Union collapsed. She had not even been a glimmer in Peter Machtchenko's eye when the most egregious of the legendary crimes against humanity committed on the premises of 'the Lubyanka' had occurred. Still, the imposing neo-baroque structure had always filled Asya with dread. It was like the dark tower from *The Lord of the Rings* movies, a place forever haunted by the ghosts of its many victims. The stories of what had happened behind those yellow brick walls were drilled into the collective consciousness of all Russians. Those walls had contained the offices of the KGB and the various agencies that preceded it, and the notorious prison for political dissidents, which had occupied a sizable portion of the complex. There was an old joke that the Lubyanka was the tallest building in Moscow, because you could see Siberia from its basement.

Much had changed since the fall of the USSR, but many of those changes were merely cosmetic. The statue of Felix Dzerzhinsky was gone from Lubyanskaya Square. He had been the founder of the Cheka, the earliest incarnation of the secret police bureau, and the man responsible for tens of thousands of political executions in the early years of the Communist regime. The statue had been replaced by the Solovetsky Stone—a chunk of granite commemorating the victims of the infamous GULAG prison system—but the building, with all its ghosts, remained. Moreover, it was still the official headquarters of the state security bureau, though the sheer size of the agency had necessitated expansion into a neighboring building, an ugly gray structure that looked like a massive cinder block.

Asya had changed, too. She was Bishop now, a deadly warrior, but the Lubyanka still made her nervous, particularly given the reason that she had returned after so many years away.

The two-and-a-half-hour flight from Yekaterinburg to Moscow, and the subsequent eight hours of cooling her heels in a room at the Hotel Metropol, had given her a little time to get over her surprise at the last-minute change to the op. The unexpected addition of two new 'pawns' —her parents—had left her anxious. She was not entirely clear on why King had elected to bring their parents along, and he had not given her an opportunity to ask. She suspected it had nothing to do with the mission Admiral Ward had given them, and everything to do with King's personal obsession with the woman who looked like their long-dead sister.

Bishop was glad for a chance to spend time with her parents, particularly with her mother, whom she felt she barely knew, but the circumstances were troubling. The team's primary mission, at least as far as she was concerned, was finding Thomas Duncan. And that mission had gone completely off the rails. Her anxiety had only deepened when, just minutes after the reunion, King had directed them all to bundle up in their newly acquired winter clothes before heading out to Lubyanskaya Square.

Against the dull backdrop of gray snow and damp macadam, the yellow brick façade seemed to glow like a warning light. She pulled her coat tighter, even though the frigid air was not the source of the chill that tingled in her extremities. "I do not like this."

Peter glanced over at her. "Do you remember the first time we were here? I took you to the ballet."

Although she had not thought about it in a long time, the memory arose unbidden. The trip had been a birthday present—her tenth. Peter, her father, had been a transient figure, always moving in and out of her life. He had been 'away on business,' her grandmother had always told her. Eventually he had decided to settle down and see to her upbringing. At her grandmother's insistence, she had begun taking ballet lessons almost as soon as she could walk, and she had shown great promise as a dancer. For her birthday, Peter had taken her to the Bolshoi Theatre to watch a performance by the famed dance troupe. They had ridden the Metro to Lubyanka Station and walked to the Bolshoi, which was just a few blocks away. She recalled that they had also visited Detsky Mir, the enormous toy store that bordered the square. Strangely, although it was right across the street, the Lubyanka building was absent from her memory of that day.

"You danced around the apartment for weeks afterward," Peter went on. "Telling everyone how you were practicing for the Bolshoi."

She knew he was just trying to put her at ease, but the memory brought up a strange stew of emotions that were equally unwelcome. She looked over at her mother and saw the sadness in the woman's eyes. Lynn had completely missed out on her daughter's childhood. She also felt King's scrutinizing stare. "What? I dreamed of being ballet dancer. So what?"

"It's not that," King admitted. "I was just trying to wrap my head around it all. How did you keep Asya a secret from me? I must have been...what, six or seven when she was born?" He turned to Lynn. "You'd think I'd have noticed a baby bump."

"You weren't a very observant child, dear," she replied. "But surely you remember that I spent a few months with your grandmother."

King's forehead creased. "Not really."

"We told you Nona was sick and that I was going to take care of her. A little white lie. Just like when we told you she lived in Germany."

"We tried our best to keep it a secret from everyone," Peter supplied. "We thought the KGB had forgotten about us, but my former handler, Vladimir—the man that is helping us get into Lubyanka—warned me that Moscow was thinking about waking the sleepers. That was back when President Reagan was pushing hard for his Star Wars program. The Politburo believed the United States was actively seeking first-strike nuclear capability. We feared that Moscow would perhaps use your mother's pregnancy as leverage to force us back into the life, so we kept it a secret from everyone. When it was impossible to hide any longer, she traveled to Russia to have Asya, while I stayed with you and...Julie."

Bishop did not fail to notice how his voice had caught, just for a second, at the mention of her older sister. *Maybe I am being selfish*, she thought. *Julie was also their daughter.*

"We had to leave Asya with your grandmother and get things back to normal as soon as we could, but I made it a point to check in on her whenever I could. It got a lot easier to do that after the Cold War ended, but we still had to be careful. Technically, we were still spies, liable for arrest if discovered. And even though the Soviet Union went away, there was always the possibility that the Russian government might try to reassert their influence."

"It must have been quite a juggling act," King said.

"It was. We couldn't have done it without help, especially from Vladimir."

"I guess I don't need to ask if you can trust the guy," King murmured.

"You do not," Peter replied. "But you need to trust me, Jack. I've been playing this game a long time. I know what I'm doing."

The plan, Peter explained, was for the four of them to join the guided tour of Lubyanka. Once inside, Peter and Bishop would slip away from the group and make their way to the basement to search one of the many archival rooms that preserved the record of intelligence gathering activities going back more than fifty years. Because of a long-standing, and probably not unwarranted, deep distrust of electronic data storage methods, the information was all in hard copy form—hand-written notes, typed reports, photographs—all filed and indexed.

"You're saying the entire history of the KGB is kept in boxes in the basement?" King asked, skeptically.

Peter shook his head. "Of course not. Highly classified documents on active operations are kept in secret locations that I doubt even Vladimir could get us into. This archive is more of a research and reference library. If an agent needs information about a particular subject who had been investigated previously, they can just go to the archive and request it. Vladimir said he would leave a set of credentials at a dead drop inside the building. That will get me most of the way in.

"Asya, you'll watch my back while I'm in the archives. Lynn and Jack, you cover for us with the tour group. If anyone notices that we're gone, tell them that I suffer from dementia and wandered off, and that Asya went looking for me. They'll probably lock the place down until I'm found, but by then we should already have what we're after."

"And if they decide to detain us?" Bishop asked.

"I doubt that will happen, but we've all had training in how to stand up to interrogation. The key is to keep it simple. This isn't Soviet Russia anymore. We're just a family of Russian ex-pats visiting the *Rodina*. It's not even a lie."

King made a deferential 'after you' gesture. "Let's get this done."

After they made their way inside, Peter excused himself to visit the restroom, where Vladimir had left credentials that would get him into the archive rooms. When he returned, they joined the queue for the museum tour.

Despite now being in the belly of the great yellow beast, as she caught snippets of conversations and studied signs and posters written in Cyrillic, Bishop began to feel strangely at home. She had spent the last few years surrounded by Americans, immersed in their culture and language. Even though she liked most of it, she always felt like a visitor. She wondered if her parents were feeling the same way.

The tour began with the museum docent delivering a perfunctory monologue about the history of the building and its role in the early years of the Soviet Union. The tour group included visiting Americans and Koreans, accompanied by hired tour guides who quietly translated for their respective groups and provided additional commentary. Managing the multilingual crowd kept the docent occupied, and Bishop was not at all surprised when Peter tapped her on the arm, indicating that the time had come to break away from the group.

She did not acknowledge the signal, but counted to ten and then, when she was certain that no one was paying attention, turned and slipped away. Peter had, by design, gotten a head start. She had to set a brisk pace to keep him in sight. She walked with her head high, projecting a confidence that she did not quite feel.

If you look like you know exactly where you are going, Peter had instructed her, *no one will stop you. No one likes to borrow trouble by interfering in someone's business.* It was a universal truth, and even more so in the Russian consciousness.

Peter navigated the halls with the familiar surety of someone who had worked there for years, and maybe he had, before taking his assignment in America. Maybe nothing much had changed. He approached an unmarked door, produced a key to unlock it and then went through, but not before turning back to make eye contact with her. He made a casual 'come here' gesture, and then stepped through.

He was waiting for her in the cramped stairwell just beyond. The dark stained concrete and musty smell suggested a route that was seldom used, but Bishop knew that such neglect was commonplace, particularly in government buildings.

"We'll stick together from here on," he told her. "We're visiting from the St. Petersburg office. I'm the senior agent and you're my aide. Got it?"

She nodded.

"Good. Follow me." He started down the stairs with the same authoritative stride.

"May I ask you something?" she said, her whisper barely audible over the rapid-fire tapping of their footsteps.

He glanced over his shoulder with a faintly perturbed frown. "Can it wait?"

It was not, strictly speaking, a 'no,' so she forged ahead. "This is about Julie, isn't it? King thinks the SVR faked her death so they could abduct her and turn her into a spy."

"If that's your question, then yes, it is about Julie. The rest... I don't want to believe it, but part of me thinks that's exactly what happened."

"If it is," Bishop pressed, "then what do you think you will find here? Surely if anything was going to be classified as top-secret, the detail of that operation would be."

"Vladimir suggested we start here. During the Cold War, the First Directorate targeted American pilots for abduction, to learn the secrets and weaknesses of American aircraft. The protocols for the operation may be here."

"But Julie...that happened after the fall of the USSR."

"I know. But the men working in this building did not change. The operation may have continued under the direction of the FSB." He made a cutting gesture. "Vladimir has never led me wrong."

"I'm sorry. I should not have asked. I know that she must be very important to you."

That stopped him. He turned to face her. "Asya, wanting to know what happened to my oldest daughter does not make me love you any less."

Bishop felt her cheeks go hot.

I should not have said that, she thought.

"I wish you had known her," Peter said. "You are so much alike."

Bishop thought about what the search had already uncovered and the nightmare they had escaped in Virginia. "If King is right, maybe I will have a chance to know her."

Peter did not respond to that, but resumed walking, faster now, as if to prevent her from asking any more questions.

They came to a corridor and followed it to a door at the far end. Beyond it was a dark room separated by a counter. The young man sitting behind the counter glanced up from the book he was reading and then grudgingly got to his feet.

Peter reached into his pocket as if to produce his credentials, then abruptly froze. A look of embarrassment came over his face. "I seem to have left my papers behind. I'll come back later."

Bishop quickly overcame her surprise at the sudden shift in Peter's focus. Something had clearly spooked him. While she did not fully understand the nature of the threat, she knew that it was critical to stay in character. She faced the clerk behind the counter and gave a helpless shrug.

That was when she saw it.

"No need," the man was saying, hands extended invitingly. "You're here. Why make another trip?"

The man reminded her of Rook—tall, blond hair and broadly built, with muscles that strained the fabric of his dress shirt. Not the sort of person one would expect to find guarding a desk in a dark forgotten corner of the building.

Peter had caught the discrepancy immediately. If his instincts—and hers—were wrong about the man, then the excuse of having forgotten his credentials would be accepted at face value, and they would be allowed to make their exit without interference.

But if they were right about the man, then it was already too late.

"No, no," Peter said, waving his arms. "We must follow procedure."

He turned for the exit, and Bishop turned, too, but not before she saw the man vault over the counter. She reacted instinctively, dropping into a crouch and performing a spinning leg sweep that took the man's feet out from under him a fraction of a second before they could touch the floor. The man went sprawling, sliding face first toward Peter.

At almost the same instant, the door behind the counter burst open. Two more men rushed out. They were big athletic men, like the phony clerk, wearing black suits and heavy coats, as if they expected the encounter to end with a trip out into the cold.

Despite the first man's mishap, the new arrivals were gazing intently at Peter, as if he was both their primary target and the greatest threat in the room. As they rounded the end of the counter, aiming their compact Makarov pistols at her father, Bishop took full advantage of that misjudgment. She sprang out of her crouch and into a forward handspring, whipping her feet up and into the chest of the lead gunman. The added momentum of the acrobatic maneuver drove the man back into his accomplice and sent them both tumbling backward in a daze. Bishop landed cat-like on her feet. She whirled around to deal with the fake clerk, only to find that Peter had already taken care of that problem with a two-handed hammer blow to the back of the man's neck.

"Run," he shouted, rising up and throwing open the door through which they had entered only moments before.

Bishop moved, but before she got even halfway, two more figures clad in heavy greatcoats and wielding pistols appeared in the corridor beyond. They were too far away for her to charge them without taking a bullet first. The fact that they had not already fired meant maybe—just maybe—the intention was to take her and Peter alive, but alive did not necessarily mean uninjured. Worse, the two men she had bowled over were already recovering—four gunmen against the two of them.

Suddenly, the rearmost of the pair at the door vanished from her view, as if plucked off the face of the Earth by the hand of God. The lead man was oblivious to his partner's fate, but a moment later, the same invisible force struck him as well. Something hit him from behind, driving him forward and snapping his head back so violently that Bishop thought she could hear bones cracking. As the man careened into the room, the face of their savior was revealed.

"Mother?"

Lynn ducked back out of view, even as something thundered in Bishop's ear. It was a shot fired by one of the men she had earlier knocked down. The round sizzled through the air where Lynn had been standing a moment earlier.

Bishop spun around, and before the man could change his aimpoint to a more immediate target, she struck him in the Adam's apple with a knife hand attack. The Makarov slipped from fingers that were now more interested in clutching his injured throat, giving Bishop all the time she needed to catch the pistol before it could hit the ground.

Or try to.

As her hand made contact with the falling metal object, the world vanished in a flash. She dimly registered the impact of something against the side of her head, and then she was face down on the floor. She knew what had happened. The other man had struck her. She knew that she was now vulnerable and exposed, and she knew that if she didn't recover immediately, she would be dead. But the message was slow to reach the part of her brain that would enable action.

Another shot cracked the air above her.

She struggled to move, flopping sideways like a fish out of water. Then she managed to roll over, hands raised to ward off the amorphous shape that was descending toward her. Her fingers made contact but she was unable to deflect the thing that crashed onto her, pinning her to the ground.

Still, she did not give up.

She pushed against the thing holding her down and was surprised when, despite its mass, it shifted away. That was when she realized it was not an attack but rather the unmoving body of the man who had struck her. Dazed, she squirmed out from under the dead man, ready to rejoin the fight, but there were no enemies left. The only people still standing in the room were her family.

King reached out a hand to help her up. "I leave you alone for five minutes..."

"Thanks for coming to the rescue," Peter said. He was bent over, hands resting on his knees and panting to catch his breath, but otherwise he appeared no worse for wear.

"It was mom's idea," King said.

Lynn merely smiled.

Bishop took the proffered hand and got to her feet. "I hope you have B Plan."

King started to say something, but Peter beat him to it.

"Actually, *I* do."

SIXTEEN

Lynn had been the first one to spot trouble. King had been watching the docent's expression for any hint that the man had noticed two people missing from his tour group, and so he had not seen the line of men in long coats moving purposefully through the lobby. Lynn's senses were evidently more attuned.

It was still hard for him to think of Lynn Sigler—or rather Lynn Machtchenko—as anything but the kindly woman who had always been there for him when he needed her, and even sometimes when he hadn't wanted to admit that he needed her. The years had blunted his memory of her sharper edges, but it still boggled his mind that she had once been a spy. He supposed that was an indication of just how good she had been at her job.

Their abrupt separation from the tour group did not go unnoticed. King had heard the docent shouting after them, but Lynn had not looked back and neither had he. They followed the group of what King assumed were FSB officers into a stairwell, where Lynn had surprised him yet again by stealthily picking off the last man in the group. She had slipped a wire garrote—which King had not even known she possessed—over his head. Then, with a sharp cross-arm pull, she had throttled the man to death. She exhibited similar cold brutality when they caught up to the rest of the group, just in time to save Peter and Bishop.

My mom's a killing machine, King thought, as he bent to relieve the fallen FSB men of their pistols. He handed one to Bishop, and tucked another in his belt. *Who knew?*

"There's another way out," Peter said, as he headed back through the doors. "There's an entire warren of tunnels underneath the Lubyanskaya. Secret passages to the Metro station and other places. We can leave through one of those."

"Not to be a spoilsport," King said, "but don't you think they'll have thought of that? This wasn't a random event. They set a trap for us. For you."

"Vladimir," Lynn murmured.

Peter pursed his lips together for a moment. "I don't want to believe that he informed on us. Maybe someone intercepted my last call to him." He turned to King again. "They meant to take us here. Hit us with overwhelming force."

"They didn't count on *our* overwhelming force," Lynn said.

Peter smiled at his wife. "They might be watching the main entrance and the passage to the Metro station, but there is one exit that I think they will not be watching. We have to hurry though. Once they realize they've failed here, they'll close in."

With Peter leading, they raced into the maze of passages, some of which looked—and smelled—like sewer tunnels. King brought up the rear, checking their six every few seconds. He didn't see any pursuers, but a few minutes after the battle in the archive office, the sound of shouting became audible.

"Here," Peter said in a hoarse whisper, leading them down yet another short passage. At the far end, a brick arch framed what appeared to be a doorway, except where the door ought to have been, there were only more bricks. The masonry appeared to be a relatively recent addition. The bricks were not as worn or discolored as those that formed the surrounding wall, and the faint extrusions of mortar that joined them indicated the work had been done from the opposite side.

"Uh, Dad..."

Peter raised a hand to silence him. "This exit was sealed a few years ago during the renovation. That's why they won't be watching it."

"Right," King said slowly. "Because it's not actually an exit."

Peter took something from his pocket and turned to Lynn. "Please tell me you brought it, *Babushka.*"

"You know how I feel about proper dental care," she said, holding up a similar object. When he saw what it was, King was speechless. Both of his parents were holding small travel-sized tubes of toothpaste.

"Toothpaste?" Bishop said, incredulous. "Are we going to brush our way out of here?"

"Something like that," Peter said. He uncapped his tube and pressed it to the wall, squeezing out a strip of blue gel that ran up the edge of the arch, around the top and back down the other side. Even before he was done, Lynn was doing the same with her tube, though her gel was a chalky white.

"Let me guess," King said, at last finding his voice. "A compound explosive. Separately, they're inert and won't react to chemical screening, but combine them and you've got plastique. Very James Bond."

"Please," Peter said with a derisive snort. He stepped aside to allow Lynn to complete her contribution. "Ian Fleming got the idea for Q section from rumors he'd heard about what KGB Fifth Directorate was developing. He barely scratched the surface."

"We should probably move back," Lynn advised, standing up straight as soon as she had finished. "The reaction usually takes about thirty seconds, but there's no telling—"

That was enough for King. He grabbed ahold of his parents, one with each hand, and pulled them several paces away from the arch. "Bish. Duck and cover."

He had barely gotten the words out when a noise like a jet engine filled the passage. A shockwave shuddered through his body, followed by a blast of heat and a wave of nitrate smoke laced with gritty debris. From the midst of the miasma, he felt both Peter and Lynn pulling against his restraining hands, drawing him back toward the source of the blast, and then beyond. Shattered bricks crunched underfoot for a moment, but as the cloud began to abate, he saw that they were now standing in a small room, or possibly the end of another tunnel. It was illuminated only by the glow of Peter's penlight.

"This way," he called out, waggling the light like a beacon.

King fumbled forward until he was mostly clear of the debris cloud. Somehow, Peter and Lynn had emerged from the blast without even a hair out of place. Bishop was covered in dust, resembling a powdered donut. King suspected he was as well.

Peter kept urging them onward, deeper into what King now saw was indeed another passage, dark and musty from years of disuse. They came to a wooden door so warped by moisture and mildew that King thought they might have to use more of the explosive to get through, but a sharp kick from Peter caused it to burst open. The passage permitted entry into what looked like a cramped warehouse, filled with pallets loaded with cardboard boxes.

Peter paused there for the first time, as if uncertain where to go next.

"Not what you remembered?" King asked.

"Of course it isn't," Peter said, a bit testily. "They remodeled the building a few years ago, closed off the old tunnels. I know where we are. I just don't know the most direct way to an exit."

"We're in basement, right?" Bishop said. "Maybe look for stairs?"

Peter gave a noncommittal nod and started forward through the maze of pallets. Unlike the supply depot in Virginia, little attempt had been made at organizing the wares. The wooden skids and their contents—some stacked too high for King to see over, others with only one or two boxes—were simply jammed in like pieces of a jigsaw puzzle. As they moved toward the center of the storage area however, they found a central structure surrounding a large freight elevator door. Alongside it was an ordinary sized door marked with Cyrillic characters.

Stairs.

"That's more like it," Peter crowed. He pushed open the door and started bounding up the steps.

Lynn was only a few steps behind, but before she disappeared from view she turned to look at her children. King thought she had an almost manic expression, like a young child at an amusement park rushing from one thrill ride to the next. "Come on, kids. What are you waiting for?"

King recognized the signs of an adrenaline high, but try as he might, he could not reconcile his memories of the kind, nurturing woman with what he was now seeing.

My mom the superspy? Nope.

He exchanged a glance with Bishop and then nodded, signaling that he would continue to bring up the rear. A moment later, he was charging up the stairs behind the others. The well-worn concrete steps zig-zagged back and forth, rising without any exits. Finally, after at least two or three stories worth of ascent, they came to a landing. Peter already had the door open.

The area beyond was cluttered with boxes and pallets, but unlike the basement storeroom, here there were windows through which afternoon light streamed in. That was not the only difference however. As they emerged from the stairwell, several heads turned in their direction. The men, laborers by the look of them, looked up from their activities and regarded them with a mixture of curiosity and confusion. Peter seemed at last to have found his bearings. He ignored the workers and led the group away from the windows, toward a pair of double doors that let out into a brightly lit service corridor. He opened the first door they came to and led them through the cluttered backroom of a retail establishment. A young woman, wearing a blue apron embroidered with a cartoon image, was sitting at a table with a mug of some hot beverage. She looked up in surprise as they passed through. A moment later, they emerged onto the sales floor of an enormous toy store.

"This is Detsky Mir," Bishop exclaimed.

"It was," Peter said. "They had to change the name when they reopened last year."

King mentally translated the name—Children's World—and made the connection. While not widely known in the Western world, Detsky Mir was nearly legendary in Eastern Europe. Built in the 1950s, it was an enormous mall filled with shops selling almost anything a child could want—toys, candy, clothing—in a fantasy-themed setting. It was several stories high with a façade of tall arches. The signs out front identified it simply as 'Central Children's Store.' He had only been vaguely aware of the building when they had arrived at Lubyanskaya Square. His focus had been on the FSB building across the street.

"A secret passage connecting KGB headquarters to a toy store," King mused. "It makes sense in a disturbing kind of way."

"We'll blend in with the crowd," Peter said without stopping. "Make our way to the Metro."

Blending in was easier said than done, particularly for King and Bishop who still bore the soot and dust of the explosion in the under-ground passage, but Peter was not wrong about the crowd. They emerged onto a balcony overlooking an expansive atrium bustling with activity. On the floor below, children frolicked in elaborate playsets that resembled fairytale castles. For the older kids, there were science-fiction environments from popular American films. In contrast to the playful innocence of the setting, the interior façades seemed almost intentionally ostentatious—like the lobby of a gentrified luxury hotel. An ornate glass ceiling rose overhead, and at the far end of the atrium, five stories above the ground floor, were the exposed gears of the biggest mechanical clock King had ever seen. A suitably large pendulum, polished to a mirror sheen, hung down from the clock, sweeping lazily back and forth above the swirling human sea.

Suddenly, a dark spot, like a drop of ink creeping across a page, appeared at the edge of the crowd, just below the pendulum. Men in black coats were pouring into the atrium.

Peter gripped King's shoulder, commanding his full attention. "Jack. Get your mother to safety."

Before King could respond, or even process the statement, Peter turned and ran back into the store. "Wait..."

Another hand held him back. It was Lynn. Some of the excitement had ebbed from her face, replaced by a more appropriate anxiety. "He's right, Jack. If we stay together, they'll catch all of us."

King gaped at her a moment, then turned to his sister. "Stay with him."

Bishop needed no further prompting. She was running after Peter before King had even finished the sentence. "Meet us in Yekaterinburg!" he added, but Bishop was already gone.

SEVENTEEN

The Ural Mountains, Russia

"In the words of the late lamented Yogi Berra," Rook said, as he stared through the binoculars at the blank white landscape, "'It's déjà vu all over again.'" He gave a heavy sigh. "I am so fucking done with snow."

Beside him, Queen said, or rather sang in an exaggerated falsetto, "Do you want to build a snowman?"

"I'm turning into a snowman," he said. "I've even got testicicles."

"You've been waiting all day to say that, haven't you?"

"It's like you're in my head," he said, ruefully.

He had actually come up with the joke during their misadventure in the Arctic Circle, but the battery-operated heaters in the custom-made winter combat suits they had worn on that outing had ruined the joke by keeping all his parts toasty warm. Unfortunately, high-tech winter combat suits didn't quite jibe with their present cover as outdoorsy adventure tourists. Nor did FN-SCAR assault rifles or any of the other tactical gear they normally would have carried with them on an op. Commercially available polypro thermal underwear and The

North Face parkas and bib overalls had kept the cold at bay—mostly, anyway—during the long ski trek to their initial objective, but now that they weren't moving, the chill was setting in.

"Let it go," Queen said. "Knight, you see anything?"

"A lot of potential snowmen," Knight replied from his perch two hundred yards away. His voice was astonishingly clear, without any of the distortion or background noise that often accompanied radio transmissions or even mobile phone calls. "Not much else."

"Roger. Blue, anything from your eye in the sky?"

Rook glanced up. It was a reflex action. There was little chance of spotting the lightweight micro-drone, which was not only about the size of a hummingbird but hovering high above in the darkening slate gray sky. The surveillance units, Aleman's own design, had a service ceiling of ten thousand feet, necessary since the drones relied on line-of sight radio signals, both for operational control and data relay. When combined with advanced miniaturized high-def digital optics, it was the perfect altitude for watching a potential battlefield. The built-in solar recharging system meant they could operate non-stop during daylight hours. But once night fell, battery-life would be more of a problem.

Deep Blue had four drone units at his disposal. It took nearly two hours for a drone to reach their current location from Ivdel, the last rural town of consequence, about eighty miles away. That meant each unit could only stay on station for about an hour before making the equally long return trip for a one-hour recharge period—not nearly long enough to bring the batteries back to capacity. That would be a problem the longer they were out in the open, but since their purpose was only reconnaissance, Rook doubted they would need Deep Blue looking out for them all night long.

"I like the term 'proto-snowmen.'" Deep Blue's reply came through as clearly as Knight's, even though he was stationed in his makeshift op center—*his warm op center*, Rook thought miserably—in a rented room in Ivdel. "Otherwise, it's a whole lot of nothing."

"Since we don't know what we're supposed to be looking for," Rook said, "how are we going to know when we see it?"

No one had an answer for him.

King's last order to them all had been to set up an observation post, conduct passive recon and wait for his arrival. That had been almost a full twenty-four hours ago, enough time for them to make their way from Yekaterinburg to Ivdel. That had been the last best place for Deep Blue to set up a command-and-control center from which to operate his micro-drones. The rest of them continued on as far as the unplowed roads and four-wheel drive would allow, after which they had broken out the cross-country skis and kept going. The ski trek fit nicely with their cover as globe-trotting adventure tourists, although it hardly mattered, since they had not seen another living soul since leaving Ivdel.

"I take it King is still maintaining radio-silence," Queen said.

"Unfortunately."

"Crap." She sighed. "It's going to be dark soon. Since we're not going anywhere, we should probably set up camp."

Rook let his head droop forward into the snow, but then pushed himself up. Queen was right about the approaching dusk. When the sun passed beyond the mountain ridge to the west, not only would they have to contend with darkness, but also plunging temperatures. Besides, a few hours of sleep, even in these miserable circumstances, would be welcome after the exhausting ordeal of skiing up the mountain passes, gaining almost a thousand vertical feet over the course of twenty miles.

"I took your advice," he said, as he clipped into his skis.

"That's new," Queen replied. "About what exactly?"

"I Googled this place."

"Russia?"

"Dead Mountain." Rook pointed to the distant peak jutting up from the ridge of the Urals to the northwest. "That's what Bish said the name translated to. Guess what I found out?"

"You found out that 'dead mountain' is a very literal interpretation and that a more accurate translation for Kholat Syakhl would be 'place with no game.'"

"No. Well, yes, I did find that, but that's not what I'm talking about."

"He means the Dyatlov Pass incident," Deep Blue said.

Rook had nearly forgotten about the open line to their handler. "Way to steal my thunder, Comrade Buttinsky. But yes, that's what I found." He debated whether or not to continue relating the strange but true story of the nine hikers who had died mysteriously, not far from the very spot where they now stood.

In 1959, a group of Russian hikers, mostly college students, led by young Igor Dyatlov, set out on an expedition into the Ural Mountains. When they failed to show up at their destination two weeks later, a massive search effort was launched and eventually located the lost hikers' frozen remains. Instead of resolving the mystery of their disappearance, though, the grisly discovery only led to more unanswerable questions.

The tent in which the nine hikers had been camping had been torn open from within, as if the victims were trying to escape from something inside the tent with them. Despite frigid winter conditions, several of the bodies were barefoot or in only socks and underwear, as if there had not even been time to get dressed. Although the bodies showed no outward signs of injury, two of the victims had fractured skulls and broken bones. One was missing her tongue, as if it had been torn out of her head. Some reports, impossible to verify or deny, said that the bodies were highly radioactive. The bizarre details of the incident had led to many outlandish theories, ranging from military-experiments-run-amok to an encounter with space aliens. The response of the Soviet government had only made matters worse. The investigation was shrouded in secrecy. Travel in the area around Kholat Syakhl had been prohibited for three years following the incident. It was as if the government was trying to cover something up, and the official finding of the investigation was that the deaths had been caused by an 'unknown compelling force.'

"So?" Queen said. "After everything you've seen—and I might add, survived—you're worried about an old ghost story?"

"Unknown. Compelling. Force." Rook enunciated each word succinctly in hopes of conveying just how freaky they sounded when put together. "You can't shoot a 'force.'"

"There's a perfectly rational explanation for everything that happened," Deep Blue said. "An avalanche may not be as sexy as UFOs or Abominable Snowmen, but it's much more plausible. The hikers heard the avalanche coming and freaked out, ripped open their tent, ran out into the snow half-naked, and then froze to death."

Rook shook his head. "Spoken like a true nay-sayer. How do you explain the broken bones with no external trauma, or the high levels of radiation on the clothes and bodies of the victims?"

"I'd be more concerned if it hadn't been over fifty years since the incident," Queen said. "The *only* incident, I might add."

"Are you sure about that? Maybe that's what happened to the other guys. Our replacements. Maybe the JV Chess Team also ran into an unknown compelling force."

"When did you become such a pussy?"

"Frankly I think an avalanche is something we *should* be worried about," Knight said, jumping in after a long silence. "We've got mountains on both sides. Nowhere to go if there's a slide."

"You think maybe that's what happened to them?" Queen asked. "The JV team?"

"It's a possibility."

"There's a stand of trees about a klick north of your present location," Deep Blue said. "That would give you better shelter from the wind and some protection... That's weird."

"Not what we wanted to hear from you right now," Rook said.

"What have you got, Blue?" Queen asked.

"Uh, well, I'm not sure. There's something weird about those trees."

"Okay, 'weird' is not really painting a very clear picture."

"There's fog rising from the trees," Deep Blue said, still sounding uncertain. "A lot of it. Almost like a steam plume."

"I can see it from here," Knight said.

"The trees could have trapped heat," Deep Blue suggested. "Now that the temperature is dropping, it could be creating a temperature inversion."

"We'll check it out," Queen said. "Knight, hold where you are. We'll link up with you there."

By the time they reached Knight's position, the vapor cloud had grown to near epic proportions, towering above the frozen landscape like some Biblical pillar of smoke. Knight stood with his back to them, staring at the spectacle. The treetops were just barely visible underneath the plume.

"That doesn't look like a temperature inversion," Rook said, leaning on his ski poles.

"No, it doesn't," Queen admitted. "Looks more like a steam discharge from the cooling tower of a nuclear power plant. Those trees could be camouflage to hide exhaust vents and air exchangers for an underground base."

Rook had been thinking along the same lines. "I guess that means camping in the woods is out."

"King told us to recon. For now, that means we watch from a distance. We'll set up a concealed OP."

Rook cast a skeptical eye about their surroundings. "Concealed?"

"I think she means we're going to build an igloo," Knight said.

Rook rolled his eyes. "Great. Where's Nanook of the North when we need him?"

"You could be Nan-Rook."

"Funny."

"I've got movement in the trees," Deep Blue cut in.

All eyes swung in the direction of the cloud column. Rook used his teeth to pull off his heavy ski-mittens, revealing the knit glove liners he wore underneath—warm enough to keep his fingers from freezing, but thin enough to fit in a trigger guard. Then he reached inside his jacket to find the comforting grips of his Desert Eagle pistols. Knight reacted just as quickly, unslinging the old Mosin-Nagant P91-30 rifle he had acquired before leaving Ivdel.

Smuggling in handguns was no great trick, but getting a rifle past customs would have been impossible. Before leaving for Moscow, Bishop had made contact with an arms dealer she trusted, but they had left Yekaterinburg before the requested weapons package had arrived. Since they were only doing recon and posing as tourists, they had figured the pistols were protection enough, but an old grizzled hunting guide they had met before leaving the small town had strongly suggested they take along some real firepower. The Mosin-Nagant looked like it belonged in a museum—and perhaps it had been stolen from one—but the old hunter who claimed to have used it to kill Nazis in the Great Patriotic War, had done a decent job of maintaining it. "You will need it if you run into wolves," he had told them, before charging them a black market premium. "Or something else."

Wolves were pretty low on Rook's list of concerns. It was the 'something else' that worried him

"Talk to me, Blue," Queen said. "What do you see?"

"Not sure. The mist is freezing over. Visibility is nil."

"I see them," Knight said. "Unfortunately, I think they see us, too."

"Them?" Queen raised her binoculars and peered in the direction Knight was staring. "Holy shit. What the hell are those things?"

Rook drew his pistols and pointed them in the direction of the whiteout. He could just make out a few dark specks, silhouetted against the wall of icy mist, definitely moving toward them.

"Put 'em away," Queen said, lowering the field glasses. "We're getting out of here."

"What do you see?" Rook growled. "Do we need to have another talk about sharing?"

"Trust me." She handed him the binoculars, as he holstered a pistol. "Those won't do us any good."

He pressed the lenses to his eyes and peered at the approaching shapes.

They were not men, although they were upright and bipedal. They were also not wolves, although they were covered in shaggy black fur, which made them easy to spot against the brutally white landscape. What they actually were, however, was harder to say. Rook thought they might be bears, but the body shape was wrong. Bears had long torsos and short legs, which made them top heavy, giving them a shambling gait when walking on their back legs. These things were hunched over, staying low to the ground, but running. Fast. They seemed almost to float across the snow.

Bears were also territorial creatures, rarely traveling in groups larger than two or three, and even then, usually a mother with her cubs. There were considerably more of the shaggy man-shapes headed their way. Rook stopped counting at twenty. There were at least three dozen of them.

He understood now why Queen had said what she had. While he had no doubt that a fifty-caliber Magnum round from his Desert Eagle would put any one of the advancing beasts down permanently, he didn't have enough bullets to take them all.

EIGHTEEN

Moscow

Bishop caught up to her father just as he was about to duck into the storeroom at the rear of the toy shop. "*Batya!*" Dad!

Peter glanced over his shoulder and shook his head brusquely. He didn't stop, but as she drew alongside him, he said. "Stay with your mother."

"King will keep her safe," she said, confidently. "I'm with you." Then, as if it was an afterthought, she added, "So, you have a plan, right?"

He uttered a short sharp laugh. "Keep moving. Don't let them catch us." He led the way back to the service corridor and into the stairwell.

"Up or down?" she asked.

Peter's answer was to veer toward the descending stairs, but then he halted so abruptly that Bishop had to throw herself against the wall to avoid colliding with him. She slipped and would have tumbled down the steps but for Peter's restraining hand. As she righted herself, she saw why he had stopped. Several men, probably those who had pursued them through the underground passages, were ascending the stairway below.

She made a furtive grab for the pocket where she had stowed the Makarov King had given her earlier, but then Peter hauled her back and spun her around so that she was facing away from the men.

"Up," he shouted. "Go!"

She went, rounding the corner on the landing and then leaping up the next flight of stairs three at a time, until the exertion began to burn in her muscles. As she reached the next landing, she glanced back and saw her father, right behind her, pointing ahead urgently.

Keep going.

It felt like the wrong choice, like they were postponing a confrontation rather than averting it. They would eventually run out of steps to climb, and then they would have to somehow make their way back down. By that time all the exits from Detsky Mir would be blocked. She told herself to trust her father, but that was easier said than done. After all, everything she had grown up believing about him was a lie.

"Get off... Next floor," Peter called out, the words coming in gasps between breaths. It was a reminder that while he possessed the skills and instincts of a world class intelligence operative, he was a bit past his prime.

When she reached the next landing, Asya headed through the unmarked door and found herself in yet another non-descript corridor. Peter passed her by, turning right down the hallway. He took the first door he came to, not a storeroom this time, but an office occupied by more than a dozen people. Most of them did not even look up from their labors to acknowledge the odd pair running through their midst.

They emerged onto another balcony overlooking the atrium, which was now four stories below. The crowded floor looked more like a mosaic picture than a collection of people. She couldn't make out any details or distinguish the hunters from the innocent bystanders, and she wondered if King and Lynn had already made their escape.

Peter did not give her more than a moment to look. He ran along the balcony, ignoring the looks of astonishment from the handful of people who were enjoying the relative solitude of the upper reaches of the department store. Behind them, men in black coats were spilling out of the office they had just exited. She sprinted ahead to catch up to Peter. From the corner of her eye, she could see that at least some of the men chasing them had broken off and headed out along the opposite side of the balcony to cut them off.

The noose was tightening, and there seemed to be nowhere to go.

She looked ahead, trying to locate another stairwell or elevator to the lobby...anything that might give her a hint as to where they were going. But she saw only storefronts and cafes. Peter did not appear to be interested in any of them. Instead of skirting the outside edge, he was staying close to the rail overlooking the atrium floor. As he rounded the corner, she could see that his gaze was fixed on something out beyond the rail.

The clock pendulum.

The impressive Raketa Monumental Clock was one of the largest mechanical clocks in the world, rivaling even London's Big Ben. It was a recent addition, not present in her childhood memories of the Detsky Mir building. As she stared at the exposed clockwork mechanism, protruding from the balcony one story above them, and the pendulum hanging down halfway to the floor, she realized what Peter intended.

My father is crazy.

Peter clambered up onto the rail, crouching like a stone gargoyle on a castle battlement. He paused there for a moment, breathing rapidly. Perspiration was beading on his forehead, but despite the frantic level of exertion, when he turned his head to look at her, he seemed preternaturally calm.

"You can do this," he said, and then, as the pendulum swung his way, he leapt out into space.

He caught the vertical support to which the enormous reflective lozenge-shaped pendulum hung, and then he immediately slid down like a fireman on a brass pole. His feet hit the top of the pendulum disc. Then with a nimbleness that astonished Bishop, he leapt from the disc to catch hold of the rail on the second floor balcony. He glanced back up at her, shouted: "Come on!" and then he let go, dropping down onto a decorative façade above the main entrance.

Don't think, she told herself. *Just do!*

She vaulted onto the rail and waited for the pendulum to swing back. She felt a brief wave of vertigo as the atrium floor yawned up at her, but she kept her focus on the support lines, which were easily close enough for her to make the same leap Peter had.

She jumped, throwing her arms wide and wrapping them around the support, hugging it close, as gravity started pulling her down. She felt her feet strike the disc, and she pushed off, bounding over to the balcony and ricocheting to the façade, where Peter waited. He had made it look so easy that she was moving before she could even contemplate the consequences of failure, and just like that, they were both dropping into the astonished crowd on the atrium floor.

The maneuver had caught their pursuers completely off-guard, but she could hear someone shouting for the crowd to disperse. Bishop knew that not all of the hunters were on the balcony high above. Peter seized her hand and together they bulldozed through the entrance and out onto the street.

They threaded their way through the cluster of people entering, leaving or simply passing by, and headed for the street and the towering Lubyanka building. It seemed to Bishop like the last place they should be going, but her father had successfully gotten them out of the toy store. There was no cause to stop trusting him now.

"Metro station," he said, still a little out of breath. "Don't stop for anything."

Then he was running again, dodging traffic on the edge of Lubyanskaya Square. She spotted the subway entrance, surrounded by a low half-wall. Then she saw an imposing figure in a dark greatcoat, rising up from the steps, eyes locked on Peter.

Instead of slowing or trying to dodge, Peter ran headlong at the man. He deftly avoided an attempt to sweep him up in a bear hug. As the man's arms closed on nothing, Peter sidestepped, pulling the man further off balance to send him sprawling on the street. Bishop leapt over the dazed man and then followed Peter down the stairs.

The subway entrance brought another rush of memories. Everything looked almost exactly as she remembered, from the white tiled walls to the air, warmed by bodies and smelling faintly of grease. Yet she knew it was not the same. In 2010, suicide bombers had targeted the Lubyanka and Park Kultury Stations. Forty people had been killed, and more than a hundred were injured. Bishop had been living in Murmansk then, but the brutal terrorist attack had nevertheless felt like a personal assault.

They pushed through the crowd, earning more than a few contemptuous looks, descending to the tunnel that led to one of two central vestibules located under Lubyanskaya Square. Peter slowed to a jog, like someone hurrying to catch a train. If he was trying to be less conspicuous, the effect was spoiled when he clambered over the ticket gate without pausing to scan his pass card. Bishop felt like all eyes were on her as she followed suit, but a few seconds later they were on the escalators, descending deeper into the station.

She scanned the faces around her, looking for FSB agents or policeman in the crowd, but she saw only indifferent commuters, unaware of the chaos that had unfolded behind them. That would change soon enough, she knew, but for the moment, blending in offered greater protection than speed. Once on the platform however, Peter resumed his frantic pace.

They descended another flight of stairs to a platform clogged with bodies, jostling their way through. Then they moved toward the end of the loading area, as if intent on boarding the last car in the next train to pull into the station.

Bishop worked the timetables in her head. A crowded platform meant a train would probably arrive any moment. If they boarded it, they would be away from Lubyanskaya in a matter of minutes, but if the pursuers guessed or even suspected what they had done, they might be able to send ahead to the next station. Instead of providing salvation, the Metro might very well deliver them into the hands of their enemies.

She was still pondering that when Peter did something that, given everything else he had done, should not have surprised her. He jumped down onto the track bed and ran into the train tunnel.

Of course he did, Bishop thought, and she leapt down after him.

It was a reckless move, even for the man who had jumped from a fourth story balcony onto a clock pendulum. Dozens of people had surely witnessed their actions. If the hunters did not already know about it, they soon would. Moreover, instead of a quick train ride to the next stop, they would now have to traverse the length of several city blocks to the next station down the line—in the dark no less. How long would that take? Ten minutes? If they didn't electrocute themselves on the third rail or get pulverized by a speeding subway train, they would almost certainly be greeted by an armed reception committee.

From the frying pan to the fire, she thought, as the light from the station shrank behind her. A smaller cone of light appeared ahead of her, Peter shining his penlight on the tracks. She quickened her pace to catch up to him.

"You know what you are doing, I hope."

"Of course I do," he replied confidently. "Always have a plan. It's the only way to stay alive."

"Just like my brother. Your idea of a plan and mine are not the same, I think." She felt a gust of wind on her face and a faint tremor rising up from the track bed. "A train is coming."

"I know." This time, there was a hint of concern in his tone. "Hurry."

She felt like screaming. *Hurry toward it?* But then Peter's light swung to the side, illuminating a shallow alcove in the tunnel wall thirty feet ahead of them.

A faint glow arose from further down the tunnel, growing brighter with each passing second. The tunnel filled with the shrieking tumult of wheels on rails, which seemed to be approaching faster than Bishop would have believed. Peter lowered his penlight again, shining it on the track bed, revealing the path they would have to negotiate. Then they were both making a mad dash for the recess.

Even though they reached it with several seconds to spare, Bishop felt compelled to press herself tightly against the wall. She felt the wind shift, as if the train was trying to drag her into its slipstream. Then it was gone, plunging them into relative dark and quiet.

As she pushed away from the wall, she saw Peter's face, faintly lit by the penlight, which he now had clenched between his teeth. He was kneeling beside her, the light shining on his hands and the lock he was endeavoring to pick. He smiled around the light as the lock yielded, and then opened the door.

What lay beyond did not immediately fill her with hope. It was little more than an electrical room—disused, judging by the dust and grease that coated the meters and gauges mounted to the wall. Peter, however, marched inside like the room contained the lost jewels of the Romanov dynasty.

"Close the door," he said, when she was inside. "We don't want anyone to know we came this way, though I suppose they'll figure it out quick enough."

"And we are just going to hide in this closet?"

"Sort of," he said. He ran his fingers along the top of the electrical panel. There was a faint click, and then the entire panel swung away on concealed hinges to reveal a passage, or more precisely, a stairway that descended into total darkness. "But not this one."

"How...? Never mind."

"This leads to Metro Two," Peter explained. "A secret subway line built by Stalin, connecting Lubyanka to the Kremlin and other key locations around the city."

"I've heard of it. I thought it was just a rumor."

"It might as well be. The line hasn't been used in decades, and from what I've heard, many of the tunnels are flooded. Getting through won't be easy, but at least they won't be waiting for us when we emerge."

Bishop nodded slowly. She felt a little embarrassed for having doubted him, but she was grateful that, for the moment at least, they no longer had to run for their lives—at least in the literal sense. "It would have been nice to know your B Plan ahead of time. What happens next?"

Peter considered the question for a moment. "It's time I met with Vladimir, face to face."

"What if he's responsible for the trap?"

"All the more reason. If he is part of this, then he will know the truth about what happened to your sister."

"What about King and mother?"

"I wouldn't worry about them." He gave her shoulder a squeeze. "King is in good hands. Your mother was always the better spy."

NINETEEN

You shouldn't have done that," Lynn said with a disapproving scowl, as Bishop vanished into the toy shop in pursuit of Peter. "Your father was right. We need to split up. One person alone is harder to catch than two moving together."

"He also said to keep you safe," King said in an equally sharp tone. "I didn't bring you here just to lose you. Maybe if we had talked about this a little beforehand, we could have worked out our contingency plans."

She wrinkled her nose, as if trying to decide whether or not to lecture him. "We have to focus on our own survival now. Come along."

She turned away, walking briskly along the balcony, heading in the direction of a nearby escalator. He caught up to her. "Are we going out the front door?"

"Those men went after your father first. They knew exactly where he would be."

"Friend Vladimir sold us out."

"So it would appear," Lynn said. "But my point is that they weren't looking for the rest of us. Vladimir didn't know your father wasn't traveling alone."

King thought back to the fight in the archive office. Had any of the FSB officers seen their faces? Had any even survived? It was a slim advantage, and one that wouldn't last long. Eventually, the police would check the hotel or review Peter's travel itinerary. They would discover that he had been accompanied by his family.

Even though they each had used bogus passports and aliases, their photographs would soon be circulated among the hunters. Still, while they had their anonymity, blending in with the crowd was the best course of action.

"So he already suspected Vladimir might betray him?"

Lynn shook her head. "No. It was merely a precaution. Healthy paranoia is what keeps a spy alive. I still have trouble believing that Vladimir would turn on us now, after all these years of protecting us."

They stepped onto the descending escalator and started down to the floor of the atrium. "Why was he helping you? What's your connection to him?"

"Honestly, I don't know. He made contact with us when we were already in our assignment. I don't even know who he really is. We never met face to face, at least not that I know of. His interest in us always seemed personal, not political. I cannot imagine what would change that."

What had changed was that the Machtchenkos were now looking into the circumstances of Julie's accident, but King did not voice that observation. "Maybe he slipped up."

"Yes," she said, and then she fell silent as they passed by two men in black coats, who were riding the ascending escalator just a few feet away. King managed a surreptitious glance in their direction and saw no indication that the pair had noticed them. There were more men circulating on the floor and scanning the crowd, but even when their eyes alit upon King and Lynn, he saw no hint of recognition. King wondered if Peter and Bishop were having similar success. Then he pushed the seed of worry out of his head. His mother had been right about the importance of focus.

As they crossed the floor of the atrium, Lynn set a slightly more determined pace, like someone eager to get home after a long day of shopping. They passed within six feet of one of the FSB men, but his roving eyes did not linger on them. They moved beneath the enormous swinging clock pendulum and into the entrance foyer.

A few seconds later, they were outside in the bitter cold, moving with the flow of pedestrian traffic along the edge of Lubyanskaya Square. Directly across the street was the FSB headquarters building, and right in front of it was one of the many entrances to the Lubyanka Metro station. Lynn caught King's eye and gave a subtle nod in the direction of the subway stairs. He returned the nod, and they eased into a group of people waiting to cross the street.

A low murmur signaled some kind of disturbance arising from behind them. King's first impulse was to feign indifference, but he immediately realized that doing so would be rather conspicuous. Everyone else was turning to look, so he did too.

The crowd parted, and he saw Peter and Bishop just a few steps behind, sprinting away from the entrance to the department store. They were pursued by several figures in dark coats. The fleeing pair—his father and his sister—bolted out into the street, dodging cars that swerved and skidded and honked in protest. They headed for the same subway stairs that King and Lynn had been approaching. Before King could even contemplate a reaction, he felt Lynn's hand grip his forearm, cautioning him to stay where he was.

He knew she was right. If he tried to interfere with the pursuit, he would accomplish nothing more than attracting notice, which he and Lynn had managed to avoid so far. But standing by and doing nothing while his loved ones were in danger was the worst kind of torture imaginable.

Dad knows what he's doing, he told himself. *Bishop is a pro. They'll get away.*

But what if they don't?

I won't leave them behind.

Across the street, a figure emerged from the Metro entrance to intercept the runners, but Peter evaded the man's grasping arms and used what looked like a judo move to send the man sprawling into the street.

King's view of the fight was abruptly eclipsed by the arrival of a trio of police cars with lights flashing and sirens blaring. They were accompanied by an unmarked black Lada Vesta SUV. The vehicles skidded to a stop on the wet pavement, blocking the way to the Metro entrance in front of the Lubyanka building.

Doors flew open and uniformed men and women emerged from the cars and immediately began establishing a secure perimeter.

That's it, he thought. Peter and Bishop were on their own. There was no way to help them now. *I hope they—*

"Julie?"

Lynn's shout completely derailed King's train of thought. Cold dread slammed into him like an avalanche.

Mom, no!

It was too late. Lynn had let go of his arm and was already in the street. She moved like someone half-caught in a dream, shambling toward the dark-haired woman who had just climbed out of the Lada.

"Julie? It's you, isn't it?"

The figure turned hesitantly to face Lynn, and King now saw what had prompted his mother's rash behavior.

When he had seen that face on a television screen all those months ago, the rational part of his brain had been able to dismiss it as a fluke. Everyone had a look-alike. Perhaps the camera and his eyes were conspiring to trick him. Maybe it was just wishful thinking.

But as he beheld the woman staring back at Lynn with an odd mixture of curiosity and contempt, he knew none of that was true. Moreover, he knew why Lynn—his sensible, pragmatic to a fault and totally-in-control mother—had just completely abandoned caution and good sense.

Now he knew for sure.

The woman standing twenty feet away was Julie Sigler.

Without even realizing it, he drifted away from the crowd, moving to Lynn's side. Julie's eyes lingered on Lynn's face for a moment, then shifted to meet his stare.

Her eyes widened in an unmistakable look of recognition.

"It is you," he whispered. "Julie."

He saw her lips move, forming a single word that she did not speak aloud.

'Siggy?' Is that what she said?

"Julie it's me. Jack. And mom."

She continued to stare at him, recognition becoming certainty, and then...triumph. Her mouth opened again, and this time she spoke clearly, in Russian and loud enough for everyone to hear. "Take them."

As men swarmed over him, tackling him to the ground, he realized what she had said. Not Siggy, but another name. A name by which Julie had never known him.

King.

TWENTY

Ural Mountains, Russia

"Do you know what those are?" Rook said, without lowering the binoculars.

"Nope," Queen said. She pivoted her skis around so that she was facing the other way. "And I'm not that interested in finding out."

"Yetis. Abominable Snowmen."

She had expected him to say something like that. Yetis, as far as she knew, were strictly a Himalayan thing, but every region seemed to have its own variation on the theme of a large undiscovered primate. In the Pacific Northwest it was Sasquatch, AKA Bigfoot. Floridians believed that a creature called the Skunk Ape roamed the Everglades.

In Arizona, it was called the Mogollon Beast. She did not doubt those stories. Strange creatures—missing links, evolutionary holdovers that weren't quite as extinct as scientists believed—did exist. She had seen it with her own eyes, with an isolated population of Neanderthals and Neanderthal-Human hybrids living in the Annamite Mountains of Vietnam.

She didn't know if these things were Neanderthals or something else, and given the circumstances, answering that particular question was not that high on her list of priorities.

"Doesn't matter. Move out. That's an order."

She planted her ski poles in the snow and pushed off, using the skating technique of pushing the skis away at an angle with each step forward, until she had built up enough momentum to coast down the slope. She glanced back to make sure that Knight and Rook were both moving, then focused on staying upright. Skiing off-piste—on ungroomed, untrammeled snow—was challenging under the best of circumstances. Despite its uniform color, there were all kinds of snow, ranging from treacherously slick ice to sticky dry powder. Sometimes deep drifts hid obstacles that could stop a skier dead in their tracks—sometimes, literally. But the way ahead looked clear, the descending gradient steep enough that she could tuck in and glide.

The journey in had been mostly uphill, which meant gravity was now on their side, doubling or maybe even tripling the rate of travel for the return trip. There was no knowing if that would be fast enough to outrun the massive pack of—

Yetis. Shit.

—creatures though, just as there was no way of knowing how far the creatures would go. Wolves were known to stalk their prey for days at a time.

But these creatures weren't wolves. They were...

"Watchdogs," she said, thinking aloud.

"What's that?" Rook asked.

She risked a quick glance back but saw only dark spots against the snow. *Closer? Hard to say.* "Later. Blue, please tell me we're outrunning those things."

"Not exactly," Deep Blue admitted. "They're moving a lot faster than I would have—oh, crap!"

"Blue?"

"They're sledding." There was no mistaking the incredulity in his tone. "Like penguins sliding across the ice."

"Damn," Rook said. "So they're smart, too. You know how this is going to end."

Queen did know. If they couldn't outpace the creatures, they would have to make a stand. She had brought along a compact SIG Sauer P228, with three full magazines. Knight had one too, along with his antique rifle. Rook had 'the girls,' but handguns wouldn't be effective until they let the things get a lot closer. And they would have to stop moving to shoot.

The slope bottomed out, quickly stealing away the momentum she had built up. To the right lay the flank of a steeper incline than the one they'd just come down. Ahead and to the left, the snowfield undulated gently, like sand dunes on a beach. She double-poled, skating furiously to maintain forward progress and reach the next decline. But in her mind's eye, she could see the creatures glissading down the slope, like drops of water sliding down a window pane.

"Screw this," she said. "Let's see them try that going uphill."

She turned right, still skating hard as she angled toward the slope. It now rose up in front of her like an insurmountable blank wall.

"Uh, Queen, they'll be on you in seconds."

Deep Blue was not wrong. "I'll try to slow them down," Rook said. "You and Knight get to higher ground. Maybe he can put that relic to good use."

It was a desperate plan, the chances of success no better now than when they had first spotted the incoming yeti wave, but it was increasingly looking like they would have little choice.

"Do it, Knight," Queen said. "I won't be any good at long range."

She expected some kind of chivalrous protest from Rook, but it was Deep Blue that challenged the order. "Shooting anything is a bad idea," he said. "The noise could bring an avalanche down."

"That's a myth," Knight said. An accomplished mountaineer and extreme skier, Knight knew what he was talking about. "Sound waves are too diffuse to break the ice holding a snowpack."

"Avalanche!" If Queen's hands had not been gripping the ski poles, she might have smacked her forehead. "That's exactly what we need."

She stabbed her poles deep and pivoted, digging the edges of her skis in for an abrupt stop, and hastily turned to face the yetis. They were still more than fifty yards away, too distant for her to see them as much more than shaggy black forms. They were throwing up clouds of loose snow as they bounded across the flats. She couldn't begin to estimate their numbers, but half-a-dozen were visible at the leading edge of the wave. Queen drew her pistol but she did not aim at the yetis. Instead, she pointed it at a spot high up on the slope looming above them. Then she started firing.

The reports echoed together into a sound like a long peal of thunder in the mountain pass, but her shots seemed to accomplish little else. The bullets vanished into the snow without any visible effect. Knight and Rook both grasped what she was attempting and added their own firepower to the effort. The combined noise of the different weapons echoing back from the mountainside was momentarily deafening.

Beside her, Knight was furiously working the bolt and shifting his aim a few degrees after each trigger pull, stitching an invisible horizontal line across the slope. Five shots in less than as many seconds. He ejected the spent magazine without lowering the weapon, and started firing again.

Rook was keeping up a constant rate of fire as well, but only half of his shots were directed at the slope. He was firing his left-hand pistol up without looking, but the one in his right fist was aimed directly into the advancing horde. The big pistols boomed like a cannon with each shot, the recoil shaking his entire body. If not for the special customized wrist-braces he wore specifically for the purpose of absorbing the murderous kick, shooting one-handed would probably have broken his wrists. A hit almost anywhere on the body would be fatal to a human. Queen didn't know if that held true for Russian yetis, but Rook's precise fire was definitely having an effect. She could see crimson eruptions as the .50-cal Magnum rounds punched holes clear through the shaggy creatures.

Four down.

Five.

But he couldn't possibly hit them all.

She gave up trying to bring the mountainside down and shifted her aim to meet the charge.

Twenty yards now, and even through the haze of disturbed snow, she could see how huge the creatures truly were. They were as big as Kodiak grizzly bears. Their black fur was matted with snow, giving them a mottled appearance, but their snarling simian faces were hairless, more like a chimpanzee than a gorilla.

More like a human than a chimpanzee.

She aimed at the nearest fanged visage and fired. The primate's head snapped back, and the creature went down in a flurry of limbs and snow. She shifted to the next, now just ten yards away, but before she could pull the trigger, one of Rook's rounds blew the side of its face off.

"It worked!" Knight's shout was barely audible over the din of the battle, but almost as soon as he said it, Queen felt a tremor rising up from the snowpack. "We should be going!"

From the corner of her eye, she could see an enormous cloud of snow rolling down the hillside. By design, they had fired at a point further up the pass, where they had been only a minute before. But as the avalanche gained momentum it also gained mass, spreading out in both directions. A rush of frigid air racing ahead of the cascading frozen wall underscored the urgency of the threat. If they didn't take Knight's advice, the slide would bury them along with the yetis, but if they tried to run, the creatures would be on them in an instant.

She squeezed off another shot, but only grazed her target. The creature stumbled but regained its stride, trailing a stream of blood as it closed within reach of her.

Hands—actual hands with fingers—swiped through the air, and would have caught her if she had not ducked under them, firing out the rest of the SIG's magazine point blank into its chest. The 9-millimeter rounds seemed to have about as much effect as poking the creature with her finger. It threw its head back and let out a strange hooting howl, then bared its fangs and lunged.

She thrust the empty pistol into the gaping jaws, driving the smoking barrel deep into its throat. The yeti flinched and thrashed, but its grasping hands caught her, holding her fast and squeezing. Just as suddenly, the creature collapsed against her. Her nostrils were filled with the smell of the thing, wet dog hair and body odor, stronger even than the sulfurous tang of burnt gunpowder. She could feel its weight, crushing against her.

Then, darkness crashed down on her, and she felt nothing at all.

TWENTY-ONE

Moscow

King never quite lost consciousness, but when his tormentors ratcheted handcuffs around his wrists and drew a heavy burlap hood over his head, shutting out both light and fresh air, he stopped resisting. He willed himself into a relaxed, almost trance-like state. He had been in stickier spots than this, and he knew that sometimes the trick to surviving was to stop fighting and wait for an opportunity to present itself.

Once shackled and shrouded, his captors had bundled him into a vehicle. Judging by the syncopation of several different sirens, it was part of a convoy moving through the streets of Moscow without stopping for anything. He suspected they might be driving in circles, but after a while he gave up counting the turns.

Ultimately, the question of their destination was not as important as the fact that he had just seen his sister.

He was even more certain of that identification now. The woman was Julie. Every detail of her face, which bore all the familial characteristics, was just as he remembered. Even her eyes were that strange hue of light brown with flecks of orange that Julie had shared with him and Asya. The likeness was so perfect, and yet at the same time, so very troubling.

Julie was his older sister. Twenty years had passed since the accident, which might have been designed to cover an abduction. Yet this woman looked *exactly* the same as he remembered Julie. Faces changed over time. Even super-models who indulged in exotic beauty regimes and bathed in the blood of newborns to keep their skin elastic and young, did not look the same from one year to the next.

So it couldn't be Julie. *Could it?*

The convoy stopped and he was dragged out of the vehicle, carried bodily a short distance and then deposited in a hard chair. More shackles were added to his wrists and ankles, and then the hood was yanked from his head, along with a generous handful of his hair. Bright light stung his eyes, momentarily blinding him. He blinked through suddenly watery eyes until the world finally came into focus.

His mother was in the room with him, seated alongside him, likewise squinting against the relative brilliance of the overhead incandescent light bulb. Her hair was mussed but she looked otherwise unhurt. Evidently, their captors had determined that she wasn't threatening enough to warrant a pre-emptive tenderization.

If they only knew, King thought, recalling the cool efficiency with which she had dispatched the agents on the stairs leading to the Lubyanka basement. Yet, there was no trace of that deadly calm now. Lynn looked like someone who had just seen her entire world turned upside down.

Sensing his scrutiny, she turned toward him. "It was her, Jack. It was Julie."

He frowned, glancing around the room to see who else was present, but it appeared that they had been left alone. The austere room with cracked tile floors and crumbling plaster walls made King think of a seedy underworld doctor's office, where disgraced practitioners stitched up bullet wounds for mobsters. There was a battered wooden table in the room, and three ancient-looking but sturdy metal chairs—one empty, the other two occupied by himself and Lynn. He did not doubt that they were being observed through a peep-hole or hidden cameras, but aside from a single windowless door, the room was a featureless cube.

"Let's talk about it later," he said at length.

"You think I made a mistake, don't you?" She shook her head. "What else could I do? We came here to learn the truth, and there she was, right there in front of me. I couldn't just turn away."

"Yeah." He didn't know what else to say.

"She recognized you," Lynn continued. "You saw that, right?"

"Yeah." The importance of that finally hit home. Julie had recognized him, but not as her kid brother 'Siggy.' Then she had sicced her dogs on them both. The latter action was yet more definitive proof that Julie was working with the Russian government, evidently in a position of some authority. If Vladimir had betrayed them to the FSB or some other agency, it would have made sense for the agents to be on the lookout for Peter and Lynn, but Julie had been completely indifferent to Lynn.

She had known his callsign.

How?

"She recognized something all right."

As if on cue, the door opened and the subject of their discussion entered. She strode forward until she was standing directly in front of King. Then she crossed her arms imperiously over her chest and sank into the empty chair. The harsh light did nothing to dispel his earlier certainty.

"Julie?"

"I don't know who this 'Julie' is," she said, her voice oh so familiar, her English perfect, with no trace of an accent, Russian or otherwise. "My name is Catherine Alexander."

"Julie is my daughter," Lynn blurted. "*You* are my daughter, no matter what they've told you."

Julie, or Catherine rather, returned a cold smile. "You're mistaken." She turned back to King. "Why are you here?"

"You tell me," King said quickly, hoping to stifle any further outbursts from his mother. "Your goons were driving the car."

"Let's dispense with the macho posturing bullshit, okay? Why are you, Jack Sigler, callsign: King, field leader of the U.S. Special Forces Unit known as Chess Team, here, in Moscow?"

King did his best to maintain an indifferent expression, even though inwardly he was reeling from the revelations. How had she learned all that? Was there a mole in JSOC? No, that didn't add up. If there was a leak, then she already knew the answer to her question.

She came here to catch Peter. She wasn't expecting me at all, but she recognized me. What the hell?

"I could ask you the same thing," he replied at length. "You're American. What are *you* doing here?"

Catherine stared at him for several seconds then turned to Lynn. "I'm sure you've been trained in all the techniques to resist interrogation," she said. King couldn't tell to whom she was speaking, but he guessed the words were meant for him. "But it seems you've brought along a particularly vulnerable pressure point."

King decided to cooperate, or rather give the appearance of cooperating, not because of the threat, but because he sensed an opportunity to answer some questions of his own. "You're right," he said. "Let's skip the posturing. I'm here because I found... No, scratch that, I *destroyed* your little supply depot in Virginia." He stopped there, studying her reaction.

Whatever else she was, Catherine Alexander was not a trained interrogator. Her eyes went wide in disbelief. "You? You did that?"

"We know what you're planning," he went on. "But you know how it is. Politicians and bureaucrats live in a persistent state of denial. More proof." He shook his head. "If a Russian army supply base on American soil doesn't convince them that Russia is planning to invade the United States, I don't know what will."

Her reaction, or rather the lack of one, betrayed her again. "How did you find it?"

So it is true. Damn.

Before King could answer, the door opened again and a man strode in. With the hanging light between him and the new arrival, it took a moment for King to bring the man's face into focus. He saw immediately that the man was shorter than average, maybe five-foot-six, but powerfully built beneath his immaculately tailored suit. Catherine jumped up from her chair, surprised or alarmed. But instead of challenging the man, she shrank back several steps. The man ignored her, advancing until he was standing in front of King, almost exactly where Catherine had been a minute before. King looked up at the man's face, fleshy but with a blandly arrogant expression, framed by thinning hair that even the understated comb-over could not conceal. King started to laugh. The man standing in front of him was the President of the Russian Federation.

"If I'd known we were going to get the VIP treatment," he said, "I would have dressed better."

The President cocked his head sideways, as if only partially comprehending what King had just said, then he turned to Catherine and spoke in Russian. "I wanted to see him for myself."

"And you are satisfied now?" Catherine replied haltingly in the same tongue.

King feigned a confused expression, hoping that they might let something slip if they believed he couldn't understand what they were saying. Of course, if they knew who he was, then they probably also knew that he spoke Russian, but it was worth a shot.

"Yes," the Russian president said. "Take him to Volosgrad. He should be able to provide what Alexei needs."

Volosgrad?

Grad was a common Russian suffix, an abbreviated form of 'gorod,' which meant 'city.' Under the Soviet regime, St. Petersburg had been renamed Leningrad, literally the City of Lenin. But there was no city anywhere in Russia named Volosgrad. As far as King knew, Volos wasn't even a Russian name.

"Hey," he said. "You guys want to share? What's going on? We were talking about your little secret in Virginia."

Catherine's eyes flashed toward him for a moment, but then she spoke again in Russian. "He's right. We should find out how much he knows. And how he learned about it."

The Russian waved a dismissive hand. "That doesn't matter now. The only enemy that can stop us is time. Go to Volosgrad. We must have the Firebird."

"What about the spy?"

Lynn flinched ever so slightly, but the reaction did not go unnoticed. The Russian turned and stared at her, studying her face intently for several long seconds. Then, he turned back to Catherine. "I will deal with Peter Machtchenko."

TWENTY-TWO

The tunnels seemed to go on forever, endless miles of old brick and mildew. More than once, they were turned back by flooded passages, but Peter never lost his sense of direction. Bishop could do little more than follow along and hope that her father knew what he was doing. Whether it was his unerring navigational abilities or just plain luck, they eventually came to a narrow staircase, carved into the bedrock. It brought them up into a room cluttered with boxes and other forgotten detritus.

Peter touched a finger to his lips, then crept through the room to another staircase, this one a rickety wooden construct. He ascended it and then eased open the door at the top. "It's clear. Come on."

The door let out into a hallway in what looked like a rundown apartment building. "Where are we?"

"The entrance to Ramenki Forty-Three. One of them anyway. Stalin built an entire city underneath the university. A shelter in which he and senior party officials could survive the nuclear war that was certain to come." Peter chuckled softly. "Nothing fuels accomplishment like paranoia."

"How did you know about this entrance?"

"I read about it on an urbex website. Urban explorers. Bored college students have been exploring the old tunnels for years, looking for new places to party. This is one of the few entrances that doesn't just lead back to the main subway line. Even if they figure out that we made it into the Metro-Two network, they'll assume that we'll have to come back up in one of the Metro stations."

They emerged from the building on a mostly deserted residential street. A light dusting of snow was falling from the night sky, the chilly air making it powdery like ash. Bishop finally got her bearings when they reached Vernadskogo Prospekt, a main thoroughfare just to the south of Moscow State University.

Peter pointed to a brightly lit yellow sign half a block away, a pair of golden arches that resembled the letter 'M.' It was a universal symbol—like the red octagon of a stop sign—that meant the same thing in almost every country on Earth. "Big Mac?"

Bishop was incredulous. "You want to eat? What about King and mother?"

"We need to get off the street. Figure out our next move. Might as well do it over food and hot coffee."

The prospect of coffee won her over, and Bishop waited until they were seated in the brightly lit plastic environment of the restaurant, savoring their repast, to address the more pressing issue. "King told us to go to Yekaterinburg."

Peter chewed a French fry thoughtfully. "Yes. You should head there. If your mother and Jack made it out, that's where they'll go."

She heard the implicit message in the statement. Peter did not intend to accompany her. "You think they were captured?"

"No. I mean, anything is possible, but your mother is too canny to fall into a trap."

"Then why are you not coming with me?"

Peter picked up another fry but just held it between thumb and forefinger, as if he could not decide what to do with it. "I have to talk to Vladimir."

"The Vladimir who set you up?"

"That's what I need to find out. If he did, then that is something we will discuss at great length. If he did not, he may be in great danger. Either way, I need to know if he is an ally or an enemy."

"What difference does it make?"

"He knows all about us, Asya. About your mother and me. If he has betrayed us, he will never stop looking." He shrugged. "And there is the question of honor."

"You mean payback."

Peter smiled. "If you prefer."

"Then I will help you."

Peter shook his head. "No. You have your own mission. And I will be more effective by myself."

Bishop frowned. As much as she hated the idea of leaving him, everything he had said was true. He had escaped from the Lubyanka without any help from her. He'd navigated the passages of the underworld, where she would have been completely lost. She would just be a burden to him. And she did have a job to do. The team was waiting for her and King to arrive.

The team!

"I should call Deep Blue. King might have already made contact."

Peter considered this for a moment. "You have a secure line of communication with him?"

She took out her mobile phone and regarded it like it was a hand grenade. Acting on King's instructions, she had not brought along one of Deep Blue's fancy quantum communicators, a decision she now regretted. But there was no reason to believe the Russian intelligence service had her number. "I think so."

At a nod from Peter, she dialed Lewis Aleman's number. The call seemed to take forever to connect, but when it finally rang through, Deep Blue answered immediately. "Bishop. Is everything all right?"

She thought he sounded unusually anxious. "I think so. Have you heard from King?"

"He's not with you?"

"We were separated." She decided it was probably best not to go into details, just in case someone was eavesdropping.

"Things here have gotten a little...sticky. We could really use your help. If it's not already too late."

Bishop did not like the sound of that. She looked at Peter, frowned and then said, "I'll be there soon."

"Yesterday would be good."

She ended the call and turned again to her father. "They need me."

He nodded.

"You will come to Yekaterinburg when you are finished?" she pressed.

"If I can. Depending on what I find out from Vladimir, I might have to go dark again, at least for a while. But I will find a way to get a message to you first." He reached across the table and gripped her hand. "I'll be fine, Asya. I know what I'm doing."

TWENTY-THREE

Ural Mountains, Russia

"It worked," **Knight** shouted. In his left eye, in magnification mode, he could see a jagged line spreading across the slope, connecting the dots where his bullets had weakened the ice sheet. A low rumble heralded the onset of the avalanche. He lowered the rifle and turned to the others. "We should be going."

Even as he said it, he realized that it was already too late. The first wave of primate monsters—Russian yetis, or whatever they were—had already reached Queen and Rook. They wouldn't be able to break contact for even a moment. The avalanche was going to hit them along with the attacking horde of yetis, and there wasn't a thing he could do to stop it from happening.

But maybe he could survive it.

He twisted the toes of his ski boots, popping them out of the quick-release bindings, and then raised his rifle to help fend off the yeti attack. He figured he would have time for only one shot.

Rook was still on his feet, acquiring targets and firing like an automaton. Queen, however, was in trouble. One of the beasts had tackled her to the ground, and despite her best efforts to fight it off, she was badly overmatched by the hulking monster. Knight sighted on the back of the creature's head and fired, killing it instantly. The dead yeti slumped over Queen's diminutive form, pinning her down.

And then the avalanche was upon them.

The first thing Knight felt was the blast of wind driven ahead of the slide. Loose snow particles swarmed around him, creating a blinding whiteout that concealed the larger pieces of ice that he knew were coming next. As soon as he felt the cascading snow strike his legs, he leaned into it. He started moving his arms in a clawing motion, as if he might somehow climb to the top of the onrushing mass. In a way, that was exactly what he was trying to do. Even when the slide slammed into him with enough force to knock the wind out of him, sweeping him off his feet, he kept at it. The avalanche spun him around, but the constant swimming-motion kept him from being completely buried. After a few seconds of brutal punishment, the energy of the slide dissipated. He was left buried up to his waist in chunks of ice and clumped snow.

He immediately began digging at the snow around him, kicking his legs to loosen the snow's grip on him. After a few seconds, he was able to squirm out of the hole. He took a moment to catch his breath, and then another to take stock of his situation.

No injuries. He still had his pack and an unused SIG P228 in a shoulder holster under his jacket, but his skis and the rifle were gone, buried somewhere under the snow. The sacrifice of the skis had been unavoidable. If he had been wearing them when the avalanche hit, he would not have been able to stay mostly above the slide. He reached up to the side of his head and found the earpiece to his comm unit. It was askew under his polar fleece cap, but still in working order.

"This is Knight," he said, only now aware that his teeth were chattering. "Queen. Rook. You there?"

There was an answer but it was not from his teammates. "Knight," Deep Blue said. "Thank God."

"Blue, where are the others? Do you see them?"

"Negative. There was too much blowing snow when the avalanche hit. They must have been buried."

Knight stared out across the newly altered landscape, looking for anything that might mark their location. He saw a few dark spots—yeti limbs protruding from the snow—but there was no sign of Queen or Rook. Still, he did not give way to despair. Most avalanche victims didn't die from the initial impact. The real killer was suffocation. Rook and Queen were under there somewhere, and he had only a few minutes to find them.

"Backscatter!" Deep Blue said, the shout so loud in Knight's ear that he winced. "You can use backscatter vision to see through the snow."

Knight nodded and blinked slowly to activate the X-ray mode in his new artificial eye. The effect was unbelievably eerie. The snow vanished completely, making it seem that he was hovering in mid-air. Solid objects, which looked like three-dimensional shadows, were floating just below him, as if suspended in the ether. He saw skeletons—dozens of them—some still moving, struggling to get free of the invisible grave in which they had been prematurely interred. The resolution of the backscatter image wasn't fine enough to allow him to differentiate primate bone structure from human—but their size alone was indication enough. He kept looking, scanning back and forth as he headed toward the approximate location where he had last seen Rook and Queen.

He spotted a ski—probably one of his own—two or three feet below, but he did not attempt to retrieve it. A few steps further along, he saw two more skis close together, and then saw the skeletal shape still attached to them.

"I found Rook!"

He knelt above the shape and began digging furiously, scooping out snow by the armful until Rook's motionless form was finally revealed. As soon as his shivering face was uncovered, Rook's eyelids fluttered open. He looked up at Knight and managed to gasp a single word. "Queen?"

Knight continued removing snow. "Not yet."

"Find her."

"Two of us will have a better chance of doing that." He gripped Rook's arm and pulled him to a semi-upright position.

"I'm fine," Rook insisted. He shook free of Knight's grip and struggled to his feet.

That was good enough for Knight. He resumed sweeping the area with backscatter vision, immediately spotting one of Rook's pistols. The metal weapon was easily the most substantial thing he had seen since beginning the search. He tried to remember how close Rook had been to Queen before the avalanche. He began walking a spiral pattern away from the place where he had found Rook.

He soon spotted a ski, almost certainly one of Queen's, but it was attached to nothing. He found a ski pole, and then another ski, this one protruding out from beneath an enormous skeletal silhouette.

Too big to be Queen. *Dead yeti.*

He nearly jumped out of his skin when a spectral black limb began moving beneath the snow.

"Not dead yeti," he muttered and kept going.

"Queen!" Rook was on hands and knees, digging at the snow. Knight had no idea what had prompted him to look in that spot. Nothing was visible there. Knight turned away and kept looking. He found a small pistol, almost certainly Queen's, and two more yeti skeletons, neither of which showed any signs of life.

But where was Queen?

"Blue, is there any way to track Queen's comms? Can we triangulate the signal?"

Deep Blue didn't even have to think about the question. "Negative. The quantum ansible doesn't work like a radio."

"There's got to be something we haven't tried. She's running out of time."

There was a short pause and then Deep Blue's voice came back. "Okay, no promises, but I'm going to send a high-frequency tone over the comm. You and Rook will need to switch yours off. You should be able to hear it, even under a few feet of snow."

"That's more like it. Shutting down now." He took the earpiece out and deactivated it, then turned to make sure Rook had gotten the message as well. He took a deep breath, held it and closed his eyes, listening for the high pitched tone that would reveal Queen's whereabouts.

At first, he heard nothing. Then, after a few seconds, he thought he heard the tone, but the more he strained to locate it, the less certain he became that his ears weren't playing tricks on him. He resumed his backscatter survey, hoping that the combination of search techniques would increase the chances of finding Queen.

"Here!" Rook shouted. "She's here."

He had scrambled over to the exact spot where Knight had found Queen's skis and the still living—or at least still moving—yeti buried under the snow. "Rook, she's not..." He stopped, not because he heard the tone, but because from a different angle, he could see that there were two skeletal forms beneath the snow. The larger yeti had blocked his view of the smaller human form underneath. The movement he had seen had been Queen, pinned underneath the yeti that he had shot in the instant before the avalanche swept over them.

He ran to Rook's side and began furiously scooping away clumps of snow and ice. In seconds they had uncovered the dead yeti. Wisps of steam were rising off its still warm body.

"We're coming!" Rook shouted. "Hang on!"

Knight grabbed a double-handful of shaggy hair, but when he tried to pull, it slipped from his grasp. The thing was prodigious, a literal 800-pound gorilla, or ape at least. He kept digging, trying to get under the creature for more leverage.

Queen's hand shot up from the snow, clutching the air. Knight could hear the tone now, a shrill pitch that set his teeth on edge, and less distinctly, muffled shouting.

He pulled the comm unit from his pocket and turned it on. Even though it was held at arm's length, the eardrum piercing tone made him wince. "Blue, we found her. Turn it off."

The comm instantly went silent, and Queen's hand curled into a fist with the thumb raised.

Rook got both hands underneath the yeti, and with a feral howl to rival anything the creature might have uttered when alive, he tried to lift it off Queen. The thing's weight immediately caused him to sink deeper into the snow, cancelling out most of the gains he was making. But it was just enough for Knight to grab hold of Queen's free hand and pull. Her head and shoulders emerged, and then, she erupted from the icy grave like a jack-in-the-box, landing atop Knight.

"Hey, she's mine. Get your own." Rook's quip sounded half-hearted, as if he was trying to use humor to cover the emotional rollercoaster of almost losing her.

Knight would have been content to simply lie back on the snow and rest, but he knew the ordeal was far from over. They were bruised and exhausted, soaked through with perspiration and melted snow, and the temperature would soon plunge well below zero. Rook and Queen, who had both been completely buried, were already looking a little blue.

"I need to keep you guys warm while I pitch the tent."

Rook's chattering teeth managed a weak grin. "Cut open the tauntaun. Stick us inside."

Knight wasn't sure if Rook was making an obscure joke or babbling in the grip of hypothermic delirium. "Only as a last resort."

He slid his pack from his shoulders and dug into one of the pouches, producing a handful of chemical hand-warmers. He activated them all, stuffing them underneath his teammates' ski clothes, where the warmers would at least keep their core temperature from dropping.

He then took the tent from the pack, unfurling it with a snapping motion so it settled onto the snow like a blanket. He unzipped the entrance and then turned back to the others. "Get in there. Now."

The tent, even in its unraised state, would act like a bivvy sack, insulating the freezing couple, while Knight finished setting it up. Queen and Rook crawled inside without comment. The two human-shaped lumps looked like dead bodies at an accident scene, covered up to hide the grisly scene from curious passers-by.

"Get those wet clothes off and keep each other warm," he shouted. "If you don't I'll have to get naked and join you."

Rook managed a weak retort. "Not the threesome I was hoping for."

With his backscatter vision, Knight saw Queen punch Rook in the gut. Hard. Then they both started shedding clothes.

That's enough of that, he thought, blinking back to normal mode so he could focus on assembling the tent. The shock-corded fiberglass rods came together easily, but he couldn't seem to make them fit in the metal grommets at the corners of the tent. The cold was taking its toll on him as well. It took him nearly two minutes to raise the tent—two minutes in which the sun dipped behind the mountains and the air became noticeably colder.

He climbed inside the tent, which was barely large enough for two people, let alone three. Rook and Queen were already huddled together beneath an unzipped sleeping bag, and after stripping down to his polypro long johns, Knight slid in with them. The change in temperature was neither immediate nor dramatic, but the combination of three living heat generators, all set to 98.6 degrees Fahrenheit, gradually took away the chill.

When his teeth finally stopped chattering, he made sure that Deep Blue's micro-drones were keeping an eye on them. Not that he had the slightest idea of what they would do if another wave of yetis or some other unknown threat materialized. Their weapons—except for his little SIG pistol—were buried under a mountain of snow. It would take hours to dig them and the rest of the gear out and render them fully functional, and even if they did that, there was little hope of fighting off another yeti attack.

He thought about Rook's ghost story about the Russian trekkers, and the missing Spec Ops team. Had they both suffered a similar fate, attacked by monsters and left to freeze to death? Then he recalled that the tent used by the Dyatlov expedition had been torn open from inside, as if the hikers had been trying to escape from something inside with them.

What if there were worse things than yetis in the snowbound wilderness?

He lay there for what seemed like hours, unable to sleep, unwilling to completely wake up, until Deep Blue's frantic voice sounded in his ear. "Guys, you need to wake up. Company's coming!"

TWENTY-FOUR

After the Russian President's departure, King and Lynn were hooded again and taken from the interrogation cell. They walked a short distance and then stood still for a few seconds, during which time King thought he felt movement beneath him.

An elevator.

A sudden change in air temperature, which he could feel on his exposed hands, indicated that they were outside. The roar of a jet turbine engine and the distinctive rhythm of rotor blades beating the air finally brought his mental image into focus. Wherever or whatever Volosgrad was, they would be going there by helicopter.

The noise inside the aircraft, combined with the heavy shroud covering his entire head, made it impossible for him to hear anything that might have offered a clue as to where they were actually going. He didn't even know for certain that Lynn was still with him.

'Take him to Volosgrad,' the Russian had said. *'He should be able to provide what Alexei needs.'*

He, King thought, *means me. They think I've got something that this Alexei wants. What? And why?*

The Russian had said something else, too.

'We must have the Firebird.'

King doubted whatever scheme they were cooking up involved an American muscle car. The only other thing that came immediately to mind was a Stravinsky ballet suite, composed in 1910 and based on a Russian folk tale about a magical creature. That made only a little more sense though. Likely, it was merely a randomly selected code-name, but whatever it meant, King evidently had something they needed to make the Firebird a reality.

It was one more maddeningly irregular piece of the puzzle. Julie...or rather Catherine, had recognized him as King. Why was that important? He felt certain that if he could just get an answer to that question, the full picture would emerge.

I need to talk to her again.

But as the minutes dragged into hours, those jumbled pieces kept coming to the surface of his consciousness. Was the woman that called herself Catherine Alexander actually Julie Sigler? Was his sister alive or not? Were the Russians preparing for all-out war with the United States? Were Peter and Bishop safe? Did his father know that the President of Russia had taken a personal interest in finding him?

He felt the helicopter banking, changing both direction and elevation, as if in preparation for landing. The maneuvers continued for several minutes, and then he felt a bump as the aircraft came to rest.

While the turbines were still powering down, his hood was removed again. He blinked to bring the world into focus, immediately noting the interior of the aircraft. From the large passenger compartment and utilitarian design, he guessed it to be a military transport. The small contingent of soldiers occupying some of the seats supported that assumption, but there were also two other people with him. They were not wearing dark green camouflage uniforms. His mother, at least he assumed it was Lynn under the sack hood, and—

Julie!

—Catherine Alexander, who was standing right in front of him.

He forced a smile. "Hey. We didn't get a chance to talk. I was going to tell you all about how I found your operation in Virginia. It's a good story. I think you'll like it."

Her stare was unnerving. No matter how hard he tried, he could not see her as anyone but his lost sister. Even her expression, a mixture of confidence and curiosity, was pure Julie. "I'd like to hear it if there's time."

"Make the time. You're the boss, aren't you?"

A wry smile. "What makes you say that?"

He ignored the question and nodded toward Lynn. "Can you take that off her?"

Catherine glanced over and then did as asked, removing Lynn's shroud more gently than she had his. As Lynn's eyes adjusted to the light, Catherine turned back to King. "Why did you bring your mother along?"

It was an odd question, and he considered his answer carefully. "How do you know she's my mother?"

"Please. Even if I didn't have files on both of you, the family resemblance is obvious. I can understand why you might want someone with her background along, but putting your mother in harm's way? That's...cold."

Her background? Files? King was certain that he was missing something very important. "Maybe she's the one who brought me."

Catherine registered mild surprise at the statement, and then something like comprehension. "Interesting. I hadn't considered that." She turned to one of the soldiers and spoke in Russian that was precise but slow and labored, a sure indication that it was not her first or preferred language. "Take them to the research laboratory."

King sensed the window of opportunity closing. "I saw you on television," he blurted.

She turned back to him, the curious look back again. "What are you talking about?"

"That's how I found your supply depot. I saw you on television with President Chambers."

"And because I resembled your sister, you tried to track me down."

King nodded. "We linked you to TSAR Data Solutions, and that led us to the warehouse in Virginia. But it's more than just a resemblance. I keep trying to find something about you that's off, but the harder I look, the more certain I am. You *are* her. That's why I brought my mother. We had to know the truth."

Catherine shook her head sadly. "All that work, undone because of a case of mistaken identity."

"Is that all it is?"

"How could it be anything else?"

"We're still talking about it. I think you're wondering if it might be true. If you might actually be Julie Sigler."

"Preposterous."

"The lady doth protest too much," King said. "Can you prove that you aren't Julie?"

Her silence told him more than her expression. At length, she turned and opened the helicopter's sliding door. "Alexei is waiting," she said, to no one in particular.

King was mildly surprised to see that the helicopter was inside a closed hangar with no obvious opening to the outside world. The air was chilly and there were clumps of snow scattered randomly about the tarmac.

Probably a retractable roof door, King thought.

The soldiers marched him and Lynn across the landing area, through a door and into a hallway that wouldn't have been out of place in a school or hospital from the 1950s. They continued into a windowless room with an examination table and other medical apparatus, which strongly suggested the latter. Catherine entered first and stood next to a young man wearing a white lab coat. He was almost painfully thin, with lank brown hair and a short beard that could not quite hide his delicate, somewhat effeminate features. There was something vaguely familiar about his appearance, but King's attention was immediately drawn to the man's blue eyes. The orbs darted about the room, never settling on any one thing for longer than a few seconds.

"You must be Alexei," King said in English. "I'd offer to shake, but..." He held up his hands, which were still shackled together.

The man in the lab coat shot him a hateful look, then turned to Catherine and addressed her in Russian. "Why isn't he sedated? Are you trying to kill me?"

There was no trace of humor or even sarcasm in the man's tone. King could almost smell paranoia on the man's skin. Catherine was not the least bit apologetic. "I do not work for you, Alexei. He's awake because I needed to question him. If you want to sedate him, do it yourself."

His dancing eyes could not meet her cool stare, so the man looked at King. "Well, we mustn't interfere with your interrogation." He turned to the soldiers. "Strap him down."

King's reaction was a moment too slow, not that he could have done much to prevent what happened next. One of the soldiers grabbed his shoulders, while another kicked his legs out from under him. An instant later, he was slammed, face down, onto the examination table. A heavy leather belt was cinched down across the small of his back. He struggled, instinctively, but with his waist already secured, he was easily overpowered. His legs were restrained, then his hands were unshackled and similarly bound to the table, leaving him spread-eagled, facing down.

"Alexei," Catherine said, her tone more irritated than pleading. "You don't need to do this. Just give him a general anesthetic."

From the corner of his eye, King could see the defiant look on the young Russian's face. "You think I'm afraid, don't you?"

Alexei bared his teeth in a feral grin. He pulled a small cart from the corner of the room, positioning it beside the exam table. On it were a variety of medical instruments. Alexei's hand trembled with anticipation as he picked up a scalpel, holding it up so King could see the glint of light reflecting off the blade.

"I'm not afraid," he whispered.

King couldn't see what happened next. He ground his teeth, but the only sensation he felt was of cool air on the skin of his lower back and buttocks. Alexei had sliced through his belt and the waistband of his trousers, exposing his right hip. He returned the scalpel to its place on the cart. Then, with fastidious care, the man picked up a trocar. The hollow needle looked almost as big as a drinking straw. He showed it to King, just as he had the scalpel, but this time he leaned close to King's face and whispered in heavily accented English.

"This is going to hurt."

He was not wrong.

TWENTY-FIVE

They watched the trees for a full thirty minutes, waiting to see if the arrival of the helicopter was the harbinger of some new threat—for which they were completely unprepared. But the activity that had prompted them to venture out into the blisteringly cold night seemed to have run its course. Darkness had returned, and the only sound was the rasp of ice crystals being blown about by the wind.

The aircraft had come from the northwest, moving fast. It had been too fast to be searching for them or anything else in the frozen wilderness. There had barely been enough time for them to pull on their ski clothes and make the short hike across the slide zone to where they had been earlier in the day. They arrived just as the helicopter dropped below the treetops, disappearing completely, as if the woods had swallowed it whole. Queen half-expected another swarm of yetis to burst from the forest, fleeing before the hovering noise machine, but if there were more creatures lurking there, they remained in hiding.

After that, there had been a whole lot of nothing.

"Is that it?" Rook said, breaking the silence.

"Looks that way," Queen agreed, hugging her arms around her body in a futile effort to stay warm. She wasn't sure if it was the actual air temperature, or the memory of being buried alive in the avalanche that now chilled her to the bone.

"If there's an LZ in there," Deep Blue said, "then there's probably a whole lot more we're not seeing. I'd say we found our secret research base."

Queen grimaced. They were in no condition to infiltrate a nursing home, much less a secret Russian research facility. Especially one they knew nothing about, beyond the fact that it had evidently been guarded by yetis. Ready or not, though, this was the mission.

As if sensing her anxiety, Deep Blue said, "I meant, once Bishop gets there."

At last report, Bishop had caught a late flight to Yekaterinburg, where she had picked up a small arsenal of Soviet-era weaponry from an old former comrade turned black market arms dealer. Her plan was to hire a bush pilot to fly her north. The flight had been on hold due to the presence of the unidentified helicopter in the area. If there was a secret base in the woods, the airspace would almost certainly be monitored with radar and possibly even anti-aircraft weapons.

"Still no word from King?"

"No."

Their last standing order from King had been to recon the site and await his arrival, but if he did not make contact soon, it would be Queen's job to decide how and when to carry out the mission.

Wonderful, she thought. *Another FRAGO.*

Deep Blue was silent for several seconds. "I'm going to take another look at the drone's surveillance feed. Maybe it saw something that I missed. Like another entrance."

"Or a fucking Ewok treehouse city," Rook grumbled.

Queen glanced over at him. "Yeah, about those...things... It feels weird calling them yeti."

"Been looking into that," Deep Blue said. "The locals call them 'almas.' Plural is 'almases.'"

"Seriously? They're actually a thing?"

"There have been a lot of sightings over the years, though they're usually described as being a bit smaller than the creatures you encountered. Five or six feet tall, with reddish-brown hair. A leading theory for the fate of the Dyatlov expedition is that they were attacked by an almas."

Rook shook his head. "Just this once, I hate being right."

"Whatever you want to call them," Knight said, "it's a hell of a coincidence, them living in the same woods as a secret Russian base."

"I was thinking the same thing," Queen added. "Those weren't just wild animals. Could that be what the Russians are doing in there? Creating an army of monsters to fight for them?"

"If so," Rook put in, "they've been at it for a while. The Dyatlov incident was over fifty years ago."

"It's a distinct possibility," Deep Blue said. "A hundred years ago, a Russian scientist named Ivanov believed he could create human-ape hybrids. Orangutans and chimpanzees bred with humans. Stronger than a man but smarter than an ape. Easier to train for absolute loyalty. Stalin loved the idea of a humanzee army. Ivanov failed though. Stalin exiled him to a gulag, and he died in 1932."

"Humanzee," Rook rolled the name around in his mouth. "I don't know if that's better than 'almas' but it fits those monkey-faced fuckers."

"Maybe he succeeded," Queen suggested. "And Stalin exiled him to cover it up?"

"Ivanov's experiments would never have worked. Not with the methods he was using."

Rook's eyes went wide. "Uh, methods?"

"Artificial insemination. With modern gene-splicing technology, I suppose it's feasible, but not then. And not in 1959, when the Dyatlov incident occurred."

"Maybe we're not dealing with humanzees after all," Knight said. "Maybe this is a different experiment. One that worked."

Queen shook her head. "This has to be about more than just humanzees. I think they were just the guard dogs. We need to get a closer look at that place."

"The only way to keep something like this a secret is to limit the number of people who know about it," Deep Blue said, trying to sound upbeat. "If they were relying on humanzees to guard the perimeter, then there probably won't be a strong security presence inside. Maybe none at all."

"Which is wonderful news," Rook said, "if we got them all in the avalanche."

Queen sighed. "Give Bishop the greenlight. Humanzees or not, we need to get in there and get this done. I don't know if the cover of darkness will give us any sort of advantage, but out here we'll stick out like a sore thumb, come daybreak."

"While we wait, I'll see if I can dig out our weapons," Knight said.

"We'll help," Queen said.

"Our shit's buried under a ton of snow," Rook said, giving Knight a skeptical look. "How are you going to find them?"

Knight tapped a finger beside his left eye. "X-ray vision."

Rook snorted derisively. "No. Seriously."

Queen didn't need X-ray vision to know that, under his thermal face mask, Knight was grinning.

TWENTY-SIX

Moscow

The phone trilled once in Peter's ear. Then a second time. He expected Vladimir to pick up then. In their past dealings, which were admittedly few and far between, the Russian mole had always picked up before the second ring.

Two was unprecedented.

Three would be cause for alarm.

Peter had spent hours creating an elaborate network of mobile relays, distributing linked burner phones all over Moscow to confound any efforts to trace the call and learn his location. It was possible that, even now, the trace had begun and FSB officers were triangulating the signal. When they found the phone, in a garbage can in Gorky Park, they would know what he had done. It was a trick he would not attempt to duplicate. If Vladimir did not pick up, it would all be in vain.

His finger moved to depress the button that would end the call, but before he could touch it, there was click and a familiar voice spoke. "Da?"

Vladimir's tone was hesitant, the lone syllable full of apprehension. Peter did not allow himself to read too much into it. "Tell me what happened, *tovarich*."

Tovarich. Comrade.

The word had once held great significance for all Russians during the Soviet era, not only as a term of endearment but also as a subtle reminder of the duty owed by each citizen to the greater good. Peter had chosen it deliberately.

"You are safe?" Vladimir sounded relieved, but Peter knew better than to accept anything the man said at face value. Whether friend or foe, Vladimir could not have survived in the spy game as long as he had without being a consummate actor.

"You know that I am. Now, tell me what happened, and make me believe it." He glanced at his wristwatch, noting the time that had already elapsed since initiating the call. If Vladimir was working with the FSB to capture him, the response was already underway.

"You did not tell me about your traveling companions."

Was he stalling? "That is not an answer."

"It is the only answer," Vladimir said. "They were looking for your son. It was a trap to catch him."

"My son?" The question was out before he could stop himself. Vladimir had deftly turned the conversation away from the matter of his own trustworthiness and placed the blame on Peter. The damage was done, so he pushed ahead. "What does Jack have to do with any of this?"

"You tell me, *tovarich*," Vladimir retorted, throwing the word back at him. "They knew he was coming. There is a leak somewhere. A highly placed source. When I learned of it, I tried to call and warn you, but there was no answer."

If Vladimir had tried to make contact when they were already inside the Lubyanka on their way to the basement archives, the call would not have gone through. But that assumed Vladimir was being truthful, and that was something of which Peter was not yet convinced.

He wanted to believe this man who had safeguarded him for so long, and protected him and his family at great risk. If Vladimir had wanted to betray them, he could have done so at any time. If everything that had led up to this moment was part of a grand scheme to win the trust of Peter and Lynn—and that was a possibility Peter could not dismiss—then why had Vladimir chosen this moment to reveal his true nature, when there was nothing to gain?

Unless there *was* something to gain. Something that Peter couldn't see.

"I am so sorry, my friend, but they have your wife and son."

Peter felt his blood go cold. "No. You're—"

Lying!

"—mistaken."

Vladimir went on as if Peter had not spoken. "They have been taken to Volosgrad, a secret facility north of Yekaterinburg. There is still time to rescue them, but you must hurry. I will..." He hesitated, as if contemplating something truly terrible. "I will meet you there, old friend. In Yekaterinburg. We will do this together."

Peter was speechless for a long time. Too long, he realized, checking his watch. If Vladimir was the architect of the earlier betrayal, then the noose would close around Peter's neck.

But if he was telling the truth?

Yekaterinburg.

Jack and Asya were to rendezvous with their team there. Surely, that could not be a coincidence. Peter had never heard of Volosgrad before, but in all likelihood, it was the very place the Chess Team had been sent to investigate. Asya was already en route, and if Vladimir was wrong or lying about Jack and Lynn being captured, they too would be headed there.

All roads, it seemed, led to Yekaterinburg. "How will I find you?"

"Go to Church on the Blood. I will find you."

Peter's instincts told him a blind date like that was a very bad idea. He knew a few ways of mitigating the risk, but ultimately it all came down to the question of whether or not to trust Vladimir. "Why? Why have you always looked out for us?"

"There can only be one answer, my friend. I am a patriot. Everything I have done, everything I do, is for Mother Russia."

It was not an answer Peter would ever have expected. "How does protecting us benefit Russia?"

"Everything is connected, old friend. Even what happened to your daughter. I will explain when I see you."

"My daughter? Julie? Is she alive? Is Julie still alive?"

There was a long pause. "I will take you to her."

TWENTY-SEVEN

He grips the base *of his seat tightly as the F-14 rolls over and stays that way, belly-up like a dead fish in the sky. The plane continues rocketing forward, the G-forces plastering him into the acceleration chair. Below him, separated by the canopy and twenty-thousand feet of air, the ocean is an endless blue-green eternity, with no hint of the storm to come.*

Then it is all gone as the plane begins corkscrewing through the sky, shades of blue shuffling like cards in the hands of a street magician... Light blue sky, dark blue ocean... Sky... Ocean... Light... Dark...

"You better not throw up, god damn it!" Julie shouts, and he doesn't think she's joking. "I mean it, King. Breathe through it."

"Then...stop..."

The spiral ends and he feels acceleration again, but this does little to quell the nausea twisting his guts, or the inexplicable pain stabbing through his lower back. It's as if someone has driven a hook through his hip and left him hanging by it.

Suddenly, the plane heels over, and he can see both sky and ocean now. A dive. He tries to shout, but no sound comes out. He tries to pound on the back of the pilot's seat, but his arms won't move. It's as if they are being held in place by some unseen force.

"Pull up! Please, Julie. You're going to kill us!"

The endless sparkling blue resolves into cresting waves, rising and falling. Close. So close.

A loud hiss fills the cockpit. Alarms sound, warning of imminent impact. He tries to reach out for the ejection handle but his arms still won't work. All around him the sounds grow louder, deafeningly loud, as the blue ocean reaches up. Then she turns to look at him, her neck craning around at an impossible angle in the close confines of the cockpit, her raven black hair falling loose around her face. Smiling as she opens her mouth to speak.

"Don't you know? We can't die."

King jolted back to consciousness, though for a moment, he wondered if it was a false awakening. Had The Dream merely shifted, as dreams sometimes do, fooling him with the semblance of a return to normalcy? Part of him still felt trapped in it. The strange pain auguring into his hip was still there—a throbbing persistent ache, like a railroad spike driven through his abdomen.

Julie's face was still there, too, hovering just above him, no longer smiling.

"Good. You are awake."

"Awake?"

He tried to rise up, but his body was still immobilized, not by a five-point harness or the G-forces, but rather by leather restraints cinched around his waist and extremities. He winced as the attempt sent a fresh wave of pain through his body. "What happened?"

"Alexei needed a sample of your bone marrow."

Alexei.

The name severed whatever connection remained, bringing him fully awake. The woman was not Julie, but Catherine Alexander. He was in some secret Russian base. A madman in a lab coat had just strapped him down and stabbed a gigantic hollow needle into his hip bone.

"He should have anesthetized you first," Catherine went on. "That's the procedure. But Alexei is..." She trailed off as if unable to find an appropriately benign euphemism for *bat-shit crazy.*

"Thanks for trying so hard to stop him," King said. Because he was clenching his teeth to endure the constant agony radiating through his lower body, his retort lost some the intended sarcasm, but Catherine picked up on it nonetheless.

"I don't give Alexei orders," she snapped.

"Really? My mistake. I got the impression you were like Darth Vader around here."

Her face registered mild confusion, as if the reference had sailed past her, then she shook her head. "Alexei is very special to the President. He tolerates the boy's eccentricities."

"Eccentricities." King laughed and then winced. "Is that what you're going to call that? Where's my mother?"

Catherine's eyes narrowed, as if she was trying to decide whether to accommodate her prisoner's request or assert her authority over him. He expected the latter, but she surprised him. "I moved her elsewhere. No mother should have to watch something like that."

"Thank you." He paused a beat, then decided to see how far her goodwill would extend. "What's 'Firebird'? And why does that lunatic need my bone marrow for it?"

She stared at him for a moment, then turned her head and addressed someone else in the room. "Wait outside."

He craned his head around just in time to see two soldiers, their AK-104 carbines hanging from slings over their shoulders, exiting the room. Catherine turned back to King and folded her arms across her chest. He tried to remember if that had been one of Julie's mannerisms. "You are special, King. Not like Alexei. In fact, you are everything that Alexei is not."

"Well that explains it, then."

"You are part of an experiment that has been going on right here in Volosgrad for more than fifty years."

"Volosgrad?"

She frowned as if disappointed that this was the question he had chosen to ask. "You must have wondered why your parents were brought together."

"Nope. Call me old fashioned, but I figured it was true love."

Catherine either did not hear him or chose to ignore the comment. "In 1892, a young Siberian man suffering from what he thought was a seizure disorder, left his family and journeyed to the Nikolay Monastery in Verkhoture. He had hoped that the monks would heal him, but instead of finding a cure, he learned the truth about his condition. A hermit named Makary revealed to him that he was part of an ancient bloodline. He was descended from a race of giants that once lived in the Ural Mountains, long before the rise of mankind. This place, Volosgrad, was named for the ancient giant city that Makary discovered.

"What the young man mistook for seizures were in fact the awakening of latent abilities inherited from his giant ancestors. Under Makary's direction, he learned to control those abilities. He was able to influence the minds of other people, and even induce a sort of psychosomatic healing state with just a touch. He saw visions of a terrible darkness that would engulf all of Russia. For many years after, he wandered the country as a *strannik*, a religious mystic, sharing both his wisdom and his healing gift, until he came to the attention of Tsar Nicholas."

King suddenly forgot all about the pain. "You're talking about Rasputin."

"A great man, unjustly reviled by history," Catherine said. "More than a man, actually. The blood of old gods flowed through his veins." She flashed an indulgent smile. "Not actual gods of course, but that is how they are remembered. During his years of wandering, Rasputin sired many children—"

"Is that what you meant by 'sharing his wisdom'?" King laughed to hide his growing dismay at the strange turn the conversation had taken.

"In fact, it is. His blood was the only defense against the darkness he foresaw. His descendants—his children and grandchildren—would be the protectors of the Russian empire and the Romanov dynasty. The light to guide Russia out of the darkness."

"The darkness being the Soviet Union," King surmised. "Well, mission accomplished, I guess."

"The Communists were only a symptom of a greater malaise."

"Uh-huh. So let's skip to the part where you tell me that mom and dad are both descended from Rasputin, which makes me practically a pureblood." He said it with an indifferent air to hide how stunned he was by the revelation—not because it sounded so implausible but because it actually made a lot of sense. "That's the big experiment, right?"

It did not require a great leap of faith to believe that Grigori Rasputin, the so-called 'mad monk' and close confidant to the ill-fated Romanov family, was a descendant of Alexander Diotrephes—or that King's own ancestry might trace through him. Nor was it hard to accept that his parents had both been recruited into the Soviet spy agency at a young age because of their unknown heritage. King could believe that they had been brought together in what amounted to an arranged marriage and sent to a foreign assignment as a way to both rarefy the bloodline and protect it from the enemy controlling Russia.

"In a word," Catherine said, "yes. Your parents are the descendants of Rasputin, Children of Adoon. You are. And so was your sister."

Coming on the heels of everything else, the familiar name for the Diotrephes bloodline did not even faze him, but what she said next did.

"I think I might be her. I think I'm Julie."

TWENTY-EIGHT

King's screams echoed after Lynn as she was taken from the examination room, dragged down a flight of stairs and locked in a small chain-link enclosure. The space resembled nothing less than a dog kennel, replete with a strong animal odor and clumps of dark fur on the concrete floor. The cage was one in a long row lined up against the wall. There was another row just like it across a narrow aisle. From her limited vantage, she could not tell how many cages there were, or if any of them were occupied. The soldiers pushed her in and closed the gate, securing it with a padlock. Afterward, they switched off the overhead lights, leaving her in the dark, alone and helpless, weeping for her son.

Lynn Machtchenko however was anything but helpless.

She remained still for a full minute, then another, listening for any sounds in the darkness that might indicate that she was being watched.

Nothing.

When she was sure that she was alone, she contorted her body until she was able to reach her right foot and take the set of miniature lock-picking tools from a hidden compartment in the heel of her shoe. She used one of the picks to shim the pawl in the handcuffs, allowing them to swing open. Then she began groping along the chain-link wall until she found the gate and the heavy-duty padlock that held it shut. She probed the lock for a few seconds with her fingertips. Then, working by touch alone, she got it unlocked in less than thirty seconds. She returned the picks to their place and then drew a thin carbon-fiber dagger from a sheath concealed in the sole of the other shoe.

Peter had always told her that she was the better spy, but her superiority owed more to the fact that most people—most enemies—fatally underestimated her skills, both physical and mental. The agents who had arrested them in Moscow had performed only a cursory pat down. After that, they had mostly ignored her, not even bothering to replace the sack hood over her head before dragging her down into this dungeon. It was a mistake that at least some of them wouldn't live to regret.

She eased the gate open a few inches but stopped when one of the old hinges let out a rusty squeal. After another minute of waiting—listening but hearing nothing—she slipped through the gap and crept out into the darkness beyond. With one hand stretched out, fingertips lightly touching the chain-link cage, she started in the direction of the stairs.

"Who are you?"

The whisper froze Lynn in her tracks. It was a man's voice, and right next to her.

In a cage, she realized. *Another prisoner.*

The question had been asked in Russian, but there was something odd about the man's speech pattern. He sounded fatigued, as if the mere act of uttering the question had left him completely exhausted.

"Lynn," she said, giving nothing more than her name.

"Why are you here?"

She turned, facing the cage, even though she could see nothing. A faint smell of sickness joined the unpleasant mélange of odors that permeated the room. It was almost certainly emanating from the other captive. "I could ask you the same thing."

"Are you with them? Is this supposed to get me to talk?" He was not whispering anymore, and now the weariness in his voice was even more pronounced. Lynn was also beginning to suspect that, in addition to whatever else was ailing him, he was not a native Russian.

His paranoia was understandable. One of the first things a captive lost was the ability to trust. It occurred to Lynn that the source of the disembodied voice might in fact be the very thing he was accusing her of being, but she discounted the idea immediately. No one had asked her anything so far, and she doubted anyone cared enough to create such an elaborate ruse to trick her. No, the man was a prisoner, like her. That made him either a potential ally or a liability.

"Doesn't matter," the man continued, mumbling now. "Those beasts. Did they get you, too?"

"Beasts?" The odd phrase used to describe their captors caught her by surprise. It confirmed her suspicion that the man wasn't as familiar with the language as he believed. "Are you American?" she asked in English.

There was a strange shuffling sound in the darkness. "How..." The word, also in English, came out in a stifled gasp. He drew a sharp breath, then in a more subdued tone said, "Yes."

"Then we are on the same side," she told him. "Are you here with anyone else?"

"Not anymore."

No wonder he sounds so beaten down, she thought. "Well, I'm here with someone. My son." *And my daughter*, she thought but didn't say. "We're getting out of here. All of us. Including you." She slipped her shoe off and retrieved the picks, then began groping for the gate to the man's cage.

"What's the use? We can't get past those beasts."

"Why do you keep calling them that?"

"What else should I call them? Monsters? Ape-men?"

Lynn realized he wasn't talking about their Russian captors but something else entirely, but judging by how agitated the man was becoming, she decided not to press the issue.

"This is where they keep them," he went on. "They went out hours ago. We won't be able to get past them all."

She found the lock, fitted the pick into it and went to work. A few seconds later, the lock fell open. She removed it from the hasp and opened the gate. "Come on. I'll keep you safe."

"Doubtful," he moaned. "But I guess I'd rather die out there than in here."

She slowly extended her hand out to where she thought he was, groping until she encountered him. A moment later, he was gripping her hand, holding onto her like she was a life-line. "I didn't catch your name."

"Joe."

"Okay, Joe. Just follow my lead."

He squeezed her hand. "Thank you."

A thin sliver of light at the top of the stairs marked the door through which she had been led. It was not enough to see by but enough to gauge the distance. Lynn found the doorknob—unlocked—and carefully cracked open the door. With the dagger poised in a backhand grip, she eased the door open a little more.

The hallway was deserted, but she stayed in a ready fighting stance as she beckoned Joe to follow.

When she got her first look at him, she was unable to stifle a gasp of dismay. When he had been merely a voice in the darkness, the mental image she had formed had been of an emaciated prisoner, dressed in rags, with shaggy hair and beard. Joe however looked like something from a horror film.

Aside from a few lank tufts, his hair was gone. There were large weeping sores on his face, and judging by the crusted blood-stains on his T-shirt, all over the rest of his body as well. His mouth was caked with dried blood. As someone who had grown up during the nuclear arms race, Lynn immediately recognized the early signs of severe radiation poisoning.

Joe was a dead man walking.

As disconcerting as that realization was, she was even more alarmed at the possibility that Joe's condition might not be the result of accidental exposure. Were Catherine and her sadistic friend Alexei conducting radiation experiments on prisoners? Was that what they were doing to Jack even now? Was it already too late for her son?

She pushed the terrible thought away, refusing to let herself be defeated before striking even a single blow. She focused on the immediate situation. The corridor was empty and as still as a tomb. "Where is everyone? Are there soldiers here?"

"A few," Joe said. "I think. Most of the people I've seen are scientists, and there aren't very many of them."

Lynn wanted to press him for more information about the facility and its purpose, but she sensed that the subject might push Joe deeper into despair. She did not take his assessment of the security force at face value, but if he was correct, then the main threat she would have to contend with would be the men Catherine had brought with her. And of course, the 'beasts' Joe had mentioned. But that seemed like a topic best avoided.

She stole down the hallway, trying to remember the route her captors had taken. As she neared a corner, she heard a door behind them open. The sound of male voices in boisterous conversation filled the space.

"—send the Army in to take over security."

"I can see why he would not want that, but he cannot keep it a secret forever."

She grabbed Joe's arm and hastened him around the bend, but then she edged out far enough to see two men—both wearing lab coats and headed in her direction.

"It will take a minimum of two years to replace the almases," the second man continued.

"None came back?" the first asked.

Lynn drew back and rushed to the nearest door, which she cautiously opened. The room beyond was dark and apparently unoccupied, so she pulled Joe in and then went inside. She left the door open just a crack, to observe the hallway. The scientists rounded the corner, still chattering, oblivious to the presence of the two escaped captives.

"None."

"What about the subhumans?"

"They don't tolerate the weather, very well."

"We have plenty to spare."

"I suppose we could put coats on them."

Lynn couldn't make out the rest of the conversation as the men moved out of earshot, but she had heard and seen enough to know that neither of them was the sadist Alexei. That was probably a good thing. If he had been there, she might have risked venturing out and slitting both men's throats from behind, consequences be damned. Instead, she closed the door and flipped the light switch.

The room contained several medium-sized metal tanks, which Lynn recognized as fermentation vats. They were useful for producing small batches of ale or wine, as well as cultivating anthrax and other biological weapons. The fermenters were empty, however, and they did not appear to have been used in a long time. Whatever else they were doing at the facility, creating bio-weapons did not seem to be a priority.

She turned to Joe. "You'll be safe here for a while—"

"No," he said quickly, straightening a little. "I can fight. And I've got some unfinished business."

Lynn didn't know or care what he meant by that. Having him along might increase her chances of escape, or just the opposite. "Suit yourself. You'll have to keep up."

Joe chuckled. "Never thought I'd hear that from someone old enough to be my grandmother."

She shot him a withering glance. "Funny. You don't look like a twelve-year-old."

His eyes went wide. "Sorry, ma'am. I just meant that I'm... ah..."

Lynn did not miss the abrupt shift in his demeanor and his deferential language. The man was a soldier, probably an American special ops commando caught spying on the facility.

He might be useful after all, she thought.

She raised a finger to her lips, and then returned to the door. She opened it a crack then waved him ahead. "I'll take point. You watch our six o'clock."

"Yes, ma'am."

With her carbon-fiber blade at the ready, she moved out into the open, walking with a quick determined pace. The two scientists were long gone, the hallway utterly deserted, as far as she could see. If her mental map was correct, her destination was just beyond the next turn.

A peek around the corner revealed two soldiers standing guard at the door to the examination room where she had last seen King. Unless they were asleep on their feet, sneaking up on them wasn't an option. Rushing them would be suicidal, even with Joe's help.

Joe's help, she thought, and a plan began to take shape. She grabbed his arm and pulled him forward. She did it so quickly that he was halfway around the corner before he realized what was happening, by which time she was already pulling him back. Off balance, he stumbled back, crashing noisily against the wall.

Lynn could hear the voices of the two soldiers, registering confusion, and then their footsteps as they moved to investigate the strange occurrence. Exactly as she hoped they would. As soon as the first man reached the corner, she struck like lighting, driving her dagger hilt deep into the soldier's temple. Even as he was slumping to the ground, she used his body to launch herself at the second man. She moved so quickly that the man barely had time to register a shocked expression before her arms enfolded his head. Her momentum toppled him backward, and as they both fell, she twisted her body—and his head—halfway around. As they hit the floor together, there was sickening crunch of bones snapping.

Not his.

Hers.

A spike of pain transfixed Lynn's ankle. Her leg buckled beneath the combined weight of herself and the soldier, and she slammed into the floor hard enough to knock the wind out of her. Stunned, she could only watch helplessly as the soldier shook off the effects of her attack and then turned toward her, his eyes red with rage. Before he could do anything more however, Joe leapt into the fray and slammed the butt of a captured Kalashnikov rifle into the side of the soldier's head.

Lynn's breath returned in a gasp. She reflexively backpedaled away from the unconscious man, but another explosion of pain in her ankle almost made her pass out.

Joe didn't look much better than she felt. It was as if the exertion required to club the soldier had taken ten years off his life. Nevertheless, he knelt beside her and began gently probing her ankle. "It's broken," he said, but then he managed a wan smile. "That was a pretty gutsy thing to do, ma'am. Sorry about the whole 'grandmother' thing."

"You were right. Maybe I am too old for this." She glanced over at the door to the examination room, just a few steps away. "Help me up. We have to keep going."

"You won't get far on that ankle. At least let me—"

She pointed at the door. "I only have to get that far. Give me a gun."

He passed over the carbine he had used to club the soldier, then extended a hand to help her up. She stood on her good leg, steadying herself by leaning against the wall. Even without putting any weight on the injured ankle, the pain brought tears to her eyes. But she was too close to stop now. Joe retrieved the unconscious soldier's weapon and then leaned down so that she could use him as a crutch.

She hobbled the last few steps and then leaned against the door frame so she could put both hands on the weapon. "Open it," she whispered. "Slowly."

Joe did as instructed, easing the door open slowly. Catherine's voice was immediately audible. "—descendants of Rasputin, Children of Adoon. You are. And so was your sister."

Lynn could see inside the room now. Catherine stood with her back to the door, facing the examination table where King was still restrained in a prone position. Aside from the two of them, the room was empty. Lynn raised the carbine, aiming it at the back of the woman's head, but before she could voice a threat or demand surrender, Catherine spoke again.

"I think I might be her. I think I'm Julie."

Lynn drew a sudden involuntarily breath.

Can it be true?

The gasp was enough to elicit Catherine's attention. As she started to turn, Joe swept into the room, his weapon trained on her. "Don't!" he shouted, the single word covering a multitude of possible violations.

King twisted his head around, staring back at Lynn with a mixture of incredulity and admiration, which quickly gave way to curiosity and then urgency. "Cut me loose, quick."

Joe took a step forward. "Lynn, cover her."

Lynn kept the weapon trained on the woman who had just admitted to being her daughter. Part of her desperately wanted to hear what Catherine...or Julie...had to say about that, but the moment for revelations had already slipped away. It was only a matter of time before someone discovered the dead bodies in the hall and sounded a general alarm. The only thing that mattered now was escape. "I have her."

Catherine raised her hands slowly, almost languidly, as if this were nothing more than a game they were all playing. "This is foolish," she said. "You'll never make it out of here, and even if you did, we're in the middle of the Urals. There's more than two hundred miles of frozen wilderness between here and the nearest town."

"That's our problem, lady," Joe said, lowering his carbine but nonetheless giving Catherine a wide berth as he moved to the table and started loosening King's bonds.

King looked up at his rescuer. "White team?"

Joe paused a beat to stare at him, then resumed his activity. "That's right. I'm King. How did you know that?"

"What's the status of your team?"

Joe's hands stopped moving again. "Three of us survived what happened out there, but now I'm all that's left."

King allowed a moment of silence to pass. "We'll catch up on that in debrief. Right now, I just need you to drive on."

A look of disbelief came across Joe's tortured face, but he resumed unbuckling King's restraints. "Debrief? Who the hell are you?"

"I guess you could call me King, Version 1.0."

"Seriously? You're Blue Team?" He glanced back at Lynn. "And you brought your mom?"

"Long story. But with a happy ending. We're gonna get you home." The last restraint was loosened, and King swung off the table. He winced as his feet hit the floor, but then he hastened across the room to Lynn. "You're hurt."

Lynn managed to smile. "I'm better now," she lied, then she turned to Catherine. "Is it true? Are you my Julie?"

The younger woman said nothing, but met Lynn's stare with a gaze that was as cool and impassive as a glacier.

"There'll be plenty of time to sort this out later," King said. "Right now, we need to focus on getting out of here."

"You heard what she said." Joe nodded at Catherine. "We're a long ways from anywhere. And there are things here. Monsters. A whole army of them. I don't mean to sound ungrateful, but it's gonna take more than you and your mom to get us out of here."

"How about a helicopter?"

Joe stared at him for a moment, then shrugged. "Yeah, that might work."

TWENTY-NINE

There were advantages in being the only foreign-born member of the Chess Team. One was not having to come up with a convincing backstory to explain to a Russian black-market arms dealer why Bishop needed several thousand dollars' worth of guns, ammunition and sundry items for causing death and destruction. She also hadn't needed a similar fiction to explain her urgent need to fly to the middle of nowhere in the middle of the night. Yevgeny, the cousin of a friend of a friend, with whom she had served in the Russian Army, was currently a low-level soldier in the Uralmash syndicate—Yekaterinburg's mafia. He had not even asked why she needed the guns. Sasha, the creaky old pilot of an equally creaky and old Antonov An-2 biplane, had complained more about her timing than her choice of destination. "Come back tomorrow," he had said from behind a closed door, his voice thick with sleep—or vodka. He had relented when she started slipping hundred dollar bills under the door.

She doubted the Russians, even those who felt no particular loyalty to the rule of law, would have been as accommodating to her American teammates.

Sasha's accommodations did not extend to helping her unload the plane when they reached their destination. But the physical labor helped banish the chill that had set into her bones during the three-hundred-mile flight to a remote mountain pass in the Urals. To his credit, the old bush pilot was a little concerned about leaving her in the frozen wilderness.

"I will come back for you," he promised. "Right here. Twenty-four hours. You will pay, of course."

"Really," she told him. "You don't need to. I've already made arrangements."

She hoped that was true. The plan Queen and Deep Blue had devised had them commandeering the helicopter that was still at the secret research facility. They would use it to escape after they accomplished their objective—rescuing the members of White Team. If any were still alive and being held there. If Chess Team did not or could not accomplish their objective, the exit-plan would probably be irrelevant.

Sasha insisted she keep the half-empty thermos of coffee he had brought along. The beverage was bitter and full of grounds, but hot enough to ward off the chill while she waited for the rest of the team to show up.

She did not have to wait long.

Almost as soon as the Antonov took off, Queen contacted her on the quantum communicator they had left for her in Yekaterinburg, to let her know that they were nearby. There was no time for a proper reunion, but they briefly recounted the story of their battle with the humanzees.

"I have never heard of such things in this area," Bishop said, incredulous.

"That's just what we're calling them," Rook explained. "But whatever they are, they're real enough and there might be more of them."

"Good thing I didn't come empty handed." She gestured to the Gator boxes that held the weapons she had acquired—five AKM rifles, each with an accompanying Type-2 bayonet, five GSh-18 semi-automatic 9-millimeter pistols, an RPG-7 reusable anti-tank weapon and four rocket propelled grenades to go with it. There were also over a thousand rounds of 7.62-millimeter ammunition for the AKMs. The rounds were already loaded into magazines, and there were several more magazines for the pistols, fifteen pounds of Semtex and a few dozen blasting caps with some radio detonators. "Don't say I never brought you anything."

The weapons were distributed amongst the team. Rook carried the extra rifle, which had been intended for King. It still might prove useful if things went pear-shaped. Bishop held onto the spare pistol. Per Deep Blue's instructions, she had also brought along a pair of cross-country skis, and as soon as they were all outfitted, Queen led the trek back up the pass to where the avalanche had nearly claimed their lives.

Bishop could sense the change in mood as they skied across the fresh slide zone. Even Rook seemed to have lost interest in providing glib commentary. For her part, Bishop had never felt more at home. While she had enjoyed the familiarity of Moscow—immersing herself in the language and culture she had grown up with—this was what she loved about the Motherland. There was a strange beauty in the harsh austerity of the natural environment, which could be appreciated only in solitude.

Except we aren't really alone, are we?

"Head on a swivel people," Queen said over the comm. "Those things could be anywhere. Blue, any sign of them?"

"Negative. Aside from that helicopter, there hasn't been any activity down there since the avalanche."

"Okay, we'll approach the woods using standard buddy teams. Rook and I will lead out. He'll get all butt hurt if I don't keep him with me."

Queen and Rook stayed on their skis, moving as quickly and quietly as possible to the woodline. Bishop peered down the iron sights of her AKM, straining to keep her teammates in view as they approached and ultimately vanished against the dark background of the trees.

"We're set," Queen whispered a few seconds later. "Move out."

Bishop slung the rifle across her back and started out across the flats, staying in the groove cut by Queen's skis. She quickly crossed the distance and ducked down behind the first tree she came to.

"Set," she said.

"Knight, do your magic eye thing," Queen said.

The one thing Bishop had not been able to procure on short notice was any sort of night vision devices. Knight's new optical implant would suffice, for him at least. The rest of them would have to play blind man's bluff. Fortunately, the forest floor was covered in snow, despite the dense overhead canopy of evergreen branches, which meant the rest of them would be able to follow Knight's trail to the objective.

"All clear," Knight reported a few seconds later. "Starting forward now."

The woods were unnaturally quiet. There were no birds or insects to provide nocturnal accompaniment to their journey. The only sound, aside from Knight's periodic reports, was the rasp of skis on snow.

"Hold," Knight cautioned suddenly. "Something really big up ahead. Made of metal."

The ensuing pause removed even the noise of travel. It was so quiet Bishop could hear her heartbeat.

After nearly a full minute, Knight spoke again. "It's a vent cover. I think we've found our back door."

"Any security?" Queen asked.

"Negative." There was not a trace of uncertainty in his answer. "It's safe to shed a little light on the subject."

"You heard him," Queen said. "Red lights only."

In the ruddy glow of their LED headlamps, the team advanced to the vent cover—a vertical structure, about the size and shape of an outhouse. There were probably several more like it scattered throughout the forested area. Knight had already begun using his bayonet like a can-opener, enlarging the opening that allowed air movement into or out of the system. He revealed a long duct about four feet square, that disappeared into the heart of the Earth.

Queen peered down into the shaft, then she nodded in satisfaction. "We can chimney slide down this. Knight, you stay on point."

"You won't be able to see through metal," Deep Blue warned.

"Maybe not," Queen answered, "but he's the best climber on the team."

Knight just nodded and crawled over the edge of the opening he had made. With his back flat against one side, legs extended and feet braced against the opposite wall, he began inching down into the darkness.

A minute passed. Five minutes. Then Knight's voice came over the comm. "You guys need to get down here. Now!"

THIRTY

Yekaterinburg, Russia

"**Let me out** here."

The taxi driver glanced back, one dubious eyebrow raised, but then pulled to the sidewalk. Peter handed him a five thousand ruble note and got out without waiting to see if the man would offer to make change.

The brisk air stung his cheeks, which gave him an excuse to pull his collar up, completely hiding his face. It was probably a futile precaution, just like getting out two blocks away from his actual destination. Three a.m. local time, was too early for even the earliest rising commuters to be up. The streets were completely devoid of traffic. There wasn't a single person to be seen anywhere on the sidewalk, which made his presence all the more conspicuous. If he was walking into a trap, then no amount of spy tradecraft or paranoia would save him.

His gut told him it was a trap, but it was also his best chance of learning the truth about Julie's fate. The fact that Vladimir had dangled that particular carrot meant that maybe there really were answers to be had. He was not likely to find them anywhere else. Escaping the trap was something he would worry about once he had them.

He began walking toward the cathedral, its white exterior and magnificent gold domes shimmering with reflected brilliance from the streetlights below. Despite its traditional Eastern Orthodox design, the Church on Blood in Honour of All Saints Resplendent in the Russian Land—usually referred to as 'All Saints' or sometimes 'Church on Blood'—was not five hundred or even a hundred years old. In fact, construction of the cathedral complex had begun in the year 2000.

The location had formerly been the site of the Ipatiev House, the last residence of Tsar Nicholas II and his family before their execution by Bolshevik revolutionaries. The Communist Party had intended to use the site to commemorate the overthrow of the bourgeois monarchy, but the opposite had happened. The Ipatiev House had become a symbol of the old Russia—the Russia many longed to see again—so the Soviet government had the historic house demolished in 1977. Thirteen years later, with the end of the

Soviet Union looming, the site was handed over to the Church for the construction of a new cathedral complex. The once despised Romanov family were canonized as saints. Church on Blood was a celebration of the end of Communism and the restoration of the Russian Orthodox Church in more ways than one.

Peter stopped at the foot of the snow-covered stairs leading up to the main entrance, partly to take one last surreptitious look around to ensure that he was not being followed, but mostly because he felt like he was about to commit an act of sacrilege. Indoctrinated from infancy in the sacred tenets of Communism, he had never identified at all with Russian Orthodox Christianity, unlike many of his countrymen who had secretly kept the faith and ultimately contributed to the downfall of the Soviet Union. That he should be looking for answers in a church felt surreal, but those answers would not be found in the cold outside.

The church itself was warm and inviting, the golden walls of the entrance hall decorated with dozens of painted icons in gilt frames, but there was not a soul in sight. Peter approached the elaborately decorated double doors opposite the entrance and opened them, revealing the much larger nave of the church, likewise deserted.

No, not quite deserted.

A cleric, dressed in black klobuk and mantle, stood before the altar, his back to the entrance, in silent prayer or meditation. Peter hesitated, wondering if he should leave and return in the morning, but then the priest spoke without turning. "Please. Join me."

The room seemed to amplify the man's voice, but Peter couldn't quite tell if it was the same as that which he had heard over the telephone on so many occasions. Was this Vladimir in disguise? Or was this the man's true identity? Had Vladimir always been an agent of the Church?

The man gestured to the altar. "This is where it happened."

Peter shook his head. "I'm sorry. I don't understand."

"Below us, in the cellar of the old house. It was midnight. They told them to get dressed and go to the cellar, where they would wait for a truck to take them somewhere safe. But it was a lie. Instead, when they were all together, Yurovsky of the secret police, read the execution order. They did not even have time to cross themselves."

Peter recognized the familiar story of the execution of the Romanov family, but he did not grasp its import. Perhaps this was just a priest, mistaking him for a late-night tourist. "I should come back later."

"No, *tovarich*. You should stay."

Peter froze.

So it was Vladimir. Peter looked around quickly, verifying that no one else was in the room. Unlike Catholic and Protestant churches, there were no pews or kneelers. The Church expected the faithful to stand respectfully for the Divine Liturgy. "Did you bring me here for a history lesson?"

"The future is rooted in the past. As are the answers you seek."

That prompted Peter to begin moving forward. "Then explain it."

"The execution of the royal family was the transformative event. The step beyond the precipice, from which there could be no retreat. It is a difficult thing to make such a choice, to change the world. Not all men are capable of such decisiveness. Lenin could not bring himself to give the order, for he knew, correctly as it turns out, that in death, the Tsar would become a more powerful figure in Russia's history than he ever could have been in life."

"I don't understand." Peter stopped alongside the man. "What does this have to do with Julie?"

"Nothing. And everything." He turned, giving Peter a look at his face, clean-shaven and intense. He was several inches shorter than Peter, though his klobuk—the traditional brimless hat worn by senior Orthodox clergy—gave the illusion of added height. He looked very familiar, but with the rest of his head covered, Peter couldn't quite place him. "I chose the name 'Vladimir' to honor Vladimir Sviatoslavich, who brought Christianity to the Kievan Rus. Vladimir the Great. The first Russian.

"Earlier," he went on, "you asked why I have been helping you all these years. Protecting you and your family."

"You said it was for Russia."

A hint of a smile touched the man's lips.

"And now you are wondering, what is the connection? Can the fortunes of one family change the fortunes of a nation?"

Peter glanced to the altar. "I suppose it depends on the family."

"Your family is very important, Peter. You and your wife both are the scions of an ancient and powerful bloodline."

This was not news to Peter. He had learned of his heritage from the source, from Alexander Diotrephes himself. What he did not understand was how this man had come by the knowledge. "You knew? All along?"

"Almost from the beginning. Of course, back then, my influence was limited. It was all I could do to whisper in the right ears to make sure that you and Lynn Sigler were brought together, sharing a long-term deep cover assignment. I wanted to keep you safe, give you a chance to grow and thrive. Raise a family." He smiled again. "You see, I have always played the long game."

Peter scrutinized the man's face more closely. Vladimir appeared to be about the same age as him. "You must have been very ambitious to have that much authority at such a young age."

Vladimir did not address the topic directly. He gestured to the far end of the nave and began walking toward it. "As the years passed, my position in the KGB became more secure, and my ability to influence senior party officials grew to the point where I was able to indefinitely postpone your activation, until the inevitable collapse of the U.S.S.R."

"What about Julie?" As he wrestled to find the right question, some of the pieces finally fell into place. "You said that she's still alive. Did you take her? Stage the accident so you could kidnap her? Is she just a pawn in your long game?"

"Not a pawn." Vladimir stopped and gave him a look that was both stern and at the same time, strangely indifferent. "The accident was real. I had nothing to do with that. Your daughter died in that plane crash."

"You said—"

"I said that I would take you to her. And I will." He resumed walking, and as he approached the door he began removing his priestly vestments, revealing a gray business suit underneath. "I told you that you are the descendants of a powerful bloodline— the Children of Adoon—but what I did not tell you is that your ancestry gives you extraordinary abilities. You are more intelligent. Stronger. You heal faster than an ordinary person." He glanced over for a moment. "We all do."

Peter was sure he knew the man, that as soon as the head covering was removed, he would recognize him instantly. Who was he?

He had not seen anyone in the KGB leadership in several decades. He tried to imagine this man thirty years younger, but he could not organize his thoughts. His mind was stuttering over this latest revelation.

Vladimir was also descended from Alexander Diotrephes. They were related.

Vladimir continued speaking. "There are certain organic chemical compounds that are deadly to an ordinary human, but in a child of Adoon, they promote rapid cell growth. They reverse aging, and instantaneously heal even a fatal wound. Adoon himself discovered the formula for the elixir of life, thousands of years ago, but he feared to share the secret—even with his own children."

"You found the secret," Peter said, breathlessly. He felt dazed, not by what Vladimir was telling him—most of it was not new information—but rather by the implications. "And you gave some to Julie. That's how she survived."

"Now you understand." Vladimir gestured for Peter to step through the doors ahead of him, and then he removed the klobuk to reveal thinning, light brown hair. "The time for the Children of Adoon to fulfill their destiny has come. There is a place for you in my new empire, Peter."

Peter felt his knees go weak as he at last recognized the man.

Before he could find words, Peter glimpsed movement in the corner of his eye. Vladimir had not come alone. Standing in the narthex, just past the double doors, were half a dozen men, all wearing plain clothes and greatcoats, but all unmistakably seasoned military veterans.

It all made sense now. He understood now how the secret of his and Lynn's undercover assignment had been preserved. The man standing before him had indeed once been a senior KGB officer in the First Directorate, and later in Directorate S—the secretive unit charged with recruitment of foreign spies. But that had only been the beginning of this man's rise to power.

Vladimir, secret benefactor and protector of the Machtchenko family, was the President of Russia.

THIRTY-ONE

Volosgrad

After hastily dragging the bodies of the two soldiers into the examination room, King set about splinting Lynn's ankle. She wouldn't be able to walk on it, which meant she would have to be carried. Catherine was an unwilling hostage, which meant that someone would have to watch her at all times. Joe was ambulatory, but he looked like he might collapse from exhaustion at any moment. King recognized the signs of radiation sickness. He knew that whether they all made it back, the mission had already claimed Joe as a casualty.

In short, situation: TARFU—*things are really fucked up*—that rarely lingered-at stage between the normal level of screwed-up—SNAFU—and the shit-hitting-the-fan catastrophe of FUBAR.

Which was both cause for optimism and concern. Optimism because things weren't as bad as they possibly could be. Concern because things could still get a lot worse.

"Joe, tell me about this place," he said, as he wound a long strip of cloth around Lynn's swollen ankle.

Joe seemed to have anticipated the question. "They didn't let me see very much of the place. I do know that there aren't very many humans here. I only saw maybe a dozen different people, mostly scientists."

"Not very many humans? What the hell does that mean?"

"The place is guarded by these...ape-monsters. A lot of them."

"Ape-monsters? Can you be more specific? Are we talking trained apes? Genetically modified animals? Hybrids?"

"Big and ugly, but smart. Kind of reminded me of the ape-men you see in museums. You know, like the Missing Link. Or Bigfoot maybe." Joe looked at him suspiciously. "You don't seem very surprised by this."

"It's not the first time I've dealt with something like it." King looked over at Catherine. "Got anything you'd like to contribute?"

For a moment, Catherine's only answer was a cold stare, but then she relaxed a little. "He's right. One of our ongoing research projects has been the creation of super-intelligent primates. We have an army of them. You'll never get past them."

"They're inside? Guarding the complex?"

She hesitated ever so slightly before answering. "Some are."

"They were keeping them in cages downstairs," Joe added. "They're not there anymore."

"That's right," Lynn confirmed. "The cages are all empty."

"You saw only a fraction of the force we have here," Catherine said. She crossed her arms. "You can take your chances with them of course, but they do tend to get carried away." She nodded at Joe. "If you don't believe me, ask him."

King could tell she was holding something back. Not lying exactly, but bluffing, like a champion poker player trying to hide a weak hand. The primates were out of play somehow, maybe patrolling outside the facility. But she was hiding something else, too.

The Firebird.

Before he could figure out how to ask without giving himself away, Lynn spoke. "Julie, we're here to take you home. No matter what has happened, you're my daughter, and I love you."

King could have kicked himself. He had been thinking tactically, trying to deal with the immediate situation, treating Catherine—*Julie?*—like a hostile prisoner, or at best, as a hostage who had developed sympathies for the enemy. He had forgotten about the very thing that had brought him here.

His sister.

"I am not your daughter," Catherine said, matter-of-factly.

"You know that isn't true." Lynn's voice was clear, despite the pain she must surely have been enduring. A mother's voice. "I heard what you said. You know it in your heart."

Catherine's face might have been made of stone. "I don't know anything of the sort. I am a child of Adoon, just like you. Whether you gave birth to me is irrelevant. Family is irrelevant."

King saw that his first impression of the woman had not been wrong. Yet he wondered if Lynn had gotten through to her. What was she thinking behind that mask? "We're gonna have to put a pin in that," he told Lynn. He gave the binding on her ankle a final check. "It's time to go."

He outlined his plan. It was ugly, but a mad rush for the goal line was the only chance they had.

"It's a lot of balls to juggle," Joe said when he was done. "If we have to fight our way to the helo, we won't be able to keep an eye on her." He nodded to Catherine.

"You should leave me," Catherine said. "Handcuff me to the table. You might actually make it out."

King spotted the manacles he had worn from Moscow on a side table. He picked them up and ratcheted one of the cuffs around Julie's right wrist.

"Good idea. But I've got a better one." He clipped the other one loosely around his own left wrist. "Looks like were in this together, Sis. Now, do I need to gag you?"

She glowered at him. "No. It would be stupid of me to draw attention to us. I might get killed in the crossfire."

"Smart girl." He gripped his captured rifle in both hands, holding it at a low ready. Then he moved to the door, pulling Catherine along as if she was not even there. Joe knelt, allowing Lynn to climb onto his back, and he followed along, holding his rifle one-handed.

The hall was empty, but King knew that there were numerous places between the examination room and the hangar where enemies might be waiting. "Don't stop for anything," he said. Then he started out.

Pain throbbed in his lower back with each step, reminding him of what Alexei had done. He recalled what the Russian President had said to Catherine.

He should be able to provide what Alexei needs.'

For the Firebird.

The pieces were falling into place. The Russians had known about him for several years. They had known about his true heritage as a descendant of Alexander Diotrephes. Perhaps they had known about him longer than he realized, as far back as Julie's accident. Or further.

Don't you know? We can't die.

Had Julie said that, or had it been The Dream?

He wasn't immortal. Not anymore. He had not wanted it in the first place, and when his long journey through history had finally ended, he had taken a serum to neutralize the effects of Alexander's immortality elixir.

He doubted the Russians knew about any of that, but if they knew about Alexander—or Adoon—then it wasn't impossible that they had learned about the elixir of life. Was that what the Firebird was? Was Alexei trying to create an army of invincible ape soldiers?

Something about that didn't quite sound right.

He glanced back at Joe, who was struggling to keep up. It wasn't just the added burden of Lynn's weight that was draining his vitality. King knew the man had routinely carried heavier loads for longer distances during Special Forces training. The fatigue was caused by radiation sickness.

They thought he was me, King realized. *They experimented on him. Dosed him with radiation to see what would happen.*

Bastards.

They reached the entrance to the hangar without encountering anyone. But as King looked out at the helicopter parked seventy-five yards away, he knew their luck had finally run out. The soldiers who had accompanied them from Moscow—all but the two that Joe and Lynn had removed from the equation—were gathered around the aircraft. The men weren't in a defensive posture, just hanging out. Smoking and joking. Vulnerable. Unfortunately, a sneak attack was out of the question. There was no way to take them out without shooting up the helicopter in the process.

But maybe there was another way.

He looked over at—

Julie!

—Catherine. "Will those men follow your orders?"

She glowered at him. "I'm not going to help you."

"We'll do it your way then." He pulled her in front of him, resting the stock of the rifle on her shoulder. "Joe, when you get a clear shot, take it."

He stepped out into the open, pushing Catherine ahead of him. She did not resist, but as they moved away from the door, she said, "You're even colder than I thought. First you drag your mother along on a spy mission, then you use your sister as a human shield. I'm impressed."

King had to force himself to keep moving. "So you're my sister again. Is that your final answer?"

Across the hangar, one of the soldiers looked in their direction, did a double-take and then was instantly on guard, shouting to the others. Almost in unison, the entire group assumed forward-facing shooting stances. Their weapons focused on the pair moving toward them. King took a few more steps, moving forward at an oblique angle to give Joe a clear field of fire, then he stopped.

"Lower your weapons and move away from the helicopter," he shouted in Russian.

The men did not comply but neither did they fire. Instead they began advancing, just as he had hoped they would, fanning out to get a better shot at him. He ducked a little lower behind Catherine, knowing that it would buy him only another second or two. Russian soldiers, particularly those in the Spetsnaz—and he did not doubt that these men were from that elite group—were trained to shoot without hesitation. Even in hostage situations.

Especially in hostage situations.

The ruthlessness of Russian Special Forces was well known. In 2002, when Chechen terrorists had taken almost 900 hostages at the Dubrovka Theater in Moscow, rigging the roof with explosives that would have killed everyone inside, the Spetsnaz had pumped in an anesthetizing gas to render hostages and terrorists alike unconscious. Of the one hundred and thirty casualties in the incident, all but two had died as a result of exposure to the gas. One of the Spetsnaz operators had called it their 'most successful operation in years.'

King didn't think these men would be quite so cavalier with Catherine's life in the balance, but if they succeeded in flanking him, one of them would almost certainly risk the shot.

"Anytime, Joe," he muttered.

"Don't shoot!" Catherine's unexpected shout startled King. For a moment, he thought she was going to cooperate, but her next utterance revealed her true intent. "We need him alive. You know what to do."

Crap!

She wasn't done. "He's trying to lure you into the open. Fall back to the—"

King clamped a hand over her mouth, stifling her, but the damage was already done. The soldiers quickly sought cover, most of them retreating to the helicopter, ducking behind the fuselage.

A burst of gunfire shattered the tense stillness. King dropped to a semi-prone position. He instinctively tried to cover Catherine with his body, even though the rational part of his brain was telling him she was supposed to be his shield—not the other way around. He couldn't tell where the first shot came from, but in an instant, the hangar was transformed into a thunderous echo chamber.

And then, just as quickly as it had begun, the shooting stopped.

King raised his head, expecting to see the soldiers closing in, but instead he saw only a pall of smoke hanging in the air above the helicopter. The soldiers were all gone.

No, not gone.

Dead. Every last one of them.

"Joe! Status!"

"We're good," came the hesitant reply.

"Then get moving. If there really is an army of ape-men guarding this place, they'll be here soon."

Joe emerged from the doorway, Lynn still riding piggy-back. "I think we may have another problem," he said. "I didn't get a shot off."

"You didn't? Then who?"

The answer came even as he asked the question. "King! Friendlies coming out!"

He whirled toward the source of the familiar voice and saw someone rise from a concealed position at the edge of the hangar.

Three more figures appeared, and then all four of them were running toward him.

King shook his head in disbelief as his teammates surrounded him. "It's about damn time."

THIRTY-TWO

Bishop was still trying to wrap her head around the fact that King and their mother were here, in the middle of nowhere. That they were at the very research facility the Chess Team had been sent to recon, and if necessary, destroy, was incredible. That her mother was riding on a stranger's back like he was a horse didn't make it any better. Then there was the matter of the woman standing next to King—hand-cuffed to him. It was the same woman she had seen on a television screen seven months before.

Julie.

King had been right after all. Julie was alive, and somehow, against all odds, he had found her. Yet, Bishop had seen and overheard enough to know that Julie was not exactly overjoyed at the family reunion.

"I see you have been busy," she remarked.

King managed a grin. "I'll catch you up when we're in the air," he said. He might have been speaking to the whole team, but his next question was clearly just for her. "Where's dad?"

"In Moscow. He is still trying to find her." She nodded at King's prisoner.

King frowned at that, but then shook his head dismissively. "We need to—"

Before he could complete the sentence, Julie dropped to the ground like the proverbial sack of potatoes. Bishop's first thought—everyone's first thought, judging by the way the entire team immediately went into a defensive posture, spinning around and searching for a possible target—was that a bullet from a suppressed sniper's rifle had felled her. But Julie was very much alive. She curled herself into a fetal ball and brought her feet together around her shackled hand. Then, like a swimmer pushing off against the side of the pool, she thrust out with both legs. There was a hideous wet crunching sound, like a cleaver slicing through meat and bone, and Julie somersaulted away.

After she had left the Russian Army, before coming to the United States to join her brother's team, Bishop had briefly worked a trap line near Murmansk. Up until that point, she had always believed the stories about animals gnawing off their legs to escape the jaws of a trap to be hyperbole, but she had quickly been disabused of that notion. Some animals were desperate enough to do exactly that.

Evidently, Julie was that desperate, too.

She did not exactly tear her hand off, but the powerful double-kick had scraped the cuff past the meaty part of her thumb, leaving a bloody ribbon of flesh behind in exchange for her freedom. She was on her feet before anyone could react, running for the passage back into the research facility. As she ran, her savaged and bleeding hand was clutched protectively to her abdomen.

King was the first to recover his wits. He bolted after her without a moment's hesitation, shouting as he ran. "Get the hangar door open. Don't wait for me."

Bishop started after him but caught herself. She turned to Queen, who like everyone else was still dumbfounded by what had just happened. Queen managed to nod, which was good enough for Bishop. As she took off after King and Julie, she heard Queen's voice over the comm, urging her to "Talk some sense into him."

She might have said, 'Knock some sense into him.' Bishop figured if one didn't work, the other would.

She was just a few steps behind King, who was about that close to Julie. The intervals separating them all were not shrinking, though. Julie was running as if the hounds of Hell were at her heels. Unlike King and Bishop, she knew exactly where she was going. She ran through a twisting corridor, passing several doors without slowing. Without any warning, she skidded to a stop and threw open a door so forcefully that it slammed against the wall with a noise like a gunshot. The brief stop allowed King to gain a few steps, but then Julie was gone again, running down a flight of stairs into the darkness. King charged after her, and Bishop followed him.

After about ten steps, what little light filtered down from the doorway ceased to provide any illumination. Bishop was forced to slow to a near-crawl, probing ahead cautiously one step at a time. The rank barnyard smell that suddenly filled her nostrils brought her to a full stop.

A smell like that was never a good thing.

She raised her AKM and started forward again. Over the sound of footsteps—King's, she assumed—she could distinctly hear animal grunts. She extended her foot for another step down, but discovered that she was already at the base of the stairs. The smells and noise were much louder now.

"King. We need to go. Leave her."

Lights began flashing on overhead, one by one, in sequence. They started at the far end of what she now saw was a long narrow aisle between opposing rows of partitioned stalls. King had come to a halt halfway down the aisle, one hand raised to shade his eyes as the lights above him blazed to life. Julie stood at the far end of the room, her hand still resting on a large circuit breaker handle. There was a look of fierce triumph on her face, as if the light switch had been her goal all along.

The fixture above Bishop, the last one in the row, came on, casting a circle of light that left the stalls to either side still mostly hidden in shadow.

Something was moving in those shadows.

THIRTY-THREE

Queen had barely gotten Lynn and the other man situated in the helicopter when Bishop's frantic call came over the comm. There had not been time for a proper introduction, but she assumed the man was a survivor from the ill-fated Chess Team White. Lynn was calling him Joe, which probably meant he was Master Sergeant Joseph Hager, the King of White Team. Most of Bishop's call was incomprehensible, but woven into the tapestry of what Queen assumed was Russian profanity, was an actual message: "Trouble. We need to go. Now."

"Damn it." She secured the clasp on Lynn's seat belt and then rose. "Knight, have you found the garage door opener?"

By way of a reply, there was a loud ringing noise, similar to an old-fashioned ship's alarm bell. It was immediately followed by a hiss of hydraulics and a mechanical clanking that sounded like an industrial trash compactor.

She stuck her head out the door opening on the left side of the aircraft and looked up at the high ceiling. It had split apart down the middle. The two halves were slowly pulling apart to reveal the black night sky beyond. Knight stepped out of a control booth in the corner of the hangar and flashed a thumb's up.

"Open sesame," Rook muttered from the cockpit of the helicopter. "Now if I can just find the button for..."

A low whine filled the helicopter, as the twin engines ignited and began spinning up. "Ha!" Rook crowed over the increasingly strident turbine noise. "Piece of cake."

Queen was not generally superstitious, but she felt like she ought to knock on wood or take some other precaution against jinxing the run of good luck.

Sure enough, the universe was paying attention.

As the rotor blades began turning overhead, Bishop burst into view, running full-tilt, with King on her heels. "They're coming!"

"Knight, bring your ass or get left behind!" Queen took a knee and aimed her AKM into the corridor behind the running figures, her finger curling around the trigger, ready to shoot the next person that came through the doorway.

Except it wasn't a person, and it wasn't alone.

Three of them appeared together. Her initial impression, in that fleeting instant as she chose a target and adjusted her aim, was that they were wild men—escapees from an insane asylum as imagined by Edgar Allan Poe. Naked men with shaggy hair, hunched over, almost but not quite walking on all fours.

She fired a controlled pair at the...whatever it was on the right. Two shots, aimed as close to center mass as its bent posture would allow. The thing stumbled and fell, sliding face first across the floor. She shifted her sight picture, looking for another target.

"Shit!"

Finding a target wasn't going to be a problem. In the time it had taken her to kill just one of them—and she wasn't even sure she had done that—a dozen more had emerged from the corridor.

She realized now that they had been wrong to call the creatures that had attacked them outside the facility 'humanzees.' While those hulking beasts bore the distinctive simian traits of a mutated primate—a gorilla or chimp—they really had not resembled the other half of the equation.

The portmanteau was a much better fit for these creatures.

These beasts were considerably smaller than their wooly cousins who had perished in the avalanche. In fact, most of these humanzees were shorter than Queen. They had the long torsos and even longer arms typical to chimpanzees. Their naked bodies were nearly hairless, with just a shaggy mane on top and tufts sprouting from the armpits and pubic region. The lack of facial hair, not to mention the complete absence of any external genitalia, suggested that they were female. But the almost obscenely swollen musculature hinted at another possibility. Either through genetic manipulation or surgical alteration, these creatures were androgynes. Sexless. The weirdest thing about them was the shape of their heads. Every detail—ears, jaw position, forehead and brow ridge, nose—was distinctly human, distinctly individual. Distinctly...distinct.

It took her only a moment to process all of this. In that same moment, she realized the futility of fire discipline. She lowered the AKM to her hip, nudged the fire selector lever up to 'full-auto' and hosed the oncoming mass.

Several of the humanzees went down, but there were more to take their place. And those that didn't fall were getting closer.

The rest of the team joined the fight, all except Rook who was still at the controls, coaxing more power from the turbines. Bishop and King had turned and were likewise firing on full-auto as they backed toward the helicopter. Knight too, was running and gunning. Their intersecting fields of fire had momentarily stalled the advance, but Queen knew it would be only a brief reprieve. As if to underscore that fact, her gun went still, the thirty-round magazine exhausted.

Overhead, the rotor disc was turning at what seemed like full speed, creating a whirlwind in the enclosed hanger that only accentuated the chaos of battle. But the raging humanzees did not seem the least bit intimidated by the tumult.

"Rook! How much longer?" She clipped in a fresh magazine, then added, "'Now' would be a great answer."

"How the fuck should I know?" Rook shouted. "Another minute, maybe? Somebody come take my place. You need me out there."

Queen knew he was just frustrated at being left out of the fight. Rook wasn't a highly trained helicopter pilot. None of them were. He had received the same familiarity training as everyone else on the team. It was better than nothing, but starting and flying a helicopter —and not just any helicopter, but a Russian Mil Mi-8 with switches labeled in Cyrillic—was most definitely not just a muscle-memory skill like learning to ride a bicycle. Rook was only in the front seat because Queen, who had a marginally better bedside manner, had been helping Lynn and Joe, and Knight had been using his Magic Eye to trace the power cables from the retractable roof to the control room.

"We need you to get this beast in the air." She punctuated the comment with another spray of bullets.

Knight had joined King and Bishop, the three of them laying down an almost constant barrage of lead as they backed toward the helicopter. A score of humanzees were down, dead or writhing on the floor in mortal agony, but the flood issuing from the depths of the facility showed no sign of abating. If the team stopped firing, even for the second or two it would take to climb aboard the helo, the creatures would swarm over them.

They needed a game changer.

Queen ducked back into the Mil's cabin, tossed her empty AKM aside and replaced it with the RPG-7 Bishop had brought along. The launcher was already fitted with a PG-7V high-explosive anti-tank warhead. All she needed to do to prepare the weapon was unscrew the safety cap covering the impact detonator at the end of the warhead. Then she cocked the hammer. The actions took less than two seconds to complete.

It felt like an eternity.

She hefted the heavy steel weapon onto her shoulder and hopped out of the cabin. In the time it had taken her to retrieve the RPG, the noose had tightened. The humanzees were not charging headlong into the hailstorm of lead, but instead were trying to circle around and attack from the flanks. Spray and pray was no longer a viable tactic. The only way to repel the attack was with selective fire. As the team shifted from one target to the next, the rest of the humanzees spread out a little more in anticipation of a concerted rush, when the opportune moment arrived.

Armed with the single-shot RPG, Queen could not do much to stop the flanking maneuver, but she could deal with the source. She shifted toward the tail of the helicopter, just enough to clear her backblast area, and took aim at the doorway.

"Fire in the hole!" she shouted, and then she pulled the trigger.

There was loud crack, like a lightning strike right beside her, as the booster charge detonated. A hiss sounded as the rocket motor on the grenade ignited and streaked toward its target.

The HEAT warhead had been designed solely for the purpose of destroying armor plating. When the charge detonated, it produced a jet of plasma that could instantly burn through ten inches of steel. That would allow the secondary explosive charge to detonate in the enclosed interior of an armored vehicle, with devastating consequences. Against an unarmored target—like the unending deluge of humanzees—the results were less spectacular, but no less lethal.

The impact fuse was triggered when it struck one of the creatures, just outside the doorway. Although Queen could not see what happened next, it wasn't hard to imagine the plasma jet shooting down the length of the corridor beyond, burning a hole through every humanzee directly in its path, and flash-cooking those that weren't. When the secondary explosion finally occurred, it seemed disappointingly small. It was just a loud bang, like a cherry bomb in a mailbox. The explosion was so far down the corridor that Queen couldn't even see the puff of smoke. Nevertheless, the RPG had broken the wave attack.

The humanzees already in the hangar were stunned, not by the physical blast, which could barely be felt amidst the swirling tempest caused by the helicopter's rotor blades, but rather by the results. Several of them stopped in their tracks, staring in disbelief at the smoke and screams issuing from the corridor. It was as if they knew that dozens of their kindred had just perished.

If not for the fact that the creatures were trying to kill them all, Queen might have felt sorry for them. They weren't enemy soldiers or radical insurgents driven by ideological hatred. The fact that they were abominations created in a laboratory only made the injustice of their fate all the more poignant. Not merely animals trained to kill like attack dogs, which was an atrocity in itself, but animals with the intellect and emotions of humans.

The moment did not last. Astonishment gave way quickly to rage, and one pair of too-human eyes after another turned back to the team, the source of their woe.

Light a candle for them later, she told herself, as she scrambled back to the door of the helicopter. The others had already seized on the diversion and were piling inside. Bishop went first, and as soon as she cleared the opening, she stood and braced herself at the edge of the door, then resumed shooting. King went next, but Knight stood his ground a moment longer.

"Queen! Go!"

She pitched the spent RPG tube into the helicopter and then heaved herself in after it. King pulled her out of the way and then shouted for Knight to climb in. Queen, still in a prone position, drew her pistol to help Bishop cover for Knight, but as soon as he was inside, the humanzees made their move.

They did not attack *en masse*, but instead continued with the flanking maneuver, circling around to either side of the aircraft, removing themselves from the field of fire.

"Rook," she hollered. "We need to go!"

She didn't know if she had bought him the minute or so he had asked for. It felt like it, but time passed differently in the fog of war. One thing was certain though. If the helicopter wasn't ready to lift off, no amount of nagging would change that.

"I see 'em," he shouted back. "Hang on to your nuts!"

The deck shuddered beneath her as the helicopter began to move, but to her surprise and dismay, it rose only a few inches off the ground before bumping back down. The impact was surprisingly forceful, bouncing her off the deck and slamming her back down.

A feral human face appeared in the doorway, and then it was reaching inside with its long, thickly muscled ape arms. Someone behind her fired point blank. The humanzee toppled back, but she could see more of them moving in, sidling along the edge of the aircraft.

They're trying to hold us down! Can they do that?

The helicopter lurched again but it didn't rise. Instead, it began to pivot beneath the rotors, spinning faster as Rook increased power to the tail rotor. The aircraft spun completely around, again and again, faster and faster with each revolution. Queen hugged the deck to keep herself from being flung out the open door. She saw several humanzee bodies flying through the air before a wave of vertigo forced her to close her eyes to keep from throwing up.

An invisible hand pressed her to the deck as the helo rose, not just a few inches and not just for a millisecond. This time it went straight up, until Queen could feel the chill night air on her face. Rook continued to rotate the aircraft several more times, then both the awful spinning and the elevator ride from hell ended.

"Everyone still here?" Rook shouted.

Knight answered before Queen could even open her eyes. "Shaken and stirred, but all present and accounted for."

Rook chuckled over the comm. "That was some Grade A, E-ticket shit right there." Before Queen could tell him to stop mixing metaphors, he went on in a more sober tone. "Can someone take a look out the window and make sure we didn't pick up any hitchhikers?"

Queen finally opened her eyes and rose up off the hard metal deck. It had already grown uncomfortably cold in the brief seconds they had been aloft. If any of the hairless human-ape hybrids were clinging to the exterior of the helicopter, they would not survive long, but she nevertheless eased her head outside and scanned fore and aft just to make sure.

Nothing.

Directly below, the open hangar formed a rectangle of light in the otherwise black void of the forest. It looked deceptively calm, like a magical gateway into another universe, instead of a portal into a hell ruled by laboratory grown demons. She pulled the sliding door closed, shutting out some—but not all—of the cold and noise, and then she turned to King.

"You finally made it," she said. King didn't have a comm earpiece, so she had to shout to be heard. "We were starting to wonder."

"You know how I like to make an entrance."

"Well the show's all yours. What now?"

King glanced back to where Lynn and the rescued Delta operator were seated. That they had succeeded in locating even one member of the team—and alive to boot—was nothing short of miraculous, but retrieving M.I.A.s was only one of their mission objectives.

They had found the secret facility, and they had discovered at least some of what was going on inside. Queen couldn't quite fathom how an army of human-ape hybrids gave the Russians a strategic advantage. It didn't seem like sufficient provocation to start World War III. But whether or not they went back and finished what they had started was King's call, not hers.

But King was not looking at the Delta operator. He was looking at his mother, and Queen realized his thoughts were on an altogether different mission. A personal one.

He had done the impossible. He had found his dead sister, very much alive, after all. And then he had lost her again. Or maybe he had not really found her at all. Queen had no idea what had transpired between them, but Julie was clearly working for the other side.

Is he thinking about going back for her?

If he was, he kept it to himself. "Now, we get the hell out of here."

THIRTY-FOUR

After the last of the horde of subhumans vanished up the stairs in pursuit of King and the younger woman, Catherine pushed away from the electrical panel and headed up as well. The subhumans weren't as fast as their cousins, the almases. They probably wouldn't catch King before he reached the hangar, but they would certainly be able to prevent him and his team from escaping.

His team. The Chess Team.

The trap had finally caught its intended victim, though not as smoothly as Alexei had anticipated. King's people had actually gotten past the almases somehow and made it inside Volosgrad, but they would get no further. And now that Alexei had his sample of King's bone marrow, the Firebird would soon become a reality. Although nothing had gone according to plan, the plan was back on track.

Her injured hand was throbbing, but the ravaged flesh was already beginning to heal. Soon, the pain would be replaced by the fierce itch of nerve regeneration. The discomfort was better than the alternative.

The report of gunfire, a lot of it, echoed down the corridors. The Chess Team was making a stand. No surprise there, but it would be a futile effort. They were hopelessly outnumbered by an enemy that was not afraid to charge headlong into a storm of lead.

Finally putting them to good use, Catherine thought.

The genetically modified primates were a holdover from another era, sidelined research that, while successful, had ultimately been deemed irrelevant. Cannon fodder didn't win wars. Human soldiers were much easier to train, house and replace. Cheaper too, especially in a country and culture as fatalistic as Russia. Stalin had figured that out almost from the start, but Ludvig the inventor had contrived a way to continue the research in secret.

The most robust lines, the big almases, named for the local version of the legendary yeti, and the smaller, but more intelligent subhumans, had been maintained for site security. What better way to keep a secret facility secret? But there was no longer any research being conducted on the creatures.

There were over a hundred subhumans, and while they lacked the size and strength of the almases, they were much more intelligent. They would swarm over the invaders like army ants, killing the weak and bludgeoning the strong into submission. King might survive, though. He was a child of Adoon, after all. And her mother?

She is not my mother, Catherine told herself, and she knew that was true in every sense except the literal. She did not know if Lynn Machtchenko was her biological mother. Her mentor had never spoken of her life before, and she had never cared to know. Her life had begun twenty years earlier when her mentor, already a senior official in the new Russian government, had awakened her from the darkness of non-existence.

I do not care what happens to that woman, she told herself.

She almost believed it.

She did not make her way back to the hangar then, but went instead to Alexei's lab. The door did not open when she tried it, so she rapped her knuckles on it and shouted to be let in. There was a shuffling sound from inside. Then the door opened a crack to reveal Alexei's agitated face.

"We heard shooting," he said. "What is happening?"

"Everything is under control. Let me in."

He regarded her with naked suspicion. For a moment, she thought he might refuse, but then he stepped away. There was more noise from beyond, the sound of some piece of heavy furniture scraping across the floor. Then the door opened a little wider.

Alexei, who was deathly afraid of sustaining even the most minor injury, had retreated several steps, so his fellow scientists could manhandle a large desk out of the way. As soon as she was inside, Alexei directed them to put the barricade back in place before addressing Catherine. "What is happening?" he repeated. "Did the subject try to escape?"

"Don't concern yourself with it," she said. "Your task is to finish the Firebird. I've already dealt with the situation."

"*He* is concerned," Alexei said, arching his eyebrows imperiously, leaving no doubt to whom he was referring.

"You called him? You had no right."

"*He* called. He wanted to speak with you. That was when the shooting started."

Catherine frowned. She had never liked Alexei, nor understood what compelled her mentor to not only keep him around but give him authority over a project as important as the Firebird. Alexei was little more than a trained technician. He had a formal understanding of the science, barely, but lacked the innovative vision needed to make the breakthrough the project required.

She understood why the President preferred to employ such creatively sterile lackeys. The technology they were working with was a double-edged sword that could just as easily be turned against him. But Alexei had other issues that made him all but impossible to work with, which was no doubt why he had been effectively exiled to Volosgrad.

A loud thump shook the room, rattling the beakers and test tubes on the lab tables.

Alexei jerked as if stung by non-existent flying debris. "What was that?"

"It's nothing," she said. "The Americans are fighting back, but they won't win."

She did her best to sound confident, but she was not so sure. She didn't know what the Chess Team's capabilities were. It was not impossible that they had brought enough firepower to actually win their freedom.

"I will call him," she said, trying to distract Alexei from the nearby battle. "I trust I will be able to assure him that he will have the Firebird before the end of the week."

"You can tell him yourself when he arrives."

The news hit her like a physical blow. "What did you tell him?" she hissed.

Then, without waiting for a reply, she stalked across the room and picked up the telephone receiver. There was no need to enter a number. In fact, the dial plate had been removed. The old Bakelite relic connected directly, via a dedicated hard line, to the President's private switchboard. She waited through a series of clicks as the call was rerouted and the subsequent buzz as the signal reached out to the only man who would ever answer.

"Da?"

"You are coming here?" she asked without preamble.

"Ah, it is you, my Ice Queen. How good of you to fit me into your busy schedule." There was more than a trace of sarcasm in his tone. "Alexei was very concerned. What is the situation?"

She knew better than to be evasive with him, as she had been with Alexei. "There was an intrusion. The American team. It's being dealt with. They freed King and..." She hesitated a beat. "The Machtchenko woman. I don't know if I will be able to capture them alive."

There was a long pause during which the only sound was the crackle of static across hundreds of miles of copper wire and the faint pop of gunfire from within the facility. She wondered if it was audible over the line.

"That is unfortunate," he said at length. There was another pause. "Am I to understand that the almases were lost?"

"I know nothing about that. Security is Alexei's purview." The excuse sounded petty in her own ears, but it was the truth. Alexei had told her only that the almases were outside the facility, on patrol.

"I am dispatching an Airborne Guards division to reinforce external security. And I am coming there to oversee the completion of the Firebird personally."

"I look forward to it," she lied.

"I hope that you will have everything back in order when I arrive. I am bringing someone very special with me. Someone who cannot wait to see you."

The line went dead before she could reply. As she stood there, still holding the phone to her ear, she became aware of two things: the first was Alexei, staring at her expectantly, his eyes dancing with a barely restrained manic energy. The second was silence.

The shooting had stopped.

She returned the phone to its cradle and turned to the man standing nearest to the barricaded exit. "Move that out of the way."

As soon as the door was clear, she threw it open, pulling a cloud of acrid smoke into the room.

Volosgrad was burning.

"Bring fire extinguishers," she shouted without turning. "Quickly."

The hallway immediately outside Alexei's lab was in shambles, littered with cracked plaster and paint flakes, but that was nothing compared to what awaited her around the bend that led directly to the hangar. The walls in every direction at the turn were gone, completely demolished, along with an enormous section of the ceiling. Surprisingly, there were no flames. Whatever had caused the smoke had already burned itself out.

The damage was not structural. The facility had been built from hardened concrete, on a foundation of native rock. Everything man-made in a fifty foot radius however, had been reduced to rubble.

The worst part however was the bodies.

Near the epicenter of the blast, there were only unrecognizable pieces of burnt meat wrapped around jagged bits of bone. She hesitated for just an instant, then began picking her way through the carnage. Further along, she encountered bodies that were more complete but no less dead. But that was not as bad as the ones that were still alive.

She quickened her pace, as eager to be away from the moans of the maimed and dying subhumans as she was to learn the fate of King and his team. As she went along, a feeling of dread settled into the pit of her stomach. Her worst fears were confirmed when she stepped out into the hangar.

When the two dozen or so surviving subhumans saw her, they immediately assumed subservient postures, just as they had been trained to do. The losses—*two, maybe three dozen left, out of more than a hundred*—were astonishing. More shocking was the empty space in the middle, where the helicopter had been.

"Where are they?" Alexei asked from behind her.

Catherine was surprised, and a little dismayed, that he had ventured out of the relative safety of his lab. She pointed at the open roof overhead. "Where do you think?"

"This is unacceptable!"

"It is unfortunate," she admitted. "But you have King's genetic material."

"A very small sample. We may require more, especially with the accelerated timetable. And we needed him for the test phase."

She stared up at the night sky, wondering how long they had been gone. "You have air defenses here, don't you?"

"A battery of Buk M3 surface-to-air missiles."

Missiles.

The helicopter would be blown apart, everyone aboard killed. King would die. Lynn—

Mother?

—Machtchenko would die.

It didn't matter. They were nothing to her. No, they were worse than nothing. They were the enemy.

"Track them. Shoot them down." When Alexei's dancing eyes refused to meet her gaze, she pressed on. "What are you waiting for? We'll retrieve his remains from wreckage and reconstitute him. You'll have all the bone marrow you need."

"There's a problem," Alexei admitted. "The missiles are radar guided."

"So?"

"Our prisoner, the other test subject. He's with them, isn't he? You know what will happen if he's exposed to a burst of electromagnetic radiation."

Catherine did know. It was the problem that had bedeviled the Firebird project almost from the beginning. It was an ironic reversal of the intended effect that, it was hoped, might be overcome with a selective introduction of genetic material from a descendant of Adoon.

"You call that a problem?" A rare smile touched her lips. "I call it an opportunity."

THIRTY-FIVE

Queen handed King one of Deep Blue's quantum ansible comm units and a Bluetooth enabled earpiece. He put the latter in place and then made his way forward to the cockpit.

He settled into the co-pilot seat and gave Rook a nod. "Good flying back there. You're officially promoted to team pilot."

"That's about as likely as an elephant winning a small pecker competition." Rook smiled, and then frowned. "Damn. I should have said 'as likely as *me* winning a small pecker competition.'"

"Yeah, but then it would have been a lie." King grinned and peered through the windshield, but saw only inky darkness. "Can you actually see where we're going?"

"Not really. Compass says we're going north and the altimeter says we're high enough that we won't run into any mountains."

"Might as well turn the lights on. I don't think there's anyone out here to see us."

Rook started examining the switches until he found one that activated a bright spotlight mounted on the nose of the craft. The light shone down to reveal craggy snow-capped peaks towering over broad white valleys several hundred feet below. They flew along for a few more minutes before Rook noticed something framed in the moving circle of light.

"Huh. What the hell are those things?"

King peered forward and saw several strange vertical protrusions erupting from the snow. Pillars of stone, twisting upward like frozen tornados rising from the otherwise flat snow-covered plateau. It was difficult to judge their size from overhead, but based on how far away they were, King guessed that the shortest of them was still close to a hundred feet high, while the tallest was at least double that. There were seven in all, standing in a haphazard line vaguely reminiscent of Stonehenge or the Moai statues of Easter Island.

"I really want to make another dick joke," Rook said, "but I don't want you getting the wrong idea."

King gave Rook a sidelong glance, raising a single eyebrow. "Uh-huh."

"C'mon, you can't tell me they don't look like a row of oversized wangs to you."

"I don't see it," King said, trying not to laugh. "But I'm not judging, either. To each his own."

"You do remember I'm boinking the only good looking member of our team, right?"

"Well as long as you and Knight are happy. That's all that matters."

Rook grumbled to himself and fell silent. He liked to pal around and argue, but he knew when he was beat.

King's smile faded as he stared at the columns. Something about them was familiar, but at the same time, wrong, like returning to a childhood home only to find it demolished and replaced by an apartment complex. He was fairly certain he had never been in this particular spot, though with three thousand years' worth of memories to sift through, it was possible he was remembering wrong. Perhaps he had seen them in a photograph. "Blue, can you do an Internet search for 'stone pillars in the Urals'?"

There was a grumbling sound over the comm. "Now I know how Siri feels. Okay, well, you're in luck. That was an easy one. Those are the Manpupuner Rocks."

Rook gave a snort of laughter at the unusual name, but offered no commentary.

"Also called the Seven Strong Men," Deep Blue continued. "There's a legend that the pillars were giants walking through the mountains on their way to attack the local tribes, but a shaman turned them all into stone."

The pillars had an anthropomorphic aspect, like colossal statues worn down by time and the elements. As King stared at them, his mind's eye saw what they might once have looked like: towering sentinels, chiseled out of the natural rock, like the Sphinx or the presidential faces at Mount Rushmore.

Is that just my imagination?

Or is it a memory?

What had Julie said about the research facility being built atop the ruins of an ancient underground city? A city built by giants, worshipped by the natives as gods?

Who were these giants?

She had also said that there was a connection between the giants and the line of Adoon. He knew that Alexander Diotrephes had been a visitor from a parallel reality, but he had been, in appearance at least, a normal, if somewhat exceptional, human being. Tall, but definitely not a giant.

But if there were other universes, then the possibilities were endless. The giants might be from some other reality, or visitors from an alien star.

He did not recall Alexander ever mentioning giants in their travels together. If a city did exist beneath the research facility, then it probably predated Alexander's time on Earth by thousands of years.

So why am I tuning in on this frequency? He shook his head. *One more mystery I'll probably never solve.*

The light slid away from the last of the strange rock formations, revealing a relatively flat and empty snowfield glinting like a field of white crystals. The image of the ancient stone guardians lingered in his mind, tugging at his consciousness, beckoning him to return. "Rook, how far have we gone?"

"Maybe thirty miles. That's just a guess."

"What made you decide to go north?"

"Flipped a coin." Rook shrugged. "North is the Barents Sea. We've got enough fuel to reach it if we think light thoughts. Everything else in our range is in Russia. We might make it to the border of Kazakhstan, but I'm not sure Borat will be much help."

King glanced over at the fuel gauge and did the math. "Light thoughts won't cut it. Come around and head south. The Trans-Siberian Railroad crosses about a hundred miles from here. We can ditch this bird and catch a train."

"Ah, riding the rails. The authentic Siberian Hobo Adventure Experience. Vladivostok is only...what, five thousand miles? Figure a week? Could be worse."

King decided not to mention that Vladivostok would not be the ultimate destination, at least, not for everyone.

King activated the comm unit. "Blue, you there?"

Deep Blue's voice sounded immediately in his ear, as clear as if he was standing beside King. "I'm here. Time to chat now?" His tone was playfully sarcastic, but there was an undercurrent of paternal ire.

"Couldn't be helped. It was a personal thing." King sighed. "And it's not done yet."

"It was her?"

"Honestly, I'm not sure. I think..." He hesitated. "Julie died in that crash twenty years ago. But I think the Russians got ahold of her remains and used a version of the regen serum to bring her back."

He did not need to explain what that meant. They had all witnessed the effects—good and bad—of Richard Ridley's attempt to create a serum that would rewrite human DNA, giving the recipient the ability to heal from almost any wound—even regrowing lost limbs. But the serum had the unfortunate side-effect of driving a person insane. They also knew that Alexander Diotrephes had created a more successful version, which had not only imbued instant healing but literal immortality as well—the elixir of life.

"That makes sense," Deep Blue said. "Your sister would be in her forties, but the woman we saw on television didn't look a day over twenty-five."

It wasn't much of a stretch to believe that a similar potion or serum could have reconstituted Julie Sigler's remains, restoring her to full health and even preserving her youth for more than twenty years.

"Yeah, but the clincher is that I saw her regenerating. She practically ripped her thumb off to get away from me, but two minutes later, the wound had completely healed."

"Okay. So mystery solved. The Russians brought her back to life and brainwashed her." He said it as if it was an everyday occurrence. "We're gonna get her back and deprogram her, right?"

King was grateful for the expression of unconditional support, but he knew that what Deep Blue had just suggested would be far more difficult than anything they had ever attempted. They were still deep in enemy territory. The last thing they should be worried about was the next mission. "Grab a pen and paper. I need you to do some shopping for me."

"Pen and paper. That's cute. This is the twenty-first century, King."

King began reciting a list of rare botanicals and other exotic ingredients. When he was done, Deep Blue let out a low whistle. "This is some pretty obscure stuff. Dare I ask?"

"It's the formula for permanently reversing the immortality elixir." King had used the same recipe on himself a few years before.

"Ah. Okay. This could take a while."

"Expedite it. I don't care if you have to hire couriers to hand deliver the stuff to you. We need it ASAP."

Rook looked over. "We're going back, aren't we?"

"Bishop can take our mom and Joe on to Vladivostok. They can find a boat to Japan or something from there. The rest of us—"

"It's cool. Felt like we left some unfinished business there anyway." Rook banked the helicopter into a spiraling turn that brought the aircraft down until the snowy plain was just thirty or forty feet below the helicopter. Then he headed due south. As he did, an alarm sounded and an indicator light on the control panel began flashing furiously.

"It wasn't me," Rook said, hastily.

King read the Cyrillic letters on the indicator. "It's a missile lock."

Rook's eyes went wide. "I don't—"

Before he could get the thought out, a scream ripped from the passenger area, loud enough to be heard over the noise of the turbines. Simultaneously, Queen's shout came over the comm. "King! Get back here!"

"What the—?" King looked back reflexively. Over the terrified wailing—an inhuman sound, like an animal caught in a trap in the path of a brushfire—he could make out the shouts of his teammates, and Queen's voice alternately cursing and calling for him.

Somebody was dying back there.

Mom?

"Deal with it," he said, knowing it sounded heartless and hating himself for it. But no matter what was happening aboard the helicopter, it could not be worse than the radar-guided SAMs that were about to take them out of the sky. Unfortunately, there wasn't much he could do about the latter threat either.

Attempting to outrun or outmaneuver the missiles would be an act of futility. The slowest surface-to-air missiles traveled at about 2,000 mph, more than ten times faster than the Mil Mi-8 helicopter. The fastest missiles could go well over 10,000 mph. It would be like trying to outrun a bullet, and not just any bullet, but one that could change directions if you attempted to step out of the way. And since Rook had the stick, about all King could do was offer suggestions and try not to be a back-seat driver.

"Those pillars," he said. "Maybe we can lose the radar lock."

"Right," Rook said. "On it."

King felt the deck tilt as Rook took the helicopter down. Just getting the aircraft down close to the ground might be enough to shake the radar lock. SAMs were designed to take down high-flying jet aircraft, not low and slow targets. Then the towering Manpupuner stone columns came into view, towering above the landscape.

Another warning indicator on the panel lit up. "We've got inbound. Five seconds. Four. Three."

Rook slid the helicopter between two of the pillars.

The indicator lights began flashing on and off. Radio waves, both from a ground tracking station and the missile or missiles hunting them, were still sweeping the sky, but the stone pillars had eclipsed the helicopter from their line of sight.

Something flashed by in the darkness to their right. A sonic boom rattled the aircraft and shook snow from the pillars.

The missile had overshot.

King and Rook both let out a sigh of relief as the warning alarm ceased, but the relative silence was immediately filled with the screaming from the cabin.

THIRTY-SIX

Deal with it?

Queen was too astonished by what she was seeing to even be angry with King. Truth be told, she wasn't really sure what she expected him to do about it. She had no idea how to 'deal with it,' and it didn't seem likely that King would either.

Joe appeared to be having some kind of seizure. He doubled over without any warning, and then his entire body went rigid. He jerked in his seat, straining against the safety belt. His head thrashed back and forth so fast that Queen couldn't see his face anymore. Beneath the rags that were his clothes, his muscles appeared to be swelling, but given the violence of the attack, Queen couldn't tell if this was an illusion or the beginning of some kind of transformation.

Lynn, seated next to Joe, had initially tried to comfort him, but now she was fighting to get out of her seat belt, and for good reason. Joe was out of control, consumed by primal fury. If he started thrashing and flailing, Lynn would bear the brunt of it.

Bishop was shouting something. Queen couldn't make it out over Joe's shrieking.

Queen unbuckled her own seat belt and started forward, but just then, the helicopter tilted. She went stumbling across the cabin and slammed into a bulkhead. The aircraft leveled out almost immediately, but Queen hugged the bulkhead until she was steady on her feet, even as Joe's wailing built to a fever pitch.

Behind her, Lynn, with some help from Bishop, had succeeded in getting free of the seatbelt, but the pitching of the aircraft had dumped both of them on the deck. Lynn cried out in pain as the tumble aggravated her broken ankle, which only added to the hellish din.

Joe jolted again, and then he went still with the abruptness of a red-lined engine seizing up. And like an overheated engine, he appeared to be on the verge of coming apart at the seams. His lips were pulled back in a rictus of pain, teeth grinding together with such force that Queen thought they might be crushed to powder in his mouth.

"Bones...on fire." Spittle flew from his mouth, as he forced the words past his clenched jaws.

Queen knew she had to do something for him, something *to* him, to prevent him from harming himself or the rest of them. Knocking him out cold seemed like the only option, but as she pushed off the bulkhead and started toward him, both Joe and Knight shouted for her to stop.

"Don't go near him," Knight added. He was on his feet as well, but making no move toward Joe. "He's hot."

Her first thought was that Knight was somehow getting a temperature reading with his new bionic eye, but then she remembered that the eye picked up on background radiation. And Joe was suffering from radiation sickness.

Not hot as in hot. Hot as in radioactive.

But how was that possible? Could a person just *become* radioactive?

Joe managed to force out another word. "Kill..."

His eyes were boring into her, imploring her to do something to end his suffering.

"You," he finished, with a gasp.

Queen felt her blood turn to ice. Joe wasn't threatening her. He was warning her what would happen if she didn't stop him first. He seemed to grasp that she understood. Then he looked at something behind her. She followed his gaze and saw that she was standing in front of the door.

Oh, God.

"No." She shook her head. "There has to be another way. We'll get you some help just as soon as we—"

A loud boom, like a thunderclap, reverberated through the cabin. Joe went rigid again, and then, as if the sonic boom had been a signal, he jerked hard against the heavy duty nylon seat belt. The mounting bolt snapped in two with a noise like a gunshot. Joe erupted from his seat and began staggering toward Queen.

She stood her ground, refusing to budge, even as Joe lurched closer, arms stretched out as if to embrace her. Then someone—Knight—was pulling her out of the way.

"No, damn it!" Some part of her knew that her protest was as futile as her refusal to let Joe reach the door. Knight wrapped his arms around her, preventing her from tackling Joe, and Joe kept going. He grasped the door handle and yanked it open.

The effort brought him to his knees. He dropped, wracked by another seizure as frigid air swirled around him.

"Joe, we can help—"

With another inhuman cry of agony, Joe heaved himself through the opening and out into the night.

Queen broke free of Knight's bear hug. She reached the door just in time to see Joe's body impact the snow-covered plateau. The helicopter was only about fifty feet above the ground, hovering, close enough that the rotor blades were churning up a tornado of blowing snow.

King's voice sounded inside her head. "Queen, what's happening back there?"

"It's Joe," she shouted. "He fell out. We need to land."

"No." Knight cut in. "We need to get the hell out of here."

Queen couldn't believe her ears. "We can't just leave—"

Knight's face was a grim mask. He pulled her back and slammed the door. "If we stay here, we're all dead. He knew it. That's why he sacrificed himself."

"Moving from where we are would be a really bad idea," Rook put in. "They're looking for us."

"Staying will be even worse," Knight said. "I don't know what happened to him, but he's throwing off enough radiation that I can see him through the door."

"Firebird," King muttered. Then in louder voice, he said, "Knight, you better not be wrong. Rook. Go!"

"Go where?" Even as Rook asked the question, the aircraft began to move, tilting and accelerating away from the shelter of the stone pillars.

"Anywhere but where we were," Knight said. "I don't know—"

That was the last moment Queen would remember before the world turned upside down.

FIREBIRD

THIRTY-SEVEN

Knight's warning, and Rook's subsequent quick action, were the only reasons why they were not instantly vaporized or smashed into a pulp. The shock wave created a moving front of air as hard as a concrete wall, and the secondary explosion as the aircraft was ripped apart in mid-air by some combination of those factors would have killed them. But they were more than a quarter of a mile away when it happened. A delay of just two more seconds—one even—would have put them that much closer to the blast, guaranteeing their deaths.

That they survived what happened next owed more than anything to simple luck.

For several seconds, or maybe minutes, after everything stopped moving, King's brain was like a computer struggling to resolve a logic error. It was locked up and not responding. Too much data flooded the processor, every sensory organ demanding first priority.

Light. Heat. Motion. Noise. Pain.

Cause or effect? Impossible to tell the difference.

Do you wish to close the operation?

Yes, he thought with a groan, but [Control+Alt+Delete] wasn't going to get him out of this mess. He opened his eyes, and even before the world around him came into view, he caught a whiff of a weird odor, like rotten fish with just a hint of ozone.

The smell—burning electrical insulation from a short in the helicopter's wiring—broke the processing deadlock.

We crashed, he thought. *Why did we crash?*

We were tumbling, out of control, damaged by the blast.

What blast?

Had there been another missile? He could not recall another warning from the alert system, but he did remember a disturbance inside the helicopter. Something about Joe...

Forget that. There's a fire. You need to get the hell out.

The world came into focus, though he couldn't see much in the darkness. The indicator lights on the control panel were dark. The only light was a faint purple glow, entering the aircraft above a jagged horizontal line that bisected the windshield.

King intuited several pieces of information from that observation, but the most important takeaway was that the helicopter was upright and at least partially intact.

He felt a glimmer of hope.

"Rook!" He turned his head, which did not hurt as much as he thought it would, and saw the silhouette of his teammate, strapped into the pilot's seat. The only answer he received was an incoherent mumble, but that was better than he had dared hope for. "Shake it off," he said, as much to himself as Rook. "We need to evac, pronto."

Now that he was finally hitting on all cylinders, he realized that the smell was starting to diminish. The electrical short had evidently burned itself out without starting a fire. That meant at least one potential threat could be taken off the board. Unfortunately, there were still plenty more on the list.

King tried to get up, then realized that he was still belted in to the co-pilot's seat. He had no memory of buckling in, but doing so had definitely saved him some pain and suffering, if not a lot more. As he fumbled with the clasp, he called out again. "Anyone else? Sitrep. Sound off."

In the long silence that followed, he could hear the incessant ticking of the turbines cooling and the groan of the airframe flexing and settling.

Finally, a voice sounded in his ear.

"I'm here," Knight said. His voice was a sluggish mumble, like someone awakened suddenly from a dead sleep. "I mean, Knight here. I'm okay. I think I'm okay."

King got the buckle loose and slid out of his seat. A quick check of Rook showed no visible signs of trauma, but King knew looks could be deceiving. Often the deadliest injuries could not be readily detected. He gently shook the other man's shoulder. "Rook. Talk to me."

"Auntie Em, is that you?" Rook mumbled, his eyes opening. "Oh. Looks like I stuck the landing. I'll understand if you want to change your mind about making me the team pilot. Unless you came across an elephant with a really small—" Rook's eyes went wide. "Queen!"

He exploded out of his seat belt, pushing past King in his haste to reach the passenger cabin. King understood his urgency. Queen meant the world to Rook. King was worried about her, too, just as he was worried about his mother and Bishop. They were all family to him, whether related by blood or not. That was one reason he had not passed Rook by. Another was that he did not want to face what might be waiting for him in the cabin alone.

He was relieved to discover everyone alive, and to varying degrees, well. Queen and Bishop were coming around, with a little coaxing from Rook and Knight respectively. The jolt of the shockwave had thrown them against the bulkhead, but the g-forces of the sudden acceleration had held them there through the ensuing tumble across the sky. A second impact had come with deceleration, leaving all of them rattled like the marble in a spray paint can. Luckily, their injuries were no more serious than bruises and strained muscles. Lynn, securely buckled in her seat, had come through with the least to complain about.

In the brief time it took to assess everyone's condition and remove the possibility of an unmanageable injury from the threat list, King became aware of another danger that he had forgotten to take into account.

It was getting cold.

With no power, the metal skin of the aircraft was rapidly conducting away all the heat from the interior. The crashed helicopter was turning into an enormous freezer. For the rest of the team, dressed in winter gear, that would merely be a source of discomfort. But King and Lynn had lost their heavy coats during their arrest in Moscow.

"Head's up, everyone." When he had their attention, King went on. "First priority is SERE." SERE was a military acronym that stood for Survival, Evasion, Resistance and Escape. "Our most immediate survival concern is the cold. Look for blankets, or anything mom and I can stuff in our clothes for insulation. Seat cushions, paper, anything that will help us conserve body heat."

Bishop immediately shrugged out of the heavy parka she was wearing and draped it over Lynn's shoulders. It was a valiant gesture, but it did not change the equation. Now, instead of Lynn freezing to death, it would be Bishop.

"Get to it," King said. "Talk and work. While you're at it, keep an eye out for supplies we might need—food, first aid kits, fuel for a fire."

The five of them went to work, searching the aircraft for anything that might help forestall hypothermia. Bishop and Queen began searching the various supply cabinets, while Knight and Rook started tearing down sheets of noise-dampening foam insulation from the ceiling. King stuffed pieces of the foam under his shirt. He did not notice an immediate improvement, but he knew it would help immensely for what would have to happen next.

"Evasion is our second problem," he said, as they began tearing apart the aircraft like scavenger ants. "They've probably already figured out that we're down. It won't be long before they send someone to investigate. We need to be long gone when they get here. So, in addition to everything else, keep your eyes peeled for anything we can use to make snowshoes, skis...maybe a sled we can pull."

"Got a destination in mind?" Queen asked.

King nodded. "Resistance. Or in this case, accomplishing our objective." His gaze flitted just for a moment to the empty chair beside Lynn, where he had last seen Master Sergeant Joseph Hager. "Our secondary objective," he clarified. "We're going to take down that research facility."

Although none of them said a word, or even so much as twitched a facial muscle, their silence spoke volumes. It was as easy to interpret. They had barely escaped, and now he was asking them to hump twenty or thirty miles through a frozen wilderness to go on the offensive against an inhuman enemy, about which they knew almost nothing.

"Well, at least it's someplace warm," Rook muttered.

"We're going to make it a lot warmer." King turned to Bishop. "You brought demo, right?"

She nodded uncertainly. "A few pounds for breaching charges."

"That place is off the grid. I'm guessing they've got a small nuclear reactor buried deep under the levels we saw. We blow that and the place is toast."

Queen mustered an outward display of confidence. "The ventilation system is that place's Achilles's Heel. We got in before, we can do it again. They probably won't expect that."

"What about Julie?" Lynn asked.

King gave his mother a hard look. "I came to terms with losing Julie a long time ago. That woman—Catherine, or whatever she wants to call herself—is with the enemy. She condoned torture and medical experimentation on a prisoner, and she's up to her neck in plans for total war with the United States. If I see her, I'll kill her myself."

He looked away quickly so he wouldn't have to see Lynn's reaction.

"While we're on the subject," Queen said, turning to Knight, "what the hell happened to Joe?"

"I only know what I saw. He started throwing off... Well, I'm not sure what it was, but the eye picked it up. There was a lot of it."

King knew that Knight had a new bionic eye, but he wasn't up to speed on its functionality.

Lynn spoke up, evidently over the earlier topic. "Joe had radiation sickness. Could that be what you were seeing?"

Deep Blue, who had been listening silently over the comm, now spoke up. "In backscatter mode, the eye is a passive radiation detector, but you get radiation sickness from exposure to radiation. You'd have to be pretty badly irradiated to actually start emitting ionizing radiation. And you would have noticed it from the first moment you saw him."

"I only know what I saw," Knight said. "All of a sudden, it looked like his skeleton was trying to burn its way out of his body. And it was getting more intense by the second. Like he was building up to critical mass."

Rook straightened as if at last connecting the dots. "That was what exploded? A person?"

Knight nodded uncertainly. "I think so."

"Is that even possible?"

"Our bodies are seventy percent water, and the water molecule is made up of hydrogen and oxygen, the same stuff that rocket fuel is made from. It's just a question of creating the right conditions." Deep Blue sounded somber over the comm.

"Turning people into walking bombs." Queen shook her head. "The next evolution of suicide bombers."

"Damn," Rook said. "No vest needed. Just walk up and go boom."

"What about the radiation Knight saw?" Queen asked. "Are we talking a nuclear explosion?"

"If it was," Deep Blue replied, "I don't think we'd be having this conversation."

"Blue, Julie told me..." King stopped himself. "The Russians are working on something called Firebird. Ring any bells?"

"Nothing relevant. I'll run it past Admiral Ward."

"It has something to do with genetic engineering." He didn't go into detail on how he had come by that information, and no one asked. "They must have tested it on Joe. The only question is whether it was supposed to do what it did, or if something went wrong. We'll try to get whatever intel we can, but shutting it down is now our primary objective."

"Which just leaves us with 'escape,'" Queen said. "You got a plan for that?"

"I'm not sure any of this qualifies as a plan," King admitted. "But if we make it that far, I'm sure we'll figure something out."

"So business as usual," Rook remarked.

"Pretty much." King checked his watch. It had been nearly fifteen minutes since the crash. "All right, save any other questions for later. It's time to go."

Rook threw back the sliding door to reveal a snowdrift completely blocking their way. "This is off to a great start," he said, as he began cautiously pushing the accumulation out of the way.

The drift was several feet thick, almost completely burying the helicopter, but the snow that had piled up around the stricken aircraft had not been caused by the weather. In fact, a hundred yards or so beyond the crash site, the ground had been virtually scoured clean, revealing bare rock at the bottom of a shallow ring-shaped crater. The edge of the crater curved away in either direction as far the eye could see. At the center of it, silhouetted in the pre-dawn twilight, King could just make out the seven colossal stone pillars, likewise stripped of ice and snow by the blast that had brought them down.

"What are those?" Bishop asked.

King turned to find his sister supporting Lynn, and both of them staring at the distant columns with the same perplexed familiarity he felt.

"Those are the Man Poo Poo Rocks," Rook supplied with a profess-orial air. "According to legend, seven Russian giants took a shi—"

King cut him off. "Mom, do you recognize them? Have you been here before?"

Lynn shook her head, but her gaze never left the stone pillars. "No. I mean, I don't think so."

"They look different," Bishop said.

Lynn nodded. "Yes. Exactly."

"Different? How so?" King hoped one of them would be able to answer the question, because he felt the same way.

"I don't know," Bishop admitted. "I've never seen them before. Never even heard of something called 'Man Poo Poo.'"

"It's Manpupuner," King said, shooting a scowl in Rook's direction.

"The three of you," Queen drew an imaginary circle in the air with her finger, "are sharing a memory."

"You mean like ancestral memory?" King asked.

"Something profound happened to one of your ancestors here," Queen went on. "Something that got written into your DNA."

"We need to go there, Jack." Lynn's voice was calm, but there was an undercurrent of urgency in her tone. King picked up on it immediately, because he felt it, too. But there were other concerns he couldn't ignore.

"We'll look as we go by," he said, even though technically they would have to go out of their way a little to reach it.

Although the bottom of the blast crater looked like bare rock, they quickly discovered that it was covered in a thin layer of slick ice that had formed from snow, vaporized by the blast. Not surprisingly, the explosion itself was a topic that no one seemed interested in discussing. Joe had been one of them, a fellow Delta shooter. His horrible death was not just evidence of the enemy's brutality, but also of their own failure to bring their fallen comrade home.

It took a full fifteen minutes to traverse the distance to the pillars, partly because of the treacherous conditions and partly because Lynn, over her protests, had to be carried in a makeshift litter. Nevertheless, as they drew nearer to the pillars, King felt with increasing certainty that it had been the right decision.

The immense pillars loomed over them, some twenty stories high. As they drew closer to the source of the explosion, King saw that dirt and frozen tundra had been scraped away along with the snow. The blast had revealed grooves in the bare rock. The channels were too straight and smooth to be the work of nature. As before, he was haunted by the sense that something important, something he should remember, had been erased from existence by the passage of so many millennia.

"King!" It was Knight. "There's something here you should see."

Knight had followed one of the grooves to where it disappeared into the stone, near the base of a pillar. "There's a void just underneath the surface."

"X-ray vision, huh? That's handy."

"It's not like it sounds," Knight replied, sounding a little defensive.

"I'm sure it's not," King said with a grin. Even without the ability to see through solid matter, he had no difficulty visualizing what Knight was describing. The channels were just that, part of a system to shunt rainwater runoff and seasonal snowmelt into a subterranean water supply system.

How did I know that?

If Queen was right about the memory of this place being imprinted in his DNA, then one of his ancestors, perhaps the very descendant of Alexander Diotrephes that had established the Machtchenko branch of the family tree in Russia, had explored the lost giant city and all its mysteries. Or maybe that ancestor had found the city by following the same ancestral memory, a memory that stretched back much further into the past—before even Alexander himself.

Julie would have known about it, too, he thought.

"Julie told me that the research facility was built on the ruins of an ancient lost city. She called it Volosgrad."

"City of Volos," Deep Blue muttered.

"This is an aqueduct. It leads straight to a reservoir in the lowest levels of the ancient city." King looked up at the others. "This is our way in."

He saw Bishop and Lynn nodding in agreement, and then he saw the looks of skepticism on the faces of the others. Queen broke the silence. "Even if you're right, how can you know that the tunnel is still intact? Still passable?"

"I think they're still using it. It will be dry during winter. And probably a lot warmer than being on the surface."

Rook studied the small hole where the channel disappeared into the stone. "If we pack some semtex in there, we could probably blow open a hole big enough to squeeze through. But there's a chance we'll collapse the tunnel."

"Then we'll think of something else."

"Found it," Deep Blue said. "Veles, or Volos, is the ancient Slavic god of death and the underworld."

"As good a name as any for an underground city."

"You know what this means, right?" Rook said. "We're going to hell."

"Pretty much."

THIRTY-EIGHT

The Mil Mi-8 helicopter settled onto the hangar landing platform. It was the same make as the military aircraft that had been stolen, only ninety minutes earlier. The resemblance ended there. This aircraft was equipped with external fuel tanks, and it bristled with antennae and defensive electronic counter-measures. Instead of spare utilitarian military appointments, the interior was lavishly decorated, with plush club chairs and sofas, wood trim, in-flight communications and video and even a restroom. It had everything needed to ensure the comfort and safety of the VIP passenger who rode aboard.

Catherine waited at the edge of the platform with Alexei and the rest of the staff. A contingent of plainclothes agents of the Presidential Security Service debarked and fanned out in a protective ring around the aircraft. Once they were in place, the President of Russia stepped down onto the platform. His gaze swept the hangar, pausing here and there to take in the scars of the earlier battle.

The subhumans had tended to their own, wailing mournfully as they carried the bodies of their fallen kin away, transporting the corpses down to the old city, far below the research levels...where *it* lived. She didn't like to think about what dwelled in the depths, or the fact that the subhumans and almases had an almost worshipful respect for both the creature and the old city. It was like a religion to them, and in a way, she supposed that was the best word for it. What was that thing down there, if not a god?

What bothered her most about it though was the fact that the creatures, which she always told herself were merely animals— trained attack dogs—were even capable of such abstract reasoning. Despite the fact that they were animals, engineered for ruthless efficiency in battle, the hybrids carried in their genes the social traits of both their simian and human progenitors. Catherine found that more than a little disturbing. They were far too human for her liking, and their loud grieving and bizarre rituals of death had driven her to Alexei's laboratory, which was, she had to admit, only a mildly preferable alternative.

Simply being in the presence of the odious Alexei felt like a punishment. Maybe she deserved that. She had allowed her curiosity about her own origin to override her need to maintain control of the situation. That had given King the opportunity to slip through her grasp.

Of course, the rest of it was Alexei's fault, and by extension, the President's. She had succeeded in every task she had been given, from ruling the Consortium to creating the supply stations.

If Operation Perun succeeded, it would be because of her, not in spite of her. She was not really sure why the President was so insistent upon carrying out the operation now. The Consortium already more or less ruled the world, and since they ruled the Consortium, his ultimate goal had already been realized. But she knew the President would not see it that way, just as he would not hold Alexei accountable for King's escape.

The bodies had all been cleared away, but there was no hiding the pools of drying blood or the damage from the RPG round that had exploded in the hallway leading from the hangar. It was glaring evidence of the security breach that had threatened her mentor's master plan. As he strode toward them, Catherine braced herself for the expected eruption of wrath.

To her surprise and dismay, the President instead embraced Alexei like a long lost son, kissing him on the cheeks. Alexei in turn swelled with pride at the attention from his benefactor. Then the President held him at arm's length and affected a more serious manner. "Now Alexei, tell me, when will we have the Firebird?"

Alexei's expression seemed to melt and his bottom lip started to quiver. Catherine thought he might burst into tears. "I am trying. I've followed your instructions to the letter."

The President nodded and clapped his shoulders. "Then you will succeed."

"I was able to prepare more of the serum using bone marrow harvested from...ah..." He glanced nervously at Catherine. "King. But he escaped before I could move to Phase Two."

"What happened?"

"We were attacked."

"I can see that. How did they get in?"

Alexei's eyes went wide. "I do not know."

"Don't you think it would be wise to find out? To prevent another such incursion?"

The young man nodded, sheepishly.

The President held his stare for a moment, then turned to Catherine. "What is the extent of the damage?"

"The facility is intact," she said. "The damage is mostly cosmetic. We're still assessing the loss of resources, but I would estimate we're down sixty to seventy percent of the subhumans. No one is certain what happened to the almases."

The President glanced at Alexei. "No? The attacking force would have had to get past them, would they not?"

"One assumes," Catherine said, dryly. "The only other loss of consequence was my helicopter. They stole it."

"And?"

"I destroyed it," Alexei said, eager to claim a victory and restore some face. "They are all dead."

"Are you certain? Have you gone to investigate the wreckage?"

"We did register a large explosion," Catherine said. "Too large to have been just the missiles. Our hypothesis is that Firebird in the test subject, whom they rescued, reacted with the radar beams from the missile."

The President nodded in understanding. "So that unfortunate side effect has finally worked in our favor. All the same, a company of Spetsnaz is on their way here. They should be arriving shortly. I will have them sweep the area of the wreckage, just to be sure." He turned back to Alexei. "Go to the laboratory. I will join you shortly."

"I will still need another test subject."

"I will provide you with one." The President clapped the young man's shoulders again and let go, dismissing him. Then he faced Catherine fully. "I've brought someone along who wants very badly to meet you."

Catherine felt great apprehension as she watched the helicopter's other passenger climb out onto the platform. She recognized the man instantly: Peter Machtchenko, the spy. Yet she knew he was much more than that. He was the father of King—Jack Sigler. That meant he was also the father of Julie Sigler. Judging by the awed expression on his face as he approached her, Peter clearly believed the same thing as his wife and son—that she *was* Julie.

And perhaps she was.

Catherine Alexander did not remember her childhood. Her first memory was of waking up in a bed, in a private hospital facility outside of Moscow. Everything before that was a blank slate. Even basic motor and language skills had been erased. She had proved a quick study however. At the urging of her mentor—he had not even been President, then—she had adopted an American persona. She had learned not only English, but American customs and behaviors at an old KGB training facility. Probably the very same facility where Peter and Lynn Machtchenko had learned how to effortlessly wrap themselves in the American Dream.

During that period of learning—relearning, she supposed—it had never occurred to her that she was missing something, missing the memories of childhood. It was not like amnesia. There was no gap, no sense of loss. No burning need to find out where she had come from or who her parents were.

Then King and Lynn Machtchenko had shown up, telling her she was Julie Sigler.

She was not oblivious to the fact of her missing childhood. It was the one thing that set her apart from everyone she had ever known. It was the reason why she saw the world and everyone in it—almost everyone—as a puzzle. They were chess problems, to be solved logically, without emotion.

Ultimately, knowing who her parents were would change nothing about who she was.

So how was she supposed to react to this man walking toward her, looking at her like she was his long-lost daughter?

She thought he would say something maudlin, perhaps attempt to embrace her or break down in tears, but he did not. Although he could not completely hide his emotions upon seeing her, he stood back a few steps, as if content to simply behold her.

"I know that you don't remember me," he said, addressing her in English. "He told me what happened, how you were brought back after the plane crash."

"There is much that you do not know, Catherine." The President paused. "Catherine," he repeated, savoring the name in his mouth. "You have always known that is not your true name. I gave you that name as a way of inspiring you to greatness. Names are very important." His tone changed, becoming cryptic, as if this last statement was another puzzle for her to solve.

"It is good that this reunion should happen now, on the verge of the next step in our journey. Everything has been leading to this. You already know much of what I am about to tell you, but you do not yet see how it fits into my broader vision.

"You *are* Julie, the daughter of Peter and Lynn. You were raised in the United States, where you joined their Air Force and became a fighter pilot. The union of your parents was no accident. They are both heirs to the ancient bloodline of Adoon, an immortal wanderer who first appeared more than three thousand years ago.

"Peter, you and your wife were brought together to refine the bloodline, and Catherine—Julie—was the culmination of that design." He turned to Catherine. "You were meant for great things. Your death in that plane crash did not change that.

"I was able to procure your physical remains and reconstitute your body using an ancient elixir developed by Adoon himself. I *grew* you, but while your body is in every way the body of Julie Sigler, the culmination of your life experience—your memories—could not be regrown. That is why you have no recollection of your past."

Catherine shrugged. The revelation was not unexpected, and as such, was of no consequence to her.

"What's this journey you're talking about?" Peter asked. "And how does Julie fit into it?"

Catherine had always believed she knew the answer to this, but she now realized that, while she understood her mentor's bold plan, she did not fully comprehend his motivations.

"Have you ever heard of a man named Genrikh Ludvig?"

Catherine had, of course, but Peter shook his head.

"In the 1930s, a man calling himself Ludvig was arrested by the NKVD. His research into ancient mysteries led him to the Vatican. Stalin thought to make him an agent provocateur on behalf of the Soviet Union. When Ludvig refused, Stalin accused him of colluding with the Vatican. He was sentenced to the GULAG. That punishment would have been a death sentence for an ordinary man, but Ludvig was not an ordinary man, a fact which did not escape Stalin's notice.

"After the war, Ludvig was put in charge of special scientific research projects. He chose to build a secret laboratory here, on the remains of an ancient prehistoric city he had learned of in his research. A city built by a race of giants, unknown to history but remembered in our folk tales. Ludvig called it Volosgrad, the city of the god of the underworld.

"His first task was to revisit the ape hybrid experiments of Ilya Ivanovich Ivanov. Stalin knew that Russia could not endure another war on the scale of the Great Patriotic War. He believed an army raised to fight the West might turn against him. But an army of loyal subhumans would give him the military might he needed to take the rest of Europe. Of course, the discovery of the atom bomb changed all that. Ludvig succeeded where Ivanov had failed, and in ways that he could not have imagined. He used genetic material recovered from the remains of the ancient giants themselves. Of course, by the time his experiments bore fruit, there was no longer any need for such an army, but the research itself proved invaluable.

"Ludvig was quick to grasp that the giants were not merely some evolutionary aberration, but they were in fact visitors from the stars. He called them 'the Originators,' for they had brought with them the catalyst to advance primates to Homo sapiens, and also the means to unlock evolution itself."

Peter had been following along with rapt interest, which Catherine found surprising given the astonishing nature of what he was being told. "Ludvig was the immortal? Adoon?"

The President regarded him thoughtfully for a moment, then shook his head. "No. But he was of the bloodline, a descendant of Adoon, who had discovered the treasured secret of immortality. All offspring of Adoon carry a genetic link to the Originators, which enabled Ludvig to utilize the evolutionary gift left by them. He not only produced man-ape hybrids, but he unlocked other physical properties undreamt of by Ivanov or Stalin. He also foresaw, as many of his age did, the possibility that humans would not survive to take that next evolutionary step. As an immortal, he might survive total nuclear war, but the rest of the human race, not to mention the bloodline of Adoon, would be wiped out.

"To remove that threat, he set out to engineer a serum that would immunize against the effects of radiation. The immortality serum could do that, of course, but only for that small percentage of the population who were descended from Adoon himself. And immortality for all would pose other problems, which might prove even more catastrophic than the bomb. Ludvig labored for many years to synthesize a formula that would make it possible for Russia to survive such a war and rise from the ashes like the phoenix of legend. He called it Firebird."

"A serum like that would have strategic implications," Peter said. "The army that possessed it would not hesitate to use nuclear weapons against their enemies."

The President raised an eyebrow, as if both impressed and a little dismayed at Peter's accusatory tone. "Ludvig did not share Stalin's vision, but he saw no other way to ensure the survival of both Mother Russia and the bloodline of Adoon. For that reason, it is perhaps fortuitous that he was not entirely successful. The

Firebird serum *did* enable the body to purge itself of radiation before cellular damage could occur, but much like the immortality elixir, it had dire side effects.

"In 1959, a group of trekkers unknowingly ingested some of the serum. At the time, wastewater from the facility fed into the reactor cooling system. The steam was vented and mixed with snow, which the trekkers melted for drinking water. A military helicopter investigating their camp inadvertently exposed them to radar beams, which triggered a reaction in their cells. Their bones began to burn inside their bodies, driving them to madness."

"The Dyatlov Pass incident," Peter murmured.

"Yes. Three of the hikers were affected. The others died from exposure as a result of the panic that ensued. Those young people had received only a very small dose, and their tissues had only trace amounts of radiation from long range exposure to atomic testing. Higher doses of radiation would have resulted in more catastrophic effects. That unfortunate accident revealed the fundamental flaw in Ludvig's research. High frequency electromagnetic radiation, whether from radar beams or the electromagnetic pulse of nuclear fission, triggered an explosive reaction. Instead of creating a formula that would enable a person to survive an atom bomb, Ludvig had done almost exactly the opposite."

Catherine well knew the truth of that. The destruction of the escaping helicopter with King and his team had been caused by an intentional application of that principal. The captured American Special Forces soldier, whom Alexei had initially believed to *be* King, had received the latest version of the Firebird and subsequent doses of radiation to test its efficacy. When the radar from the air-defense system had swept the helicopter, it had triggered an explosive reaction.

The President continued. "Ludvig realized that, just as with the immortality elixir, human tissue could not withstand the underlying process. He recognized that there was some unique trait in the genes of the bloodline of Adoon that enabled them to survive, where an ordinary person could not—even when the bloodline was severely diluted. This, of course, was before the discovery of the DNA molecule or the sequencing of the human genome. With such technology at his disposal, he would surely have succeeded then and there. Instead, he turned his attention to restoring the line of Adoon. It would be a monumental task, but if there is one thing an immortal has, it is patience."

Catherine saw Peter's eyes widen in surprise.

He's figured it out, she thought.

"You're Ludvig?"

The President inclined his head. "One of the drawbacks of being an immortal is that people start to notice that you aren't aging. For a time, I was able to create the illusion of age with theatrical make-up, but to succeed in my plan, I knew it would be necessary to become someone else. Someone with resources not available to a mere scientist, and a former dissident at that, in the Soviet Union. What better place to start than in the heart of the enemy camp? I created a new persona, joined the KGB and began my climb to the top, all the while secretly engineering the downfall of the Soviet empire from within. I told you, Peter. I have always played the long game."

To her surprise, Peter's face darkened with rage. "So all of this? My marriage to Lynn, my family, what you did to Julie... It was all so you could have more lab rats? An unending supply of DNA to help you perfect your serum?" His eyes darted back and forth as his brain made yet more connections. "You told me... You sick bastard. You told me this was all a setup to trap Jack. You said that Lynn and Jack had been caught, but what you really meant was that you have them."

He turned to Catherine. "Are they here? Your mother and Jack? Damn it, Julie, you have to tell me. He took your mother and brother so he could experiment on them. That's the only reason he brought you back. Don't you see? That's all we are to him. A means to an end."

She regarded him with her usual cool demeanor. His appeal to the family bond meant nothing. Yet, she could not help but recall how the President had ordered her to Volosgrad to allow Alexei to harvest her bone marrow and be his lab rat.

Abraham offering up his children on the altar of his own ambition.

Peter turned back to the President. "You're ready to do it, aren't you? Start World War III? Nuke the United States without fear of reprisal because you've got the secret of how to survive the fallout?"

The President's eyebrows came together in a frown. "The Firebird is a safeguard to prevent the Americans from using nuclear weapons against us. Their power to destroy has made them arrogant. When I have taken their power away, Russia will achieve a greatness that even the tsars did not dream of."

"You don't care about Russia," Peter countered. "You don't care about anything but yourself. That's all you've ever cared about, and you'll sacrifice anything and anyone to have your empire."

"Our empire," the President hissed. "It is true. I needed the DNA of Adoon to complete my work, but you and Lynn, and your children, are so much more to me than living tissue donors."

Peter let out a disgusted snort.

"You see," the President went on. "Despite my efforts, I was unable to locate any other branches of the family tree. There was only one way to ensure that the bloodline did not die out."

Catherine looked up sharply, as the significance of what he had just said hit home.

She had always believed her parentage to be an irrelevant detail, and learning that she was indeed the child of Peter and Lynn Machtchenko had not changed that belief at all. But now she understood that it was of the utmost importance, for it not only established her connection to the line of Adoon, but also to the man who had, in every other way, been a father to her.

"You...?" Peter seemed unable to say anything else, but Catherine—

No. I'm not Catherine. I never was.

—knew what he was thinking, because she was thinking it, too. She was Julie Sigler, the daughter of Peter and Lynn Machtchenko, and the granddaughter of the President of Russia.

THIRTY-NINE

The journey through the aqueduct was not quite the hell Rook had expected. From what little they could see of it in the green glow of the chem lights clipped to their clothes, the scenery never changed. But it was actually a pleasant, if somewhat claustrophobic experience. The air was frigid, but nowhere near as cold as the outside temperature had been. Because there was no wind to steal their body heat away, the act of walking actually kept them comfortably warm inside their winter clothes. The round tunnel—more of an enormous pipe, wide enough for two to walk abreast—was smooth, with the appearance of finished concrete. It was uniform, except near the bottom, where the passage of water over the millennia had worn away the cement a little to reveal the underlying rock.

King verified that it actually was man-made concrete. It was not just any concrete, but to all appearances, a formula similar to what the ancient Romans had used to build monuments, roads and aqueducts that were still mostly intact two thousand years after their construction.

"So we should be good," Rook said, "as long as nobody flushes."

There seemed little danger of that. The tunnel floor was bone dry, although there were some trace amounts of fresh ice, caused by snow melted in the earlier explosion—not from their breaching charge, but the blast that had uncovered the plateau. The explosion nobody seemed to want to talk about.

There was no time to talk about much of anything. All their energy was being expended in the effort to reach the end of the conduit. They took turns bearing Lynn's litter, though that particular chore was no more arduous than packing the extra weapons.

An hour passed, then another. Rook had to struggle to remain vigilant, poised to react at the first sign of trouble. The walk down the long unending cylindrical passage felt like a journey down the barrel of the world's longest rifle. Rook wondered if they were headed for the muzzle or the bullet.

Midway through the third hour, with Rook pulling the front end of the litter and Bishop at the back, Deep Blue's voice snapped him out of his semi-hypnotic trance.

"Head's up," he said. "I sent the drone north to cover the crash site. Two choppers full of tough-looking hombres just showed up. Probably Spetsnaz."

"Better that than more of those goddamned monkey-faced fuckers," Rook muttered. His voice reverberated weirdly in the long tube.

"Have they figured out where we went?" King asked.

"Not yet, but they know you didn't leave through the snow. They're sweeping the crater. Eventually they'll find that hole you blasted."

"We've got a good headstart on them," King said. "They won't be able to catch us."

"No," Knight said. "But they will be able to cut off our escape route."

"I don't know about you, but I have no intention of coming back this way."

"What if they know where this leads?" Queen asked. "They could have someone waiting at the other end."

King had no ready answer for that, so Rook filled the silence. "Bring 'em on. I'm getting blue balls, here."

No one laughed, but King managed a smile. "Keep us posted."

The silence returned, but the spell had been broken. Rook was fully alert now. He knew the next sound they would hear, aside from the soft slap of their boot soles on the bottom of the passage and the even softer huff of their breathing, would be Deep Blue announcing that the hunters had their scent.

He was wrong.

Knight stopped abruptly, raising a hand to signal everyone to freeze. Several tense seconds of absolute silence followed, then Knight whispered, "Do you smell that?"

Rook sniffed the air. Though faint, he could definitely make out an earthy odor, like mildew or compost.

"Could be a reservoir," Queen suggested.

"We're close." There was an eerie certainty in King's voice, as if he was remembering a prior visit.

"Stink at the end of the tunnel," Rook said. "That's a new one."

As soon as the echo of his words died away, a different noise filled the void of silence. A low rumble, like a freight train passing in the distance. It was oddly punctuated every few seconds by a sharp rise in frequency, almost like the growl and bark of a dog.

Or an ape.

Rook grimaced. "More monkey-faced fuckers," he said. "Well, at least they don't shoot back."

King raised a finger to his lips, then pointed to Knight and Queen, giving them the go-check-it-out signal.

Wordlessly and without making any sound whatsoever, the pair crept ahead. Within a few seconds, the darkness swallowed them whole. For nearly five minutes, the rest of them waited where they were—not moving, not speaking, barely breathing. The silence would have been absolute if not for the ominous growl in the distance.

Quiet was good though, Rook knew. It meant Queen and Knight had not been discovered by the simian guardians. And now that he thought about it, the presence of the humanzees—and he did not doubt that was what they were—meant King had been right about finding a back door into the research facility.

Then Deep Blue delivered the bad news they had been expecting. "The soldiers are gathering around your entry point. I'd say they figured it out."

King subvocalized into his comm mic. "Are they coming in after us?"

"Not yet. It looks more like they're just going to sit on the spot. Could be waiting for reinforcements. I'll let you know if and when they come your way."

"Guess we're definitely not leaving that way," Rook whispered.

"That was never the plan," King replied.

"Your plans," Bishop muttered, irritably.

"What about my plans?" King sounded just a little defensive.

"Kids," Lynn said in a soft but firm voice. "Behave."

Rook chuckled. "Sibling rivalry rears its ugly head."

A few more minutes passed before Queen called in. "Found something," she spoke in a low voice, but not a whisper. Keeping quiet was evidently no longer a primary concern. "You're gonna need to see this for yourself."

There was an uncharacteristic undercurrent of anxiety in Queen's transmission. Subtle, probably too subtle for anyone but Rook to pick up on, but it was there, and it concerned him. He had heard that same note of apprehension during the briefing at Limbo, when Ward had told them they were going to Russia to stop World War III.

It was not fear. Aside from a former Mossad operator with a medical condition that had left him physically unable to experience fear, Queen was damn near the most fearless person he had ever known. This was something else. An acknowledgement that, no matter how fearless or tough they were, the problem was simply too big for even the extraordinary Chess Team to surmount.

Although both his hands were occupied with the task of supporting the litter, Rook mentally rehearsed what he would do if a herd of humanzees came charging down the tunnel toward them. It probably wasn't going to happen. The creatures would have to get past Queen and Knight first, which would give him plenty of time to set Lynn down, draw his Desert Eagles and start firing, but it still paid to be mentally ready.

The expected attack did not materialize, however. The strange animal sound grew more distinct as they neared the end of the tunnel, some two hundred yards from where they had stopped. It did not seem much louder though, even when the tunnel opened into a chute—like a half-pipe. The chute continued on for another fifty feet, and then there was only empty black nothingness.

"Up here," Queen said. She was crouched down on the deck to the right of the chute, still speaking in a low voice but well above a whisper.

Rook took a moment to survey what he could in the low-light conditions. The platform on which Queen was situated appeared to curve inward, rising slightly at a steady rate, like a ramp. The wall behind her and above the mouth of the tunnel was carved from native bedrock. It rose thirty feet before curving smoothly into a ninety degree turn to form a ceiling overhead. Like the floor beneath, the ceiling exhibited the same constant rise, like the spiraling thread of a bolt-hole. The scale of what he could see was enormous, but there was nothing to immediately explain Queen's subdued apprehension.

Knight came into view over her shoulder. "This is your lost city, all right," he said, in the same hushed tone. "There's a cistern about two hundred feet down. Not sure how deep it is, but it probably fluctuates seasonally. So right now it's probably lower than usual. There are several large bore pipes running all the way up to the top. Metal pipes. Modern manufacture."

"They're drawing water for the base," King said. "Those pipes will lead us to the reactor."

"The cistern is about two hundred yards across," Knight went on. "The city spirals around it like a corkscrew."

So basically, we're screwed, Rook was about to say, but before he could utter a sound, Queen held up a hand to silence him. "I know what you're gonna say, Sweetie. Hold that thought until you hear the rest."

"There are six levels above us," Knight went on. "Well, technically speaking, it's all one continuous level, but you know what I mean. There's not much below us. Higher up, I can see openings in the wall. Probably entrances to home, though..." He paused a moment. "You remember how Blue talked about the old legends of giants? Those openings are twenty feet high. When you consider that our doorways are usually a foot or two taller than the average height..."

"Got it," King said. "Giants. So where's that sound coming from?"

Knight and Queen exchanged a look. "Show them," she said.

Knight took a chem light from his pocket and bent it to break the glass ampoule inside, mixing the chemicals to create the phosphorescent reaction. When the plastic tube was glowing brightly, Knight drew back his arm and hurled the glowstick out over the chasm.

As it began to descend from the peak of its parabolic trajectory, Rook could just make out the distant side of the spiraling platform. It took a moment longer—a moment in which the chem light fell away into oblivion—for him to register what he had just seen.

It was an ape-like creature with dark fur, more like the monsters that had attacked them on the mountain slopes near the forest than the smaller hairless humanzees they had fought in the hangar. But it was very different from both. Its eyes had glinted the reflection of the falling chem light, leaving little doubt that it had seen the team. It was watching them from the darkness.

Rook only saw the one, which made sense. The odd animal growls they had heard in the tunnel had definitely been from a single creature, not a large group. One was enough, though, because the creature was enormous. Its bulk occupied two-thirds of the space between the ceiling and the platform on which it was sitting—and it was sitting on its haunches, which meant its standing height would have been even greater.

Thirty feet from floor to ceiling, which meant the mutated animal—humanzee or almas or whatever—from monkey head to monkey ass, was at least twenty-five feet tall when standing upright.

There *were* still giants in the ancient city.

"You can say it now," Queen said.

"Say...? Oh." The quip was more appropriate now, though he could not remember why he had ever thought it was funny. "Yeah. Screwed."

FORTY

King stared out across the chasm as the light vanished into the depths below. In an odd way, the darkness revealed more than the transient light of the glowstick, for in the absence of light, his ancestral memory, or whatever it was that made this place so familiar, filled in the blank spaces. While it would have been a stretch to say that he could have navigated the city blindfolded, he knew with unwavering certainty that the ancient giants had built their city in a spiral. Spiral architecture was an essential component of giant technology, though King did not know how he knew that either. At the top of the spiral, they would find a way out, and access to the research facility above.

What was absent from his memory was the giant ape-thing that sat watching them from out of the darkness. And yet, there was something. Not quite a memory, more an intuition really, about the creature and why it was here.

"Looks like another variation on the humanzee experiments," Queen said. "I wonder why they stuck it down here."

"Variation?" Rook said, shaking his head. "That's King fucking Kong over there."

"It's Volos," King said. "Or the thing the ancient people living here called Volos. That's why they avoided this place."

Queen was skeptical. "A giant ape living underground?"

"I don't think it was always an ape. Maybe the Russians who made those...what did you call them? Humanzees? Maybe they messed with him, too."

"Why does it not attack us?" Bishop asked.

"Maybe he already ate," Rook suggested. "Or could be he's just lazy."

King kept staring at the spot. "He's in our way."

"We could ask him to move. Politely, of course." Rook turned to Queen. "Maybe he likes blondes, like in the movie. 'Twas beauty that tamed the beast.' Wanna give it a try?"

Queen regarded him with one dubious eyebrow raised. "I don't think Apezilla over there will be quite as susceptible to my charms as you were. Oh, and it's 'beauty *killed* the beast.'"

"Knight, with your new eye, you could make that shot, right?" King asked.

"I could hit that thing blindfolded, but I'm not sure anything we've got could take him down."

"What about the RPG?"

Knight's face screwed up in thought. "The rockets tend to get a bit wobbly past a hundred yards. At that distance, the odds of actually hitting it are fifty-fifty at best."

Rook laughed. "What are the odds of royally pissing it off?"

"I just told you. Fifty-fifty. And hit or miss, we could do some structural damage."

"If you've got a better option, let's have it."

"Actually, I might," Deep Blue said. "I can send a high frequency sound pulse through your comms. The electronics are solid enough to handle high volume high frequency sound, for a few minutes at least."

"I remember," Queen said with a groan.

"Apes have about the same hearing range as humans. Big boy there might actually be a little more sensitive. A tone of 4000 Hertz should send him packing."

"And us, too."

"Yeah, you'll probably want to wrap something around your ears to muffle some of the sound."

King weighed this less violent approach. He wasn't as confident of its success as Deep Blue, but there were many advantages, not the least of which was maintaining a degree of stealth as they made their way up the levels of the ancient city. "We'll give it a try, but be ready with that RPG."

Knight nodded and began prepping a rocket. As soon as they were ready to move, King gave the go ahead to Deep Blue, and a shrill tone filled the air. Even with scarves and coats wrapped around their heads to dampen the noise, the high-pitched whine was like nails on a chalkboard. The sound bounced back and forth in the vertical cylinder, setting up an interference pattern, the tone rising and falling in a nausea-inducing pulse that was even more excruciating. King and the others gritted their teeth and kept moving.

"Oh, he doesn't like that," Knight reported, shouting a little to be heard over the tone.

"He is not only one," Bishop remarked with a grimace.

"He's moving."

"Which way?" King asked.

"Up." Knight's head bobbed slightly as he followed the figure that only he could see. "Now he's gone."

"Gone?"

"He went in one of the passages. I can't see him anymore."

King did not like the sound of that, but since the sonic deterrent appeared to be working, there was no reason not to keep moving. "Keep your eye on him."

They moved at a fast walk up the gentle slope of the spiraling balcony, and soon they reached the first of several enormous openings cut into the rock. King performed a cursory inspection to ensure that none of the ape-creatures—*humanzees* seemed to be the term favored by his teammates—were lurking within, waiting to spring out at them. The space beyond was empty save for a scattering of what looked like irregularly shaped black rocks. They were as thick around as a football and some were longer than King's leg. *Animal droppings*, he realized, *dried out, nearly petrified by the look of them.* Nothing had been in this place for a long time. Months, maybe years.

The lower reaches of the city looked to be the sovereign realm of the giant ape. It was probably an attempt by Russian scientists to hybridize a primate with DNA recovered from the ancient occupants of the place—not unlike similar alleged experiments to recreate extinct species, like the woolly mammoth. A giant ape monster wasn't very useful from a strategic or tactical point of view, which was probably why the creature had been exiled to the abandoned city. Of course, if the subterranean realm was a dumping ground for failed or useless hybrids, then Volos might not be the only long-term resident.

They pushed onward, occasionally checking for signs of activity in the passages and residences they encountered along the way. Mostly they trusted haste to get them through. The pungent smell of fresh scat reached their nostrils as they neared the spot where Knight had first sighted the giant ape. There was no sign of the creature itself, nor did they detect any activity when they reached the passage where it had disappeared.

The tension, accompanied by the constant sonic bombardment, was enough to drive King into a homicidal rage. He tried to channel it into a sense of urgency, quickening their pace to a jog. No one complained, not even Lynn, who was being shaken up and down with every step.

They finished a full circuit, and then another. They were a third of the way to the top, then halfway. And then, as they were completing the fourth circuit, the thing King had been both dreading and expecting finally happened.

Whether the ape had simply been biding its time, lulling them into a false sense of security, or it had simply reached the point where rage overcame the pain of the sonic assault, the creature was done hiding.

The attack did not take them completely by surprise. Knight, who had been trailing the group and checking their six every few seconds, saw it coming and shouted, "Down!"

As King went to the prone position, he twisted around so that he was facing down the slope, the same direction that Knight was aiming the RPG. He could not see anything in the darkness behind them, but over the insistent shriek of the sound pulse, he could just make out a series of rapid grunts—the heavy breathing of a charging animal.

Knight shouted another warning, letting his teammates know to cover up to protect themselves from the deadly backblast. Then the insistent whine in King's ears was replaced by the slightly lower ringing of tinnitus, as the rocket booster motor detonated. With a thunderous boom, the warhead blasted out of the launch tube. The shockwave hit King like a kick to the gut. Then he felt the hot rocket exhaust wash over him, but he did not look away as the rocket streaked toward its target.

There was a flash, no more than seventy-five yards away, as the warhead detonated on impact. In that fleeting light, King saw the beast clearly. It was enormous—even bigger than his first estimate. Although it was hunched over, holding itself up on its knuckles, like a gorilla, it almost completely filled the space between floor and ceiling. King had, without even realizing it, brought his rifle around, aiming at the briefly illuminated target. But in the instant that he saw it, he knew that if the RPG did not take the creature out, there was no hope for any of them.

The light was gone as quickly as it appeared, vanishing even as the report of the explosion reached King's ears. There were more loud pops from Rook firing blindly with his Desert Eagles, and then over the tumult, there was a shrieking sound. It was like a bull elephant trumpeting, only much, much louder.

Knight loaded a second grenade into the tube, a process that took all of one second. He raised it to his shoulder, but instead of shouting another backblast warning, he began crying out repeatedly, "Ceasefire!" He waved his left hand in front of his face, the universal military signal for the same.

Rook got the message, and in the stillness that followed, King realized the animal noises had stopped, along with the shooting. Over the stink of rocket exhaust and high explosives, King's nose detected the distinctive odor of burnt hair and cooking meat.

"Knight, talk to me."

"He's gone. He went over the side."

"Dead?"

Knight hesitated a moment before answering. "He had a great big hole clear through his chest. If that didn't kill him, I don't know what will."

That was good enough for King. "They probably know we're on our way now, so we're done being sneaky. Rook, I'll take your place on the litter. You take point. Shock and awe."

"Testify, Brother," Rook said, raising his pistols in the air like a supplicant praising a deity.

"Blue, can we turn off the noise?"

The harsh tone softened but King could still hear it faintly. He cautiously held the comm unit closer to his ear. "Blue, is it off?"

Deep Blue's voice came through clearly. "It's off."

"Must be my imagination," King said, fitting the earpiece into place.

After a moment, the sound went away, but then he heard something that definitely was not his imagination. An enraged growl, as loud as a jet engine, was echoing up from the depths.

FORTY-ONE

If that didn't kill him...

Knight's own words had come back to haunt him.

He had seen the gaping hole, big enough to reach his arm in without touching burnt flesh or bone. It went right through the center of the monstrous ape-thing's torso. The warhead's secondary charge had gone off an instant later, blasting the creature off the platform and sending it into the depths.

Now it was coming back.

His backscatter vision showed the monster, an enormous skeletal wraith of black smoke, heaving itself up the spiraling levels of the city like rungs on a ladder. It would reach them in a matter of seconds.

And the hole through its middle was gone. Completely healed.

If that didn't kill him, I don't know what will.

"It's a regen," he shouted, hefting the RPG tube onto his shoulder and aiming it straight down at the bounding primate. "King, get your mother to safety. I'll try to slow it down."

"Do what you can," King answered. "But don't be a hero."

Knight knew King had done the math. If the creature caught them, they would all die, probably with just one swipe of its massive arm. But if Knight could knock it back down, it might buy the rest of them the time they needed to reach the top of the city.

Something moved beside Knight. He glanced over quickly and saw Rook standing next to him, a Desert Eagle in each hand, both trained on the nearly invisible mass rising up from below.

"King Kong is a regen," Rook said, shaking his head. "Outstanding. Can this day get any better?"

Regens—humans, animals or hybrid mutant combinations thereof, imbued with rapid healing abilities verging on actual invincibility—had been the bane of the Chess Team's existence almost from the beginning. There were different ways to go about making a regen, ranging from gene-splicing to exotic botanicals. Most of them shared the same vulnerability: healing was tied to neural function. Destroying the brain or severing the head of a regen was usually enough to put it down permanently. Volos's huge head would be an easy target, but whether it could be destroyed was another matter entirely.

Knight knew it would be a waste of time and breath trying to convince Rook to leave with the rest of the team. And if there were any weapons in their arsenal that might be capable of doing some serious damage to the monster in the event that he missed with the RPG, it was Rook's .50 caliber semi-automatics.

He looked down again, sighting in the RPG. The creature was just three levels down, less than a hundred feet away, a grinning death's head made of black smoke, looking right at him.

"Smile, you son of a bitch." He pulled the trigger.

The warhead lanced down, driven by a tongue of fire, and the monstrous visage vanished in a flash and a puff of smoke.

"Well?" Rook shouted, still aiming his pistols into the void.

A smoke-skeleton, shrunken to ant-size by the distance, splashed into the water at the bottom of the cistern. Knight increased magnification and the X-ray image tripled in size. It showed him in full detail the damage wrought by the armor-piercing HEAT round. Half of the enormous skull was gone, along with an entire arm and a portion of the rib cage.

But the creature was still moving, thrashing to stay afloat. As he watched, Knight saw the damaged bones lengthening, as if someone was pouring smoke into an invisible skeleton mold. Judging by the speed at which the bones were filling out, he estimated they had less than a minute before the creature was fully reconstituted.

"Down but not out. This thing is going to keep coming back."

Rook shook his head ruefully. "Like my hemorrhoids."

Knight raised his eyes and saw the rest of the team on the opposite side of the chasm, halfway into the next circuit. Queen in the lead, King and Bishop trailing with Lynn's litter suspended between them. Further up, the spiraling ramp fed into an opening in the gray concrete ceiling, a relatively recent addition, like the water pipes that also disappeared into it. The exit was too small to allow the ape creature through—probably designed for that very purpose.

It would be a journey of two, possibly three more minutes to reach it.

"We better move." He loaded another warhead—their last—into the launcher, and then he and Rook were sprinting up the spiral ramp.

Not a minute later, another roar of primal fury erupted from the chasm.

"Time for some Preparation H, Knight," Rook shouted.

Without slowing, Knight got as close to the edge as he dared and looked down. As before, the ape creature was moving vertically, scaling the levels in dynamic bounds that seemed impossible for so massive an animal. It was already half-way up and moving on a trajectory that would put it between the exit and the team.

"Damn it!" He skidded to a stop, shouldered the RPG, aimed it at a point just above the wraith-like figure and fired, all in one abrupt motion. The rocket streaked across the chasm, but just before it impacted, the smoke-skeleton swung to the side, as if telepathically sensing its proximity. The warhead detonated an instant later, the shockwave shaking the creature loose, but as it tumbled back down into the abyss, it somehow managed to snag hold of one of the water pipes, which buckled under the sudden load. Then it whipped itself around, flying through the air like a gymnast vaulting onto parallel bars. Knight felt the ramp lurch beneath him as Volos caught hold one level down from where he was standing.

There was another roar, this one louder even than the detonation of the rocket, and then the ape monster heaved itself onto the ramp. Knight tried to hit the deck, but a trailing foot almost as long as Knight was tall, caught him a glancing blow. The useless RPG launcher flew from his grasp as he went sprawling across the ramp.

The unintentional hit knocked the wind out of him and left him struggling simply to stay conscious. He rolled over, fumbling for a weapon, and he was knocked flat again, this time by a blast of hot ape breath that reeked of rotten meat. The creature was bent over him, roaring, its fanged simian face—more like a baboon than a gorilla or chimpanzee, or any of the hybrids they had faced—was close enough to touch. It raised its fists above Knight, preparing to squash him like a bug. Each looked the size of a Volkswagen.

But before the death blow could come, the creature's head began twitching. One massive hand, then the other, came up to swat the air in front of its face. Through the haze of pain, Knight could hear the throaty report of Rook's pistols. The heavy caliber rounds weren't really doing any damage—mosquito bites to a creature that size—but they were keeping it busy, giving Knight a chance to slip away.

As soon as he started to move, though, the creature's full attention came back to him. The enormous fists were raised again. This time it did not stop until it had smashed them both onto the stone floor.

But Knight had already slipped away, darting between the monster's pillar-like legs. Rook took advantage of the confusion to reload. Then he resumed shooting, pumping rounds from both pistols directly into the creature's face. He focused his fire on the somewhat more vulnerable eyes and mouth. One grotesquely curved canine tooth shattered, spraying the area with flakes of calcium.

The barrage got the creature's attention. It forgot about Knight entirely and turned its full rage against Rook, who stood less than fifty feet away—a couple of strides for the monstrous ape. It leaned forward, preparing to charge, but Rook stood his ground until both pistols were empty again.

From the creature's blind spot, Knight saw what was about to happen. His only weapon was a SIG pistol. If Rook's Magnum rounds had been nothing more than bothersome mosquitos, the 9-millimeter bullets would be like gnats against the ape-thing's shaggy hide. Still, if gnats and mosquitos could ruin a hike, maybe there was something he could do to keep Volos occupied. He just needed a shot.

He realized the monster did have one vulnerability that was practically staring him in the face. Its feet, shaped a little like deformed human hands, with fingers—or maybe they were toes—as long and big around as a man's leg. Before the creature could take a step in Rook's direction, Knight drew a bead on one knuckle, and started shooting.

Little explosions of red marked the hits. The bullets were barely man-stoppers, and probably didn't penetrate much further than the top layers of skin, but the wound had the effect of stepping on a Lego block while barefoot. The ape-thing let out a cry of agony oddly disproportionate to the injury, especially considering the punishment it had taken from both the RPGs and Rook's Desert Eagles. Then it twisted away, lost its balance and crashed down on the ramp, clutching its injured toe.

Knight was so stunned by the success that he could only stand and stare in disbelief. Then he heard Rook shouting, and knew it was time to start running. He barely made it to Rook's side before Volos shook off the injury—or more likely, regenerated the damaged tissue—and was back in pursuit.

"Split up!" Knight shouted as he ran past. It was about the only thing he could think to do. They had used up all their tricks and most of their luck.

In the back of his mind, Knight recalled the old joke about two hunters running from a bear. One man, ready to give up, told the other that he would never be able to outrun the bear, to which the second said, 'I don't need to outrun him. I just need to outrun *you.*'

It was a grim thought under the circumstances. Given the distance separating them from the top of the city, not to mention the creature's intelligence, there was little guarantee that the creature would settle for just one of them.

Knight felt the stone rampart shudder beneath him as the creature started forward, each footstep sending a tremor through the rock. Even without looking, he could guess its pace. At ten or fifteen feet per stride, it would be on them in seconds.

But then the footsteps stopped. He risked a look back and saw the beast once more trying to protect its face from some unseen nuisance. Rook was still running, staying close to the city wall, which meant the shots were coming from somewhere else.

Over the monster's roars, Knight could hear the faint pop of gunfire from multiple weapons. Some of the rounds struck the stone behind the ape-creature, but most struck its head and upraised hands. One and a half levels up and opposite them, the rest of the team had reached the end of the ramp—the city limits. They were now providing covering fire to give him and Rook a chance to escape.

The rifle bullets were higher-powered, designed to go farther and penetrate deeper, but it was still like trying to bring an elephant down by throwing sewing needles at it. Nevertheless, the distraction was working.

A little too well.

The creature knew the origin of its torment. It let out another primal howl, and then pivoted off the platform, catching it with one outflung hand. It swung there for a moment, gathering momentum, and then swung itself up to catch hold of the next highest level. It was now just half a circuit away from the end of the ramp and the rest of the team. It did not climb up, but continued swinging hand over hand along the edge of the platform, covering twenty or thirty feet at a time.

Knight couldn't see what was happening above, but he knew that in saving him and Rook, their teammates had brought the creature's wrath upon themselves. He kept running, struggling to keep up with Rook, who was likewise sprinting at full-tilt, no longer running away from battle but toward it.

But just as before, Knight knew there was no way they would reach the end of the city in time.

FORTY-TWO

Peter strained against the leather restraints that held him fast on the examination table. But he was no more able to break free of them than he had been the grip of the Presidential bodyguards, who had held him down and fastened the thick belts around his limbs. The rational part of him knew that his efforts would be futile. He would accomplish nothing more than wearing himself out. But the primitive reptilian part of his brain compelled him to keep struggling.

He was angry. Angry at himself for walking into the trap that he had known was a trap. Angry at the man he had known as Vladimir—his father? He still wasn't ready to accept that—not only for this latest betrayal, but for an entire lifetime of treachery and manipulation. Angry at his daughter for not being who he thought she was, and then angry at himself again for not being able to save her.

The door opened, and the person foremost in his thoughts entered. "Hello, Peter."

He stared back at her. "What am I supposed to call you?"

"Julie," she said, though her tone was uncertain, as if she was trying the name out for the first time. "That's who I am, right?"

"If you're Julie, then you should call me 'Dad.' I'm old fashioned that way. Kids today, addressing their parents on a first name basis..."

He gave a snort of disapproval. "Too familiar. And you know what they say about familiarity?"

"I don't, actually."

"It breeds contempt."

She stared at him in consternation.

"Like the contempt your grandfather seems to have for his offspring," Peter went on. He used the word 'grandfather' deliberately, just as he had when suggesting Julie call him 'Dad.'

"You don't understand what he's trying to do," she said, immediately defensive.

He wiggled his arms and legs in the restraints. "I'll admit, it's kind of hard for me to see him as a benevolent visionary."

She pulled a chair away from the wall, positioned it near the table and sat facing him. "You don't need to be afraid. Whatever he does...whatever he has to do...he can bring you back. That's why he wanted to test the Firebird on King...on Jack. Because only the Children of Adoon can be brought back."

"You make it sound like he's doing us a favor. Where I come from, when someone does medical experiments on their children and grandchildren, we call social services." He stretched his hand out, palm up, in an inviting gesture. "I'm sorry I couldn't bring you back, Julie. But the fact that he did is no reason to trust him. He's using you. Using all of us. That's not love. That's not what fathers are supposed to do."

"You don't understand," she said again. "He's doing this to save the world."

Peter sensed that he would gain nothing by trying to force the issue, but the fact that she had sought him out was reason for hope. "He told me that your mother and brother were captured. Is that true?"

She looked away. "They were here."

"But they aren't now? What happened to them? Are they okay?"

"You will see them again."

He realized that what he had taken for guilt at having imprisoned her closest relatives was actually embarrassment at having lost them. *She's not really Julie at all*, he thought. "So what happens now? He's going to test this Firebird on me, right?"

"Yes. But you don't need to worry. The latest generation of the serum utilizes your son's DNA. It should provide complete protection from nuclear radiation, with no attendant side effects."

"Wonderful. So I'll survive the end of the world."

"We all will." She frowned, realizing too late that his comment had been sarcastic. "There won't be a nuclear war. NATO is already finished, and once the Americans realize that atomic weapons are useless against us, the war will be over before a shot is fired."

"You're as naïve as he is arrogant."

Julie's lips curled into a patronizing smile. "Great men are often accused of hubris by their rivals, while the masses cheer for them in secret. The world craves a leader like him. Bold. Fearless. With this courageous step, he will forge a new Russian empire, and we—the bloodline of Adoon—will rule beside him."

"Just like Julius Caesar crossing the Rubicon. I seem to recall that didn't work out so well for him."

She opened her mouth to reply, but just then a resounding thump shook the room. Her forehead creased in sudden alarm and she bolted to her feet. She turned toward the door, but it opened before she could reach it, revealing the would-be emperor himself.

"We're under attack," he snarled.

Julie shook her head in disbelief. "How is that possible? Our early warning system—"

"They are coming up from the old city."

"Who?"

"Who do you think?" The President flashed an angry look at Peter.

It's Jack, Peter thought. *Jack is attacking them.*

"We should leave," Julie said. "Alexei can finish his research elsewhere."

"We will not flee before our enemies." The President continued staring at Peter, his rage solidifying into resolve. "This attack will fail. Send the remaining subhumans down there. And have Alexei bring the Firebird. We will test it now."

FORTY-THREE

King could pinpoint the exact moment when the ape-creature figured out where the attack was coming from. Its fiery orange eyes, squinting against the storm of incoming bullets, seemed to be staring right at him.

With eyes that big, it was probably staring at all of them, but somehow it felt personal, which was fine with King. The creature was no mere wild animal protecting its turf. It was a smart, deadly predator. A carnivore, possibly even a cannibal, depending on how closely it was related to the partially eaten humanzees, the remains of the creatures the team had fought in the hangar. Evidently, Volos was part of the local waste removal system.

"That got his attention," King shouted, unnecessarily. They could all see the thing swinging along the edge of the spiraling platform like the mutant monkey it was. "Fall back."

They had already taken Lynn through the narrow opening in the concrete slab that sealed off the ancient city. The slot was barely wide enough to permit a person to pass through.

Once they were inside, Volos would not be able to follow them.

Queen squeezed off several more shots at the approaching primate before shouting, "What about Rook and Knight?" Her tone was grim, determined, but with a hint of desperation.

The beast would be on them in a matter of seconds. "Right now, we're in more danger than they are."

He loosed a burst at one of the enormous grasping hands, hoping the shock of impact might cause the creature to lose its grip and fall. But the beast was moving so fast, it was impossible to tell if he even scored a hit. Abandoning the effort, he drew back from the edge, shouting again for Bishop and Queen to fall back.

There was a rush of movement as the ape-beast heaved itself up and onto the platform. It landed so hard the floor shook and almost knocked the three of them over. King emptied his weapon into the creature's face, all the while shouting for the others to move, but they were doing the same thing he was.

We're gonna have to have a talk about following orders, he thought.

He spun on his heel, grabbed ahold of Queen and Bishop by the arms, one in each hand and propelled them toward the slot. Something crashed down right where they had been standing, and the stone floor lurched again. He glimpsed a series of fracture lines shooting up the gray concrete wall, but then they were inside the narrow corridor, half-running, half-stumbling.

A roar filled the passage, and King knew without turning that the creature was looking in at them, filling the opening with its bestial visage. Then he heard a rustling noise, something scraping against the sides of the corridor.

It was reaching in for them with the full length of its massive shaggy arm.

He shoved Queen and Bishop ahead of him, stumbled and went face down on the concrete. Something struck his foot and he recoiled, as if from a fire or deadly snake. As he scrambled forward on all fours, he looked over his shoulder and saw the hand, dark leathery skin, chipped fingernails...huge. And just out of reach.

The hand drew back a little, then came forward as the beast tried to jam its whole arm deeper into the slot. The corridor shook and more cracks appeared in the walls.

"Okay," he said, panting to catch his breath. "He's a little pissed off."

Queen was staring...no, glaring at him. "We aren't leaving Knight and Rook."

"Of course we aren't," he said, and then as if to give further reassurance, he activated the comm device. "Knight, Rook. What's your status?"

"Still here," Knight said. "Unfortunately, I don't think we can get to you."

"There's a great big monkey-ass blocking the exit," Rook put in.

King gave Queen an encouraging nod. "Just keep out of sight until he loses interest and goes back to his hidey hole."

Another tremor rattled the passage, loosening pieces of dust and grit from the ceiling.

"He does not seem to be losing interest," Bishop remarked.

"He will," King said, sounding more confident than he felt. *What if he doesn't?*

He picked himself up and looked further down the corridor to where they had left Lynn. She was on her feet—or rather, on her good foot—leaning against the wall, a borrowed pistol in one hand. Her attention was divided between the team's narrow escape and the far end of the passage, which presumably led into the research facility. "Blowing the reactor is the mission. Everything else is secondary."

"Everything?" Bishop asked, one eyebrow raised.

His answer was to push past her and continue along the corridor, but he had not missed the none-too-subtle accusation. Perhaps he deserved it. Even now, in the back of his mind, he still wondered if it was possible to save Julie, to break the hypnotic spell she seemed to be under. Nevertheless, he intended to heed his own admonition. There was no guarantee any of them would make it out alive, but he was going to make damn sure that Volosgrad and all its secrets were wiped off the face of the Earth before he went down. That was priority one. A safe exit for the team and his mother was second on the list. Finding Julie was a distant third.

He allowed Lynn to drape one arm over his shoulder, and they continued along the passage and through the door at the end of the corridor, which opened onto a stairwell. Bishop went out ahead of them.

The stairs—utilitarian metal grating on a frame of steel I-beams—went up ten feet through a vertical channel cut in the slab of solid concrete that kept Volos a prisoner of the abyss. As they rose above it, King saw that they had not reached the end of the ancient city after all. The cylindrical shaft continued up, as far as the eye could see, which was not very far given the low light conditions. The new tenants had made some additions, using the cap as a foundation for the modern subterranean facility. The stairs kept going up the exterior of a flat wall that bisected the shaft, almost certainly the outside wall of the facility to which Julie had brought him and Lynn. Somewhere up there was the hangar and a possible exit to the surface. But without an aircraft to bear them away, it was a less than ideal objective. They would have a better chance making their exit through the ventilation system.

First things first.

Opposite the wall, the top of the concrete slab continued all the way to the far side of the cylindrical shaft. The space was mostly empty, save for a domed concrete structure that looked like a squat grain silo with several metal pipes of varying dimensions sprouting from it. Some disappeared into the slab and others rose straight up and out of view.

"That looks about the right size to hold a small pressurized water reactor." He pointed to a line of steel elbow pipes rising from the slab and connecting to the side of the containment building. "Those are probably feeding the coolant system. We blow those and this thing will go critical in half an hour. There won't be a thing anyone can do to stop it."

The floor jumped again, and this time the cracks spread all the way to the top of the slab. Volos was still at it, and by the look of things, angrier than he had ever been.

"Maybe you don't need to blow reactor," Bishop observed. "Giant monkey is going to do the job for us, I think."

"I'll give him an assist." He eased out from under Lynn, shifting her onto Bishop's shoulders. "Help Mom get up those stairs. Queen, go with her. I'll set the charges."

Queen glowered at him. "Women and children first, is that it?"

King knew the real source of her ire was the fact that she wanted to stay behind to make sure that Rook and Knight—one her boyfriend, the other her oldest and dearest friend—made it out. That was understandable, but not acceptable. Getting them all home was his responsibility, not hers. And he had a plan.

"That's an order," he snapped, but then added a little less forcefully, "Take care of my family."

Queen's expression softened a little, then she nodded to Bishop. "Let's go."

As the three women started up the stairs, King started out toward the containment building at a run, reaching it just a few seconds later. He worked quickly, pressing all but one of the remaining blocks of semtex around the pipes and affixing blasting caps to each block. All of them were daisy-chained to a radio-controlled detonator, and he set it all up while trying to ignore the intermittent tremors.

Volos was still trying to tear concrete apart with his bare hands, and judging from the tumult, he was succeeding. The steel pipes creaked and flexed with each new assault. King could feel heat coming off the pipes, and he tried not to think about what else might be radiating from the containment building. Bishop had not been wrong about the level of damage the creature was doing, and if one of those pipes ruptured prematurely, he wouldn't live to see the meltdown he was trying to initiate. Although it would take time—as much as half an hour—for the nuclear fuel in the reactor to reach a critical temperature and melt everything in the ancient city to slag, the steam eruption from a bursting pipe would parboil him instantly.

With the explosives set, he turned and headed back for the stairs. He could just make out the others, slowly climbing the steps, their progress hampered by Lynn's injury. Even with the headstart, he would have no trouble catching up to them, provided of course that what he was about to do next did not go horribly wrong.

"Knight, Rook, you guys still hanging in?"

Rook's voice sounded immediately. "There was a traffic jam, so we decided to stop off and get Frappucinos. Who knew there was a Starbucks down here? Knight's hitting on the barista. Beck is going to be pissed when she hears about it."

Rook's inclination to meet every crisis with a joke was either refreshing or infuriating depending on the circumstances. Counterintuitively, the worse the situation was, the more King found he appreciated Rook's sarcastic wit. He could imagine Rook fighting alongside the Spartans at the battle of Thermopylae, taunting the overwhelming forces of the Persian emperor, laughing in the face of death.

"I'm gonna blow a small charge in the tunnel. Just enough to give Volos a hotfoot. If it works, he'll probably pull back for a second."

"Give this guy five more minutes and he'll tear open a hole big enough for all of us to get through."

"Yeah, I don't actually want him to do that," King replied. He hopped down the steps. Then at a considerably more cautious pace, he advanced into the crumbling passage.

The ape's huge hand was systematically crushing the cement, breaking off boulder-sized chunks like pieces of an old Styrofoam cooler. The effort was shredding the leathery skin of his fingertips, but the damage was healing almost as quickly as it was sustained.

King got within about twenty feet of the thrashing hand. Close enough. He slipped a silver-colored blasting cap, already wired to another receiver unit, into the wrapped semtex block, then placed it on the floor and nudged it forward with a gentle kick.

"Operation Hotfoot is a 'go,'" he said, backing away. "Standby for the signal to run."

"Now would be a good time," Knight said, cutting off any further humorous observations from Rook.

King backed out of the passage and climbed back up onto the slab. He had to stay close to the mouth of the passage to guarantee simultaneous detonation of all the charges, but far enough away to avoid getting blasted by either explosion. He skirted along the base of the vertical wall about fifty feet, trying also to put some distance between himself and the reactor. Then he flipped off the safety on the 'send' unit.

"Ready?" His finger hovered above the trigger.

"As we'll ever be," Rook replied, with just a trace more apprehension than usual.

At the same instant, Queen shouted, loud enough to be heard even without the comm. "Contact high!"

As soon as the words were out, the shooting started.

It never just rains, King thought, and shouted, "Fire in the hole!"

And then there was.

FORTY-FOUR

Queen didn't know if she was madder at Rook or King. Rook for being a hero and standing with Knight against the giant killer ape. King for showing up out of the blue, taking over and doing what, as their leader, he was obligated to do—namely sending them into harm's way but being the first in line to pull them back out. Or was she madder at herself for being mad at either of them?

Ultimately, it didn't matter. Anger was what she needed right now.

It had begun with a door, two stories above them, bursting open and slamming against the wall with a bang like a gunshot. Then they were everywhere. Humanzees poured down the stairs like a waterfall of flesh and teeth.

They were the same variety that had attacked them in the hangar, or more probably the veterans of that battle—the survivors. The metal grating of the stairs allowed her to see them coming, but it was an effective bullet screen. She would have to wait until they were practically face-to-face to start firing. It was going to be a very close, very ugly battle. Even though the enemy couldn't shoot back, the three of them were outnumbered ten-to-one. She shouted a warning to her teammates, a military habit more than anything else, and then she waited for the creatures to step into the open.

Lynn actually got the first shot off, drilling the first humanzee to come around the corner. She dropped it in its tracks and in the way of the onrushing mob. Then all three of them were firing into the descending wave.

The front rank perished in an instant, their bodies tumbling down the steps like unstrung puppets, exposing the creatures just behind them, who met a similar fate. For a few seconds, the tide of battle was against the humanzees. A third of their force was dead or injured, piled up on the steps like a deadly obstacle course between them and their objective. In the face of such carnage, even the bravest human soldier might have hesitated before charging into certain death. But the humanzees appeared oblivious to their losses. They kept coming, bounding nimbly over the corpses strewn in their path.

In the midst of the chaos, Queen did not hear King's warning or the subsequent explosion of the containment building. The shockwave that shook the stairs was barely a blip on her radar. A cloud of smoke hung in the air around them, mixed with the smell of blood and death. Spent brass was piling up atop twitching bodies that had slid all the way down the steps and come to rest at their feet.

The magazine in her rifle lasted longer than she expected it to. In the fog of war, she must have made a counting error in her favor. She had a spare in hand, and changing it out took less than a second, but it was a second in which the front line advanced almost within reach. They were pushed forward by the mass of creatures behind them. Beside her, Bishop changed her magazine with similar haste, and Queen did her best to cover the brief slackening of their defensive fire, but as she swept the muzzle of her rifle back and forth, raking the advancing line of humanzees at point blank range, she realized the creatures weren't going down. Although their bestial semi-human faces were contorted with death throes, sightless eyes clouding over as they stared into oblivion, they were still upright, still advancing.

They're using their own dead as shields, Queen realized.

And then her rifle went empty again.

She reversed the spent weapon and jammed the wooden stock forward, connecting solidly with the skull of a humanzee that was probably already dead. The blow knocked the creature aside to reveal the head of the living enemy right behind it, and Queen put a round from her pistol through its eye.

Then the crush was upon them.

Queen was knocked back, as a wall of dead humanzees pushed by the dozen or so living ones that remained, slammed into her. She managed to stay on her feet and leaned into the advancing horde. Gripping a blood-slick corpse, she pushed back, but it was like trying to stop a bulldozer.

With a cry of pain, Lynn lost her footing and went tumbling down the steps. Bishop made an instinctive grab for her, and suddenly the humanzees were everywhere.

FORTY-FIVE

"**Fire in the** hole."

On the far side of the concrete slab, and with Volos's arm and body plugging the only opening through it, Rook barely felt the subsequent detonation. But the giant ape snatched its arm out and recoiled like it had been hit by an electric charge. Rook caught just a glimpse of the thing's hand before it was clutched protectively against Volos's body. The explosion had smashed it into an unrecognizable pulp.

"Go!" Knight shouted, bursting from their hiding place like a racehorse out of the gate.

Rook wasn't quite as fast as Knight over long distances, but less than twenty-five yards separated them from the opening. Over that short interval, the difference was negligible. Rook stayed on Knight's heels the whole way.

The passage was strewn with rubble and gore. All down its length, chunks of concrete had broken away, exposing inch-thick steel rods. At the midpoint, the explosion had opened a four foot wide gap in the floor.

"Hole!" Knight shouted, leaping over it without breaking stride.

The warning was almost drowned out by a thunderous roar, and the sound of something rushing down the passage behind them. As Rook made the jump, he felt a concussion wave buffet his back. It was followed immediately by a sound like boulders smashing together. Beneath him, the hole suddenly doubled in size, the floor crumbling away to reveal protruding spikes of broken rebar right where he was about to touch down. There was nothing he could do to extend his leap, but he twisted sideways as he came down, trying to avoid the protrusions.

It almost worked.

A blossom of fiery pain erupted on his left side as the fractured steel tore through his coat and gouged a bloody weal across his ribs.

His breath was stolen by the impact. For a fateful second, he saw only stars. He flailed and clawed for a handhold, anything to keep him from plunging through the hole, but his fingers glanced off the rebar. Then something slammed into his left armpit. He could feel his arm rip at his shoulder...

As the initial haze of pain subsided, he realized it wasn't quite that bad. Without actually intending to, he had caught the piece of steel under his left arm. The impact had strained the ligaments and probably torn some muscles, but his bunched up coat had provided a little cushioning, and more importantly, he hadn't plunged to his death.

Not yet, at least.

The floor shook with another impact, as Volos drove his arm deeper into the passage, and more concrete crumbled away.

Knight wheeled around and then threw himself flat on the rubble strewn floor like a baseball player making a headfirst slide into home plate. He caught hold of Rook's coat and with a single seemingly superhuman heave, he dragged Rook out of the hole.

Rook could feel the floor collapsing beneath him and the steel tearing at his flesh, but a moment later he was back on more or less solid ground, half-entangled with Knight and rolling away from the breach. His side, where the steel had gouged him, was hot and cold and sticky and wet, all at the same time. But pure adrenaline was a potent anesthetic. He felt only a mild sting, like a bad sunburn where the steel had gouged him. His shoulder wasn't hurting either, at least not until he tried to get up and his left arm folded underneath him.

Knight scrambled to his feet, and before Rook could protest, dragged him the length of the passage. As they reached the base of a metal staircase, the floor lurched from another impact. Suddenly half of the passage behind them vanished. A chunk of the ten-foot thick slab had broken away, collapsing down into the cylindrical chasm, around which the ancient city had been built. The falling debris obliterated huge sections of the spiral ramp as it fell, which in turn triggered still more tremors.

The giant ape, emboldened by this success, thrust both hands—the limb damaged by the blast already fully recovered—up through the hole in the slab. He began tearing away more of the damaged concrete.

Rook found his breath. "I'm good," he gasped, trying to shake loose of Knight's grip.

He wasn't good by any means, but he knew if he didn't stand on his own, they would both get pulverized. He grabbed on to the stair rail and heaved himself up. As he did, he caught a glimpse of what was happening a few flights up. He couldn't make out any details. It was just a mass of bodies writhing on the stairwell, punctuated by a few pistol shots. But he knew one of those bodies was Queen and that she needed him.

As he charged up the steps, with Knight at his side, Rook drew his Desert Eagles from their shoulder holsters—or rather he tried to. His attempt to cross-draw was doubly foiled when his groping right hand found only an empty sheath on the left side. The pistol had been torn away during his close encounter with the exposed rebar.

Well...shit, he thought. *Another one bites the dust.*

It wasn't the first time he'd lost one of *The Girls* in the line of duty. The other half of the set was still in its holster on the right, but his left arm didn't respond to his attempts to reach the holster on the right. He somehow managed to contort his right arm around and got the pistol out before he and Knight reached the melee.

Lynn and Bishop had taken a tumble down half a flight, and four of the hairless humanzees were monkey-crawling along the stair rail in an attempt to reach them. Rook blasted two of them with an equivalent number of shots. The heavy caliber rounds not only punched fist-sized holes in their torsos, but blasted them off the rails. Knight concentrated his fire on the creatures closest to the beleaguered women, making up for any deficit in stopping power with quantity, which gave Bishop an opening to empty her pistol into the remaining attacker.

Rook leaped over the two women and charged up the remaining distance to where Queen was all but buried under a mass of humanzees. He couldn't risk a shot into the group, so instead he swung his fist, and the pistol in it, at the nearest monkey-head. Then at another and another, hammering skulls with berserker fury until he at last caught a glimpse of Queen's blonde hair. The creatures had driven her to her knees, but she was still fighting, slashing her bayonet back and forth, streaked with the blood of her foes like some ancient Norse war maiden.

Now that he could see where she was, and more importantly, where she wasn't, Rook stopped using his pistol as a bludgeon. Instead he used it as a pistol, dispatching the four remaining attackers with four rapid headshots.

It was only as the last headless corpse pitched backward that Rook realized the humanzees were the least of their worries. Below them, the gates of hell were opening, and the devil was coming through.

FORTY-SIX

Volos exploded through the slab, sending car-sized chunks of concrete flying in every direction. The eruption shook the staircase. If Bishop had not already been in a semi-supine position on the steps, one hand clutching her injured mother, she would probably have been flung out along with the rest of the debris.

Below them, the ape creature wormed its way out of the hole it had created and immediately turned its attention to the miniscule figures that had invaded its realm and attacked it. The creature grasped the base of the stairs and gave it an experimental shake, as if curious to see whether the stairs would bear his weight.

The metal skeleton supporting the stairs creaked and flexed. Anchor bolts broke loose from their moorings and shot out like bullets. Miraculously, the stairs remained upright and intact. Bishop knew they would not continue to do so much longer.

Knight knelt beside her and slipped an arm under Lynn's back. He was shouting something, urging her to flee.

Why? What was the point? They would never be able to reach the top of the stairs before the monster brought it all down.

Nevertheless, she struggled to her feet. As Knight lifted her mother, she threaded her own arm under his so that Lynn was suspended between them. The stairs groaned and swayed like the deck of a ship on a stormy sea. She gripped the rail with her free hand and lurched up one step at a time.

She saw Rook and Queen, shoving humanzee bodies out of the way, trying to clear a path for them, but before they got there, Volos let out another roar and shook the stairs more forcefully. Bishop clutched the rail, kneeling and she somehow managed to avoid tumbling back down. More bolts and rivets exploded from the staircase. Over the bestial roar, she could hear the distinctive report of a Kalashnikov.

Shooting? Now someone is shooting at us?

The shaking stopped but the shooting and the roaring did not.

No, not shooting at us. Shooting at him.

On the floor below, a hundred yards from the staircase and kneeling at the base of the concrete wall, King was unloading a rifle at Volos.

Idiot, she thought. What was King thinking? Bullets couldn't hurt the beast. They would just piss it off.

Which was, she realized, exactly what King was trying to do.

As if to confirm that, a shout sounded in her ear. "Queen. Get them the hell out of here!"

Rook answered first. "Not leaving you, boss." As if to punctuate the statement, a shot thundered from the steps just above Bishop, the bullet disappearing into the fur on Volos's broad back like a pebble thrown into an ocean.

"Damn it, Rook! Ceasefire." King shouted. He fired another long burst into the beast's face, then switched out the magazine without lowering it. "If you don't get out now, none of us will. Queen. You've got your orders. Follow them for once."

"You heard him," Queen called out. "Move."

Bishop knew her brother was right. If they stayed one second longer, they would all die. Her. Their mother. The team. And King, too.

"Trust me," King said between bursts.

Bishop looked over at her mother. Lynn couldn't hear King's side of the exchange, but she knew what was going on. She nodded slowly.

Trust him.

The staircase shook again, but only a little, as Volos charged into the storm of bullets from King's rifle. The entire slab shook with each footfall, fractures radiating across the concrete like cracks in thin ice. King stood his ground, firing until the magazine was empty again. Then he simply stood there, waiting as Volos raised his massive fists and brought them down.

Bishop knew her brother would dodge, knew that he was simply waiting for the last instant, for the beast to commit fully. He wasn't suicidal, and he knew that staying alive and keeping Volos occupied was the only chance the rest of them had at escaping.

She was not wrong. As the monster brought his fists down, King darted forward, sprinting between the beast's legs. Volos's fists came down through the emptiness where King had been standing only a moment before, and then the floor heaved as the fists went right through the concrete like a pair of wrecking balls.

A long fissure—not merely a fracture but a crack several inches wide—shot out from the point of impact. It was like a black lightning bolt racing between Volos's legs, across the floor toward the crater from which the monster had emerged. The halves of the floor lurched. King stumbled, fell and slid toward the widening crevasse. He threw his arms out wide, arrested his slide, and then he rolled away from the fissure, toward the wall.

Toward the creaking staircase.

Volos whirled around, spied his elusive prey, and lurched forward. As his foot slammed down, the broken slab collapsed completely and fell away into the yawning chasm below. Volos scrambled for a handhold, but everything he touched crumbled beneath his weight. With one last howl of fury, he plunged into the darkness along with everything else.

A long section of the wall behind the stairs broke loose and joined the rain of debris, exposing the unlit bowels of the research facility where the humanzees had lived in their pens. The staircase remained intact, hanging out over the abyss, anchored to what was left of the wall.

Queen found her voice first. "King! Come in. What's your status?"

There was no answer.

"Knight, do you see him?"

Knight leaned over the rail and scanned the darkness. "Shit," he muttered. "I don't see King, but Kong is coming back for more."

Queen's eyes went dark with helpless rage, but aside from that, her expression was as cold as ice. "Then it's time for us to go."

FORTY-SEVEN

The room shook so violently that the table Peter was strapped to rose several inches off the floor before slamming back down. There had been several smaller tremors in the minutes since Julie's departure, but nothing of that magnitude. Peter wondered if the entire under-ground facility was about to cave-in.

The Russian President seemed to be thinking the same thing. He turned to his bodyguard. "Gather up your men and take the helicopter up."

The man, clearly conflicted between safeguarding his charge and doing as he was told, frowned. "Come with us, sir."

The President clapped him on the arm. "Go. I am in no danger here, but if the helicopter is damaged, we will all have a long walk." He laughed and the bodyguard laughed, too. It was a nervous, insincere sound, though. Then the man grudgingly left to carry out his orders.

"Is this how you imagined your long game would play out?" Peter asked, when the two of them were alone.

The President was unflappable. He circled around the table, positioning himself on the side opposite the door, and leaned over Peter. "The advantage of the long game is that you always win in the end, no matter what happens, if only you stay the course."

"You've bet everything on the Firebird. What if you can't make it work?"

"It will work. If not today, then tomorrow, or next year. I can wait."

"I don't think you can. My son forced your hand, didn't he? You have to do this now, or it all falls apart. And if you don't have the Firebird, you can't risk war with the West. Your empire dies before it can be born."

The other man smiled. "Yes. Exhilarating, isn't it? A game without stakes is not worth playing. But I will tell you a secret. The Firebird does not matter."

Peter shook his arms against the restraints. "Then let me loose."

The President went on as if he had not spoken. "Oh, it will give us an advantage to be sure, but it is like a..." He waved his hand in the air, as if grasping for the appropriate simile. "A crash helmet. The days when the Americans would have been willing to use nuclear weapons have long since passed. They are weak, too concerned with how history will judge them. But I tell you, history will remember only that a once great nation went into decline, as all nations do. It will remember that a great Russian empire rose up to take its place as the world's only superpower."

"But if you're wrong," Peter pressed, "you would risk everything."

"Not everything." He seemed about to expound on the cryptic statement, but at that moment the door opened. Julie entered, followed by a young man Peter surmised must be Alexei, the mad scientist tasked with creating the Firebird.

Peter had noticed Alexei in the hangar, speaking to Julie and the President. He was a haughty sycophant, lording over his little domain, while slavishly worshipping the President. Now, he looked positively terrified. His face was pale, almost ghostly, and he carried himself with his hands against his chest, clutched in protective fists. He looked like a person trying to shrink himself into nothingness.

If the President noticed Alexei's discomfort, he gave no indication. "Ah, the moment of truth has arrived. Now you will see what comes of playing the long game."

Alexei's eyes were darting about nervously, as if he feared the ceiling might come down at any moment. "Perhaps it would be safer to conduct the test in Moscow," he said. His tone was tentative, as if he feared to give offense.

"We will test it now," the President said, his tone flat and emotionless, and yet somehow indisputable.

Alexei ducked as if trying to avoid a blow. "Of course."

The young man took a capped syringe from the pocket of his lab coat, and started toward the examination table. Julie held back at the edge of the room, staring at Peter with cool indifference. He would get no help from her.

"So how is this going to work?" Peter asked. If he stalled long enough, maybe the President would accede to Alexei's obvious desire to postpone the test, or perhaps Julie would have a change of heart. "You stick me with that and then...what? Dose me with radiation and wait a few weeks to see if I die?"

Alexei tittered nervously, but it was the President who answered. "I won't let you die, Peter. You are family."

"You're correct, of course," Alexei said, taking a step closer and cautiously removing the safety cap from the syringe. He held the hypodermic as he might a poisonous snake, keeping his fingers well-clear of the business end. He depressed the plunger until a drop of amber-colored liquid oozed from the tip of the hollow needle.

"We won't know how effective it is against radiation for several days," he continued, taking another tentative step toward Peter and lowering the syringe toward Peter's arm. "What we're really hoping for is to overcome the electromagnetic saturation reaction. We can test that right away. If you don't blow, we'll know we've made a breakthrough." He paused, then affected a guilty expression. "I probably shouldn't have said that out loud."

Peter jerked away instinctively, but the leather restraints allowed almost no movement whatsoever. "Julie! You can stop this."

She might have been a statue for all the emotion her face revealed.

"Please," Alexei said. "Try not to move. I don't want to injure you accidentally. This is going to hurt bad enough, as it is."

Peter did the only thing he could. He didn't think Alexei would take the chance of wasting the precious Firebird serum by trying a blind stick, so he started thrashing his body, as if in the grip of a seizure.

The President reached across Peter's body and clamped a hand down on his left forearm, pinning it to the table. His other arm went across Peter's throat and gripped the left shoulder, completely immobilizing Peter. "Do it now, Alexei."

The young man hesitated, his eyes full of inexplicable fear. "Maybe someone else should—"

"Do not be afraid Alexei. He cannot hurt you."

Peter struggled against the vise-like hold, determined to sow doubt about the assurance, but his tormentor was unbelievably strong.

Alexei swallowed nervously, and then moved in with the syringe, lowered it to Peter's arm and then with excruciating slowness, drove it in.

FORTY-EIGHT

King hugged the ground, grateful to at last have something under him that wasn't pitching back and forth. He allowed himself exactly one long deep breath, exhaling it as a sigh of relief, before pushing himself up to his knees and getting a look at where his desperate mad scramble from the crumbling concrete slab had taken him.

The collapse of the floor and walls had opened a new, albeit uncertain, path of escape. In the split-second he had to consider his options, anything that didn't end with him plummeting to certain death in the chasm seemed preferable.

He was in a large room, though in the dimness it was difficult to say for certain how large. It bore a passing resemblance to the room where he and Bishop had almost caught up to Catherine...Julie... whatever...and subsequently encountered an army of humanzees, but there were differences. Instead of pens, the walls held enclosures made from chain-link fences. They were cages, meant to hold something bigger and stronger, and perhaps a bit harder to control than the human-chimpanzee hybrids they had fought. The cages, thankfully, were empty.

He turned around and saw the empty space where the wall and a portion of the floor had been. He took a cautious step toward the edge of the abyss. Volos was down there in the darkness, still alive and mad as hell, and probably on his way back.

"Queen, what's your status?" Not *is everyone okay?* or *Did you guys make it out?* He kept the request vague, making an effort to avoid tempting fate with optimism or specificity.

No answer.

"Queen? Bish? Anyone copy?" Still nothing. "Deep Blue, this is King. Do you copy?"

When there was no reply, he dug into his pocket and took out the quantum ansible unit, or rather, the pieces of the high-tech device. It had been crushed during his mad scramble to avoid a similar fate. "Guess I'm talking to myself."

He discarded the fragments and edged closer to the chasm, peering out at the ruin Volos had wrought. The slab had not completely collapsed, though what was keeping it up, King could not say. The portion with the reactor containment building was still there, though the pipes leading into it were mostly gone. Steam was billowing from the holes where they had been. Without water to bear the heat away, the reactor was heating up, rapidly building toward a critical event.

To his left, he spied the staircase, suspended out over nothingness like the end of a fire escape. It was too far away to jump to, and even if he managed to make the leap, it looked like it might collapse if he looked at it wrong. He thought it might be possible to climb out to it, but it would take time, something that was in short supply.

The stairs weren't an option, but he was in the research facility now, and there were other ways out of it.

Before setting out to find a better exit, he did a quick equipment check. He had lost the rifle and the comm unit, but he still had his pistol. He also had thirty rounds of ammunition to put through it and the bayonet. Not much, but at least he'd wouldn't go down without a fight.

He picked his way through the dark room and to an ascending stairwell. A door at the top opened into the familiar corridors of the research facility. The hall was littered with debris, and the walls were spider-webbed with stress fractures. There was no sign of activity whatsoever. The place looked completely abandoned, which given the level of damage and impending reactor meltdown, made a lot of sense.

He quickened his step, trying to keep his internal compass oriented away from the shattered wall separating the old giant city from the modern facility. He passed locked doors and a few that were standing ajar or blown completely off their hinges.

He knew where he was now. He was near the hallway where Queen had fired the RPG to break the humanzee charge during their first escape. The hangar was just ahead. He made a cursory examination of the open doors, just to make sure that nobody would attempt to ambush him as he passed by, but each room was as deserted as the rest of the place.

And then he heard voices.

"You can stop this."

King froze. *Dad?*

Of course it was his father. Peter was looking for Julie; it was inevitable that he would have found his way here.

"Please," another voice said, likewise familiar. Not Julie, but the mad scientist, Alexei. "Try not to move. I don't want to injure you accidentally."

Injure? King could still feel the spot of pain in his hip where Alexei had drilled into him to harvest his bone marrow. It was merely a nuisance; he had endured much worse. But whatever was happening to Peter almost certainly *was* much worse. He started forward again, trying to pinpoint the source of the voices.

A scuffling sound came from behind a wall to his left, and then there was another shout. "Do it now, Alexei."

King, his pistol at the ready, moved to the edge of the door and began slicing the pie. Just a glimpse was enough for him to recognize the room, the same room where he had been held and violated just a few hours before.

And now it was his father strapped to the table.

Alexei mumbled something, and then the Russian President spoke, urging him to carry out whatever diabolical new experiment they had devised. King fought the urge to charge into the room prematurely. He wouldn't be able to help his father if, in a fit of tunnel vision, he charged into the room and got blown away by a squad of soldiers with nothing better to do than watch the door.

But there weren't any soldiers. Just Alexei and the President, hovering above his father, and off to one side, Julie, looking on with complete detachment.

King stepped forward. "Get away from him!"

All eyes turned toward him, but his focus was drawn to the syringe protruding from his father's arm, and Alexei's pale finger poised to depress the plunger.

"Do it, Alexei!"

The President's shout startled the young man. He looked away from King, looked down at the needle and his finger started to move.

But King's finger moved first.

FORTY-NINE

A single 9-millimeter bullet from King's GSh-18 punched into the back of Alexei's head. It entered near the base of the skull, deforming and exiting in an eruption of bone, blood and brain matter that sprayed the Russian President's face. Along the way, it obliterated Alexei's brain stem, severing the connection between his autonomic nervous system and his body. That not only killed him instantly, preventing him from consciously depressing the plunger on the syringe, but it also ensured that he would not be able to do so as an involuntary death reflex.

The cruel young man slumped over Peter, his hand falling away from the syringe, the needle still embedded in Peter's arm.

King moved the front sight of his weapon a few degrees and centered it on the spot between the President's eyes. There was no need to utter an assertive command or a victorious taunt. King telegraphed his intention with stark clarity.

Move and it will be your brains splattered all over the room.

But it was a bluff. No matter his crimes or ambitions, the man was a head of state. Short of launching a full nuclear strike on Moscow, there could be no more provocative act. King was trying to prevent a war with Russia, not start one.

Maybe the other man recognized that as well, or maybe he simply didn't care. Whatever his motivation, the rage simmering behind his blue eyes and the mask of gore on his face, spiked to a boiling point. Heedless of the weapon aimed at him, he leapt over the table and launched himself straight at King.

King had only a moment to brace himself for the charge. At the last instant before contact, the President shifted to the side, grasped hold of King's shoulders and spun around, turning King's forward lean into forward momentum. Before he knew what was happening, he was flying backward, through the open door and across the debris-strewn corridor. He slammed hard into a damaged cinder block wall with enough force to dislodge several of the bricks.

King flailed for a handhold, the pistol clattering to the floor, his brain still racing to catch up with what had happened. Eyes ablaze with raw fury, the Russian stalked toward him in a familiar low fighting stance. His fists were cocked at his hips, and with a harsh bark, he pulled his left hand back. In the same motion, he unleashed his right directly into King's chest, punching him completely through the broken wall.

King felt rough concrete scouring his body for a moment, and then he was falling—falling much further than the two or three feet that should have separated him from the floor.

Falling into a vast darkness.

As he fell, a random memory flashed through King's head like a stray cat. He recalled that the Russian President was known to have advanced black belts in Taekwondo, judo and *kyokushin* karate. Unlike most western politicians, who preferred a soft moneyed life of luxury, the Russian had cultivated the hyper-masculine public image of a warrior-leader, to include a regime of physical fitness and martial arts training. Foolishly, King had been so concerned with the threat he posed to the world leader, and by extension, world peace, that he had not considered that the man might actually pose a real and immediate threat to him.

The fall ended with King crashing into something that gave a little beneath him, just enough to cushion the blow, but not ward off the rain of broken cinder blocks that followed him. His grasping hand encountered a cold steel mesh, like a net. As his head cleared a little more, he recognized it as a chain-link weave. In the corner of his eye, he could just make out the emptiness where the opposing wall ought to have been. The distant but all too familiar growl of an animal—a gigantic animal—rolled in through the gap.

He was back where he'd started, in the room with the animal pens, lying atop one of the cages. The Russian President stared down at him through the hole, a bright spot in the dark wall, twenty feet above his head. Then the man was moving, crawling through to finish what he had started.

King heaved himself to the side, rolling out of the way a fraction of a second before the man landed, feet first on the chain-link. The flexible mesh bowed like a trampoline and rebounded, catapulting King out over the edge. He crashed down on the floor, the wind knocked out of him. His mind raced like an engine, but the transmission of his body was stuck in neutral.

Volos's grunts of exertion were louder now. The beast was close, close enough that King expected to see a great hairy hand reaching in to crush him. But his human foe struck before that could happen. The President descended on him with a knee drop aimed at his chest. King just managed to roll to the side, so that the knee glanced off his ribs—painfully, but not fatally—and the Russian, off-balance, spilled onto the floor.

King kept rolling, putting some distance between himself and the other man, then he sprang to his feet. He felt a little vertiginous, still not quite able to draw a breath, but he knew how to fight through pain and disorientation. The Russian's decisive attack had put King on the ropes, but ultimately, the man's martial arts accolades were no match for King's many lifetimes of training and experience.

The Russian assumed the fighting position known as a 'cat stance,' and then started toward him. His movements followed the rehearsed choreography of a simple taekwondo form or karate *kata*, but much, much faster. King was faster still.

He blocked the incoming punch, sweeping it aside with his forearm, then blocked the follow through. He delivered a lightning fast front kick that knocked the Russian off his feet. As the man flew through the air, arms windmilling in a futile attempt to catch himself, the rage fueling him slipped a little. It revealed the astonishment of someone whom, despite years of training for a fight like this, had never really been hit by someone who meant it. He crashed down on his tailbone and went sliding across the floor.

King leapt after him, seized the Russian's shirtfront even before the man had stopped sliding, lifted him up and then shoved him away again. The Russian collided with one of the mesh cages, then bounced back, right into King's fist. Blood and broken teeth exploded from the Russian's mouth as he fell back against the cage. Amazingly, he did not lose consciousness.

Some of the fury returned to his eyes, though. He spat out a gobbet of blood, and rasped, "You killed that precious child."

The statement caught King off guard, not because it was said in Russian but because it took him a moment to realize the man was talking about Alexei.

"You killed him," King countered in the same language, "when you told him to inject my father with that shit."

The Russian glowered at him, but the fury did not abate. "I will hunt down and kill everyone precious to you. Father. Mother. Wife. Everyone you love."

King took a menacing step forward, balling his fists, but the Russian remained uncowed. "Will you kill me, then? What are you waiting for?"

"I'm wondering the same thing myself," King muttered, and he threw a roundhouse that probably broke the other man's jaw.

Nothing had changed, of course. Killing this man would be a mistake of epic proportions, but kicking his ass? King couldn't see a downside to that. In fact, with the man's monumental ego, he would probably never admit to having been beaten.

A roar shook the room. King whirled to find the gap in the missing wall filled by an enormous simian face. Volos had arrived, and Volos was an enemy King could not defeat.

The creature's hand appeared, reaching into the room, reaching for him. He backed away quickly, and caught a flash of movement. The Russian was back on his feet, running for the steps leading out of the room.

King ran too, as much to catch the Russian and stop him from making good on his threat, as to escape the rampaging beast-god behind him. The floor quivered underfoot as the monster slammed his arm in, trying to enlarge the hole, cracking the research facility open like the world's biggest coconut.

King barely made it to the stairs before the floor collapsed completely, the pieces tumbling away into the abyss as Volos, gripping the walls with his powerful hands, climbed inside. As King bounded up the steps, taking them two at a time, one of those hands came after him. It obliterated the stairwell like a stack of Jenga blocks. King slipped twice as the steps vanished beneath his feet, but he caught himself on his hands, emulating Volos's primate cousins.

The tumult died away as he reached the corridor, a few steps further behind the Russian President than when he'd started, but it grew louder again as he neared the hole in the wall opposite the room where Peter was being held captive.

As the other man neared the examination room, King reached down into his reserves for one final burst of speed, but it wasn't enough. The Russian disappeared inside, and it seemed to take an eternity for King to make the three-second-long journey to the same destination.

This time, he did not approach with caution, slice the pie or do any of the other things that he had been trained to do. Instead, he rushed inside, stopping only when he saw Julie and he realized that she had retrieved the pistol he had lost earlier. She had the muzzle pressed to Peter's head.

FIFTY

The Russian stood to one side of the exam table, hands resting on his knees, breathing heavily after the mad dash. He looked up as King burst into the room, his eyes now fully ablaze with raw hatred. Then he turned to Julie. "Kill him! Kill both of them!"

Julie did not move.

"Do it!"

She flinched but did not pull the trigger. "We need them to finish the Firebird."

"There is no Firebird," the President snarled. "Alexei is dead."

"Alexei was nothing."

Judging by the lethality of the stare the Russian now directed at Julie, it was evident that was absolutely the wrong thing to say. Judging by her reaction, it was evident that Julie recognized it as well.

"The Firebird was your creation," she said, taking a softer tone in an effort to clarify her meaning. "Alexei was the instrument of creation, but it was your genius at work, not his."

The attempt fell flat. "There is no Firebird," the Russian repeated, his voice taut, like a wire about to snap. "My precious Alexei is dead. What do I care if the world burns? Kill. Them. Now."

King straightened and raised his hands. "Julie, you don't need to do what he says anymore."

Her eyes met his but her expression was utterly unreadable. The gun did not move.

"I'm here. Dad is here. It's time to come back to your family."

He did not dare to hope that she would simply melt into a puddle at the invitation. He half-expected her to meet the offer with hostility. Her loyalty to the Russian President was like a classic case of the Stockholm Syndrome. Julie's reaction however did not seem to come from anywhere on that spectrum.

She tilted her head sideways, lips pursed together in an expression of consternation, as if King had failed to grasp a childishly simple concept. "Why on Earth do you think I would want to do that?"

He had no answer except the obvious. "Because we're your family. We love you." He glanced at Peter, who was still trussed up like a sacrificial offering. "Tell her."

She shook her head before Peter could speak. "You keep going on about family, like it's so important. It's nothing. It's a set of biological imperatives reinforced by environment. We're all related here." She pointed with her free hand at the President. "Him. Me. You. Your father. It's completely irrelevant."

King was momentarily speechless. He did not know if it would be possible to reason with her, but this certainly was not the time or place for it. "Just come with us," he said. "Trust me, you don't want to stay here."

As if to reinforce his point, Volos let out a thunderous roar. The facility shook again, as yet another wall crumbled beneath his relentless assault. With his hands still raised, King took a step toward the table.

Behind him, the Russian President started to laugh. "You speak to her of family. You know nothing about her. I am her only family."

"Look around, Julie," Peter said. "You know what he wants. What he's planning. Is that what you want? War? A world in flames?"

"What I want," Julie said, "is for the Children of Adoon to take their rightful place as rulers of this miserable world."

"You'll rule over ashes."

Now a smile cracked her icy visage. "There won't be a war. It's all theater. A pretense. Symbolic military posturing. The America that could have stood against us ceased to exist long ago."

"If you truly believed that, you wouldn't need the Firebird."

Before she could answer, a bestial roar shook the room, followed almost immediately by an impact that collapsed one wall of the room. Julie staggered back a step. King took advantage of the distraction to move closer, but Julie quickly reasserted control, aiming the gun directly at his chest.

"Do it!" The Russian President hissed again.

King did not know why she had not already done it. He wanted to believe that it meant something, that the real Julie was still in there somewhere, fighting for control. But when he looked deep into those eyes that were so like his own, he saw that she was going to pull the trigger.

"They are of the line of Adoon," she insisted, as if this was the only salient point.

"He killed Alexei," the Russian said. "I can sire more offspring, but Alexei can never be replaced. Kill them and be done with it."

"Julie," Peter implored. "He's your brother."

"He's not my brother," she snarled, her finger tightening on the trigger. "And I'm not your daughter."

Peter's face contorted with grief, as if those words were more hurtful than anything Alexei might have intended, but then his hand moved, as fast as lightning, and he struck her in the chest.

A cry of surprise tore from her lips, rising in pitch to a shriek of pain or terror or perhaps both. As she staggered back, the gun fell from her fingers. King saw the syringe protruding from her chest, the needle embedded next to her breastbone, the plunger fully depressed. Peter had just injected the contents directly into her heart.

FIFTY-ONE

"No!" King heard the shout, but did not immediately realize that it had come from him. Even though he knew the woman was not really Julie, not really his sister, he felt as if the needle had stabbed through his own heart.

Peter, unencumbered by the leather restraints despite all appearances to the contrary, had rolled off the table, landing cat-like on his feet. His expression was utterly blank. Remorseless. He was no longer Peter the father of Julie and Jack and Asya, but Peter the spy. Peter the killer. He had somehow managed to slip out of his restraints, probably while Julie had been following the battle between King and the President, and he had secreted away the syringe as a weapon of last resort.

With practiced efficiency, he now delivered a knife hand blow to the Russian President's throat with such force that King actually heard a popping sound, as the man's larynx was crushed. In almost the same motion, Peter whirled around, seized King's biceps and propelled him toward the exit.

They emerged from the room to find the hallway almost completely reduced to rubble, and Volos the giant ape was forcing his way into the research facility. Peter faltered, staring in disbelief at the monstrosity. Now it was King's turn to take the lead, pulling his father along, racing down the battle-scarred hallway toward the hangar.

He did not allow himself to dwell on what had just happened. There would either be time to deal with both the emotions and the consequences later, or there would not. Survival was the only thing that mattered now, escaping the wrath of Volos and getting as far from the doomed research facility as they could before the reactor went critical.

He did not know what waited for them at the end of the passage. A troop of humanzees that would tear them apart? A squad of Spetsnaz, ready to blow them away with automatic weapons? Either option seemed preferable to the hell they were desperately trying to escape, but he nevertheless slowed to a jog as they neared the exit.

The hangar was completely empty. There were no hostile forces waiting for them, and no helicopter to bear them to safety. Above, the retractable doors were wide open, revealing a cool morning sky that seemed impossibly far away.

King drew to a stop and surveyed the area anew, searching for some other means of egress, and he found it. In the far corner, next to the control booth, a metal maintenance stairway rose up to a suspended catwalk that ran along the perimeter of the hangar doors. At one end of the walkway, a metal ladder continued up to the ceiling and what he could only assume was a trap door to the surface.

"There!" He pointed to it and broke into a run, charging across the vacant platform and mounting the stairs. The proximity of salvation was a stronger motivation than even the prospect of a gruesome demise.

As they neared the top of the staircase, King heard a familiar roar. Not the growl of the ape creature, but the harsh mechanical noise of a jet turbine and the persistent chop of rotor blades. He quickened his step, seeking the relative cover of the catwalk. He hunkered down there with Peter at his side, as the source of the sound—a Mil Mi-8 helicopter—descended into the hangar.

Even before it touched down, several men armed with automatic weapons emerged from the cabin and moved toward the mouth of the passage.

"Think they saw us?"

Peter shook his head. "They're here for him."

"Hopefully King Kong has already disposed of the evidence."

"What do you mean?"

"You killed the Russian President, Dad. That's kind of a big deal."

Peter let out a soft rueful chuckle. "I wish. He's not dead, Jack. I don't think it's possible to kill him. He's immortal, just like Alexander."

King stared at his father. "Still full of surprises, aren't you."

"His real name is Genrikh Ludvig. He was a scientist from the Stalin era—"

"I know about Ludvig," King said, cutting him off. "Are you sure?"

For a moment, he felt something like relief at the revelation, but then he saw its place in the big picture and knew that it would have been better if Peter actually had killed the man.

Peter nodded, and then added in a distant voice. "He's my father. Your grandfather."

King managed to keep his emotions in check as the last piece of the puzzle fell into place.

"Family, huh?" Peter said. "It can be a real bitch sometimes."

The catwalk swayed under them, rippling with the seismic waves of Volos's ongoing destruction of the facility. Maybe the problem would solve itself after all.

"Let's move."

They crept the remaining distance to the ladder. King climbed it and threw back the trap door. A sprinkling of snow fell down on his face and in spite of everything, he smiled as he climbed up into the daylight.

"King!"

He turned and saw Knight emerging from behind a nearby tree, a look of naked relief on his face. "You made it. We thought you bought it."

"Not today," King replied, nodding. "The rest?"

"Bumps and bruises. The usual. They're heading out. Getting clear before this place blows."

"Yeah? Why the hell aren't you with them?"

Knight grinned. "A little thing called hope." He glanced down as Peter emerged from the trap door. "You found your dad in there?"

"Yeah."

Knight hesitated a moment before adding, "Anyone else?"

Without quite knowing why, King glanced back into the opening. "No. That's everyone. Let's get out of here."

They made it to the edge of the wooded area before the sound of the helicopter, rising from the concealed hangar, reached their ears. King crouched down, fully expecting the aircraft to begin circling above them, scanning the area for the escapees. Instead it sailed past without slowing. While he was grateful that fate had not chosen to throw one more obstacle in their path, he knew who was aboard the helicopter. He knew what its flight portended. Their mission to destroy the research facility had succeeded, but they had not averted the apocalypse. In fact, that eventuality now seemed more certain than ever.

"Let's move," he said, and as they hiked out into the open across packed snow, he turned to Knight. "Where do we stand on exfil?"

"Bishop's working something out with a local bush pilot."

"Something goes right for a change," King remarked. He hoped it was the start of a trend.

Then, as if the universe was tuned in to his wishful thinking, the world lit up with a flash more brilliant than the sunrise. King barely had time to shout for them all to get down before the blast was upon them.

FIFTY-TWO

The first gasp felt like breathing chips of broken glass, but the pain helped the Russian focus as life returned to his body. He sat up and saw Alexei...beautiful Alexei...sprawled out on the floor beside him.

The boy's face was gone.

Beautiful no more.

Tears bled through the mask of blood drying on the President's face, but gradually, the sound of screaming penetrated the fog of his grief.

Julie's screams.

The memory of what had happened burst through the surface of his resurrected consciousness like a breaching submarine. Peter Machtchenko, attacking him, stabbing his own daughter through the heart. Stabbing her with...

The Firebird.

He rolled over onto hands and knees, crawled around the end of the examination table and saw her, writhing, shaking, as if her bones were on fire. That probably wasn't far from the truth. The serum had permeated her bloodstream, bonding with her cells. It would be spiking toward critical mass, despite the fact that she had not, to the best of his knowledge, received any long term exposure to nuclear materials or been subjected to EM radiation.

The room shuddered, reminding him that there were other immediate dangers. Volos had broken loose from his prison in the depths and was systematically tearing the research facility apart.

No matter. His work here was done.

There would be no going back to the drawing board this time. The Firebird gambit had failed, but the endgame was at hand. He might not win, but there was no way he could lose.

He would have his empire, or the world would burn. Either outcome was acceptable.

He got to his feet and made his way unsteadily across the pitching floor. He passed through the doorway as the walls to either side crumbled. He thought he saw Julie's body tumbling away into the chasm with the rest of the debris, but before he could look to be sure, a voice reached out to him.

"Sir! This way!"

Through the rain of debris, he spotted the head of his protection detail, urging him toward the exit.

He had always tolerated having bodyguards because it was expected that someone of his stature needed protection, but now he was grateful for their presence. As he ran toward them, Volos broke through, overfilling the corridor with his bulk.

"Stop him!" The President cried out as he pushed his way into the protective circle they had created for him. "I must get away."

The men exchanged a nervous glance, but then shouldered their rifles and began firing into the approaching simian visage, as the President ran for the hangar. As soon as he spied the helicopter, he raised his hand and made a circling gesture, signaling the pilot to take off as soon as he was aboard.

There was no reason to wait for the protection detail. The shooting had stopped almost as quickly as it had begun. His men were already dead.

He hurled himself through the open door, shouting for the pilot to take off. His voice was drowned out by the whine of the turbines spinning faster, and then he felt the deck lurch beneath him as the aircraft lifted off.

The ape exploded through the wall, showering the hangar with debris. Chunks of concrete pinged off the armored exterior like ricocheting bullets.

The helicopter rose.

Fifteen feet. Twenty.

Through the open door, the President met the creature's gaze. He saw the ancient hatred locked behind those animal eyes. Volos, the entity that had guarded the tombs of the Originators from times immemorial. He had been reawakened by the President's early experiments with human-ape hybridization, transformed by an infusion of his own potent immortal genetic material.

"*Do svidanya*, brother," he whispered, as the helicopter passed through the hangar doors and ascended into a bright morning sky, rising above even the creature's long reach.

Volos was magnificent, but far too dangerous for this fragile world built by mere humans. Perhaps there would be a place for the creature in the future he would create.

Or perhaps not.

As the helicopter banked away from the city and headed south, a flash briefly illuminated the portholes, followed a moment later by the buffeting of a shockwave. After a few moments of riding out the disturbance, the pilot called back on the intercom to report a massive explosion behind them, but the President did not even bother with an acknowledgment.

The fate of Volosgrad no longer concerned him.

He had a war to start.

FIFTY-THREE

The air above instantly became furnace hot, a burning gale force wind that felt powerful enough to carry him away. The snow beneath him was whisked away and flashed into steam, depositing him on soggy tundra that lurched beneath him as the seismic wave raced to catch up with the wind. The wind fell off abruptly, and then just as suddenly, it reversed as the vacuum created by the shockwave sucked the air back into the center with a great gasp.

King felt someone grip his arm. Knight? No, it was Peter, but Knight was there, too. He was battered and slightly parboiled, but otherwise no worse for wear. Peter's mouth was moving, but King couldn't hear anything but a persistent ringing in his ears.

He made a circle with his thumb and forefinger, then pointed questioningly at Peter, who nodded, and at Knight, who returned a thumb's up.

Maybe our luck is holding after all, King thought, and then he regretted thinking it, as rocks and chunks of metal and concrete began raining from the sky.

"Cover up," he shouted, or thought he did—he couldn't even hear his own voice. He pulled his shirt up over his mouth and nose, and then curled into a fetal ball, trying to make himself as small as possible. He felt numerous impacts, pebble-sized pieces of debris that stung but did not penetrate his clothing, and then that too passed and the world was still again.

He raised his head cautiously, saw that his father and Knight were still with him and then looked out at the landscape. It had been utterly transformed. The wooded area they had just passed through was gone. The trees were flattened in a ring around a column of smoke that reached into the heavens before curling over like a mushroom.

The initial explosion had been mostly contained underground, the energy channeled upward by the cylindrical shape of the ancient giant city. That was probably why they were all still alive. It also had not been a true nuclear explosion, like an atomic bomb, but something more akin to a volcanic eruption, as the super-heated gases trapped in the reactor reached a flashpoint and ignited. King was a little surprised that it had happened so quickly, and he wondered if perhaps the rampaging ape-creature had somehow hastened the process. Or something else.

The Firebird, perhaps.

That was a mystery that would remain unsolved. Volos and everything else in the city that bore his name, had almost certainly been reduced to radioactive slag. If by some fluke, enough of the monster's tissue remained intact to begin the regeneration process, whatever eventually resulted would be imprisoned in a tomb of molten rock.

After the initial blast of thermal radiation and the physical effects of the explosion, the next greatest danger was from exposure to fallout. Radioactive particles would soon begin falling like black snow from out of the cloud. There was only a minimal risk from skin contact. The real danger was inhalation or ingestion. So as long as they avoided breathing any of it in, the chances for survival were good, provided they got clear as quickly as possible.

Knight pointed them in what King assumed was the direction where they would find the rest of the team. They set off at a jog, each man alone with his thoughts until their hearing gradually returned.

When they at last caught sight of the others, Peter rushed ahead, embracing Lynn as if it had been ages, rather than mere hours, since they had last seen each other. King arrived just as his mother drew back and asked the question he had been dreading.

"What about Julie?"

King exchanged a glance with Peter. "That woman—Catherine— might have had her face, but she wasn't Julie. Julie died in a plane crash, twenty years ago."

As far as King was concerned, it was the absolute truth.

FIFTY-FOUR

Novo-Ogaryovo, Russia—Four Days Later

The Russian President listened intently as the men arrayed around the large oval-shaped conference table gave their reports. He studied their faces, reading their emotions. Each one was an open book to him.

The generals and admirals, in their immaculate dress uniforms festooned with ribbons and decorations, were barely able to conceal their excitement at the prospect of what lay ahead. Not since the Great Patriotic War had there been such an opportunity to wrap themselves in glory. Everything else, the skirmishes in Georgia and Crimea, the long and utterly futile campaign in Afghanistan—some of these men had been junior officers in that meat grinder—and before that, the shadow wars in Southeast Asia and Central America, all would pale into insignificance alongside this: a war to truly end all wars.

An expeditionary force of motorized riflemen from the Sixth Army and tank divisions from the Twentieth Guards Army were poised on the border of Estonia. A hundred Sukhoi Su-27 fighter jets stood ready to provide air support as needed. The balance of the nation's forces were on high-alert status, ready to meet reprisals from any quarter, on land, in the air or at sea. The full arsenal of RT-2PM Topol mobile strategic missile platforms were deployed, constantly on the move and conducting round-the-clock readiness drills. The same was true of the officers and crew of ballistic nuclear missile submarines positioned in deep waters around the world. More than a hundred thousand reservists had been activated and ordered to report for duty. All that was needed was the order to execute.

The men in plain suits—bureaucrats and cabinet ministers, the *apparatchik*—were less sanguine. He could smell their apprehension. They wanted to believe his promises that the Americans and NATO would simply look away as the tanks and troop transports rolled into Estonia, but these men were perennially cautious creatures, incapable of bold and decisive action. They were inherently fearful of anyone who was.

They told him that emergency meetings of NATO and the United Nations Security Council had been called for. American forces around the world were at an unprecedented Defense Condition Two. The Bulletin of Atomic Scientists had moved the hands of the infamous Doomsday Clock to two minutes to midnight. Stock markets around the world were in free fall. The American President was still waiting for someone in the Kremlin to pick up the phone.

All of which, the men in suits told him, choosing their words carefully, meant that he'd won. 'You've reminded them that Russia is not a former-anything, but a superpower, not to be trifled with.'

'Glory is a fine thing,' they went on, 'but think of the expense, not merely in the short term, but down the road, if the conflict went on for a year or ten years.' Defeat was unthinkable of course, but victory would be costly, too.

He smiled and thanked them for their diligence, wondering which of them, if any, possessed the backbone to attempt a coup.

Who is Cassius? He thought. *Who is Brutus?*

It was a pity that his Ice Queen had not survived to see this. She would know who was plotting against him, and which of them had the inner fortitude to wield the knife. He did not doubt that secret negotiations with the Americans were already underway, but he also knew that the men in suits believed that eventually he would back away from the brink of total annihilation.

Fools and weaklings, he thought.

When the last report was concluded, he stood. "A sealed package has been sent to your respective duty stations. It is to be opened only by you, and only in the presence of your immediate second-in-command. The package contains seven sealed envelopes, each marked with a specific code designator known only to me."

The generals and admirals all nodded eagerly. They understood the need for such elaborate security measures. Three of the envelopes contained detailed war game scenarios. Live fire exercises conducted on, but not across, the Estonian border. The other four contained elaborate invasion plans, likewise with scales of time and intensity. Only one of them—code-designation: Perun, named for the Slavic god of thunder and fire, the counterpart of Volos, god of the underworld—was the actual mission. The others were just misdirection, in case the enemy got their hands on the package.

"At precisely 19:30 this evening, you will receive a call on your secure line with a matching code designator. At that time, you will open the package, select the corresponding envelope and follow the instructions contained therein." He gestured to the door. "Go. You are dismissed."

Nineteen-thirty in Moscow would be three-thirty a.m. in Washington, D.C. When the sun rose over the American capital, the North Atlantic Treaty Organization would already be history. The nations of Europe would renege on their obligations under Article Five, and the greatest alliance in the history of the world would be broken.

The American President, Chambers, would threaten unilateral military action, but without popular support from his own people, he too would step aside and let it happen.

And then the true war would begin.

While the eyes of the world were on Eastern Europe, Russian Airborne and Spetsnaz units would sweep across Washington, D.C. capturing the American leadership in one fell swoop.

The unexpected discovery of the supply base in Virginia had accelerated his timetable, but the loss of its contents would have little impact on the overall strategy. The seven remaining bases in the D.C. metro area contained enough food, water, fuel and ammunition for several months of sustained operations. He did not expect the Americans to hold out that long. They were a fractured, contentious populace, and if opinion polls were to be believed, many of them thought he—the Russian President—was a stronger leader than their own elected Chief Executive.

They would welcome his empire with open arms.

It would be a bittersweet victory, though. The true prince of the Russian empire, the chosen one of God, precious Alexei, was gone.

Part of him secretly hoped that NATO and the Americans would find the nerve to stand against him. Then he could cleanse the world with fire.

As the last of the men left the room, another man wearing the uniform and rank of an Army colonel stepped inside and quickly closed and locked the French doors.

The Russian President looked up, his bland expression mostly concealing his irritation at this unwanted intrusion. "Get out."

The colonel turned to face him, removing his peaked hat and tossing it aside with a flourish that, as intended, diverted the Russian's attention away from the gun that seemed to materialize in his hand.

The President's eyes widened in surprise, not because of the weapon pointed at him, but because of who held it. He tensed, filled with a primal urge to leap across the table and throttle the intruder. It was the man who had killed his precious Alexei. "You!"

The man—Jack Sigler, Peter's son, the American operative known by the callsign: King—gestured with the gun. "If you want to go another round with me, fine, but first we talk."

"There is nothing to talk about." He pushed away from the table, rising to his feet. "I don't know how you got in here, or what you hope to accomplish, but you of all people must realize how futile this is."

King wagged his head ruefully. "I guess it's true what they say. You can't choose your relatives."

This gave the Russian pause. "Peter told you the truth?"

"He told me what you told him, which I think we both know wasn't quite the whole truth, but close enough for me to figure the rest out." He cocked his head to the side. "You should be taller."

"Taller?" The President felt some of the fire leave him.

"Did she know who you really were?"

"She?"

"Julie. Catherine. She's the one who told me the story about Brother Makary and the Children of Adoon, but I don't think she understood how it really connected to you. I should have realized it right then, but I had other things on my mind. The clues were so obvious. The story of how you supposedly died...poisoned with cyanide, shot in the head, then dumped into the river to drown or freeze or both. I read somewhere that they cut...it...off. Is that true?" King shuddered in mock horror, but then his face became deadly serious. "Knowing what I know about the immortal—the man you call Adoon—it was pretty easy to recognize the signs. I knew him by a different name: Alexander. I also know that he was very protective of his secrets. What I don't get is why he chose to share it with you."

"You knew him?" The Russian President settled back into his chair. His gaze was still fixed on King, but his thoughts were being inexorably drawn into the gravitational singularity of memory. "You are right about him. He knew from the very start that I was his descendant. He revealed to me the truth about my heritage. Showed me that I was meant for greatness. He taught me many things. He showed me how to make use of my extraordinary natural abilities. But you are wrong about one thing. He did not give me the elixir. Not until...after."

"After you were dead."

"Two and a half months dead. I don't know why he did it. To soothe his conscience, perhaps." The Russian narrowed his eyes. "You are right about one other thing also. I was as tall as you before I went in that coffin."

"I'd say you lost more than just a few inches," King said, coldly.

"When I awoke, the world I knew was gone. It had been utterly swept away." He fell silent, still caught in the memory.

"That's why you wanted to bring Alexei back," King said, and this time there was no judgement in his tone.

"They murdered him. That precious child. If I had been there, I might have been able to stop them." He shook his head, trying to push back the upwelling of emotion. "He gave me the elixir, but he would not share the secret of how to make it. I raged at him, threatened him, but he spurned me. Laughed at my despair and cast me out. I spent years searching for the formula. Decades studying science, history, theology. That is how I learned of the city of the Originators. I thought I had discovered the gates of hell, guarded by the devil himself."

"Volos."

"That is what I called it. In truth, I don't know what it was. A genetic experiment, left behind by the Originators. It assimilated the genetic traits of anything it came into contact with."

"Starting with you," King said. "Your immortality transferred to it, made it unkillable. Then you fed it the scraps from your humanzee experiments and turned it into King Kong."

"Volos made it possible for me to synthesize the serum I used to bring your sister back to life."

"That thing wasn't my sister," King said, his tone suddenly sharp again.

The Russian President ignored the outburst. "I was able to reconstitute her from just a few grams of DNA, but I could not replicate the effects with Alexei. She was a child of Adoon. Alexei was not."

"Obviously, you found a workaround."

"With the help of Richard Ridley. I believe you and he were acquainted." The mere mention of the maverick geneticist had clearly ruffled King's feathers. "But Ridley's serum was flawed as well. Alexei returned to me, but his body was not healed of the affliction he had inherited from his mother."

"Hemophilia," King murmured.

"Nor was he made immortal. In fact, he barely survived the process. When he eventually recuperated, his mind was not what it once had been." The Russian smiled sadly. "But he was Alexei, the Prince of Russia, and I loved him just as I loved him a century ago."

King shook his head. "Alexei Romanov, the son of Tsar Nicholas II and Tsarina Alexandra. Now I understand why you were so fond of him, despite the fact that he was obviously batshit insane. Or maybe that was something you two had in common. In any case, it was another clue I should have picked up on right away. Just like your name. It was right in front of us all the whole time...Rasputin."

He said it with a faint pause after the 's,' to emphasize what followed.

The Russian folded his arms across his chest. "You know who I am. You know that you cannot kill me. And you must know that you cannot escape. So why come here? What foolishness possesses you?"

"Two reasons," King replied evenly. "First, I didn't know for sure. I had my suspicions, but there were still a lot of questions I needed answers to. Like whether Alexander—the man you knew as Brother Makary—gave you the formula for the elixir of life."

"You want it for yourself?" The Russian allowed himself a smile of satisfaction. "I would never give it to you, not after what you did to Alexei."

"Been there, done that," King replied. "You think you're old? You're practically a toddler compared to me."

This unexpected revelation caused the Russian to sit up a little straighter. "You are the son of Peter and Lynn. I know this to be true."

"It's a long story." King leveled the gun at him. "And I'm afraid your time is about to become very precious."

The Russian laughed. "Go ahead. Shoot me."

"Which brings me to the second reason," King said, and to the Russian's complete astonishment, King did exactly that.

The gun in his hand gave a loud pop—though not nearly as loud as an unsuppressed pistol—and the Russian felt a sharp pain as something struck him in the chest. His hand came up reflexively, but instead of a wound gushing blood, his fingers encountered a cool metal cylinder, tipped with a needle that was stuck in his skin. He pulled it free and stared at it in consternation. "A tranquilizer dart? I give you credit for creativity, but you must not know as much about the elixir as you think, if you believe that you can drug me."

"It's not a drug. It's a counter-agent to the elixir. Alexander gave me the formula for it. I think you'll find mortality to be very liberating. I know it's taught me to appreciate the little things."

The Russian threw the dart down as if it was a scorpion trying to sting him. "You are lying."

King shrugged. "If you don't believe me, we can go a few rounds. Finish what we started in Volosgrad."

"So this was your plan? Make me mortal, so you can kill me?" The Russian chuckled, but behind his façade of indifference, his heart was hammering with fear. He did not feel any different. Perhaps King was lying. Perhaps this was a bold bluff.

Easy enough to test, he thought.

"I'm not going to kill you," King said, derailing his train of thought. "Actually, I'm done here. I needed to know if you had the formula to counter the counter-agent. Obviously, you don't. Whatever happens next is up to you."

"What happens next is that I will have you executed as a spy."

King shrugged. "You can try. But I made it in here without any trouble. I think I can find my way out again."

He turned for the door and opened it, but stopped before going through. "You're mortal now," he said. "You can die like everyone else. And if you go through with this plan to start a war, you very well might, along with everyone else. That's one possible ending for this story.

"Another is that you stand your forces down. Tell the world that you've made your point: that Russia is still relevant, a force to be reckoned with. It's a win and you know it.

"It's your move now. Destroy the world out of spite and everyone loses. Take a step back and you get to keep everything you've already won, and live out the rest of your days like a king. Either way, your empire will die with you. It's just a question of when."

Then he was gone.

The Russian jumped to his feet and ran to the door. "Arrest him," he shouted, pointing his finger at...

King was gone.

"The man who just left," he said, answering the questioning faces of the military officers and bodyguards waiting outside the conference room. "The colonel. Where did he go?"

More blanks stares and an exchange of nervous looks.

"Lock down the grounds. Blockade the roads." His mind raced to frame the appropriate response, but even as the people around him began moving, frantically trying to carry out the vague orders, he knew that it would be in vain.

He turned back into the room, closed the door to seal out the tumult and returned to the table.

'You're mortal now.'

No, it can't be true.

He seized hold of a crystal water pitcher, emptied its contents and dashed it against the edge of the table. Then he stooped to retrieve a glinting shard. He raked his thumb across the sharp edge, then squeezed the digit until a steady flow of blood was dripping from the cut, splattering the table top.

"Heal," he whispered. "Heal, damn you."

The blood continued to flow.

He fell back into his chair, staring at the cut.

'You can die like everyone else.'

No! No, no, no...

King had said something else, though. *'I needed to know if you had the formula to counter the counter-agent.'*

I can reverse this, he thought. *The elixir of life is still out there. I can find it. Become immortal again.*

Or I can let the world burn.

As he contemplated these diverging paths, King's partings words flashed through his mind. *'Your empire will die with you. It's just a question of when.'*

No, he decided, *I won't allow that to happen. My empire will live on.* I *will live.*

And with trembling hands, blood still oozing from the cut on his thumb, he reached for the telephone.

FIFTY-FIVE

Richmond, Virginia—Three Days Later

King laid the wreath at the base of the headstone, then straightened and took a step back. He gripped his father's hand. Hugged his mother, carefully so as not to unbalance her on her crutches. Then he hugged his sister, and lastly, Sara, his wife.

No tears were shed. There was no need to revisit old grief. Julie had been dead a long time, and although she was missed, even by those who had never known her, time had healed the wound of her absence. They had come here to pay their respects, not to weep for her afresh.

"You know," Bishop said, as they walked to their car, "she saved the world."

King threw her a questioning glance.

"If you had not seen her face on television," she went on, "we would not have known what was happening."

"That wasn't Julie," he replied, his tone soft but emphatic.

"No, but it was her face."

King considered that. Bishop was right, in more ways than one. It had been Julie's death all those years ago that had inspired him to pursue a military career, which had led to his saving the world many times over.

The news that Russian forces were withdrawing from the Estonian border had broken while King was surreptitiously making his way back home. Even with his Chameleon adaptive camouflage system

—a bit of old Chess Team tech that Deep Blue had managed to restore to working order—rendering him virtually invisible, getting out of Russia had been no mean feat. It would have been considerably more challenging if the Russian President had actually gone through with his mad scheme.

King supposed that, even if he had not been chasing Julie's ghost, the team still might have been sent on the covert mission, but the outcome might have been vastly different.

He knew now that the leak of information about Volosgrad had been intentional. It was bait for a trap designed to lure him specifically to the research facility, so his DNA could have been harvested to perfect the Firebird serum. Without his discovery of the supply depot in Virginia—a direct result of his search for Julie—the team would have gone in blind, and the trap might very well have worked as planned. Moreover, they would not have been able to thwart the plan without the assistance of Lynn and Peter, who would not have been along if he had not seen the woman with Julie's face.

His search for her had accomplished something else, too. It had brought his family back together.

After Julie's accident, Peter had abruptly left the family, returning to Russia—though King had not known it at the time—to raise Asya. The resentment King had harbored toward his father had been somewhat ameliorated when the rationale for that decision came to light. For King, those events were literally ancient history now, but their relationship with one another had never quite regained a sense of normalcy. They had all lived too much of their lives apart and held on to too many secrets.

Maybe that would change now.

No, he amended, *no 'maybe' about it.*

He had told the Russian President—his grandfather, if the man had not been lying to Peter—that regaining mortality had taught him to appreciate the little things, and it was true. There were no do-overs in life, but there were second chances.

For the moment however, the family reunion at Julie's grave would have to suffice. War with Russia had been averted, but there was another pressing matter—a different sort of family matter—that demanded his attention.

They said their goodbyes at the airport. Peter and Lynn boarded a plane for Seattle. Sara caught a flight back to Atlanta. Even though the Russian situation was de-escalating, the CDC remained on heightened alert, and Sara had to get back to her team. King and Bishop caught a military transport to Fort Bragg, where the rest of the team was waiting in Limbo.

They all looked none the worse for wear, with the exception of Rook, whose left arm was cradled in a sling while the torn ligaments in his shoulder healed.

Admiral Ward was waiting there as well. "Congratulations," he said, shaking King's hand. "You did the impossible."

King was uncomfortable with the praise from the man who had, up until that moment, barely tolerated his existence. Fortunately, Rook quickly filled the awkward silence. "That should be our team motto. 'We do the impossible.'"

"I'm afraid there were still a few things even we couldn't manage," King said. "Like bringing White Team home. I know it's cold comfort, but without their sacrifice, we might not have pulled this one out of the fire."

Ward nodded. "Those men knew the risks and took the job. They're heroes. Just like you."

"So are we finally off the no-fly list?" Rook asked.

"Off the list and back on the roster." Ward caught himself. "If that's what you want, that is."

King looked around the room at the faces of his teammates, but he already knew the answer. "We've got some unfinished business, sir."

Ward nodded. "Duncan."

"You said you would give us whatever support you could. With all due respect sir, you owe us. A great, big, fat blank check."

Ward shuffled nervously but said nothing.

"He's out there somewhere." King was looking at Ward, but saying it to all of them. "We're going to find him, whatever it takes, and we're going to bring him home. He's part of our family. And you all know there's nothing I won't do, nowhere I won't go, to keep our family together."

"I wish I had something to tell you," Ward said. "But right now, we've got no leads, and no ideas about who was behind this."

"Leads or no leads," King said, "starting right now, finding Tom Duncan is our only mission."

EPILOGUE

Unknown Location

How long had it been?

Days? Definitely.

Weeks? It was possible.

Months? Probably not that long.

Weeks, then, maybe two, maybe less.

He had tried counting the passage of time by the number of times his captors brought him food or came to empty the bucket that served as his toilet. Always two men—probably not always the same two, but he couldn't be sure. They wore hoods and masks to conceal their physical features. One of them kept a Taser gun aimed at him at all times. They never spoke, communicating with brusque gestures. If he mistook their intent, he would receive a hard backhand slap. But after the sixth visit—*or was it the seventh? Eighth?*—he realized that they were staggering the intervals between visits. There could be only one reason for that. They were trying to disorient him, a prelude no doubt, to interrogation.

He was almost certain that he was on a submarine, partly because the tiny room in which he was kept looked like it belonged on a naval vessel—a particularly cramped naval vessel. But mostly because no other vessel could have gotten close to the secret detainment facility where he had been kept. In fact, he couldn't think of any other way in which his captors could have approached the black site without anyone noticing. They certainly had not arrived, or departed for that matter, by land or air.

All he really knew with any certainty was that a group of men wearing white camouflage and carrying automatic weapons had stormed the Alert facility and brutally gunned down his jailors. He did not see what happened after that, because the commandos had dropped a heavy sack hood over his head. His other senses were still supplying him with information, but without a visual context it was difficult to make sense out of what he was experiencing. His captors—his new captors—did not utter a single word, at least that he could hear. They could not entirely conceal the fact that he was being moved, though. There had been a short journey on foot, no more than a quarter of a mile, across the frozen Arctic landscape. After that he had been manhandled onto a ladder.

Up? Down? Up then down? He couldn't be sure, but after that, the world had gotten a lot warmer. He had spent the next few minutes being herded slowly along a hard walkway—metal judging by the feel of it underfoot. After that, he had been strapped to a chair and left alone for a period of at least a few hours. It was long enough for his stomach to begin rumbling and his bladder to begin cramping. Even before the hood was removed, he could feel a change in the air pressure—another sign that he was probably on a submarine. Aside from that one clue, all he really could tell was that he was no longer outside.

Eventually, the hood came off and the chair was taken away. He was left in the small room with metal walls, with just a threadbare blanket and a bucket to piss in. Every meal was the same—cold, sticky rice in a plastic bowl, served without utensils. He was also supplied with a paper cup full of water. There was almost enough room on the floor for him to stretch out and sleep or do calisthenics—the two activities that occupied most of his time.

He could not help but speculate about the identity of the mysterious commandos who had taken him from his prison. There were so many possibilities. Were they soldiers or spies sent by a foreign power? Mercenaries working for a private interest or a global criminal conspiracy? A rival intelligence service within the United States government? All seemed equally possible, and each carried with it a different set of motives and outcomes. The only thing he was certain of was that at some point, someone would begin asking him questions. That was the only conceivable reason for keeping him alive.

The door opened and he saw the two men waiting outside. He was expecting meal number eighteen—give or take a few—but instead, the lead man tossed a ball of fabric at him. He caught it, and as soon as he realized what it was, he knew that the time for his interrogation had arrived.

Here we go, he thought, slipping the hood over his head.

They led him down the same corridor, manhandled him up the ladder—definitely *up* this time—and then he was forced to lie flat on a platform...

No, it was the deck of a moving vehicle. A truck or van.

A bumpy ride followed, lasting ten or fifteen minutes, and then he was removed from the vehicle and forced to walk a short distance. He felt solid ground underfoot. Concrete or macadam, or possibly hard-packed earth. Then he was moving up a ramp, into a building of some sort.

A hand on his shoulder signaled him to stop moving. He stood still, waiting. Wondering.

"You may remove the hood."

The voice—a man's voice—sounded muffled through the heavy fabric, but there was something odd about it. Odd and oddly familiar.

He did as instructed and found himself in a small room with a bed, a sink and a commode. There were no windows, but there was a large mirror on the wall opposite the bed—almost certainly a concealed observation window. The door next to the window had no knob.

My new cell, he thought.

It was a step up from the austere conditions aboard the submarine, but it fell well short of a Michelin four-star rating.

"Welcome, President Duncan. I'm sure you have many questions. We have many questions for you. But please, first take a moment to freshen up. A hot meal will be brought to you shortly."

The voice was coming from a speaker in the ceiling, and now that he no longer had his hearing obstructed by the sack hood, Duncan recognized it immediately. The odd inflection and cadence, each word enunciated as if completely disconnected from the next—his captors were using a text-to-speech program to further mask their identity. A clever idea, but not without its faults. If he could keep the person on the other end of the conversation talking long enough, a grammatical or idiomatic slip would help him figure out who had taken him.

Knowing that was the first step toward figuring out how to escape, and escape was most definitely a priority for Duncan. He might have been an ex-president, but he would always be an Army Ranger. Long before he took the Oath of Office, he had learned and memorized the soldiers' Code of Conduct.

If I am captured, I will continue to resist by all means available. I will make every effort to escape.

Resist, first.

"Let's cut the bullshit, all right? No one back home is going to pay a red cent to ransom a disgraced former president, which can only mean that you want something from me. Probably some kind of classified information that you think only I can share. Well, you're barking up the wrong tree. Any information I might have is already several years out of date. You'd have better luck looking it up on Google."

He waited, curious to see what the response would be. After nearly a minute passed with no reply, he wondered if silence would be the only answer. Then the artificial voice spoke again. "Very well. You are correct. You have information that we require."

"I told you. I don't know anything that would be of value to anyone."

"In 2009, you authorized the LCROSS mission for NASA." The automated text reader spelled out the acronyms letter by letter.

L-C-R-O-S-S.

N-A-S-A.

"Uh, I guess so."

"What was the true objective of the LCROSS mission?"

L-C-R-O-S-S.

"I...I don't recall, off the top of my head," Duncan lied. "Something scientific, I'm sure. Presidential authorization isn't required for routine NASA missions."

They know about LCROSS. His mind was racing. *Or they suspect. Who are these guys?*

Another long silence. Then, "Why don't you take a moment to freshen up. A hot meal will be brought to you shortly. Then, you will tell us the truth about LCROSS."

"I told you. There's nothing to tell."

"Then you are going to be here a very long time."

ABOUT THE AUTHORS

Jeremy Robinson is the international bestselling author of fifty novels and novellas including *MirrorWorld*, *Uprising*, *Island 731*, *SecondWorld*, the Jack Sigler thriller series, and *Project Nemesis*, the highest selling, original (non-licensed) kaiju novel of all time. He's known for mixing elements of science, history and mythology, which has earned him the #1 spot in Science Fiction and Action-Adventure, and secured him as the top creature feature author.

Robinson is also known as the bestselling horror writer, Jeremy Bishop, author of *The Sentinel* and the controversial novel, *Torment*. In 2015, he launched yet another pseudonym, Jeremiah Knight, for two post-apocalyptic Science Fiction series of novels. Robinson's works have been translated into thirteen languages.

His series of Jack Sigler / Chess Team thrillers, starting with *Pulse*, is in development as a film series, helmed by Jabbar Raisani, who earned an Emmy Award for his design work on HBO's *Game of Thrones*. Robinson's original kaiju character, Nemesis, is also being adapted into a comic book through publisher *Famous Monsters of Filmland*, with artwork and covers by renowned Godzilla artists Matt Frank and Bob Eggleton.

Born in Beverly, MA, Robinson now lives in New Hampshire with his wife and three children.

Visit Jeremy Robinson online at www.bewareofmonsters.com.

ABOUT THE AUTHORS

Sean Ellis has authored and co-authored more than twenty action-adventure novels, including the Nick Kismet adventures, the Jack Sigler/Chess Team series with Jeremy Robinson, and the Jade Ihara adventures with David Wood. He served with the Army National Guard in Afghanistan, and has a Bachelor of Science degree in Natural Resources Policy from Oregon State University. Sean is also a member of the International Thriller Writers organization. He currently resides in Arizona, where he divides his time between writing, adventure sports, and trying to figure out how to save the world.

Visit him on the web at: seanellisthrillers.webs.com

WHEN THE DAIKAIJU ARRIVE
THERE IS ONLY ONE WAY TO FIGHT:
SUPPORT
POINT
BASE
TOGETHER
UNITY
A KAIJU THRILLER BY JEREMY ROBINSON
JUNE 2016

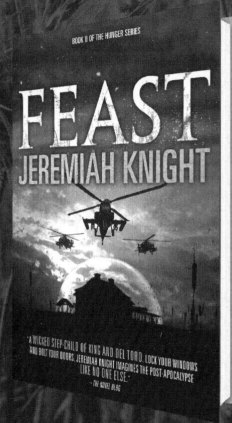

Made in the USA
San Bernardino, CA
08 May 2016